CHASING THE STORM

A STEALTH OPS NOVEL

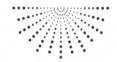

BRITTNEY SAHIN

D0006592

EMKO MEDIA

Chief Editor: Deb Markanton

Editor: Arielle Brubaker

Proofreader: Judy Zweifel, Judy's Proofreading

Cover Design: LJ, Mayhem Cover Creations

Image/Model: Joseph Cannata

Ebook ISBN: 9781947717312

Paperback ISBN: 9798534993332

❀ Created with Vellum

For Kamel

You always believed in me. Supported me. And you were such a bright light of positivity.

I'll never forget you.

The world lost a truly great person.

PROLOGUE

LOS ANGELES, CALIFORNIA – JANUARY 2013

Finn stood outside the cemetery in Pasadena, his gaze fixed on the dimly lit entrance as he tried to convince his booted feet to proceed inside. This was his third attempt to walk through the damn gate, and time was running out. He only had twenty-four hours before he was due on a flight back to Virginia Beach. Over the past three days on leave, he'd repeatedly swung by and committed to memory more and more details about the cemetery and its overall lack of upkeep. At least, based on what he saw while standing on the outside.

He'd observed visitors come and go during the daytime, telling himself he'd return when it was less people-y. But when darkness fell, it was just too damn depressing to follow through with the mission he'd given himself. Besides, under the veil of night, the place felt haunted.

Finn's attention journeyed from the concrete pathway beneath his black, beat-up boots to the arched entryway, its

1

wrought iron barely visible amidst twining green vines with sparsely sprinkled small, fragrant flowers. He recognized the scent as honeysuckle, one of his mom's favorites.

There was a chill in the air, so Finn unrolled his plaid button-down shirt sleeves, blinking away cool droplets of water clinging to his eyelashes as the rain drizzled down almost as if in slow motion.

He'd left his jacket and Red Sox ball cap in his rental, not expecting to be there long or for the clouds to choose this exact moment to open up and rain. As if nighttime in a cemetery wasn't eerie enough.

So, where was the spooky fog, the howl of a lone wolf? Or the specters lurking between headstones to freak him out? Aside from the old-world-style streetlamps fashioned to look like torches that basked the walkway in a soft, yellowish glow, there was nothing that screamed, *Graveyard, enter at your own risk*. He'd have gladly welcomed a vampire to slay. It would be a nice change from the AK-wielding enemies with a distaste for the Western world he normally faced.

But there was no one, neither human nor vampire, in his line of sight. Because who went to a cemetery on a Friday night? *Well, other than me?*

And why in the world was it more difficult to visit a grave in a cemetery than do callouts in Baghdad searching for terrorists?

Finn was just about out of time, though. He'd soon be heading to Jalalabad as part of task unit Dozer. His platoon, Golf, would be combined with Alpha to handle some "issues" the government wanted swept under the rug as quickly and quietly as possible. The idea of J-Bad didn't bother him. No goose bumps or cold, prickly sensations crept up his spine like he experienced now.

He felt like a chickenshit because he couldn't walk

beneath a gate to visit someone he hadn't, well, visited since he dropped out of USC at the start of his junior year to join the Navy. And in the decade since he'd joined the Teams, he hadn't set foot in Los Angeles at all.

His parents had moved the family from Methuen, Massachusetts, to Pasadena when he was fifteen for the sake of his older brother's music career. Pasadena was eleven miles northeast of Los Angeles and considered one of the coolest places to live in LA, known for its Craftsman-style architecture, annual Rose Bowl game and parade, Jet Propulsion Lab and CalTech, among other things. But he would always and forever be an East Coast soul, and when he'd wound up as an East Coast SEAL, Finn had decided it was fate.

But fate or not, there was no valid reason he'd stayed away for ten years. He hadn't even made an effort for a quick, one-day visit. Not. One. Flipping. Time.

So here he was, staring at the cemetery while trying to conjure up every excuse in the book not to go inside.

The palm trees on the other side of the fence swayed gently when the breeze started to kick up as the rain turned from a drizzle to a downpour. A sign from God to leave? Or to go in?

Indecision, as well as habit, had Finn bringing a palm to his jaw to rub against his beard, forgetting his face was now as smooth as a baby's bottom. Last week, the higher-ups had ordered the men to shave because the brass had decided beards were a no-no. He looked forward to going overseas, where facial hair was viewed as a lifesaver, a way to blend in.

I'll come back tomorrow, he lied to himself while turning about-face and walking to his rental. The Honda Civic was a replica of the car he'd driven when the *Fast and Furious* movies were all the rage, and everyone wanted to be just like Vin Diesel and Paul Walker.

Now Finn alternated between a truck and a Jeep from year to year whenever he was in Virginia between deployments.

After leaving the cemetery at twenty-two hundred hours, he made his way through the streets of Old Pasadena. It was a Friday night, and the traffic was heavy even at that hour.

He passed through the Playhouse District and drove toward Madison Heights, then hooked a right onto Arden Road and slowed his vehicle before stopping in front of the brick home he'd lived in from age fifteen until college.

The one-story, three-bedroom house was less than fifteen hundred square feet and recently sold for 1.3 million. A price his parents never would have been able to afford back in the day. A child's scooter sat in the driveway, and a new basketball hoop had been added since he'd lived there.

Finn rested his wrist over the steering wheel and dragged his free hand over his mouth, emotion choking him up.

At some point, he managed to press his foot on the gas pedal and leave. The houses and city became a blur as he drove through familiar streets, almost as if he'd never left Pasadena. When the loud honk of a horn jolted Finn into awareness, he found himself at an intersection, with no recollection of having stopped for the red light, which had apparently turned green. He'd been so lost in thought that he'd forgotten he was behind the wheel. Not good.

He needed a drink, but he'd be walking from the hotel to a nearby bar. After parking the Civic, he made his way to a local Irish pub that'd seen better days based on the barely blinking green sign that read, O'Malley's.

A few drinks in, the surrounding sounds and chatter in the

4

bar melted into a barely audible white noise, and Finn's focus drifted back to his past.

Why were the happy memories buried so far below the surface that he was unable to reach out and touch them? Not a single one?

Finn gripped the glass, brought it to his nose, and sniffed. His mom had always said his father's bourbon smelled like nail polish remover. She wasn't too far off.

"You good, son?"

Finn blinked and pulled his focus from the tumbler of Four Roses single barrel Kentucky bourbon to the bartender now eyeing him. "Yeah, I should cash out."

The horrible knot that had taken root in Finn's stomach the moment the plane's wheels touched down at LAX three days ago had been steadily growing, and as he left the pub, it burgeoned into the size of a heavyweight fighter's fist, punching relentlessly as the rain fell.

His stomach grumbled like the roll of thunder overhead, and he glanced at his watch, checking to see how late it was. Almost twenty-four hundred hours. *Right, I skipped dinner.*

An angry male voice caught Finn's attention, but the sharp sound of glass breaking in an alleyway around the corner caused Finn to pause in his tracks.

Did he really want to chance a look around that corner, get involved in something that was none of his business? The only fuel in his body right now was bourbon, and he had no sidearm or knife.

Sure, he'd been in martial arts since he was a teen. Third-degree black belt in karate. Throw in some Muay Thai kickboxing and wrestling, and yeah, he was decent at hand-to-hand combat.

Karate classes and a passion for *Star Wars* had helped him get through some tough times. Saved him from going down a dark path when he'd been surrounded by what felt like a black hole trying to suck his soul from his body.

So, SEAL training or not, Finn could protect himself. That didn't mean he loved the idea of possibly bringing fists to a gunfight.

And who knew what he might be up against?

But fuck it.

When he peeked around the corner to gauge the situation, he discovered the alley was more like a long hallway with too many doors that momentarily brought him back to Iraq. His least favorite place to be during an op was in a hallway. What was behind door number one? Who was behind door number two? Or three?

A large man wielding a broken beer bottle had a teenager up against the brick wall, the broken bottle neck at the boy's throat. "Pay up, dirtbag. Or you're done."

Finn quickly mulled over what to say. *Why not pick on someone your own size?* felt too cliché even with a few bourbons in him.

"Hey," Finn called out, opting for a *less is more* approach. "You want money?" He lifted one hand, palm facing the older guy wearing a backward ball cap, ripped jeans, and a black leather jacket.

"Who the hell are you?" The man eased the bottle away from the kid's neck a fraction of an inch at the distraction. *Yeah, keep moving that bottle out of range.*

"A hundred bucks if you let the kid go." Finn slowly reached around to his back pocket and went for his wallet, making a show of pulling it out so as not to spook the guy, and plucked two fifties.

The man's eyes moved from the money and up to the metal overhang protecting them from getting wet. Was he contemplating the offer? "What's in it for you? You want to save some punk-ass druggie?"

Finn's stomach clenched at the man's words, and he found himself drawing a step closer to the both of them. What kind of drugs? Were there track marks beneath the kid's jacket sleeves? How old was he? Fifteen? Sixteen?

"I asked you a question," the man barked out. The bottle was still in the guy's hand, but he'd lowered it to his side.

Finn needed to distract the asshole for a few more seconds, and then he could move in and knock the bottle from his hand before he had a chance to puncture the kid's neck. "Are you his dealer?" he pressed. "How much does he owe you?"

"More than what's in your hand," the man growled out. Based on the glassy eyes and aggressive behavior, the guy partook of his own product.

But what kind of drugs? Meth? PCP? Would the man come at him with Hulk-like strength, or would he fall flat on his ass with an easy punch?

"I'll take you to an ATM. Just let the kid go," Finn offered as he took another step closer. The shadow from the light above the door off to Finn's right shifted, enabling him to get a better look at the boy's face. Dark, vacant eyes, pale skin, and hollow cheeks.

Finn nearly froze when the kid stared right at him without any plea or hope in his eyes.

"Hey, fuck face. Back up."

Finn blinked and looked to the asshole who'd released his grip on the boy to fully face him. Well, mission accomplished. Now it was game on.

Finn dropped the money in a split second and rushed the guy, quickly blocking a wild bottle swing with one arm to land a punch square across the guy's jaw.

The son of a bitch didn't flinch.

Hulk it is, then.

"Run," Finn shouted at the boy, risking a glance to see him grabbing the two fifties off the ground before taking off. Sadly, Finn knew there was no more he could do. He turned his attention back to the game at hand and narrowly missed the big-ass man's fist as it swung clumsily toward his face.

With the kid safe, Finn blocked the punch and sent a palm heel strike between the eyes.

Still no reaction aside from the bottle falling to the ground.

"You can't hurt me." The man barked out a laugh and flung all of his weight at Finn, who quickly moved to the side and took advantage of the guy's momentum to shove his face against the wall.

Hulk shook his head a little and turned around to face him. Finn was half expecting the guy to remove his jacket and crack his neck like they were in some 1980s action flick.

He didn't have time for this, so he utilized a combination of moves that'd always worked for him in the Middle East whenever forced into hand-to-hand combat.

A few quick maneuvers and Finn managed to get the beast on the ground. And after another minute, he knocked him unconscious.

"What the hell were you on?" he muttered as he knelt alongside the guy and patted him down for a phone. Luckily, it was a basic burner, no lock. Finn checked the last five calls, all to one number he hoped belonged to the kid, but no one answered.

For one crazy, fleeting moment, Finn contemplated that maybe he'd been compelled to return to LA for a different reason than a long overdue visit to the cemetery. Maybe he was supposed to save that boy?

He added the number to his phone, then dialed the police with an anonymous tip. He had no desire to stick around and make a statement. When the familiar flash of blue and red patrol car lights appeared, Finn ducked out of the alley and slowly walked the short distance to his hotel.

With every step, his thoughts grew darker, tumbling around in his head, threatening to overwhelm and drag him under until he reached the hotel parking lot.

And then he worried he might be hallucinating. *But I wasn't punched, was I?*

A tall, well-built guy stepped away from the dark SUV he was leaning against and removed his black ball cap even though it was still raining. A woman bundled in a thin black raincoat with a matching umbrella over her head stood by his side. One hand casually tucked into her pocket, her eyes razor-sharp on Finn.

Finn redirected his focus to the man that had Teamguy written all over him, from how he carried himself to the intense way he scrutinized Finn. He conveyed the irrefutable confidence essential for a SEAL to accomplish a job that very few others could. "Luke Scott?" he damn near whispered, doubt penetrating his tone. Because why would a legend who'd supposedly up and quit the Teams be in a shitty, slightly shady hotel parking lot?

"Yeah, it's me." His gruff tone was on point with a Teamguy, too.

Finn tossed a look at the woman again, wondering what in the hell was going on as he closed the remaining gap between them. "What are you doing here?"

"Can we talk in your room?" Luke tipped his head toward the old two-story building with a faded red roof.

"Uh, yeah." Finn motioned for them both to follow him to his room, which was on the first floor not far from where he'd parked the Civic. "Everything good?" He opened the door and quickly flipped on the lights.

The cheap lamp by the bed buzzed and flickered. And there was the spooky, Alfred Hitchcock movie effect that'd been missing at the cemetery.

"I heard you left the Teams rather abruptly. Was that a rumor?" Finn slowly eased his body down onto the bed as if he'd just done a grueling leg workout at the gym while the woman collapsed her umbrella and Luke shut the door.

"Yes and no." Luke pinned him with the look of a master chief about to tell his team they were going into hostile territory with empty mags. "This is my sister, Jessica. She was a CIA officer up until last week."

Okaaaay. The word dragged out long and slow in Finn's mind as he worked to wrap his head around why these two had come to LA. The only people who knew Finn's current whereabouts were his master chief and commanding officer, which meant someone felt the need to provide Luke with Finn's coordinates. *Shit. Not good.*

"I'm going to cut straight to the point." Luke's hat was back on his head, and he crossed his arms over his navy-blue shirt. "We're here to recruit you."

Say what? That wasn't the counterstrike he'd mentally prepped. Not even close. *Recruit?* Finn pictured the Army recruitment poster he'd seen hanging in a storefront window once before he'd dropped out of college. It'd been a vintage shop, and the poster was of a soldier holding a flag that read, "Your flag. Your future."

For some reason, he'd never been able to shake that image from his head. And, of course, instead of joining the Army when he'd decided he wanted the military to be his future, he'd gone the Navy route like his favorite uncle on his old man's side had done.

"Recruit me for what?" Cue dramatic music. Another effect that'd been missing from the cemetery. He almost laughed, but damn, Luke didn't look like the type to make a special appearance for the sake of a joke.

The room next door suddenly turned on some beats that were of the smoke-some-dope variety. Finn considered pounding on the wall for them to turn it down, but maybe it'd be better to have some cover for whatever conversation was about to go down.

Luke's gaze flicked across the slightly stained burgundy and flower print wallpaper and back to Finn. "The Navy believes I retired. My family does as well." He glanced at his sister. "Well, aside from Jessica here. But the truth is, my sister and I will be handling a team of ten SEALs, one of them being myself, to run off-the-book ops for the President, CIA director, and Secretary of Defense." Luke's matter-of-fact tone of voice had dropped a few octaves, almost too low to hear over the music next door.

"And before you ask," Jessica began as if reading Finn's racing thoughts, "this won't be like the covert group of Delta guys already running missions for POTUS. Or like DEVGRU."

DEVGRU. The elite of the elite. They were more commonly known by the public as SEAL Team Six, made famous, much to the government's dismay, after Osama bin Laden had been eliminated.

"We'll handle imperative missions that haven't been given the green light by the government. Sometimes on U.S. soil." That last bit of information had Finn rising to his feet.

U.S. soil? Yeah, that's not exactly legal. He continued to carefully assess Luke's sister. It didn't take but a second for him to observe the intelligence in her eyes. To see the mind of a CIA officer at work. It wasn't his habit to blindly trust

11

the Agency, but something in his gut told him she was solid.

"Dalton," Jessica went on, but Finn held a hand up at the use of his given name.

He rarely used his first name, preferring "Finn," short for his last name of Finnegan. "Finn," he corrected with a small smile, grateful the knot in his stomach seemed to have disappeared despite the odd conversation he was engaged in.

But work talk had always been easier than discussing anything personal.

"*Finn*, we want you on our team." She raised her voice as if worried he'd missed the information train and hadn't processed the hammer of news they'd thrown at him.

But no, it'd hit him square in the head. With his feet planted firmly on the cheap burgundy carpet, he asked, "You want me to leave my platoon and lie to everyone about what I do?"

"Yes." Luke's answer had Finn's gaze swiveling his way. "You'll still technically be active duty. But to your family, friends, and well, to the world, you'll have retired and moved into the private sector." He drew a hand over the stubble on his jaw as if he was still digesting his own words.

"More specifically, the private security sector," Jessica added.

Finn tucked his hands into his jeans pockets, his knuckles still a bit sore from his unexpected Edward Norton in *Fight Club*–style alleyway encounter not too long ago. "Why?" He cleared his throat. "Not why me, but why does POTUS want this team? Aren't we violating some laws by doing this?"

Jessica retrieved a phone from the pocket of her rain jacket. She tapped at it a few times and offered it to him. "That reporter recently captured in Tehran was executed two nights ago. She didn't have to die, but the CIA was denied

12

approval for a mission to save her." She motioned with her finger for Finn to swipe right. More and more images of lives lost because no branch of American government was permitted to carry out a rescue or recovery mission.

Each loss weighed heavily on Finn's heart. How could they not? And this was one reason he didn't watch the news. It hurt too much to peer into the eyes of someone on screen, knowing that his people might have been able to save them.

"We *are* needed. And sometimes, rules are meant to be broken when you're saving a thirteen-year-old girl from terrorists." It was as if the woman had dipped into his head, then reached for his very soul and tugged.

A few seconds later, Finn swallowed around the giant lump in his throat, tore his eyes free from Jessica's ice-blue ones, and returned her phone. "What if I say no? Isn't it risky approaching me without having me sign some nondisclosure documents first?"

Jessica and Luke swapped a quick look, and Luke tipped his chin as if prompting his sister to take the lead.

"You'll be thirty this year. You have nearly ten years dedicated to the Navy. You're a rule follower, but from what I've heard, you're also willing to put people over policy when need be. You had a tough life, but you never quit. Never let adversity hold you back. You fight for the people you love. You stop at nothing to do the right thing."

Her words gripped him by the throat, and he fought the urge to reach up and claw away the invisible hands.

Memories.

Painful. Fucking. Memories.

They haunted him every night before bed.

But didn't every Teamguy have them?

He needed to shut out the pain and focus.

"I know a lot about you, Finn. Your favorite junk foods

13

are beef jerky and Twizzlers. In your opinion, the best Star Wars movie is *The Empire Strikes Back*. And you—"

"I get it. You did your research on me." Finn didn't need to hear any more about himself. He was painfully aware of the details of his life. How many times had he wished for a way to go back in time without triggering some freaky butterfly effect? "You knowing random shit about me doesn't explain why you'd assume I'd say yes to this."

As Finn watched Jessica tuck her phone back into her pocket, the answer dawned on him.

This tough-as-nails CIA officer—*excuse me, former CIA officer*—had preyed upon his emotions with those photos.

"Those cases you showed me." Finn shook his head. "The lives the military couldn't save. You knew I'd say yes because of them. *For* them."

"According to your teammates, you can't seem to stop yourself if you know someone is in trouble. You never back down," Jessica confirmed his theory. "And we want someone like you on our team."

"You just described every SEAL I know," Finn remarked with a forced casual shrug, trying to keep his emotions in check. Of course, why bother hiding from this woman? She was able to read him as if she had the master key to his innermost thoughts.

Loud moaning began to compete with the music in the room next door, and Finn bit back a smile when a blush crawled up Jessica's neck and onto her cheeks. Ah, so there was more to this woman than *Just the facts, ma'am*. Good to know.

"Okay, okay." Luke didn't bother to hide his grin as the music and moaning was joined by the headboard rhythmically banging against the wall. "You came highly recommended."

Finn smiled, doing his best to ignore the awkward entertainment from next door. "Who?"

"Wyatt Pierson. And Chris Hunter," Luke quickly answered.

Finn had worked with Wyatt a few times. He was well-known to everyone on all Teams. British born but an American citizen. One of the best snipers in the world, right alongside Liam Evans.

And Chris was from the Boston area, like Finn, and they'd bonded over that fact whenever their paths had crossed in the Middle East.

"They'll be on this team, then?" It'd be nice to work with familiar faces *if* he were to say yes.

"Yeah. Two teams. Bravo and Echo. I'll head up Bravo, and we've tasked Wyatt as Echo One. Our second sniper will be on Bravo. Looking to recruit Liam Evans." Luke paused for a moment. "We need a medic, so we were hoping you'd join Echo."

"You have a medic for Bravo?" Why did it feel like he already committed?

"Charlie Bennett." Jessica's cheeks bloomed even brighter as the woman next door proclaimed to find God.

"Ah, you mean Knox." Jessica wasn't on the DL with nicknames, huh?

Finn brought a fist to his mouth and coughed, a feeble effort to distract from the antics in the adjacent room. Knox's dad was rumored to run for President one day. How would that work?

But what he really needed to be asking himself was how the hell would this new team prevent the world from learning their identities when not even the Department of Defense was able to keep a lid on what DEVGRU Tier One guys did?

"We have a cover story," Luke answered his thoughts as

the couple next door finally finished. Thank God the man was a sprinter and not a marathon-type guy. "Scott and Scott Securities. Cyber protection. Bodyguard jobs. Kidnap and rescue. And so on."

"And we'll have retired SEALs working actual cases to keep up with appearances." Jessica's rigid stance eased up a bit. "Maybe we'll even take a few jobs between ops in the beginning. But if we're ever captured or identified on a mission, the President won't take responsibility for our actions. We'll say we were hired as private security."

"So, it's our asses, not POTUS's." *Isn't that how it is every day, anyway?* It was the men and women outside the wire who risked their necks, so this wouldn't be much different, right?

"We need an answer soon," Luke said. "I know this seems fast, but we'll be heading to Argentina for our first op in two days."

Two days? Fuck. "You're expecting a group of ten guys who will be new to working together to drop in on a target without knowing each other all that well first? Or without prep?"

"Of course not. That's why we're getting there early," Luke commented with a slow smile crossing his lips.

"You'll need to sign some NDAs once you say yes," Jessica noted.

She knew damn well he wasn't going to be able to turn her down. "Can I ask you something? Has anyone you tried to recruit said no?"

Luke and Jessica exchanged another quick look. "No."

"Is Liam your last recruit?"

Luke nodded. "What do you say? I know it's a big ask without much time."

"I'm supposed to be reporting to Jalalabad and—"

"POTUS has it covered," Luke cut him off.

Finn closed his eyes and thought back to the cemetery he'd been unable to walk through. Then he thought about the phone number he'd pulled off the drug dealer. "I need a day to do something first." His lids slowly parted to look at them. "And then I'm all yours."

CHAPTER ONE

NEW YORK CITY, NEW YORK – PRESENT DAY,
MAY 2022

FINN TOOK A SIP OF HIS COKE AND OBSERVED HIS "assignment" as she sat across the room in the trendy Tribeca bar, looking bored out of her mind as her date for the evening chatted away.

Casually holding her martini glass by the stem, Julia Maddox leaned against the back of the booth, obviously disinterested in whatever her date was saying since her gaze kept shifting around the room as if searching for someone. Or maybe she felt the need to do Finn's job for him. Scope out the place and keep an eye out for possible threats. But wait . . . she didn't believe any of the threats were credible, did she?

There were only a few instances during the last two weeks when Julia had been nice to him. And he was pretty sure it was purely accidental. She wasn't a fan of having a shadow and usually peered at him with an icy stare that'd freeze most hearts.

After nine-plus years of spinning up on countless

dangerous ops as Echo Five, never once did Finn imagine he'd be called to duty as a babysitter. Okay, bodyguard. Well, more like keep-my-sister-safe duty as defined by Michael Maddox, the man who'd hired Scott & Scott and, by extension, Finn.

This wasn't so much a job as it was a favor. The world owed a great debt to Maddox for his service and sacrifices on and off the battlefield. Michael was a Marine turned millionaire entrepreneur who committed all of his time to help veterans pursue their dreams. Everyone on Bravo and Echo would do just about anything for the man.

So, when Michael approached Luke Scott three weeks ago and requested bodyguard services for his sister because she was receiving threats at work, how could they say no? Michael was occupied with moving his family to Charlotte, and all of his Marine buddies were tied up.

Finn was already acquainted with Julia Maddox in a roundabout way. Julia had joined his self-defense classes back in January. What he hadn't known at the time was that she'd registered under a fake name.

Finn had taken up teaching the classes in Manhattan whenever the teams had downtime and he was in town. He'd always been somewhat of a drifter, bouncing around from city to city for stretches of time. But in the last few years, when his teammates began settling down and having kids, most of Bravo and Echo lived either in New York near the Scott & Scott HQ office or around the DC area. So, Finn now alternated between the two locations, content to play the role of favorite uncle.

And at a recent engagement party for his two friends, Finn had bumped into *Lois* and discovered her real name was Julia. She'd immediately ditched his classes after that, which was a month ago.

Finn had held back on flirting with her while she was in his classes because he didn't want her to think he was some creepy guy who only taught self-defense to hit on women. But once she stopped attending, he'd considered looking her up and asking her out.

And then her brother called in a favor, and well, now, Finn had no plan to ask her out on a date even when this job ended like he'd initially considered.

Finn focused back on the friends he'd dragged out tonight with him. Roman and Harper were the most recent, and the last two of his coworkers, to give up their single status.

He was ridiculously happy they'd finally come to their senses and were now engaged. Their journey had been a road fraught with danger and pitfalls, but they'd made it happen.

Roman had been with the teams since the beginning, but Harper joined them in 2019 after leaving the CIA. She was their intelligence gatherer and analyst and overall badass go-to for ops. Often the brains behind Echo Team missions, as was Jessica for Bravo.

"She hates me," Finn casually remarked.

"Julia doesn't hate you, and you know that. She hates the situation." Harper poked the ice in her glass of water with a straw, pushing the cubes around instead of meeting Finn's eyes.

None of them were allowed to drink tonight. They were on "hurry up and wait" orders from the President, which meant they'd be operating soon, they just didn't know when and where. So, no drinking. That also meant Finn's stint as bodyguard to the millionaire would end soon as well. At the time of Maddox's request, none of the retired SEALs who worked security for their cover story, Scott & Scott, had been free, so Finn had drawn the short straw on Echo Team.

Finn had no clue what they would say to Michael when

the time came for him to hand over duty to another guy from Scott & Scott. He didn't want Michael to think he was ditching his sister, even if it was pretty much true. Michael was completely unaware that Finn was much more than a bodyguard.

Not that he had anything against being a bodyguard, he'd just rather be in Pakistan right now with Bravo Team. Taking down an arms trafficker who was funneling weapons to an up-and-coming wannabe terrorist group was preferable to having Julia reminding him every second how much she didn't want or need a "babysitter."

"She's certainly selling her hate for me pretty damn well." Finn's back was to the bar in order to keep his assignment in his line of sight. Thankfully, it was after ten at night, late enough for the dinner crowd to have dispersed, yet too early for the late-night partygoers. Plus, it was a Monday.

In the forty-five minutes since their little entourage had arrived, Finn had only clocked two quasi-suspicious men, and that was because they appeared to be undressing Julia with their eyes rather than mapping out a plan to toss her into their trunk and run off with her. Besides, they'd taken a look around, seen that the place was devoid of single women, and left.

At the moment, Finn was fairly confident he was the only single person there. Hell, even the employees were all wearing wedding rings.

"If looks could kill," Finn added, shaking his head in frustration when Julia met his gaze while sipping on her overpriced cocktail. He'd rather get kicked in the nuts than pay thirty bucks for a martini. Not unless Emily Blunt herself poured the drink into the glass would he put up that much cash for a drink.

He also kind of hated that Julia happened to resemble his

celebrity crush. He didn't have a clue what color Emily Blunt's eyes were, but Julia's were a take-no-prisoners blue. The kind of blue that made a guy want to commit a crime if she were the arresting officer. Let her put him in handcuffs and . . .

What. The. Actual. Fuck? And did I seriously just channel Ryan Reynolds's voice in my head? For some insane reason, Julia had felt the need to let Finn know that the actor was her type. He mentally rolled his eyes as he continued to observe the woman who had managed to get far, far beneath his skin.

She'd changed her hair color since their run-in at the engagement party in April. What was once an inky black was now a light brown with some blonde strands woven in. Her hair was soft and wavy and hung like a pool of silk draped elegantly over her white blouse. Not a single hair out of place. Her makeup appeared perfect as well. Natural colors to enhance her bone structure, some mascara and liner to play up her bold blue eyes.

Finn squeezed the bridge of his nose at the mental image of that luscious hair wrapped around his fist, tugging her head back as she surrendered to his kiss. Willingly giving him those pouty blood red lips of hers.

And then he chastised himself. Kissing Julia Maddox would be a very bad idea. The woman was the devil in disguise, the snake in the Garden of Eden. No doubt she lured men, like this poor bastard, into her lair and did away with them. Why else was it rumored she never dated the same man twice?

Finn imagined the beautiful Julia drawing him in, pressing her lips to his, coaxing his mouth open only to bite down on his tongue and knee him in his painfully blue balls. The thought had him choking on his own spit.

"You good?" Roman hooked his arm behind Finn's back

to slap him twice as if he had a martini olive stuck in his throat.

"Yeah," Finn coughed out the answer while attempting to banish his ridiculous thoughts and calm his rapid heartbeat.

He took a deep breath and swept the room with his gaze again, checking for newcomers.

Michael had provided Finn with the threats that had been sent to Julia's office. At least, those her admin had intercepted. Apparently, Julia had tossed quite a few.

The letters were handwritten with a standard blue pen and were fairly tame. No serial killer vibes. There were no personal details mentioned about Julia, and the death threats were unoriginal. It was almost like a kid in eighth grade was bored and felt like stirring up some trouble.

Michael may have been overprotective, but he had valid concerns. Concerns Julia didn't seem to share. And it didn't help that the letters had stopped the moment Finn began looking out for Julia. That or she paid her admin to shred any new ones.

"But really, that woman's intense stare is vicious. It could scorch off my"—Finn thought the word *dick* rather than saying it, not wanting to be one in the presence of Harper —"well, you know what I mean."

"Tell him she doesn't hate him." Harper elbowed Roman. He blinked as though startled out of a daydream. Finn was confident Roman would prefer to be back at the loft he and Harper had moved into last week having sex rather than sitting at this pretentious bar.

The things Finn would rather be doing?

Freezing his ass off while running from a polar bear in the Russian ghost town, Pyramiden.

Playing hide-and-seek with the Taliban.

Or a nice game of guess who's the bad guy behind door number eight in Syria.

Anywhere but here, guarding the devil.

Finn mentally slapped his hands together in prayer pose and begged the powers that be to spin up Echo Team soon so someone else could watch over her.

Or, at the very least, he prayed for "Lois" to return.

Lois was kind. Sweet. Funny. Hell, even flirty.

Finn would also take the Julia he'd met at Roman and Harper's engagement party in April. They'd barely spoken that night, but she'd been nice enough.

This Julia was a force to be reckoned with. That movie *The Perfect Storm*? Yeah, Julia Maddox was the storm. And she'd thrown a gale force of negativity his way from the moment she learned her brother hired a bodyguard after she'd specifically told him no.

Dalton, what are you doing here? Julia had asked when he walked into her office two weeks ago. *Sorry, I mean Finn.* She'd smiled as if his presence was a welcome surprise and stood from behind her bright white modern-looking desk, then brushed her hands down the sides of her red pencil skirt paired with a black silk blouse.

Your brother didn't tell you? I'm here about the threats. Someone, uh, wants you dead.

Her smile had quickly transformed to a frown. *Someone always wants me dead. Comes with the territory of being a successful woman.* She'd gracefully returned to her chair and focused on her laptop. *Michael is overprotective. Your services are not needed.* Julia had begun typing as if she fully expected Finn to walk away.

And not-so spoiler alert, he didn't leave.

After a lot of heated back-and-forth once her brother arrived at the office, Julia had managed to renegotiate the terms of the deal. Finn sure as hell wouldn't want to go up against her in a board meeting or whatever the hell rich businesspeople did for a living.

She'd settled for allowing Finn to keep an eye on her everywhere but at home, insisting she trusted her building security and the 9mm she kept by her bed.

Thankfully, this was Julia's first date in the thirteen days and fourteen hours (yes, he was counting) since he'd begun guard duty, which meant they'd spent more time together than either liked.

The fact he screened every meeting beforehand, business and personal, including this wonder boy she'd met last month on Instagram, sent Julia over the edge.

Hell, if he had a sister who found her dates online, he'd be relieved to have someone ensure they not only looked like their profile photo but weren't of the psychopath variety. Julia should be thanking him instead of sending him death stares every five minutes.

You sure these letters aren't from someone you met online? he'd pressed earlier that day in her office.

I haven't been on a date in over a year.

Finn had been standing close enough to breathe in her perfume. She always wore the same fragrance. Subtle. Sexy. A hint of something familiar he couldn't quite put his finger on. Her intoxicating scent combined with an almost imperceptible trace of sadness he detected in her words had him wanting to gather her in his arms, comfort her.

Until Julia had glared straight into his eyes and jabbed the white-painted nail of her forefinger to his chest. *Not that it's any of your business.*

Damn. His friends back in Massachusetts always warned him to stay away from women who wore white nail polish. They said it was a sure sign of a heartbreaker.

"Julia's clearly trying to scare you off," Harper went on. "Drive you nuts, so you'll quit. It appears she's working damn hard at it, too." Harper bit her lip which did nothing to hide her smile. "She's obviously independent and most likely stubborn. But no, she doesn't hate you. She's just pissed that her brother arranged protection."

Finn stroked his jaw, forgetting he'd trimmed his beard last week and it was much shorter than it'd been for months. He regretted the decision. It was too short. Prickly and itchy. *Sort of like Julia's personality.*

"You guys set me up for this gig, didn't you?" Finn asked a heartbeat later. Harper and Roman had been exchanging odd looks ever since they'd arrived, and a little voice in the back of Finn's mind told him something was up with those two. Maybe they could see their plan was failing.

When Harper lifted her eyes to the ceiling, Finn knew she was searching for a lie. Roman only grinned.

"You all made sure I'd draw the short straw when Michael asked one of us to keep her safe. The whole thing was rigged. Damn you all." Finn shook his head and *tsk*ed, feigning disappointment. But he wasn't all that surprised. After all, he was the only single guy left on the teams. "Your game of matchmaking was an epic failure."

"No, we weren't trying to set you up." Harper's voice was pitched a touch higher than normal, and she fluttered her eyelashes one too many times. The woman was totally bluffing. "But come on, would any attached guy on Echo want to tell their wife or fiancée they had to glue themselves to a hot millionaire businesswoman as her bodyguard?"

"Bullshit." Finn looked over at Julia's table to verify she hadn't ghosted him and slipped out the back. That was more likely to happen than any real danger striking. "No. You're definitely trying to set us up."

Echo Team had been dubbed the FSGs. Forever Single Guys. And now, it was simply TSG. *The* Single Guy.

But he was okay with that.

Mostly.

Harper frowned. "Oh, come on, you don't want to be single. I know you don't."

"I'm fine with being single. I only hate it on days that don't end in Y." Finn shot Harper a wink, and Roman laughed.

"Mm-hmm. Sure. It's not easy being single. It kind of sucks, actually." Harper was likely speaking from experience because of the difficult path she and Roman had taken to get to where they were now.

Finn stepped back and brought a hand over his heart as if her comment about him being single did indeed hurt. "Single sucks, hm? Salt right in the wound. Just rub it in. Yeah, I'm feeling pretty shitty now that you keep reminding me." He couldn't hide his smile, but then he remembered he was technically working, so he glanced at his "target" once again to ensure she was still alive and kicking and in no imminent danger.

When Finn returned his focus to his friends, Roman was ogling his fiancée as she feathered her fingers down the column of her throat to the low neck of her pink blouse. She normally wore silly graphic shirts and jeans, but this place had a dress code, so she'd worn a dressy top with skinny black pants and heels.

Harper turned back to Finn. "I was hoping you'd dress up tonight to help with the whole winning-her-over thing. You know, wear something a little less Roman-like."

"What's wrong with my clothes?" Roman complained, looking down at his gray long-sleeve tee, the top few buttons undone, then on to his black jeans.

Harper laughed. "I love how you look, babe. But Julia is a stylish, high-powered businesswoman. Look at her, she's like a goddess, so maybe—"

"I should change myself for her?" Finn shook his head. "Hell no. And wait, why are we discussing this? There is no 'winning-her-over thing' happening." He pushed his sleeves to his elbows. "And also, I'm not dressed like Roman."

With pursed lips, Harper skated her gaze over Finn. His jeans were a little lighter than Roman's, his shirt slightly darker, and they both wore boots. Okay, so maybe they did dress alike, but they were guys. Best friends. What'd she expect him to wear, a suit and tie? If Julia didn't like him for who he was, then . . .

Whoa, what am I thinking? I don't want her. It doesn't matter.

Harper carried her attention to Finn's face, one dark brow lifted in challenge. "You're practically twins tonight. Plus, you have the same hair, beard, bodies and . . ."

"Bodies, huh?" Roman asked with a cocky twitch of his lips. Harper let loose a laugh that quickly turned into a yelp when he playfully slapped her ass. "If Finn and I are so similar, why'd you end up with me?" Roman challenged, an easy smile parked on his face.

"Oh, simple." Harper shrugged. "He doesn't have any ink. I'm a sucker for a few tatts. Annnd, he didn't ask."

At that, Roman swatted her ass again, causing the full glass of water in her hand to bobble and nearly spill. Finn chuckled. Oh, she was going to get it when they were home. And damn, Finn envied their relationship. More than that, his dick mourned the fact it'd been about five million years since he'd had sex.

It may have taken them forever to end up together, but Finn was happy that his buddy and Harper had finally achieved their happily-ever-after. Roman really was a lucky man. Harper was smart as hell, gorgeous, and a total sweetheart. Some people believed men and women couldn't be platonic friends, but Finn disagreed. He'd always thought of Harper like a sister, same as Jessica Scott. Now Jessica Hayes since she'd married Asher, Bravo Three.

Even though it'd been years since Marcus, the first man to hold the title of Bravo Three, was killed and Asher replaced him, there were still times when the loss of Marcus reared up and hit Finn hard. Marcus had been the only Teamguy married at the start of their new jobs in 2013, and Luke had initiated a no-marriage rule after his death. He didn't want any more widows. But then Luke went and fell in love, and like dominoes, the rest of the guys found their soulmates, too.

"Regarding your matchmaking plan, it'll fail. I am who I am. She has no interest in me. Not even a quarter of a teaspoon worth of interest."

"Who are you, Mary Poppins?" Harper chuckled. She set her water onto the bar top, then slapped a hand on his shoulder and peered into his eyes. "Picture this, an enemies-to-lovers romance. You argue. Act like you hate each other. And then"—she comically waggled her eyebrows a few times—"it's game time. You two fall head over heels in love."

Finn turned to check Roman's reaction. He couldn't possibly believe this insanity Harper was concocting. What had wedding planning done to the woman?

"Or just get Tinder. Swipe left or right. Or—"

"What do you know about dating apps?" Harper swung her focus on Roman, interrupting him.

"The man is our human Wikipedia. He knows something about everything," Finn reminded Harper of her future husband's big brain as well as the nickname the guys had given him. But he also knew Roman was just getting back at her for saying he and Finn dressed like twins.

"Mm. Have you ever swiped left or right?" Harper's narrowed eyes were locked on Roman as a low, rumbly laugh erupted from deep in his chest right before he grabbed her waist and pulled her into him for what should probably have been a private moment.

"Nothing is going to happen between Julia and me," Finn declared while Roman whispered something into Harper's ear. "As soon as her brother finds a replacement, I'm done." He rechecked her table, setting his eyes on her date, who looked nothing like Ryan Freaking Reynolds, the actor she claimed was her "type."

This guy was a six-foot Italian who worked for some famous plastic surgeon and probably took advantage of all the services because who had skin that freaking smooth and tight? He also shared more selfies of his abs on Instagram than you could shake a stick at. According to his profile, he had no permanent address. *A man of the world* was what he'd posted beneath his photo.

Whatever happened to meeting someone the old-fashioned way? Shit, and now he was drawing a blank on what the "old-fashioned" way even was.

Probably why I'm single at thirty-nine.

He was always working nonstop, though. This current break between missions wasn't the norm. Their last op had rocked the boat, and POTUS had been holding off on having them operate until the dust settled.

Although, at this very moment, Bravo was taking down some baddies, so the dust was finally where it should be. And his people were ready to roll.

Finn focused on the happy couple, and Roman now had

his arm around Harper's back with her tight to his side. "Any word from Bravo?"

Harper checked her watch and smiled. "Not since you asked me ten minutes ago."

"If we have to leave in the middle of the night, is anyone free yet to step in for me?" Finn dropped his voice lower despite the fact there was no one near them at the bar.

"I, um, did find one guy at Scott and Scott who is free. I have him on standby," Harper answered.

Finn simulated the blades of a helo and spun his finger in the air. "Call him now. Let's swap." This was the best news he'd heard all day.

"You really want Ladies Man Kevin watching Julia?" Roman asked, a note of hesitation in his voice like he expected Finn to have an issue with the guy.

"Kevin? Sure, why not." Kevin was a good guy, but he was also a charmer. *But hell, better him than me, right?* So why did Finn have an uneasy feeling about it?

"*If* we get the green light, he'll handle her." Harper checked her watch again and faked a yawn. "Getting late. I think it's time we head home. What do you say?"

"Yeah, I'm beat." Roman patted Finn on the shoulder a few times. "Good luck, man. Hope you survive the night."

"You and me both," Finn grumbled and said goodnight, then returned his attention to the corner booth across the room where Julia was supposed to be.

Annnnd she was gone. *I suck at this bodyguard thing.* He was about to rush to the ladies' room and barge in, but he didn't have to.

Julia was emerging from the back hallway, but instead of going toward her table where her date remained seated, she started straight for Finn.

Her long, wide-legged black pants hid whatever heels she

32

had on, and he did his best not to focus on the sway of her hips as she moved with confidence. Her cleavage peeked above the deep scoop neck of her silky white top, too.

"We're leaving." Julia remained rooted in place, though.

"When you say 'we,' who exactly are you talking about?" Finn glanced over her shoulder at her date still sitting in the booth.

Julia merely waved a hand between herself and Finn in answer. Their close proximity allowed him to get a whiff of her perfume as she lifted her chin. Whatever she wore, it was most likely expensive. And for some insane reason, it made his dick twitch ever so slightly as he stood and gazed down at her.

She was only five-six or so, and he was a solid six feet. A legitimate six feet, too. According to Julia, any man claiming to be six feet tall on social media was actually five-ten. And a six-two guy was six feet. So, he'd brought a tape measure with him the next day so she could verify his height for herself.

I'm not dating you. No need to check your honesty, she'd said.

No, but for the time being, your life is in my hands. I'd think you'd want to know that I'm trustworthy, he remembered responding only to get chilly silence for a return.

Julia still hadn't budged other than to stretch her long neck as though trying to make herself look taller or more intimidating. Which only resulted in Finn noticing how smooth and creamy her skin was there. "Why aren't you moving yet, sailor?" A dark brow rose even as her eyes stayed riveted on his.

Here we go again.

Finn broke first and blinked, then gave her an insincere smile. He wasn't interested in playing chicken with a pro like her. "Not calling me a commando this time?" He allowed his phony smile to stretch so she knew her little jibes didn't get under his skin as he lowered his face closer to hers.

He studied her features for a moment, not that he hadn't already memorized every inch of her that wasn't covered in clothing. Her oval face, straight nose, and high cheekbones didn't require any filters or magazine touch-ups. She was perfect, at least to him. Irritatingly perfect. And those ridiculously kissable lips . . .

Finn focused on her mouth that constantly wreaked havoc with him, whether she was driving him nuts by bossing him around, refusing to follow his suggestions, or doing that damn pouty kiss-me thing like she was doing now.

Dealing with Julia Maddox was HARD. And if she didn't stop biting on her plump bottom lip, he'd need some private time to deal with something else that was hard.

As soon as her lip was no longer captive to the hint of white teeth, she whispered, "I'm walking home tonight."

Why did she sound so breathless? For that matter, why was he feeling slightly dizzy?

What just happened?

He blinked, realizing she'd turned and already started for the door.

"It's raining now," he called out after her as the hostess scurried to open the door for Her Majesty.

Julia waved her hand in the air without turning back, already stalking toward the crosswalk as if she'd set her sights on her prey. "I'm not the wicked witch. I won't melt."

"Could have fooled me," he said when he caught up with her, which earned a quick over-the-shoulder scowl his way.

There had to be something wrong with him because no matter how often Julia treated him like dirt on the bottom of her Manolos, her sass and attitude continued to turn him on.

Right now, he wanted to pin her to the closest building and tell her exactly what that rain-soaked white blouse was doing to him. Share the dirty thoughts running through his mind.

Of course, he wouldn't. At least, he didn't think he would.

But damn, the vivid images he'd conjured up of the two of them ravishing each other had his blood running hot. He'd swiftly pin her against the brick building at his three o'clock, whisk her arms over her head, and trap her slender wrists with one hand. Startled, she'd stare at him, her pouty, red lips forming a perfect O, her breasts heaving with deep, angry breaths. And then she'd give in and plead with him to make a move. To suck her lip. Feel her tits over the material of her blouse now nearly sheer from the rain.

"Are. You. Coming?"

Finn jerked his head to see Julia standing on the other side of the crosswalk with her hands on her hips and her perfect hair growing wet.

Am I coming? Hm. Sadly, no.

It'd been way too long since he'd had sex. And that wicked mouth of hers was just—

"Dalton, damn it."

His given name snapped him back to attention yet again. He really needed Kevin to take over for him. On a scale of one to ten, Finn was a negative five tonight in terms of professionalism.

He hurried across the street to join her and prayed for an act of God to prevent him from ogling her blouse and slipping back into that never-will-happen fantasy in his head.

"What is wrong with you? You truly suck at this job."

"I know." He smiled. "But you actually waited for me," he replied in a glib voice as he worked to pull himself together. All Harper's talk about dating must've screwed with

35

his head. *Both* heads. "And I only suck because you don't make shit easy, princess."

She faced him, and he was proud of the fact he kept his eyes up top.

For all of two seconds, and then his eyes latched on to the beads of water sliding along the column of her slender neck, taking a nice ride down, down, down into her cleavage.

She was wearing a bra, at least.

"Eyes up, sailor."

Why did her words turn him on so much? He'd swear she was two seconds away from hitting him in the head with her purse. "What happened with your date, by the way? Strike out?"

She combed her fingers through her hair, her purse strap nearly falling off her shoulder in the process. The longer they stood there, the more drenched they'd both get.

But the alleyway up ahead made him a little uneasy, and then he turned to the side to put eyes on the sidewalk behind him. No one was on his heels or suspicious from what he could tell anywhere nearby.

Did someone spike his drink? Why was he so off tonight? This woman made him nuts, so it would seem.

"The date was fine. Last date I'll be going on, though."

"Wait, what? That bad?" He replayed her words, unsure if he'd heard them correctly. Did he need to go clock the guy? Did the man-boy back there say something wrong? Get handsy? "What happened?"

"Just . . . never mind." And was that a flustered breath?

She was already on the move, but this time to hail a taxi. The woman didn't believe in Uber, huh? There were still yellow taxis in New York, though, and she'd managed to get one.

"What happened to walking?" he asked once they were

both in the backseat. "Hey." Finn redirected his attention to the driver when he caught the man's eyes in the rearview mirror, trying to catch an eyeful of Julia's soaked blouse. "Eyes on the road."

"Mm. Hypocrite," Julia muttered under her breath while crossing her arms as if chilled.

"Can you turn on the heat?" he asked the driver in a nicer tone this time.

"Don't do me any favors," she tossed out, and Finn had no clue if she was talking to him or the driver.

She remained quiet the rest of the way back to her building, her gaze set out the window, and he did the same. He thought back to that alleyway, which had him remembering the night Luke and Jessica had recruited him. *Whatever happened to that kid?* He'd never been able to track him down, and he'd always been curious what became of him.

"We're here," the driver said upon arrival as if Julia wouldn't recognize her own building.

She was quicker on the draw with paying the fare than Finn, which irritated the hell out of him. "Let me pay you back for the ride," he insisted as they walked past her building security to get to the set of elevators.

"Hell no." She pressed the top button and avoided eye contact in the reflective golden doors. "You don't need to ride up with me."

"Doing my job, even if I suck at it," he said.

When the doors opened, she quickly stepped inside. "The threats are most likely bullshit. I wish you would believe me and walk away."

He waited for the doors to close before answering, "I don't walk away from people." He slowly turned to put eyes on her. "How long have you actually been receiving threats?

Is that the real reason you took my classes? You wanted to protect yourself?" The questions had been floating around in his mind for two weeks.

Julia swept a hand across her collarbone as if brushing away any remaining water droplets rather than buying herself time. "There's nothing wrong with wanting to be able to protect yourself."

What are you hiding? There was something in those cerulean-blue eyes, rain-smeared mascara now beneath them, that told him she was keeping secrets. Probably from her brother, too. And those secrets might get her killed. "You're right, but—"

"Stop where you're at. You can't help me." She eased a step closer and lifted her chin to continue holding his eyes.

"Help you?" he whispered, his stomach tightening. Worry settling hard and deep. "Why can't I help you? That's what your brother hired me to do."

The doors chimed and opened but neither exited.

"No, he hired you to keep me safe, not to help me." Her eyes dropped closed for a second before flashing open. "All you've done is get in my way." And like that, she peeled out of the elevator and started for one of only three apartments on the floor.

"Julia, wait," he called out, hating the desperation in his tone. "Please."

She'd already slipped inside her apartment and was on the verge of closing the door, effectively shutting him out, but he quickly pushed his booted foot into the slight opening.

"I don't want you. Go away."

Her words had him recalling someone else's voice. Their words that'd been a knife to the heart so long ago. *I don't want you. I can't look at you. Go away.*

"Julia." Her name escaped his barely parted lips as he

forced himself to focus on the present. "Please, don't make this so hard." He'd shove open the door if he had to, but he was stupidly hoping for an olive branch of some kind. For her to let him in. Talk to him.

What'd he expect from a woman who'd gone out of her way to push him away for two weeks, though?

"I'm home now. You're off the clock." Why the hell was there a tremble to her tone this time? A chink in that steely defense she'd erected.

"We need to talk. I need to know the truth."

"Sure, remove your boot from the door, and I'll pour some tea and we'll have a heartfelt chat." And there was the woman he'd come to know. The woman who wanted him gone. Ninety-nine percent sour with rare and accidental glimmers of sweetness.

Harper was right.

It was an act.

Julia had slipped up tonight. Let him know there was a hell of a lot more going on than just some notes sent to her office.

"Go. I won't ask again." He couldn't see her face through the slim crack. She must have turned her back to the door, too afraid to look at him because he might witness the truth in her eyes.

"If you change your mind, you know how to reach me." He was terrified he'd come to regret this decision, but Finn slowly slid his boot from the opening. "Lock up. Be safe."

The door clicked shut a moment later, just as his work phone began vibrating in his pocket.

"Hey, Harper," he answered while starting for the elevator, his heart heavy and his thoughts weighing him down more with each step.

"Wheels up at zero nine hundred. Catching a military

ride," Harper cut straight to the point. "Kevin will meet up with you at Julia's apartment in the morning to swap places so he can take her to work before you head to the hangar."

Shit. He paused outside the elevator, knowing she wouldn't answer the door anyway if he went to her apartment now. He'd wait until the morning to tell her he was, in fact, walking away. Doing exactly what he'd told her he didn't do. But it was what she wanted.

"Where are we going? Did Bravo get a location for us?" He punched the call button and waited.

"Yeah, we're heading to Egypt."

CHAPTER TWO

JULIA CAREFULLY SMOOTHED HER FINGERS OVER THE TINY ballerina atop the plain, brown antique jewelry box. The ballerina's pink tutu was now faded and she no longer twirled, but she'd survived being passed down from mom to daughter for three generations. According to Julia's mom, the Swan Lake Waltz had stopped playing long before Julia was born.

She still loved the little box, which sat on the dresser in her one-bedroom Tribeca condo. It held only three pieces of jewelry: her grandmother's emerald ring, her great-grandmother's sapphire pendant, and military ID tags.

She opened the box, lifted the chain, and held the two silver ID tags in her palm, then smoothed her thumb over Tucker Lucas's name. She'd been in college when her boyfriend died. For years she'd worn Tucker's tags around her neck religiously, terrified that if she took them off, she'd lose all the happy memories they'd once shared.

Tucker's brother, Oliver, had been the one to remove the chain from around Julia's neck five years ago, telling her it was time to let go. To let *him* go.

41

But now more than ever, Tucker's memory hung heavy and thick around her. He was the reason why she and Michael focused on helping veterans pursue their dreams. Helped them transition from the service to civilian life, start businesses.

Tucker hadn't opened up to her about his struggles, and if she could go back in time and . . .

Stop. You have to stop doing this to yourself, Oliver's voice appeared in her head. *It's not your fault. It was an accident. You can't possibly blame yourself.*

"But I do blame myself," Julia whispered the same response she always gave Oliver as she tucked the tags back inside the box and lifted her eyes to the mirror hanging above the dresser.

She was still wearing her floor-length silky black robe, and her thick mass of hair hung like a sheet of silk over her shoulders. Her makeup for the workday had already been applied—winged black eyeliner, mascara, and light brown eyeshadow. A touch of bronzer on her high cheekbones and bronzed-toned lipstick, all of it selected to match a nude-colored fitted knee-length dress. Simple beige heels would complete the look.

Why she kept purposely wearing things she knew would garner a reaction from Finn was beyond her? He appeared to be a legs and ass man based on the times she'd caught him checking her out. And the dress she was about to put on would emphasize her assets.

Despite the fact she'd been horrible to him, there'd been desire in those intense looks he'd given her during the last two weeks.

An unexpected rush of warmth radiated through her body, followed by a strong urge to clench her thighs together at the thought of Finn picking her up, tossing her onto her bed, and swiping the millions of decorative pillows to the floor. After which he'd make her pay for every asshole remark she'd slung at him by giving her orgasms and . . .

Damn it. Why did he have to be so sexy and sweet? Why couldn't he be a jerk? It would make it a lot easier to be mean if he wasn't such a good guy undeserving of her bad attitude.

When her phone began buzzing on the nightstand, she hurried over and snatched it. Sighing with relief at the sight of Mya's name on the screen, Julia did a quick mental prayer that she was calling with news.

"Hey." Julia sat on her bed and set one slightly trembling palm on her thigh. "It's early."

"It's even earlier here," Mya returned with a light chuckle. "I'm still in Vancouver wrapping up an assignment."

Mya Vanzetti had been a beat reporter in the city but gave it up to become a freelance investigative journalist a few years back. These days, her stories often led to the takedown of some pretty nefarious people around the world, and she regularly worked with Julia's brother's Marine friends to make it happen, which was how they'd first met. And they'd instantly bonded.

So, naturally, Julia would go to Mya for the particular kind of help she needed. But she'd made Mya promise not to breathe a word to any of Michael's buddies. They'd run straight to her brother, and he'd flip out about what she was trying to do.

"But you have news?" Julia asked, eager to know why Mya had called. She was answered with the sound of a long, drawn-out yawn.

"Sorry, I haven't gone to bed yet. But it looks like all your work sweet-talking the assistant online paid off. I was able to access his boss's schedule. We have the plastic surgeon's next location." Excitement replaced her sleepy voice. "I have to say, you should consider trying your hand at clandestine work. Maybe join us. You were pretty sneaky at mirroring his phone without him noticing."

"Boobs," Julia blurted as she stood from the bed, thankful they finally found the man she'd been looking for. "They can be distracting."

Julia's brother still had an office at their location in New York, and she knew exactly where he kept all of his "toys," such as a mobile phone capable of cloning another one. Luckily, he had several and hadn't noticed one was missing. Not yet, at least. Probably distracted by all the shenanigans involved in moving his family to North Carolina.

Last night on her date, she'd merely had to butt her phone right up against Lorenzo's for thirty seconds while he droned on about himself. The man loved to show off from what she'd gathered by basically stalking him online for three weeks to learn everything about him—from his favorite food to the type of woman he was attracted to. She'd gone as far as changing her hair color to that of the women who were always in photos with him, too.

Julia had convinced Lorenzo to stop over in New York for an evening on his way back from Toronto. Thank God he'd shown up. She was short on time.

And now she had a replica of his phone. She'd uploaded all of its data just as Mya had instructed and sent it to her electronically last night after Finn dropped her off.

"Unfortunately, I'm lacking in the boob department. I have to rely on my ass for distracting guys," Mya said lightheartedly. "But anyway, before I tell you where his boss is heading next, you should know all my resources are tied up. I've got no one to send there. That said, I know you're going to want to go on your own, but I strongly advise against it. I think it's time we tell your brother. Or at least Mason or Connor."

"You know I can't do that." Julia paced the room, trying to come up with a plan. A way to ditch Finn so she could dash to the airport as soon as possible.

Connor Matthews and his brother, Mason, were two of her brother's best friends. They both worked in private security, and they treated her like a sister, which meant there wasn't a chance in hell they'd let Julia follow this lead if they knew what she was really up to.

"Just tell me where his boss is going," Julia pleaded. "Please. Where will Giorgio be?"

A long sigh filled the line. "Aswan," Mya reluctantly replied. "Giorgio Ferrari is staying at some fancy hotel by the Nile for a few nights."

"He must be meeting with a new client. This is my chance to talk to him. I have to go."

Another pause . . . and Julia knew what Mya was about to suggest.

"This isn't just any doctor you're trying to chat with. You need to take someone with you. How about Dalton? Tell him it's a work thing. You can be vague. I'd feel a lot better knowing you had a former SEAL watching your back."

"A SEAL is always a SEAL, right? Nothing former about that man." *Did I just say that?*

"Ah, so you *still* like him."

She may have mentioned her attraction to Dalton once, okay maybe ten times, when she was taking his self-defense classes. She now regretted opening her big mouth.

Julia resisted the old urge to bite her thumbnail. Chewing on one's fingernails wasn't exactly millionaire mogul behavior. Then again, she wasn't the typical millionaire. Her bank account and millionaire status were originally due to her brother. After the Marines, Michael had invented intelligence software that subsequently sold for over three hundred million dollars, and he was the pay-it-forward kind of guy, so they worked together to help finance and launch businesses for veterans.

"And how is the friends-with-benefits thing with Mason holding up? Catch feelings yet?" Yeah, two could play at this game.

"He's dating someone new. So, there are noooo benefits. Plus, we rarely see each other anymore. Most of our work together is virtual." Mya didn't sound bummed, so that was good. She wasn't the type of woman to catch feelings anyway. "There is something I have to confess."

And now Julia felt the need to sit back down. She was short on time. Finn would be there soon, and she needed to book a flight to Egypt without him knowing.

"Julia . . ." Oh, that slow start from Mya had Julia's stomach turning. "Um, I'm the reason there's someone assigned to follow your every move. Not specifically Mister Hottie, but I figured your brother would go all alpha caveman and hire protection for you since his buddies are tied up and he was in the process of moving to Charlotte with Kate and the kids."

Setting the phone on her lap, Julia put Mya on speakerphone, then reached up and began massaging her forehead. "You aren't serious. You wrote the death threats sent to my office?"

"You refused to tell your brother that you'd taken matters into your own hands even though he promised he'd handle it. And yes, you're not doing it alone, I'm helping you, but I can't have you getting killed because of my help, now can I?"

"We've been at this for months. Why the sudden worry?" Julia's chest tightened with emotion, and she brought her hand to her throat as anxiety attempted to claim her control. "Is it because we actually found a lead? Or are you suddenly beginning to question this entire thing, just like Michael?"

"No, I believe you. But it's been a long shot from the beginning, and when we found out about the doctor, I just . . . I'm worried, okay?"

"Mya, I know you're only looking out for me, but this little stunt of yours was uncalled for," Julia chided. "I've been a total bitch to this man for two weeks. Trying my hardest to drive him away and get him to quit so he wouldn't discover what I'm doing. All for no reason." She muted the speaker, clutched the phone to her ear, and slowly stood. *God, why did it have to be Finn?*

"Let's call it fate that the hot self-defense instructor you couldn't seem to stop gushing about not too long ago wound up at your door for this assignment."

"Nice try, Lois Lane. Can't distract me." She'd given Mya that nickname because of her job, so when she'd signed up for Finn's classes, the name Lois had popped into her head, and she'd scribbled it down on the form. "Not fate. This is grade A Mya interference."

"Hey, I run great interference, which is why you came to me for help," she reminded her in a teasing voice. "And you love me."

Julia mentally ran through the long, long list of horrific, embarrassing, and just plain mean things she'd said to Finn to get him to back off. She couldn't risk him stepping in and stopping her when she had a life to save but playing the part of a demanding bitch went against her nature.

"I owe him a Plymouth Rock–sized apology." Her shoulders sagged with guilt. He didn't deserve the attitude. He was just doing his job.

But that apology would have to come later. Even if she

could fake a last-minute work trip to Egypt, Finn would in all likelihood come along as her bodyguard. And he'd be sure to get in her way. No, she had to ditch Finn to get on that plane.

The last thing she needed was a stubborn, six-foot-tall roadblock standing between her and her mission, no matter how handsome he was.

"Please don't go to Egypt alone. I have a bad feeling." Mya's words weren't delivered with her usual confident punch. Her friend's typical fierceness also seemed to have deflated with the reality and gravity of the situation.

"Then you shouldn't have helped me." Probably a low blow. Kind of the truth, though, right? Without Mya's investigative skills, she'd be nowhere. This endeavor was entirely over her head.

"And if I go, are you going to call my brother? Fabricate an even more dangerous threat hoping to provoke a bigger response, like house arrest?" Julia asked as her doorbell rang.

She'd granted permission to building security to allow Finn direct access to her apartment. He'd gotten annoyed about having to be approved and buzzed in every single morning, and she finally gave in despite her best efforts to drive him nuts.

And all this time, his presence was due to Mya. Julia was tempted to wring her neck the next time she saw her. But then again, Julia wouldn't have this promising lead without Mya. "He's here," she said when the bell rang again. "And he hates me, you know."

"But he still wants you, am I right?"

"It's just . . . tension." The kind of tension Julia would normally handle on her own. But she'd been experiencing an orgasm drought lately, unable to even get herself off, and it was surely stress-related.

Although, the mere thought of Finn a few moments ago

had her clenching her thighs together when a jolt of lust shot through her body. And that was pretty damn shocking.

Great. Mya had successfully distracted her.

"Yeah, tension of the sexual nature," Mya teased. "Take him to Egypt with you. That's not a request."

"No." Julia tensed, worried Mya would choose her safety over her request not to call her brother. "Do not tell Michael," she reiterated when Finn rang again.

Finn wouldn't worry that she hadn't answered yet. She usually made him wait until the fifth ring. Yeah, she'd been a real winner to him.

"Maybe your brother will have success. You have to be optimistic."

"I told you that he's losing faith. The more he studies the evidence, he just . . ." She couldn't get herself to finish that sentence.

Mya was quiet for a moment, then whispered, "Just don't go to Egypt by yourself. Promise me."

Julia opened her bedroom door and started down the hallway in a hurry. "I gotta go. That's ring number five. He might just bust down the door if he gets to six."

"Call me as soon as you're at the office."

"No, you get some sleep. Well, after you message me the hotel details of where I'm going."

"Julia." Mya dragged her name out in warning.

"Talk soon. I forgive you for the Finn thing, by the way."

"So, it's Finn now, huh?"

"Don't start. Talk later." Julia ended the call and hollered out, "I'm coming. Don't shoot your way inside or something." She quickly unlocked the door and yanked it open. And by the shocked look on Finn's face, you'd have thought she was naked. His green eyes went almost feral for a heartbeat before his focus traveled slowly south.

Shit. The robe. At least it was black and not her cream-colored one. But her nipples now stood at attention with the good sailor reporting for duty. Another oddity considering the dry spell she'd been having for the last couple of weeks. *Months, Julia. It's been months.*

As slowly as it had skated down her body, Finn's gaze swept back up to her face and pinned her with a dark look that propelled her back a step. Was he throwing out anger or lust? Maybe a bit of both.

"I wouldn't breach your place with a gun, FYI," he responded, his voice husky and rough. Like he'd been rudely awakened from a deep sleep . . . *after* having had the best sex of his life.

What is wrong with me?

A black ball cap was parked backward on his head, covering most of his brownish-black hair. He had on faded denim jeans, a black Under Armour tee, and dark sneakers. A watch on his wrist. Plus, he was sporting his standard look of concern-slash-annoyed by her overall existence.

"We need to talk." She noticed the green of his irises appeared more vibrant than usual—a hit-the-trails outdoorsy green. And for one second, she caught a glimpse of nature and freedom and all of the things she yearned for from her childhood, right there in the look he was giving her.

She'd grown up in North Carolina, frequenting the beach in the summers and the mountains in the winter. Most people wouldn't have taken her for an outdoorsy girl, but she loved nature. The fresh mountain air. The calming sounds of the water running from a nearby stream. The feel of granite beneath your palms while rock climbing. *Just* all of it.

"What's wrong?" she said quietly, aware that she should probably move aside and allow him the opportunity to enter the apartment. But she remained frozen in place, using her body as a wedge to prop the door open.

"Can we talk inside?" Finn's voice still sounded rusty, which made her pause. It was the same type of voice Mya had used to deliver her confession moments ago. Did he have bad news?

Julia wanted to flee to her bedroom, plop onto the bed, and cover her face with her palms.

Now that she knew the threats were bogus, which she'd felt in her gut from the start, he couldn't possibly have stumbled upon an actual bad guy trying to hurt her, right?

"Come in." She finally moved from the doorway, and he slowly walked inside. After a couple of steps, Finn came to a halt, scratched the back of his head, and stared at the blank wall off to his left, carefully avoiding eye contact.

Oh right. My nipples. "I'm going to change first."

"Um, okay," he responded in a gravelly tone, and she hooked a right down the hall to her room. The condo was small since she was only usually in New York a few months a year, bouncing back and forth between her offices in Charlotte and Boston. She'd been in New York since early December, though, which was the longest she'd stayed in one place in a long time.

Julia passed by the few family photos on the wall, catching sight of the framed photos of her nephew and her niece on her way. Their parents were thrilled that Michael and Kate had decided to move back to Charlotte since they had remained in North Carolina.

Julia had no clue if she would ever give her parents grandchildren or if she even wanted kids. *But I have time, right? I'm only thirty-four.*

She quickly removed her robe and second-guessed the form-fitting dress since she planned to make a beeline for the

51

airport in hopes she'd somehow buy her way onto a last-minute flight across the Atlantic.

But Finn would be suspicious if she came out in yoga pants and a loose tee. Her typical travel gear. *Dress it is for now.*

When she returned to the small living room that overlooked a multimillion-dollar view of the city, Finn's back was to her, eyes on the framed picture hanging over the couch. "This one of your photos?"

She came up alongside him and viewed the framed photograph. "That view is from the porch of my parents' home on the beach in the Outer Banks. I happened to catch a wild horse running on the sand with my lens." She crossed her arms and smiled at the memory. As a kid, she was never without her camera, taking it along everywhere. And now, well, she supposed her phone was always with her as a camera, but she rarely found herself viewing things through the eye of a photographer anymore. Her interest in capturing life's moments seemed to have waned over the years. "They just put the place on the market, though."

She felt his eyes on her and peeked over at him.

"Anyway." Why had she told him that, and with such sadness in her voice? "So, what's going on?"

Finn turned to fully face her. "I have to go out of town for an emergency work thing."

"Oh." She blinked in surprise at the turn of events. "Perfect." Turning away from him to hide her face, Julia looked toward the window. "I mean, you know how much I—"

"My replacement is on his way."

Her shoulders fell at the news. Now she needed to ditch a new guy. Would that be harder or easier? "Is he a SEAL, too?"

"Yeah. Been out for three years now."

She slowly faced him. "I thought you said last night you don't walk away from anything."

His gaze dipped for a brief moment, his eyes racing over the length of her fitted dress and down to her tan legs. "I don't, but this job is important."

She took one small step closer, her heels adding a few inches to her height, putting her at about five-nine now. "So, what you're saying is that I'm not important?"

"I thought you were ready to let me go?" he asked, clearly confused and frustrated. "Isn't that what you've been saying for two weeks?"

"I don't approve of a replacement. Not going to happen. Call him and cancel." She swatted a dismissive hand in the air. "It's you or no one."

With mere inches between them, Finn dipped his chin and narrowed his eyes at her.

What was that cologne he was wearing? He smelled incredible.

And why was she squeezing her thighs together again? Was she cured in the south-of-the-border region? Twice in one morning she'd been blindsided with sudden lust.

Finn angled his head, not backing down. "So, you do want me." He shot her a cocky smile and winked before straightening to his full height.

"I don't want to train someone new."

He set a hand to his chest and frowned as if offended. "So, what you're saying is you consider us like dogs to be house-trained?" He was teasing, but she deserved it. "Or like a pair of new high heels? Gotta break us in, huh?"

He pointed to her shoes, and she followed his line of sight, noticing how it lingered on her legs instead of her heels.

"If everything goes well, I'll be back in three days," he went on when she didn't speak. "You can manage three days without me. Kevin's a good guy. A bit flirty, so I apologize in advance."

"What do you mean *if* everything goes well? What do you anticipate might happen?" Julia folded her arms, wondering why she felt a stab of worry about whatever the hell "emergency work thing" he was heading off to for three days.

Clearing his throat, Finn brought a fist to his mouth for a moment as if to buy himself time. She'd seen that look before. On her brother's face back in the early days of the Iraq War, right before he deployed. A look that said he wasn't quite sure how to say goodbye.

What was going on?

"I just meant the trip could get extended." Finn casually shrugged.

"You're lying," she snapped out on impulse and tightened her arms across her chest.

"Am I?" Mimicking her posture, he crossed those bronzed, muscular arms over his chest, sending a whiff of that amazing cologne wafting her way. And with his forearms crossed, the veins popping—now she was the one fixating on his body. "I'm more than a bodyguard, by the way."

"What do you do?" *Look up. Stop staring at the arm porn.* "What else do you do, I mean?"

"Security work. PMC. You know, like the stuff your brother's friends do."

"They aren't private military contractors. They sort of bypass government regs." When she met his eyes, he blinked a few times as if trying not to expose a secret or a bluff. "So, you're working for the government on this three-day job?"

"Nah." He lightly shook his head. "Something else. Just a quick assignment."

"One that you believe is more important than me." Why was she challenging him, keeping up the bitchy act? After finally getting a lead, granted, it was a small one, but it was better than nothing, this was exactly what she wanted. But Finn leaving her in the hands of this flirty Kevin guy, like she was just another job, hurt a little. Besides, the last thing she needed was a new guy possibly botching shit up. She knew how to operate around Finn.

And time was running out with only three weeks remaining. If the lead on the doctor was a bust, she might be back to square one.

"I'm going out of town today. Overseas," she blurted out like a *So there, what're you gonna do about it?*

"What?" And there was that knee-jerk reaction she'd expected. "Why didn't you give me a heads-up?"

"I didn't know until five minutes before you showed up. I'm actually going to be heading to the airport now." She swallowed and looked around her sparsely furnished condo for her laptop.

The framed photograph on the wall was the only decoration in the living room, and the furniture consisted of a white couch which was too uncomfortable to sit on, a glass coffee table in front of it, and a TV stand minus the TV.

She spied her laptop on the marble bar top separating the living room from the kitchen where she'd left it last night. "Once I get a ticket, that is."

"Where are you going? Does your brother know?" Suspicion filled his tone.

"No, and you can't tell him. Please." Two quick steps and she was within kissing distance to the man. Of course, her heel chose that moment to go wonky. Her arms instinctively flew out, and her hands braced against the nearest object, which was Finn's chest. "Client–bodyguard privilege."

He lowered his gaze to peer at her hands on his chest. "I think you mean doctor–patient privilege. I'm no doctor." He closed one eye briefly. "I was a medic in the Navy, though."

"I didn't know that." For some odd reason, she couldn't pry her hands away from the hard planes of his torso. At least she fought the urge to rub her palms over all those muscles.

He cocked his head slightly. "A lot you don't know about me, princess."

"I hate when you call me that."

"And now you know how I feel when you call me commando. Makes me feel like I'm in some shitty eighties movie slashing my way through a jungle with a bandana wrapped around my head."

In a jungle, huh? She almost laughed at the image he'd painted. She really did owe him a few apologies.

And then she remembered what was going on, and he'd be leaving her. "Choose me," she whispered, then added in a stronger, almost surprising tone, "Pick me."

He smiled. "Isn't that a line from a movie? Not a SEAL movie, either. But I swear it sounds familiar."

"You a movie guy?"

He shrugged.

Why am I still touching him? She stepped back and lifted her hands as if a police officer had asked to search her for a weapon. "Please. Choose me over this other job. I don't want to go to Egypt with a stranger."

His green eyes thinned in a hurry, and he was the one stepping back now, a stunned look on his face. "Egypt?"

"Why is that so hard to believe?"

His mouth became a hard, firm line. And his eyes cut to the Brazilian hardwoods beneath their feet as though he might be considering her request. "Where in Egypt?"

"Aswan. I assume I'll need to fly to Cairo first and then get a connecting flight."

Finn held a finger between them and lifted his eyes to hers. "Say that again."

She repeated her words, still not following his odd reaction.

He dragged a hand over the light bit of growth covering his square jaw and bit out, "Why are you going there?"

"An investor's traveling there, and I've been working hard to get a meeting with him." She sucked at lying on the fly, damn it.

Finn's attention went to the door, then back to her. "I need to step out and make a call. Just, um, wait here."

"It is my place," she reminded him, still perplexed as to why the hell *he* was acting so odd.

"Yeah, okay. Be right back." He left the condo, and she took the chance to hurry to her phone to see if Mya had texted her the hotel details.

She breathed a sigh of relief at the text containing the address. Mya had followed it with a plea.

Mya: *Do. Not. Go. Alone. I will call your brother. I can't have you running around on your own chasing what could be the start of a big storm.*

Shit. And Mya would call Michael if she knew it'd save her life.

She glanced at the door to the hall, then looked back at her phone.

Julia: *Finn is going with me. You don't need to tell my brother. I'll text you later. Get some rest.*

Mya: *You promise?*

Julia: *Yes.*

And hopefully, Finn would choose her over his other

57

assignment, but after how horrible she'd been to him, she wasn't so sure.

A knock at the front door a few minutes later had her pulse racing, and she hurried to let him back in.

He set his hand on the frame outside of the door as she held it open with her back, waiting for him to come in. But he remained in the hall, studying her.

Finn had once been part of an elite unit of operators. Of course, he'd be able to read her like a book. And from the look on his face, he knew something more than a business trip was taking her to Egypt.

"You're coming out of town with me," he announced firmly.

"Wait, what?" She expected him to explain further, but when he remained silently scrutinizing her, she asked, "Where are you going?"

"My assignment . . . it's also in Aswan, Egypt."

Now she understood his shocked expression a few moments ago. How could this possibly be a coincidence?

"There aren't any commercial flights available today. We're catching a free ride another way. A pit stop in Algiers first. We should be in Aswan tomorrow by four or five a.m. local time."

She followed the line of muscle in his tense forearm with her eyes as his palm remained firm on the doorframe. "Who else is going?"

"My teammates. Harper, Roman, Wyatt, Chris, and A.J. We won't be bringing Bear on this one."

"Bear?"

"Our canine."

Oh. Hm. Okay. Weird. "And you won't tell me why you're going there?" Bad idea to ask because she knew he was about to follow up with the same question and probably push for a real answer this time. An answer she knew if she provided, he'd take straight to her brother, and no one would let her on that plane.

"Only if you tell me why you're going." His lips twitched. Part smile. Or maybe worry.

"I need to pack," she said quickly before he changed his mind.

"One condition," he began, and she had a feeling he was about to lay down some ultimatums. "You stop being so damn mean."

CHAPTER THREE

"MA'AM, IT'S WHEELS UP IN FIVE. YOU NEED TO GET situated," a soldier, or maybe a sailor, wearing a bluish-gray uniform announced, his voice deep and his Southern accent thick, as he breezed past her.

"He called me ma'am," Julia said, feeling slightly insulted, as they walked in through the back of a military cargo plane located inside a hangar on the outskirts of the city. A government site she had no idea existed.

Finn held on to her elbow and navigated them around the cargo and heavy equipment buckled down to the floor of the massive plane.

"Do I look old?" When he side-eyed her with a playful smile, she rolled her eyes. "Don't answer that." She'd promised to stop being "so damn mean," but acting the role of the villain for the past few weeks had somehow become routine around Finn, and she was worried she'd forgotten how to be herself.

"The team is already here," was his answer to her. "Somewhere."

She'd witnessed her brother board such planes back in the

day when he was in the Marines, but Finn and his team were civilians, so why the special treatment?

"So, because you guys are PMCs, the military gives you free rides? They make extra stops like this for you?" Julia did her best to withhold the sarcasm from her tone as they made their way through the plane.

"Yeah, we, uh, called in a favor."

Mmhm. Sure you did. What was he hiding? Not that she could talk.

She let go of a deep breath at the sight of a familiar face.

"Harper." Thank God for another female in this sea of testosterone.

"Nice to see you." Harper's greeting was pleasant enough, but there was a hint of coolness in her tone. She was dressed in jeans and a white tank with the words, *I can explain it to you, but I can't understand it for you* written in black on the front.

Yeah, I need that top. "Thank you for allowing me to join you all."

Harper responded with a polite tilt of her head and a smile that didn't quite reach her eyes. And those dark eyes were giving Julia the once-over as though carefully considering whether or not she could be trusted.

Julia took an uncomfortable step back and looked to her left to see the rest of Finn's teammates huddled around a crate, talking in hushed voices.

One of the guys, who she recognized as Wyatt, looked her way. He smiled and gave her a quick nod, then focused back on the others. Were they talking about her?

Wyatt was the British one, from what she remembered. Roman, of course, was Harper's fiancé. Then there was Chris and A.J.

Somehow, she'd met all of Finn's teammates at different

62

points over the years because of Michael's friendship with Luke Scott, but she'd never encountered Finn until this year. Maybe Mya was right, and it was fate. The world had kept them apart only to go the other extreme and throw them together, practically 24/7 except when she was home or sleeping.

And shit. The sleeping arrangements. Would he let her have her own hotel room in Egypt? Considering what she was planning to do, did she even *want* to be alone there?

"It's going to be a long trip. The seats suck. I'll hang you a hammock later." Finn pointed to what looked like a fishing net.

Julia frowned. "Yes, because that looks far more comfortable."

"They're not too bad," Harper commented while gazing at Roman.

Maybe not if you were sharing with someone you loved, Julia supposed, then awkwardly swallowed the lump that popped up in her throat when she noticed Finn's eyes still focused on her.

"I probably won't sleep. I have some books to read on my Kindle to keep me busy," Julia added.

"Oh?" Harper crossed her arms, then glanced Finn's way. "Romance novels by chance? Maybe a hot enemies-to-lovers book?"

"Huh?" Julia caught Finn in her peripheral view, vigorously making chopping motions in the air with his hand as if telling Harper to drop it.

What was he trying to get her to drop? Now Julia was curious.

"Anyway." Finn rolled his eyes and made a face at Harper. Julia bit back a laugh. He looked like a big brother who was annoyed with his little sister. It was a look Julia was quite familiar with because Michael had perfected it years ago. Finn gave Harper one last glare, then looked back at Julia. "So, it'll be Algiers first to drop off some supplies. The stop shouldn't take more than an hour or two."

He scratched the light bit of growth on his jaw before turning toward the rest of his teammates, who were now gathered around an open laptop. Not a standard-issue one, but the kind Julia had seen her brother use whenever he had meetings with the Department of Defense. A sturdy, black case that could probably withstand a grenade blast.

Hmmm. The cargo plane. The serious look on all of Finn's teammates' faces. The laptop. They must have taken a government job, which was most likely why he wouldn't share any details with her. It also explained why he couldn't say no to the job when she'd asked back at her apartment.

"Oh, by the way," Finn began, swiveling back around sporting a grin. "Ever jumped tandem?"

"Say what?" Her hand went to her stomach since she was fairly certain he was referring to skydiving.

"I mean, in case we need to exit this plane a different way." Finn winked, then continued on his way to his teammates.

"He's kidding, right?" she asked as the backloading ramp closed, sealing out the natural light.

"Yeah." Harper smiled. "Probably." She motioned for her to sit on a metal bench attached parallel to the wall, which offered Julia a view of Finn's backside.

Well-worn jeans on a man had never looked so good as the denim stretched over his glutes, which he must have worked out regularly.

Finn was leaning forward over a crate to view whatever was on the laptop. Wyatt appeared to be the one talking, holding the attention of everyone around him. Was he their team leader?

"So." That one word had Julia bracing herself for what might follow. Finn probably asked Harper to grill her for intel with the intent of uncovering the real reason she needed to suddenly go to Egypt.

"How's wedding planning?" Julia interrupted the unspoken words dangling in the air between them.

Harper's attention immediately skated to Roman, a smile crossing her lips.

"Find a location yet?" Deflect and distract. Hopefully, she could dodge those impending questions with a few of her own.

"No. And Chris and Rory are also getting married this summer."

"Didn't Owen and Luke marry their respective wives in a double ceremony? Vegas, right?" Julia asked, remembering when her sister-in-law, Kate, had hosted a combination Christmas and proposal party for the Scott & Scott crew. Owen had proposed to Samantha that night, and they were now married with a young son. She didn't know Owen well, but Luke Scott was fairly tight with Michael, and Julia had met his wife, Eva, a couple of times.

"It ended up being a triple wedding." Harper's smile stretched. "Bravo Four and . . . I mean Liam."

Bravo Four? Did they still use call signs in their civilian lives?

"How could I forget that?" Julia shook her head. "Liam married Emily." Emily's brother, Jake, had served with Michael in the Marines, and they remained best friends to this day.

So many weddings and happy couples. She wasn't bitter

about that, but she was losing hope she'd ever meet the one. "So, what about a double wedding?"

"Or another triple," Harper tossed out, eyes glued to Finn when he straightened and looked back at them briefly, eyebrows raised as if silently asking whether Harper was on the verge of mission success in pulling out the truth.

"Finn dating someone?" *Why did I ask that?* She resisted the urge to cover her face and instead leaned over and set her bag next to her pink Adidas sneakers. Anticipating a long and probably uncomfortable flight, she'd worn sneakers, black leggings, and a pale pink lightweight sweater.

"No, Finn hasn't dated anyone for quite a while, at least as far as I know. It can be hard to make time to date in our line of work." Harper crossed her long legs and leaned the back of her head against the fuselage. "Pretty much everyone we work with wound up together because of unusual circumstances."

"Aside from you and Roman," Julia pointed out. "And I think Jessica and her husband, Asher. Y'all work together."

"I forgot you're from North Carolina originally." Harper laughed. She was easing up on the suspicious scrutiny, thank God.

"Oh, did I let a 'y'all' slip out?" Julia smirked, feeling surprisingly comfortable despite being on a military plane with zero plans in place for when she arrived in Egypt. But she wasn't going at it alone, and Mya had been right. She was in good hands. "We have a family home in the Outer Banks. I may buy it from my parents since they put it on the market. There's a great private beach with wild horses. You should get married there."

"Ah, that sounds amazing." Harper pointed to Chris. "I can totally see Rory and Chris marrying on the beach."

"Not you?" Julia twisted a little on the bench, which felt

like it belonged inside a high school gymnasium. The government should at least invest in a little comfort for their servicemen and women when they travel.

"I don't know. I just want to marry that man. I don't care where or how." Harper let go of a soft sigh. Oh, she had it bad for Roman. "So, are you going to tell me why you're really going to Egypt?"

And . . . Whiplash.

Damn.

Julia had just been played. Harper had employed the same espionage tactics that Julia had seen a million times in movies. She'd gotten her talking until she lowered her guard and then, bam, hit her with the hard questions. Obviously, Harper's experience was *Jack Ryan* level, while Julia's was more like Jamie Lee Curtis in *True Lies*.

Harper slowly turned her head to peer at Julia.

"To be honest," Julia began, "I'm hoping to have a meeting with a plastic surgeon. He's well-known, always traveling to meet elite clients, and he's impossible to get a one-on-one with unless you're a real somebody. I found an opportunity, and so, I'm taking it." Technically, that wasn't totally a lie.

"You want plastic surgery?" Harper looked her up and down, and her tone of voice called *bullshit*. "You know I used to work for the CIA, right? I'm not an idiot."

Blunt. "Yeah, I know."

Harper lifted her head away from the wall, pinning her shoulders back as her dark brown eyes narrowed with suspicion. "Secrets are dangerous." Her gaze quickly moved to Roman as he laughed at something it appeared Finn had said.

Finn had an arm slung around Roman's shoulder, his back

no longer to Julia so she could see his white teeth as he laughed at Roman's response.

You have a great smile.

Finn really was a handsome guy in a rugged, mountain-man-reared-in-Boston kind of way. Which meant he looked like he fit in whether he was teaching self-defense classes or hanging out in a trendy Tribeca bar. His brownish-black hair was thick and had a slight wave to it when he wasn't wearing his hat, similar to Roman's. His jaw was masculine and strong and covered in a light dusting of facial hair.

While his nose might be considered a bit wide, it fit him perfectly. His lips, fully visible now that he'd closely trimmed his beard, were a bit dry like he'd spent lots of hours outdoors and needed a good Chapstick. Or a woman who wore great Chapstick. And last, but no less attractive, were the crinkles at the edges of his green eyes that appeared whenever he smiled or laughed.

She thought back to the first time she met Finn in his self-defense class in January. The man had taken her breath away from the moment he'd said hello. And even though he was listed as the instructor, there were weeks when he'd missed a few classes. Now she knew why—he was off doing mysterious stuff.

Finn had taught his students more than just martial arts moves and self-awareness techniques. His classes had also focused on how to get out of zip ties or escape a locked car trunk. She hoped she'd never have to use those skills, but when Mya began investigating the case, Julia decided she ought to be prepared for anything life might throw her way.

"We can do the whole back-and-forth thing for the duration of this long flight, but it'd be easier if you just fess up now."

Julia looked back at Harper. Her directness should've

been expected because she had been in the CIA, and yet, Julia still felt unprepared for it. People didn't talk to her like that. They danced around the truth and walked on eggshells here and there since she was the boss, and sometimes she could be intimidating, she supposed. They didn't call her on her shit, well, except for Finn since day one as her bodyguard when she began her performance as the villain in the story.

But no, she was trying to find the villain. She had to. Because she refused to accept all the lies everyone kept telling her, and she was worried Michael was starting to believe those lies as well.

"Secrets are dangerous," Harper continued as Julia's heartbeat only ramped up as she tried to find the words to share. "Roman kept some pretty big truths from me and the team because he thought he was keeping us safe. And now he makes me breakfast in bed every morning, among other things, in an effort to apologize for what he did." A quick grin met Harper's lips at whatever "among other things" meant. "He doesn't need to say he's sorry anymore because it all worked out, but I kind of like the—"

"Orgasms and eggs?"

Harper chuckled, and both Roman and Finn swung their gazes their way.

Shit, how loud did I say that? And Roman blushed. *Didn't see that coming.*

Finn simply looked amused, lifted a brow, then looked back at Wyatt, who was talking to Chris and A.J. about something that looked sort of important based on the concerned look in their eyes.

"As I was saying, secrets are bad."

"Not from where I'm standing," Julia teased. "But no, I get it," she added in a more serious tone.

"Chris's fiancée, Rory, kept stuff from him and she

regretted it. We got kidnapped, came up against wannabe pirates, the whole nine yards of crazy danger. If she'd been upfront and honest—"

"I don't have secrets. I'm just trying to help someone," Julia finally gave in.

"Who are you trying to help?"

Julia's gaze fell to her lap, and she drew in a deep breath. If she revealed any more, they'd feel obligated to tell her brother, and he'd lose his mind when he found out she'd lied to him when she promised to let him handle the situation. But the legal way wasn't working, so what choice did she have but to go around the law?

"Someone I care about is in trouble, and I'm trying to help him. That's the extent of it. I'm not in danger. Please trust me." Julia dipped her hand into her bag and grabbed her Kindle.

"He'll get the truth from you at some point."

Julia looked at the "him" Harper was referring to, not expecting to see Finn peering straight at her, lips parted as if he had so much he wanted to say but wouldn't cut across the ten feet of space to get to her and say it.

"I hope it's not too late," Harper added before popping to her feet and joining her teammates. Roman pulled her tight to his side, and his hand slid up and down the small of her back.

Julia did her best to look away and opened her Kindle.

It wasn't a romance but rather a true crime story. A murder mystery. Which was fitting since she had her own true crime to solve and three weeks left to do it before someone she cared about was executed.

CHAPTER FOUR

ASWAN, EGYPT

"This is a dream, right?" Julia opened her eyes to find herself lying in bed, a soft, white cotton duvet covering her body. She slowly lifted the covers and peeked underneath to see if she was naked, figuring if she were, that would confirm she was dreaming. And the vision of Finn standing at the window, in front of a picture-perfect view of a country she'd only dreamed of visiting, was just a fantasy.

She was *not* naked.

A devilish grin slowly swept across Finn's face as he advanced closer to the bed, those attractive wrinkles at the corners of his brilliant green eyes making her stomach do a little flip. Beneath his playfulness lay shadows she hadn't noticed until now. An intensity revealed by a look Julia could only describe as haunted. It stirred something inside of her on what felt like more than just a physical level.

"Do you dream about me often, then?" he asked seductively, his tone strikingly similar to the one used by the sexy male lead in a recent Netflix movie.

Three-Sixty Something? She'd watched it for the plot. Yup, the plot. Not the hot guy or the sex. Actually, who was she kidding? She'd hoped that movie would help her get over the strange, impossible-to-orgasm hurdle she'd been dealing with since January.

Startled back to reality upon discovering she was indeed wearing clothes and that this was not one of the many dreams she'd had in the last two weeks starring Finn, she cleared her throat.

"I, um. You know I didn't sleep on the plane ride over like the rest of you, and I"—she glanced at the clock by the bed—"guess I slept longer than planned."

Fortunately, Finn had been joking about the whole jumping-out-of-the-plane thing, but she'd been a tense ball of nerves the entire flight and hadn't slept at all. She must have crashed the second Finn left her in *their* hotel room early that morning.

He'd insisted they stay together. *No,* demanded. Wyatt was across the hall. A.J. and Chris were bunking in the room off to her left. And Harper and Roman shared the room to the right. She was fully surrounded by protection at the swanky hotel that sat on the Nile River. But Finn went so far as to also mount a microcamera across the hall focused on their door. He'd said it was to keep an eye on her if she happened to be alone. She was pretty sure the camera was also to make sure she didn't sneak away while he was working with his teammates in one of the neighboring rooms.

"You needed the rest." He removed his hands from his pockets, turned, and opened the French doors that led to a small balcony with a two-person table.

Julia stood from the comfy bed and took a minute to stretch before joining Finn on the balcony. When they'd arrived, Julia had been more interested in sleeping than checking out the view. It had still been dark then anyway. But now, the sun was at high noon, mercilessly beating down on the city. The view of the Nile, the saturated colors of the buildings, even the sand on the other side of the river that appeared to be baking in the sun was rather breathtaking.

"Beautiful," she said softly. "I've wanted to travel here ever since I was a kid. I was obsessed with those *Mummy* movies. You know the ones, right?" When she stole a look at him from over her shoulder, he was eyeing her instead of the scenery. Unsure what that was all about, Julia swallowed and braced her hands on the black, iron railing and peered back at the river.

"Why haven't you visited before?"

Good question. "I haven't had a reason to, I suppose. Most of my work is stateside. And when I travel for pleasure, I wind up in a bungalow on a beach, hoping to avoid that people-ing thing. You know, just me, the ocean, sun, and a good book."

"An introverted movie and book lover, huh?" Finn sounded surprised.

"You don't believe me?"

"I just didn't know we had that in common."

She caught him shrug from the corner of her eye, probably wondering what to make of the fact they had anything in common after the hell she'd put him through for the last two weeks.

"So, what's your favorite movie?"

Finn quietly stared at her, a confused look on his face, seemingly contemplating whether or not she'd just asked a trick question.

"I don't care so much for superheroes lately," Julia plowed on without waiting for him to answer. "Like *Superman* or those *Avenger* movies." *Why am I rambling?*

73

Why does he suddenly make me nervous by being all broody and quiet while staring at me? "I think those movies can set unrealistic expectations. Real heroes aren't without vulnerabilities. They bleed. Suffer. Feel pain." Her stomach knotted as she thought about Tucker. "They die." Memorial Day was just around the corner, too. A reminder of those who hadn't made it home. Tucker made it home, though, he just . . .

"Julia, you okay?"

She closed her eyes and gathered in a deep, relaxing breath, and as if she were in yoga class, the soft voice of her instructor guided her in calming down.

"Yes, I'm fine. Just forget the movie question. And what I said after that." She pivoted, but he reached for her wrist.

"*Star Wars.* I'm more of a Darth Vader and Kylo Ren fan, though. Not the heroes. Weird, I know. When I was a kid, I probably just thought they were cooler because of their masks."

For a long, silent moment, she stared down at his large hand gently wrapped around her wrist, and when she looked up to meet his eyes, a slight smile crossed his lips.

"I've never seen those movies," she whispered.

He jerked his head back as though she'd spoken blasphemy, then smiled and released her wrist. "Well, we need to change that. I'll trade you one *Mummy* movie for one *Star Wars* film. But once you get started, you won't want to stop. I promise."

"Oh yeah, we'll see." She focused back on the river where a felucca moved along the water. The sail on the wooden boat had just caught the wind, propelling it forward. "Didn't you say you had somewhere to be around lunchtime?"

"I do. I want you to come with me, though. Prefer not to

leave you alone." He motioned for her to head back into the room, and she noticed the Nikon camera sitting on the coffee table in front of the red couch where Finn said he'd sleep tonight.

"Is that a Z50?" She picked up the camera, forgetting how good it felt to have a real one in her hands instead of just her iPhone.

"It is. That's right, you're a photographer."

She smoothed a hand over the red and gold strap connected to the Nikon and handed it over to him. He put the strap around his neck, and the black camera hanging against his chest stood out like a target against his plain white tee. "Not a professional. It's been forever and a day since I've been behind a lens."

"What made you stop?"

Realizing she ought to change, Julia went over to where her luggage sat on the floor and bent forward to root through the bag.

At the sound of a throat clear, she looked over her shoulder to find Finn's eyes pinned to her rear end. Apparently, the bold letters that spelled out PINK—in bright pink, of course—on the ass of her gray sweat shorts had garnered his attention.

He cleared his throat again and fidgeted with the camera, clearly searching for a way to transition away from the fact she'd caught him checking her out.

"So, why'd you stop?" he repeated.

She picked out a dress and clutched it to her chest, her thoughts landing squarely on the reason why she quit. *When Tucker died.* "I should get ready if you want me to go with you to play tourist," she said instead. "That's what we're doing, right?"

He nodded, and she headed toward the connecting

bathroom but stopped and turned. "Do I have time to shower?"

"Are you capable of getting ready in five minutes?"

She smiled. "Challenge accepted," she responded in a spunkier voice than she'd intended, which seemed to catch him by surprise because what appeared to be a sincere smile crossed his face before she shut the door.

The room felt a little steamy and carried a hint of Finn's aftershave or cologne, so she assumed he'd showered while she was asleep.

After making fast work of washing off the travel grime, she slipped into her dress and twirled around to make sure the white fabric wasn't see-through. Egypt was a predominantly Muslim country, and while there were no hard-fast rules regarding female fashion, it was considered inappropriate as well as impolite for women to wear anything sleeveless, above the knee, or revealing. But it was wicked hot outside, and a white dress would keep her somewhat cooler. She hoped, at least. It was knee-length with capped sleeves, so it shouldn't offend anyone.

Julia patted her wet hair with a towel, then secured it into a side braid. A little lip gloss and mascara, and she managed to finish in under five minutes.

When she opened the door, Finn's eyes were on his watch. "Four minutes and fifty-seven seconds. Not bad." He lifted his gaze to look at her and frowned.

She frowned right back at him. "What's wrong?"

"You realize we're in Egypt?"

"There's nothing wrong with this dress. I double-checked."

"Walk into the light." He pointed toward the open French doors.

"You can't be serious." Based on the tight draw of his lips, he was most definitely serious, damn it.

"We're trying to blend in. *Not* draw attention."

"So, a tourist uneducated to the local customs and norms wouldn't be such a stretch, right?" She gave him a sweet smile.

"Just please step into the light. Let me check before we go," he rasped, his tone borderline pleading.

"Fine." She brushed past him and walked along the wall of windows, past the open doors, then twirled and moved in the opposite direction. "Am I good?"

"No." He shook his head. "You're wearing nude panties."

"Yeah, because white panties would stand out more." *How the hell could he tell the color? Was he that stealthy?* "It's just a bad angle. I'm fine." Based on the heat radiating into the room through the French doors, she should change into a white string bikini and walk around in that. Not that she'd ever do something so offensive, but damn. It was already over a hundred degrees outside, and she hadn't thought to pack sunscreen for her last-minute trip.

"I don't give a damn about angles. Or fucking quadrilaterals, for that matter." His mouth tightened before he said more forcefully, "There are going to be lots of men here who aren't used to seeing a woman dressed like that, and I don't want to have to kill a guy in broad daylight."

How did those words manage to coax chills to pop on her arms despite the heat?

She bent over to rummage through her suitcase for something that wouldn't cause Finn to commit murder. Hell, murder was the very reason she was in Egypt. "Do you only kill guys when it's dark out, then?"

"Usually," he said in such a humorless tone, she wasn't so sure he was kidding.

"My shorts don't go to my knees, so dresses will have to work for you, sailor." She retrieved a similar dress in baby blue, then held it up to the light, and he offered her a nod of approval.

A hint of a smile revealed a dimple she hadn't noticed before on his left cheek.

"Roger that, ma'am." He shot her what was probably meant to be a playful wink, but it came across as far too sexy.

And she felt a stir between her legs that not even the actor from that Netflix movie had been capable of producing.

She started for the bathroom to change and cast a quick look back his way to find his eyes super-glued to her ass again. "Those angles again, huh?"

CHAPTER FIVE

"YOU BOYS PLAN ON TELLING ME WHO YOU'RE surveilling?" Julia asked as they walked the pathway through the hotel grounds that led to the exit into the city. "I mean, that's what you're doing, am I right? Following someone, or searching for someone? Or maybe it's a some*thing*."

Chris and A.J. were walking in front of her and Finn, but they both stopped and turned to face them.

"Jeez, by the looks on your faces, you'd think I just asked why men seem to love doggy style so much."

Finn had just taken a swig from his water bottle and immediately choked, then gasped in a breath and began coughing.

"Down the wrong pipe?" Julia slapped him on the back.

He chucked the now-empty bottle in a nearby trash bin and shoved his sunglasses into his thick hair. Widened green eyes stared back at her.

"What?" She looked at Chris and A.J., then back at Finn. "I may act like I have a stick up my ass most of the time, but that doesn't mean I can't joke, too."

Finn reached for her elbow with his free hand and gently

pulled her closer to put his mouth to her ear. "I think maybe we shouldn't talk about your ass anymore," he whispered.

Chills chased down her spine at his words and the sexy "or else" implied in the warning.

Now she couldn't help but visualize Finn shifting her to all fours and taking her hard, the headboard in that hotel room colliding with the wall.

It has to be the heat making me like this. But at some point, sooner rather than later, she needed to focus on her mission, the reason she'd come to Egypt.

Julia had texted Mya that she was safe and with Finn before leaving the hotel room, but she was most likely still asleep, given the time difference.

Now that she was here, though, she most likely needed to tell Finn about Lorenzo and his boss, Giorgio Ferrari—that he was also in Aswan. And she needed to talk to him.

Though, what she would say when she finally approached the doctor was still unclear.

Hey, I hear you surgically alter the faces of people who want to fake their own death. By any chance, did you perform an operation on—

"Well, shit, it's hotter than a billy goat with a blow torch out here, so I think maybe we should split up to get this done faster," A.J. suggested, failing to hide a smile pointed Finn's way.

"What he means is that—"

"I speak Southern," Julia joked, cutting off Finn. "I'm from North Carolina, remember?"

"So, why don't Chris and I take the east side of the city, and you two go get some grub, then?" A.J. slapped his palms together, anxious to get out of there from the looks of it.

She didn't exactly blame him. She did just mention

"doggy style" to three Navy SEALs. *Yeah, the heat alright. Or I've actually lost my mind.*

"I assume your target is located somewhere on the east side of the city?" Julia asked. "Or you wouldn't be shooing us off to go eat."

"Right, um, you two have fun now," Chris spoke up, then quickly slapped a hand over Finn's shoulder before saying, "Good luck."

"They weren't too obvious," Julia said when Chris and A.J. were out of sight. Finn pointed to the gated exit up ahead and motioned for her to walk in front of him. "But I suppose you can't divulge why you're here, so I won't push."

"That doesn't mean I won't be pressing you for answers," Finn was quick to say.

As much as she hated to admit it, Julia knew she had that coming, but still, she spun around to confront him, slamming into a solid wall of man, the Nikon the only thing separating them.

Finn quickly reached out to steady her, then slowly ran his hands up the sides of her arms as his eyes held hers captive. "What is it, Julia Maddox? What is it you're not telling me?"

Julia shivered at the feel of his slightly rough hands and dragged in a breath. "Care to know my middle name for the full effect of trying to—"

"I already know it."

Of course, you do. "I hate to disappoint, but I'm not ready to talk. Plus, I'm getting a little hungry. Can we grab something to eat?"

"Yeah, I don't need to deal with an angry you. Been there," he said with a small smile as he released his hold on her arms and tried to play off the strange moment they'd just shared, "done that."

Sorry hung on the tip of her tongue, admittedly an inadequate apology for her bitchy behavior over the last few weeks, but her hunger pains and moaning stomach won out.

After a few minutes of browsing lunch options, they grabbed lamb gyros from a food stand and ate in silence as they continued to walk through the city.

Julia came to a stop in front of a home painted bright baby blue, which would've been lost in a sea of similar homes featuring a selection of cotton candy colors if it weren't for the seven-foot croc.

"Why is there a fake crocodile hanging outside on the wall of that home?" She tossed her trash into a nearby bin while Finn did the same.

He patted his hands on the sides of his shorts as he answered, "It's a mummified croc."

"So, it was once real. Makes perfect sense to mount a massive reptile outside of your house."

Finn hid his hands in his pockets and faced her. "This croc hanging here also means they have live ones inside for viewing. Well, so I've heard."

Julia stumbled back a step, nearly knocking into a traveling street vendor passing by, the talismans hanging from long gold chains clinking as he pushed the cart up the gently sloped pathway they were standing on.

"So, then that's a no to going inside for a look?" Finn smirked, then resumed walking. "Back in the day, crocodiles were given divine status in hopes they wouldn't attack people."

"I don't remember that from the *Mummy* movies." Julia slowed as they neared the bank of the Nile and studied the long dock that stretched out onto the water. It was jammed with people milling about dozens of pop-up shops displaying their wares. "And how'd the divine-status thing work out for the Egyptians?"

"We can get closer to the water and find out." Finn unexpectedly nudged her in the back when they were within falling-in distance to the water, and she just about jumped out of her skin.

"Dalton Finnegan." In one fluid motion, she swirled around to face him.

"Want my middle name?" He lifted his sunglasses to showcase his eyes and let her know he loved every second of this.

"As a matter of fact, I would like to know. What is it?" She took a few safe steps away from the bamboo-like grass, papyrus maybe, near the water and eased herself closer to him.

"Samuel." Shades now back in place, he abruptly moved past her only to crouch in front of a kid selling jewelry. She watched with curiosity as he patted the boy on the head and smiled. The kid remained seated on a red-and-blue-patterned carpet, little trinkets splayed proudly before his crossed legs. Julia's heart gave a little tug as she witnessed the ease and sincerity on Finn's face as he chatted with the boy.

After a few moments of animated conversation during which Finn repeatedly glanced toward Julia, as if ensuring she was safe, he pointed to her. The boy's attention followed, and his eyes lit up. Then he grinned and quickly nodded. Finn handed him a fifty, which she assumed was more than the going price, and the boy gave Julia a thumbs-up sign after handing something to Finn.

Finn waved goodbye to the kid, who couldn't have been more than seven years old, and Julia's heart gave another tug. The man was so damn sweet.

"I'm gonna take a wild guess and say this isn't real, but

here you go." He grinned as he took her hand and opened her palm, but rather than focus on what he was doing, she peered up at him instead. He'd pushed his aviators into his hair, and now she was able to get a good look into those deep, forest-green eyes of his. She remained still for a moment, barely registering the fact he'd set something in her palm.

He subtly cleared his throat, released her hand, and lowered his glasses back in place as if he didn't want her looking too closely. She wondered if he, too, was holding on to painful secrets.

Looking down to examine what he'd given her, she saw a smooth, flat silver circle on which a small flower had been painted. The disc was connected to a thin silver chain.

"It's a blue water lily." Finn casually pocketed his hands like it was no big deal that he'd impulsively bought her a necklace. "The flower opens in the morning and closes at night. In Egyptian culture, they represent regeneration and rebirth."

"That's beautiful. Like every day is a fresh start." Her voice was a little dry, and she blamed the heat, not the gesture.

"I was hoping he had lily of the valley but nope."

"Why?"

"They're poisonous." He lightly chuckled. "Kidding. Well, not about the flower but about giving you a necklace with one on it."

"Sure you are." She handed him the chain, turned around, and shifted her braid over her shoulder, hoping he'd get the message to hook it around her neck.

As Finn's fingers gently touched the back of her neck while he worked to secure the clasp, Julia gazed at the amber desert off in the distance. Shimmering heat waves rose from the sand, creating a mirage that looked almost like a lake.

"Sorry, my hands are—"

"Big," she blurted loudly, then cringed. Over the last two weeks, she'd ogled his masculine hands like a perv. Well, whenever she was certain he wouldn't catch her staring.

Strong hands and forearms with prominent veins, like Finn's, were basically an aphrodisiac for her. And it'd been so long since she'd had any sort of intimate touch that the mere act of his fingers skating against her neck had her core clenching in desire.

"There," he said softly.

Julia felt the loss of his presence immediately when he stepped away, and she clutched the pendant. For years she'd kept her neck bare after removing Tucker's military ID tags. It felt strange to have anything else there.

Sweeping away the emotions that threatened to overwhelm her, Julia walked onto the dock with Finn close behind. They passed delicious-smelling roasted nuts, handmade Nubian dolls, Sudanese swords—well, that's what Finn said they were—and then she paused by one vendor selling miniature statues of ancient Egyptian gods. "Isis."

Finn looked left and right, his hand going to his waistband as if ready to draw fire. Did he have a gun on him? "What, where?"

"Sorry," she quickly sputtered. "Not *that* ISIS." She forgot for a minute who she was talking to.

He relaxed and followed her finger to the little carved statues on the blanket.

"Goddess of the moon. Protector of children. Healer of the sick." Julia smiled as she explained the significance of the winged Egyptian figure with a red moon above her head.

"Ah. You want her?" He started to crouch, but she set a hand underneath his arm, motioning for him to stand. "No, thank you." But this woman had a baby tucked safely in the crook of her arm, and Julia wanted to help her. She reached for the small purse she'd slung over her shoulder and unzipped it.

Julia lowered before the woman and offered her two hundred dollars. The woman shook her head and spoke in what she assumed was Arabic.

"She doesn't want pity money," Finn translated. "My Arabic isn't so hot these days, but roughly translated, she said she'll only take the money if you also take something. It would only be fair, she said."

"Oh, tell her I'm so sorry. I didn't mean to offend." She motioned to the figurine of one of the Egyptian gods, and the woman's face tightened.

Instead of releasing hold of the statue when Julia accepted it from her, the woman placed her other hand on Julia's wrist, closed her eyes, and began speaking again.

Not wanting to be rude, Julia didn't move a muscle until the woman finished what sounded like a lecture, released Julia's wrist, and accepted the money.

"What'd she say?" Julia asked as soon as they walked away.

"She, um." Finn paused, and his throat moved with a swallow. "She said Osiris is the god of the underworld, and she said if you pursue the path you're on without Osiris's blessing, you'll get caught in the storm without oars or something like that. And . . ."

"And what?"

"Nothing."

"What did she say, Finn?"

"Let it go. She doesn't know what she's talking about."

"Roughly translated, huh?" Julia's stomach clenched. It felt an awful lot like a threat, or a bad omen, so she attempted to shake it off with humor. "Sounds like she was trying to tell me I'm about to be up the creek without a paddle, Egyptian-style."

Finn didn't seem to find that the least bit funny.

"Like I said, my Arabic might be off. It was never great to begin with." He motioned toward the direction of the hotel. "We should get back."

Cradling the statue under her arm, she wondered if she ought to give it away or if that would only bring bad luck.

As they walked in silence, she couldn't help but think about the woman's words. And it reminded her that Mya had said something about a storm, too. But Mya wasn't prophetic, and surely this woman wasn't either.

Let it go.

When they neared the hotel entrance, Finn suddenly stopped walking and reached for the camera she'd forgotten lay around his neck. He removed the cap from the lens, and as if a switch had been flipped, he was suddenly in operator mode.

What or who was he looking at?

She followed his line of sight but didn't see anything unusual or suspicious.

He lowered the camera from his eyes. "I need it to look like I'm taking photos of you. Can you walk about ten feet away and pose?"

"Okay. I'm not usually the one in front of the lens, but sure." She did as he asked, then added, "Watch those angles, though."

Not even a hint of a smile. He was in full stealth mode or whatever former military guys called it. *Former military? Nah.* Technically, he may be retired, but this man would be a SEAL forever. It was in his DNA now, she could tell.

He began snapping photos, and she did her best to act like a tourist, holding the statue up and smiling. But that just gave her eerie vibes, so she lowered it and twirled so her back was to him.

It was then Julia spied a beautiful blonde woman standing alongside a man in a suit. And at that moment, she knew who held Finn's attention. At least she thought so, but when she faced him again, his attention seemed locked on to her instead.

Click.

Click.

He snapped more photos of *her*.

"We done?" Julia strode toward him, the heat really starting to get to her. She was sweating so much that she definitely needed another shower.

"Yeah." He capped the lens but kept his eyes on the couple as they entered the hotel where Julia and Finn were staying.

"Who is that?"

"Someone I wasn't expecting to see," Finn quickly answered while adjusting the Nikon camera strap around his neck. "I need to talk to Harper and the others." He set a hand to her back and urged her to get a move on.

Her back was hot and sticky, and no doubt her dress now clung to her curves showing more of her "angles," but his hand on her still felt oddly normal. A little comforting, even.

As they entered the hotel lobby, it was Julia who stopped in her tracks this time.

Standing amid the ornate architecture of what was once a Victorian palace was Giorgio Ferrari, Lorenzo by his side. And they were talking to the couple Finn had been taking photos of outside.

What in the hell was going on?

"Julia," Finn hissed.

The urgency in his voice had her tearing her eyes away from the group to see Finn yank off his sunglasses.

And the next thing she knew, he was backing her against the nearest wall, which happened to be next to the hall leading to the restrooms.

"Don't let him see me, okay?" she whispered, knowing he'd spotted Lorenzo.

One of Finn's large hands went to the wall over her shoulder, and he must have assumed people would figure they were a newlywed couple stealing a hot moment together.

She removed her shades and positioned her eyes on the dominating force caging her with his broad frame.

With a dark look in his eyes, he leaned in and placed his lips against her ear, which sent goose bumps scattering across her skin.

She shut her eyes, surprised by the sudden arousal between her legs, and released a shaky exhale.

"Julia," he repeated, this time on a breathy exhale that caressed the shell of her ear. "Why is your date talking to a man who finances terrorists?"

CHAPTER SIX

"WHY THE HELL AREN'T YOU ARRESTING THAT MAN IF HE'S known for funding terrorists?"

Finn's jaw nearly unhinged in surprise at Julia's question. The instant they were alone in their hotel room, she went off like an IED. Every inch of her body appeared to be vibrating with anger, and it looked like she wanted to slap him across the face.

"Are you out of your damn mind?" he asked, watching in amazement as she chucked the "death statue" onto the bed and tossed her purse to the floor. "Who do you think I am? Do I look like the FBI?"

Finn clenched his teeth. He should have been meeting with the team and handing off the Nikon so Harper could double-check an ID from the photos. But instead, he felt compelled to try and rope the truth out of this woman who drove him crazy six ways to Sunday. One minute he wanted to put her over his knee for being a brat, and the next minute he wanted to put her over his knee for an entirely different reason.

Less than an hour ago, Julia had looked every bit a

goddess in that blue dress, her hair shining as she stood beneath the harsh rays of the unforgiving sun while he snapped photos, his pulse increasing with each click of the shutter.

Finn should kick his own ass for having been so distracted by her he'd nearly lost track of the fact Tariq, a Saudi who bankrolled terrorists for shits and fucking giggles, had entered his team's hotel.

"Maybe we're both out of our minds." Her voice was softer but no less intense as she went for the clasp at the back of her neck. Was she planning to fling the necklace clear across their room, too? And why exactly was *she* angry?

He should have been the one in need of blowing off some steam. She was keeping a pretty big secret if her date from the other night was meeting with Tariq and she'd followed him across the Atlantic to . . . do what? Finn couldn't imagine, but with Julia, anything was possible.

"You're going to break it, damn it." He huffed and strode toward her, twirling his finger, demanding she spin and lift her hair.

"I need to shower," she said in a breathy voice as he managed to undo the clasp much quicker than he'd secured it earlier.

He handed her the necklace, expecting her to throw it, but she kept it curled inside her palm. When her gaze slowly lifted to his face, he had to remind himself he was frustrated with her. That soulful, haunted look in her blue eyes was spellbinding, though. It was the very same look she'd given him when she'd told him she didn't care much for superhero movies. *Real heroes aren't without vulnerabilities.*

Real heroes. She'd lost someone, hadn't she? Someone who served, maybe. And she hated that he or she hadn't been invulnerable. Finn had read it in her eyes, recognized the look of loss. The kind of loss that kept a grip around your heart, always squeezing and never letting go. He felt it himself every moment of every day his heart continued to beat while so many others' had stopped.

"I'm sorry." She'd dragged out the words as if they were hard to say.

"Sorry for lying to me? Or for going all hurricane mode on me for no apparent reason?" He wanted to reach for her and pull her in for a hug, but that'd be absolutely insane. So, he folded his arms across his chest and took two steps back to maintain a safe distance and keep himself from touching her.

"Sorry for yelling at you. I was nervous and scared, and I wanted to divert the conversation away from me, I guess."

It took him a second to absorb the fact she'd just been honest.

Julia had turned away and was now standing at the window looking out. The sunlight pierced through the thin material of her dress, which was clinging to her curves like it'd been glued to her silhouette. Finn had to use every ounce of willpower to keep his eyes off her ass.

Maybe he should reply with a little bit of truth since she'd finally opened up? Build some trust between them.

"I would take that man down if I could, you know. He's off-limits at the moment. Believe me, if we ever get the go-ahead from . . ." *Wow, was I about to say POTUS?* "I did a background check on your date, Lorenzo"—Finn pivoted back to the issue at hand—"but I didn't look too deep into his boss, or I assume I would have found a reason to prevent you from going out with Lorenzo."

This was more proof he was a poor excuse for a bodyguard, but in his defense, he hadn't expected Julia to date someone with ties to terrorists. Why would he?

Julia faced him again, still holding the pendant. "There is

93

more to my story. To why I'm here. And I feel like an eight-year-old saying this, but I have to keep this to myself because if my brother finds out, he'll put a stop to what I'm trying to do."

He erased those two steps he'd placed between them. "And you won't tell me what you're trying to do?"

She opened her palm and eyed the necklace. "It's not that I don't want to, but my brother is overprotective. The man is paranoid. Bulletproof-glass kind of paranoid. And that was before what he went through with his wife. If he knew I was chasing leads in Egypt, he'd lose his mind."

Chasing leads? What had she gotten herself into? "As any big brother should," he finally said around a tight swallow, shoving thoughts about his own big brother aside. "And what leads? Who is this surgeon to you?"

Her lips pursed for a moment, her gaze seeming to snag on his tee melding to his frame from the heat. "If you promise not to involve Michael or try and stop me—"

"I can't make that promise unless I know what's going on." He cupped the side of her arm, drawing her a bit closer.

She quickly pulled free of his grasp. "Then I'm going to take a quick shower. I'm dripping with sweat from this heat. And you need to talk to your colleagues, teammates, or whatever y'all call each other, right?"

Shit, she was right. "Don't leave," he ordered, pointing toward the hall as a reminder of the camera directed at the door, then pulled out his phone and opened the app to monitor the hall for when he left the room.

"You don't have a surveillance camera in here as well, do you?"

Oh, this woman was ready to go again. Round two? Had she forgotten she'd apologized for her behavior less than a minute ago?

It was hotter than Hades outside, but that wasn't the only reason the air felt hot and soupy. Things between them had been tense since day one in her office two weeks ago, but he'd swear when he pinned her to the wall and whispered in her ear he'd felt something shift between them. Something he didn't know how to identify.

He wasn't sure if she was even aware she'd arched into him in the lobby as though urging him to press his body against hers.

He blinked, forcing away the memory so he could focus on the current issue. Tornado Julia. He'd decided she was less hurricane and more tornado because there was no warning when she was about to change direction.

"You didn't really ask me if I put a camera in here, did you?"

Her cheeks, already flushed from their hour-long walk, deepened a touch pinker. "I think the heat is getting to me."

Annnd nice Julia is back. Or was this just the calm before another storm? He closed one eye, half-expecting another mood shift, or at least some category-three winds.

"What?"

"Just not sure what to expect from you minute to minute." He grinned, attempting to lighten the moment.

He watched Julia's expression grow dark when her gaze cut to the statue on the bed. Whether or not there was any truth to the words spoken by the woman on the dock, it was a reminder Julia was potentially in danger.

"Don't be bullheaded," he found himself blurting. "You're in over your head. It's obvious. And you're scared." His worry for this woman had him feeling the need to pull out his deep, military and authoritative tone in hopes she'd bend to this command, one that kept her alive. He'd witnessed too many die, and he'd be damned if he lost her.

"I may be scared, but like you, I'll walk through the fires of hell for a friend." She ripped her focus away from the statue and turned to Finn. "What did that woman say to you?"

He considered playing dumb, but he knew she'd never buy it. His stomach tightened as he found himself whispering words he'd hoped not to repeat. "She said you're going to die."

* * *

FINN ENTERED HARPER AND ROMAN'S SUITE AND HANDED OFF the Nikon to Harper. His blood pressure was probably sky high after spending time with Julia, and he needed a second to breathe before he dropped the news on the team. News he should've delivered ten minutes ago.

Roman and Wyatt were in the room, but A.J. and Chris hadn't returned yet. The cell service was garbage in the city, but they'd managed to get a text through. They'd found the target and were moving on with part two of the plan, which was to plant a tracking device on his vehicle in order to pin down the exact location for the weapons sale that Bravo had learned would go down tomorrow night.

Once they found where the arms dealer was storing the weapons, Echo Team would move in before the exchange could happen. The guys would pose as a local rebel group looking to hijack the arms, then make it look like a botched robbery before escaping. The real mission was to tag the weapons and trace them to their final destination to learn the identity of the new group hoping to become the next regional threat to the Western world.

"I think I know who's behind the weapons sale," Finn finally shared. "Tariq." He pointed to the camera now in

Harper's hands as she removed the chip. "Just need to confirm I'm right."

"*The* Tariq?" Wyatt asked in surprise, and Finn nodded.

There was no need to use the man's last name. They all knew Tariq well. There was only one Tariq on their FSL (Fucking Shit List). A man they'd been gunning to take down ever since they'd learned he'd been behind funding various acts of terrorism overseas during the last five years.

But the U.S. government had placed Tariq on one of their own lists. The Off-Limits one. The Department of Defense and the CIA had weighed the pros and cons of targeting a cousin to the immediate Saudi royal family, and the powers that be in Washington opted to ignore the evidence linking Tariq to criminal activity. *His blood money never killed any Americans, so it's not our business,* had been the actual line that came from the Intelligence Committee.

"You know what will happen when I run this up the line." Harper sat at the desk and opened her laptop.

"They're going to ask us to destroy the weapons and get out of Dodge instead," Finn remarked. "Forget this whole thing."

"They don't want another Iraq War, only this time with the Saudis. Russia will get involved. Iran." Wyatt was trying to be the voice of reason, but Finn knew he hated this as much as they all did. "And they firmly believe if the U.S. takes out a member of the royal family, we'll be stepping into some deep shit."

Finn dropped into the armchair by the desk and looked at Roman standing over Harper's shoulder as she uploaded the photo of Tariq into their facial recognition software for an identity confirmation.

"Oh, and shit, that's not even the lead story." He tossed a hand in the air at his forgetfulness. "The plastic surgeon Julia told you she wanted to meet up with in Egypt," he began when Harper turned in her chair to look at him, "was just talking to Tariq in the lobby."

This had Wyatt standing from where he'd been working on the bed. "You're not serious."

"I really wish this was a joke." Finn rotated his neck, working out the kinks he was certain Julia had put there from worrying about her.

"I had a feeling there was something off about Julia's story," Harper said. "So, while you were in the city, I did a deep dive into his background. Giorgio Ferrari isn't just any plastic surgeon. Ferrari is his alias. A cover story or whatnot. He specializes in the change-your-face-to-fake-your-death kind of business."

"Well, that's just spectacular." Finn lowered his gaze to his phone on his thigh to check the app of the camera positioned on the hotel door. "What are we thinking? Did Julia start chatting up this Lorenzo guy on Instagram as a way to get to his boss?"

"But why in the bloody hell would she want to talk to some face-changing criminal doc?" Wyatt asked the million-dollar question. He looked at Finn as if he had a damn clue.

Not. At. All.

"Someone has to be helping Julia with all of this, right?" Harper pointed out. "Unless she's a cyber genius that we don't know about."

"She may not be a cyber guru," Roman said, "but her brother invented a lot of tech the military uses."

"Maybe Michael knows more than he let on when he asked us to be her protection. Could there be more than the office threats?"

"I'll have Luke call Michael. Bravo is still in Pakistan

until we're done here. But if anyone can pull intel out of Michael, it'll be Bravo One," Wyatt suggested.

"And since Bravo's intel about their op didn't include Tariq's name, I guess it's a good thing I happened to stumble upon him here." Finn stood, feeling antsy at the idea Julia might get caught in the middle of all of this. But if he hadn't brought her with him, she may have found a way to ditch Kevin and come to Egypt anyway. The idea of her alone here unprotected made him sick to his stomach.

"I hate that we won't be able to stop Tariq. And we'll be sent on our merry damn way back home." Wyatt grunted with frustration.

"What good are we?" *Why do our teams even exist?* "We're supposed to be able to do the shit the military can't, and I say Tariq falls under that 'do shit' category. We can blame his death on someone else. It's not like the CIA hasn't done that five thousand times before."

"I don't know, brother," Roman joined the conversation. "No clue. But I would like to know why Tariq's meeting with this doctor."

"Right. He doesn't need a face-change, get-out-of-jail-free card when he's living it up," Finn continued his line of thought. "Unless it's for someone Tariq is working with."

"Which is more likely, and that someone can't safely travel yet," Harper said. "I just don't get how Julia is connected to all of this. You should go try and talk to her again. See if you can get her to open up." She set her laptop aside. "Julia said she's trying to help someone. But who? Does someone she knows need a new identity?"

"I'll try to find out. But I'll fail again unless I agree to her terms."

"And what are her terms?" Roman's dark brows lifted in question.

"We don't stop her from trying to complete her mission or tell her brother," Finn said after a sigh.

"Talk about a red flag." Wyatt grimaced. "Just say what you have to say to get her to open up, and we'll go from there. I hate saying that, but what choice do we have?"

Finn had to say yes to Wyatt even if he wasn't thrilled to lie to Julia. Chain of command. Wyatt was Echo One, the team leader. And he was most likely right. "Roger that." Finn started for the door, his thoughts drifting to the words from the woman who'd sold Julia the Osiris mini statue once again.

"I'll let you know when the boys are back," Wyatt said as Finn opened the door. "We're ready for tonight. All squared away for the plan unless POTUS wants to change it with Tariq being in town. For now, just focus on Julia."

Focus on Julia. That sounded like a recipe for disaster, but he followed orders, tucked his phone into his pocket, and went back to their shared hotel room.

The bathroom door was shut when he entered their room. She must've still been in the shower.

"Julia?" He rapped at the door with his knuckles when he didn't hear any running water. "You okay in there?"

"Yes, but I'd prefer you not to be in the room while I'm wet and naked."

Finn set both palms on the door and bowed his head. "Thank you for that image," he muttered sarcastically. "Fucking thank you."

Instead of focusing on how to handle this Tariq-meets-the-plastic-surgeon situation, Finn's thoughts were on handling Julia in the shower. Lathering up her gorgeous body, making sure to give her nipples special attention as the water rolled down her curves. Pushing her wet, glistening hair aside and slowly licking her neck before sucking on her smooth skin like it was nectar from a peach. Yeah, he'd give her a hickey right there. Mark her as his.

"Finn? You still there?" she asked in a soft voice.

Focus, man. "No."

"Funny. But I left my clothes out there. I only have the hotel robe."

I've seen you in a robe before, he considered reminding her. And he was fairly certain the hotel robe was thick and white and wouldn't show her nipples like the black silk one she had on yesterday. "I can hand you what you want to wear."

He went to her open suitcase on the floor, surprised it wasn't a Louis Vuitton or something he'd assume rich women like the Kardashians would own.

Unsurprisingly, Julia was tidy and organized. She had little pink travel bags inside her suitcase separating everything. One for shirts. Another for pants. And, of course, her undergarments.

"No, I don't need you rifling through my things," she said while opening the door.

Finn released the bag that had her panties inside and slowly stood to face her.

Her skin was wiped free of makeup, and damn, she was beautiful. The white waffle-pattern robe was not as thick as he'd thought it'd be, but it did the job of hiding her body.

"Everything okay with your team?" she asked as she padded into the room toward her luggage.

Finn noticed her toenails were painted white like her fingernails. And then she leaned forward to search through her suitcase, and he almost surrendered to his shit-for-timing desires and spoke his mind.

But instead of letting her know that sass of hers and all

that came with it was a total turn-on, he sat on the bed and kept his mouth shut.

She started for the bathroom, clothes in hand as vestiges of steam from what must have been a really hot shower floated into the bedroom. Hadn't she been trying to cool off, though?

Just before she disappeared into the bathroom again, Julia turned toward him. Finn studied her, watching a series of emotions play out on her face—disappointment, fear, indecision—before she took him by surprise and said, "What would you do if a friend of yours was in trouble? The kind of trouble that's life or death?"

Her blue eyes shimmered as if this tough woman was on the verge of tears and fighting to keep it together the same as before her shower.

"I'd walk through hell and back for them." He glimpsed the figure of Osiris still on the bed. "Please tell me who is in trouble and why you need to talk to this doctor."

She was quiet as if mulling over his question, and then her eyes made the slow journey to his face. "I need a copy of his client list to see if someone who is supposed to be dead really isn't . . ."

"So, you dated Lorenzo to get to Giorgio?"

"Yes," she confirmed. "A friend helped me. I'm not a pro at this undercover work."

Undercover work? He needed to know all of the details, damn it. "Giorgio's clients are criminals, and that makes him one, too. You think he'll confess his sins to you and let you walk away after?"

She squeezed her eyes closed.

He turned and looked toward the glass French doors and out at the view of the river and desert in the distance. "I'm not one hundred percent certain, but it's possible your problem and my situation are connected," he hesitantly revealed, "so I'll get his client list for you."

At the feel of her hand on his back, he turned to find her standing an arm's length away. "You will?" she whispered. "How?"

He wasn't sure what the hell he was getting himself into with this woman, and he hadn't totally followed Echo One's orders yet, but damn that sad look in her eyes . . . how could he not help her?

"The good old-fashioned way." Finn forced a smile, hoping he wasn't going to regret this. "I'll steal it."

CHAPTER SEVEN

"IT'S FAR TOO HOT TO EAT OUTSIDE," JULIA GRUMBLED.

Finn looked up after gathering a forkful of kofta, the Egyptian version of meatballs flavored with local spices, and studied Julia's pouty face while he slowly savored his bite of food before speaking.

"So, eat on the bed or at the desk in the room," he suggested as he tore off a piece of naan and dipped it into tahini sauce.

He'd refused to let her leave the room, even for dinner, while Lorenzo and his boss were somewhere in the hotel. No telling what might happen if Lorenzo spotted her. Not to mention, Finn still had a mission to accomplish, and he couldn't let some plastic surgeon blow his op.

Julia pointed to the fan over their heads. "This thing just blows hot air around."

"Is this your favorite pastime activity lately?" he teased. "Complaining?" Oh yeah, he knew that would earn him a scowl.

"Hilarious." She listlessly poked at a lamb kebab but abandoned her food to take in the view of the Nile. The deep azure of the sky was melting into a hazy purplish blue as the sun began to fade into what Finn could only describe as a romantic sunset. Add in the exotic location and delicious meal, and it almost felt like he was on a date. If only he weren't sitting across from *this* particular woman.

When was my last real date? He had no clue.

Finn's thoughts quickly shifted when Julia carefully and deliberately set down her fork, then lifted a petite hand to her throat. Mesmerized, he watched as she dragged her palm down the length of her slender neck and continued the journey toward her cleavage. She had on yet another dress, this one too sexy to wear in public, but since she was now a prisoner to the room, he supposed it didn't matter. Except for the fact that the red cotton dress had a plunging neckline. And when she crossed her legs off to the side of the small table, the entire length of her tan legs was exposed.

And how could he not take notice?

That "doggy style" comment she'd made had nearly killed him earlier, and it'd played on a loop in his head ever since. He had to order himself not to picture . . .

Look up, asshole. She's going to see you staring at her chest. And too late. She caught him. By the time he planted his eyes where they'd belonged, she'd shot him a look that said *I saw you, buddy.*

"I'm not always a pain. Or mean."

"You just save this award-winning personality for me, huh?"

"I'm tense. Very, very tense. For a lot of reasons."

He sat taller and scooted his chair a little closer to their tight two-person table. "So, tell me, what's got you tense, sunshine?"

"I'm not a hurricane anymore?"

"Ha. More like a tornado. But hey, let's not split hairs." He winked. She pretended to hate it. He assumed, at least.

"I am not a tornado. Maybe a bit of a wrecking ball lately, but only because of—"

"Stress. Tension. Got it." He was tempted to snatch his sunglasses to shield his eyes from her view, but it was growing dark out. "So, tell me the truth. I know you were being a bit of a bully in New York to try and get me to quit, but now you need me, and you have me, so talk."

"I have you?" Why was there a touch of sadness blooming through her tone as if she didn't believe she really did have him?

When her hand plummeted to her lap, disappearing beneath the black wicker table, he replied, "Of course." And then he remembered Wyatt's orders and added, "I won't tell Michael about this. I'll help you. So yes, you have me."

He hoped like hell that wasn't a lie. He never wanted to be considered a liar. His brother had lied and lied. So many lies. And where had those lies gotten him?

"I'll make you a deal. I'll tell you everything after Harper and Roman retrieve Giorgio's client list."

And speaking of that, Finn checked his watch. Harper and Roman were currently implementing the plan Echo Team had come up with on the fly two hours ago after Finn promised Julia he'd steal the list.

Over the course of the nine years they'd been operating, Echo Team had accessed criminals' laptops dozens of times, so this would be an easy task. Harper and Roman were replicating a maneuver they'd pulled in Chechnya two years ago, which required that they check into the, thankfully vacant, room next to the doctor's.

According to the "friend" who'd provided Julia with intel, Giorgio was initially registered at another hotel. Finn guessed he most likely made the last-minute change to this one because Tariq had requested or demanded it.

"If the laptop is in his room while Giorgio's not there, then they'll download the files," he said with easy confidence. "And if it's not there, then we go with plan B." He refilled their glasses with the bottle of water from the ice bucket sitting on the ground by the table. The silver bucket was sweating from the heat and useless out there. Lukewarm at best.

"And if Giorgio put his computer in a safe while he's at dinner?"

"They'll breach the safe. No big deal."

"What are you all, a bunch of MacGyvers?"

He smiled and leaned toward her. "Even better." He set a finger to his lips. "But don't tell anyone." And honestly, he wasn't kidding about that part. She already knew too much about them.

"Why do I get the feeling bodyguard duty isn't your usual gig? That this," she began while spreading open her arms, "is more your speed?"

He contemplated an answer that wouldn't make him a liar, then decided to deflect. Echo Team didn't technically exist. "I didn't think Lorenzo was your type. Makes more sense that you used him. He looks nothing like that actor you like."

Julia took a sip of her water, and he'd swear she was fighting a smile. "You're right. That man is nowhere near my type. But it's Ryan Reynolds's humor I'm attracted to. Looks-wise, I'm not really attracted to him."

"Who are you into, then?" *You idiot. Get back on track.* He cleared his throat, preparing himself to guide the conversation back in the direction of discovering her secrets.

"I don't know," she said softly. If her voice hadn't

trembled slightly, he might have believed that answer. "Not military types, though."

"Wow." Finn slapped a hand to his chest. "I feel a little offended on behalf of myself and your brother. And everyone who has ever served or still does."

She rolled her eyes and pinned her shoulders back, then sighed and let them fall a touch. "It's not like that. I just can't handle the worrying. When Michael was serving, it was hard. I pride myself on being a strong and independent woman, but it takes a special kind of person to marry someone who is active duty. And then . . ." Her words trailed off as her eyes cut to the river. "The man I hoped to marry back when I was still in college had been in the service," she said around a swallow, and shit, he had a bad feeling where this was going, "two deployments in Iraq. He, um, didn't handle civilian life so well after that, though."

Finn wished he had a whiskey, so he'd be able to digest what he was worried was coming next. Something to dilute the pain a little. To soften all the blows he'd been hit with over the years that would surely rise to the surface when she revealed her past. *If* she kept sharing, that was.

"He's dead because of me," she quickly said, and that was definitely not what he expected to hear. "He had a drinking problem. I didn't realize it at the time because I was busy with a double major at UNC. I guess he took up drinking while between jobs after the Army to the point he was a high-functioning alcoholic, and he hid it from me." Her lips pursed into a disappointed-in-herself frown. "So, when I asked him to pick me up from a party one night because I didn't want to drink and drive . . . I was completely unaware he'd been drinking when we talked on the phone. I was a pathetic girlfriend."

"Pathetic? God no." He kept himself glued to his seat as

his heart raced, and he did his best not to go drop by her side. To take hold of her delicate hands and protect them inside his big, rough ones. To take away her guilt and pain. How could she think it was her fault?

Then again, don't I still blame myself for—

"He was killed in a car accident on the way to pick me up. So, you see, it was my fault."

"Fuck," he said under his breath.

And now he understood some of those layers Julia wore so well. He wore a few layers himself.

Finn pinched the bridge of his nose as he tried to find it in himself to get through this conversation without succumbing to his own demons. He sure as hell didn't want to make this about himself. And he also needed to keep his mind sharp for later.

As it stood, POTUS wanted Echo to charlie mike. Continue the mission.

Their orders regarding Tariq were "watch" and "do nothing."

A few hours earlier, Chris and A.J. successfully confirmed the location where the weapons were stored for tomorrow's exchange, which meant the boys would move out as planned at zero three hundred.

"So, I guess I avoid dating guys who are or were in the service because I'm worried I'll miss the warning signs if there's ever a problem. I failed once before, and I can't let that happen again."

Finn rubbed his chest when an unexpected lump of emotion hit him center mass as if he'd had a plate on but had been shot, which still hurt like a motherfucker. *Been there, done that.* He preferred not to take another bullet again if he could help it.

Had this tornado of a woman just made herself vulnerable?

"I didn't mean to lay all of that on you," Julia said softly, her eyes fixed on her barely eaten plate of food. "I honestly have no idea why I told you all of that. I don't think I've said that out loud before." Her voice broke on the last words.

Honestly, he was used to people confiding in him.

Harper had shared the fact that she and Roman had been secretly sleeping together long before anyone else on Bravo or Echo had known they'd gone from friends to lovers and back to friends again (and now engaged).

Other friends and teammates had dropped truth bombs on him as well over the years. Was there something about him that made people want to share?

You're a good listener, his brother always told him growing up, even at a young age. *The problem solver in the family.*

Finn hadn't solved every problem. And some secrets weren't easy to bear.

"It's okay. I'm glad you told me, and I'm sorry for your loss." A shaky breath followed, and he looked down to see his hands clutching the chair arms. When did that happen? "Not your fault, though. Don't blame yourself."

"That's what Oliver always says," she whispered in a sad voice.

"And who is Oliver?"

Her forehead tightened, and she was the one releasing an exhale now. "Oliver is Tucker's brother, and he's the one I'm trying to save."

CHAPTER EIGHT

A LOUD KNOCK ON THEIR HOTEL ROOM DOOR DASHED FINN'S hopes of Julia elaborating on that particular truth bomb she'd just dropped. She shot out of her chair like the fire alarm had gone off and hurried to the door.

"Look through the peephole," he called after her.

She turned and threw him a look that left no doubt she thought he was an overbearing dumbass, and maybe he was, but she'd just shared an incredibly emotional story, and he wanted to be sure she was thinking clearly.

When Harper and Roman joined them in the room, it was obvious by the expression on Roman's face they had both good and bad news.

"We accessed Giorgio's files. His client list and appointment schedules are heavily encrypted, so it's going to take some time to decipher, but once I do, we'll find out who he's performed surgery on," Harper quickly explained, hanging just inside the room and acting fidgety, as if they were short on time.

And were they short on time? Their op wasn't a go until

zero three hundred, and it was only twenty hundred hours. Was there a problem?

Out of the corner of his eye, Finn noticed Julia biting her lip, face pale, and arms banded tightly around her torso. She'd been on edge since they'd arrived in Egypt, and now Finn knew the reason for her distress. She was there to try and save the brother of the man she'd hoped to marry. But save him from what?

"We don't have time right now to play the twenty-question game for me to uncover what you're hiding, but it would make things easier if I knew the name of the person you're hoping I find on the list." Harper may have been blunt, but she managed to keep her tone gentle, probably not to spook Julia. Her CIA tradecraft skills with performing interviews over the years came in handy.

A mere two days ago, Finn wouldn't have thought Julia to be the type of woman who possessed an ounce of fragile or soft. Nor a woman who'd easily spook.

Hell, someone was sending her death threats and she'd been casual about it. And wow, now that he thought about it, were the threats even real? Did Michael suspect Julia might run off and try to help her friend and get herself involved in something dangerous? Would he have come up with a bogus reason to force a bodyguard on her? That didn't seem like Michael, and why wouldn't he have told the guys the truth? Unless Julia begged him not to say anything, which Finn could see happening. But damn.

"Ario and Kaira Zare," Julia revealed to Harper. "He was a building developer living in Dubai. Over the years, he lived in both the States and Saudi Arabia before moving to Dubai with his wife. I need to know if he had an appointment the first week of January this year."

"*The* Ario Zare? The man thrown out of one of his firm's

skyscrapers under construction in Dubai?" Roman joined the conversation, and of course, he'd heard of the guy. "Killed by one of his bodyguards." Roman took one step forward, now wearing the focused expression that Finn knew meant the puzzle pieces were coming together fast, like always. "The bodyguard was formerly American military. It was in the news." He drew his hands to his hips and shut his eyes as though going through the catalog of facts stored in that big brain of his. "Oliver something." Roman's brown eyes flashed open. "And he's going to be executed soon."

Finn's gaze swiveled straight to Julia. And there it was. Oliver was going to die, and this woman would do everything in her power to save him. But had Oliver really committed murder?

"Yes, and I . . ." Julia's eyes cut to the floor. "I can't be responsible for both Tucker and Oliver dying," she whispered.

Finn's stomach plummeted as he watched her step out to the balcony.

She sure as hell wasn't responsible for her ex's death, but why would she blame herself for what was happening to Oliver?

He turned to follow her, but Roman grabbed hold of his arm. "That conversation is going to have to wait," Roman said. "Boys are prepping for the op now. We leave in five minutes."

Finn frowned and looked back and forth between him and Harper. "Why now? It's not even fully dark yet."

"Our timetable was moved up," Harper said. "The boys will explain. I'll keep an eye on Julia and make sure she's okay. But you won't have radio access to me, and the cell service here is spotty."

Roman glanced at the balcony to ensure Julia was out of

earshot. "We really need to roll out, brother. Natasha has eyes on the transport vehicle, but once they get within range of the restricted airspace of the airport, which is where we think they're heading, the Agency will have to pull our eyes in the sky."

Natasha was their liaison with the CIA, as well as Wyatt's wife. She and the director were the only people at the Agency aware of the existence of Bravo and Echo Teams, which made it tricky. But having her on the inside for the last twelve months had proved helpful on multiple occasions.

*"*Great." That wasn't the original plan. The op they'd prepped for was a bust, and from the sounds of it, they'd be rolling on the fly. Most likely a vehicle interdiction. "I have to at least say goodbye first. I'll be fast."

"Yeah, okay. Hurry." Roman pulled Harper in for a pre-mission goodbye kiss while Finn went out onto the balcony.

Julia had her hands wrapped tight around the railing, eyes pointed toward the desert on the other side of the narrow part of the Nile.

"I have to go handle something. I shouldn't be too long. Timeline changed. I hate leaving you like this, but it's kind of a time-sensitive situation." He kept his tone level as he stood alongside her.

She side-eyed him for only a second before fully facing him. "Everything okay?"

Hopefully. "It should be." He turned toward her, surprised when she placed her palm on his forearm. In all of his years serving, he'd never had any pre-mission goodbye moments. On the rare occasion he was in a relationship, notice of deployment had resulted in him and his girlfriend parting ways prior to shipping out.

So, why did this feel like one of those goodbye moments?

And now, an odd, unsettling feeling struck him in the gut.

Was this how the rest of Echo felt when they kissed their loved ones goodbye and prayed it wasn't the last time they saw them?

She's an assignment. A favor, Finn reminded himself. Nothing more.

Yet, there was a tremble in his arm beneath her delicate palm.

"We'll talk when I get back, okay? I hate leaving you like this, but I don't have much of a choice. I'm sorry," he admitted, carefully treading around the truth without lying.

She held his gaze, her eyes a little glossy as if holding back tears. "You do what you need to do. I'll be here. And I'll stay in the room like you asked."

"Thank you." He forced an awkward smile as she slowly lowered her hand. Almost as if she hadn't wanted to let go. He filled his lungs with a deep pull of the hot evening air and held it as he gave her one last look before walking back into the room. As soon as his back was to her, Finn released the breath he'd been holding.

"Keep her safe," he said, opening the door.

"Of course. Stay safe, too." Harper gave him a tight smile.

"Roger that." Finn went to Wyatt's room, where Roman was in the process of swapping his clothes.

A.J. and Chris weren't there yet, so he assumed they were securing the vehicles.

Wyatt held a large duffel bag in one hand, which had the weapons they'd need for the mission inside. Using his thumb to motion over his shoulder, he said, "Get dressed. I'll update you on the rest of the mission details when we're in the car."

Finn strapped on his titanium-and-steel-armor-plated vest that could withstand a hit from an AK-47 to the back or chest, then pulled on an oversized black polo to hide it. Lastly, he swapped his pants for khakis. He wrapped a white-and-black-checkered shemagh around his neck and over his head. He left his face exposed for now, but he'd cover everything except his eyes once on the op.

The scarves were common in the desert heat, which made for convenient disguises, but Finn was used to wearing them on military ops as well.

Once they were outside, Finn and Wyatt joined A.J., who sat behind the wheel of a beat-up old Land Cruiser. Roman and Chris rode in the second vehicle behind them.

"So, what the hell is going on?" Finn cut straight to it as they rolled away from the hotel.

Wyatt twisted in his seat from where he sat shotgun to look back at Finn. "Tariq paid the weapons dealer an hour ago, and he's already back at the hotel."

Finn hissed under his breath. "Damn it, and CIA intel had suggested the exchange wasn't going to happen until tomorrow."

"Earlier, Chris and A.J. followed the arms dealer to the site five klicks outside the city, then Natasha directed the site to be monitored by drone. Tariq and the dealer exchanged money, then Tariq left three of his men there and returned to the hotel," Wyatt explained. "His men started loading some odd-shaped containers into the back of a big rig-type truck. They rolled out a few minutes ago, and Natasha believes they're heading for the airport, which is about forty minutes from the site."

"Now that it's no longer possible to plant trackers with the weapons to follow them to this new hate group, are we going to destroy the weapons like Bravo did in Pakistan?" Finn asked.

"The CIA has decided to follow the money now that we know Tariq is the financier," Wyatt replied.

"Wasn't that our original suggestion?" Finn shook his head. But the higher-ups called the shots, so what could they do?

"Tariq is still off-limits, but our new orders are to glue ourselves to Tariq in hopes he leads us to this group he's funding for whatever purpose," Wyatt went on, but his attention kept moving around. Left and right out the windows. Head already on a swivel as if they were in the middle of the op and a sniper might be in the wings. This wasn't his typical behavior pre-boots on the ground. What was up with that?

"And when it comes to that fucker, who the hell knows what he's really up to. No rhyme or damn reason as to the groups he's funded in the past," A.J. tossed in his two cents. "He's a hopper. Gets bored. Jumps from terrorist group to terrorist group."

"Maybe now he's decided to form his own group." *Group?* Yeah, right. Like they were a Barnes & Noble book club. "With the weapons destroyed in Pakistan and then after tonight, Tariq is going to start looking over his shoulder."

"Which is why POTUS needs us to monitor him. Can't put a DEVGRU team on his arse," Wyatt replied, still seemingly on edge and a bit distracted, and Finn wanted to probe and find out what bothered him aside from the fact they were going to pull off an op without prep, but he kept his mouth shut. "But it's also why we're still posing as a local rebel group. It's not unusual for the rebels here to learn of a big transfer of arms like this and make an attempt to jack it."

"So, we're crossing our fingers, toes, and whatever the hell else is crossable," A.J. drawled, "in hopes this cousin to the royal family doesn't connect the dots that we're on to his bad guy shenanigans?"

And that was the problem with Tariq—his royal

connections to the Saudis. The main reason he was off-fucking-limits. Total bullshit.

"Looks that way," Wyatt grimly replied.

What would Finn do about Julia? He couldn't bring her with him to wherever Tariq might lead them next. But how could he turn his back on her now?

"I'm sorry, brother," A.J. said as if reading Finn's thoughts.

"What are the rules of engagement tonight?" Finn asked instead, needing to bury the noise and worries so he didn't wind up with a bullet to the head, or worse, let something happen to one of his brothers. Men he'd die for any day of the week. They had loved ones. Families. They had something to live for.

What do I have? I have the teams. No one else.

An image of Julia's face gathered like a sudden storm in his mind, and his stomach ached at the thought of leaving her behind, which didn't make much sense.

He shook off the strange thoughts. Thoughts that had never before occupied his mind prior to a mission, so he wasn't sure what to make of this turn of events. *Focus, man. Not going to die tonight.* Override and focus on the mission.

"The ROE is the same as before." Wyatt faced forward again as if sensing Finn's thoughts were on some sort of tilt-a-whirl, and he needed a moment to regroup. "So, like I was saying," he continued after a heavy throat clear, "we're acting as though we're part of the local rebel militia looking to hijack the truck of weapons, and when they resist, we'll light them up. The weapons will *accidentally* be destroyed in the process. And hopefully, Tariq buys that story."

Finn always did hate *hopefullys*. He much preferred guarantees, which was probably why he also stayed away from committing to a woman for more than six weeks. There were no guarantees when it came to relationships outside of the teams.

"Finn, can you get Harper on the phone to see if she has an update from Natasha on the truck's current path?" Wyatt's voice sounded faraway, and Finn fought to hear him over the noise of thoughts that were all wrapped up in his past once again. A past he couldn't seem to escape even when his boots were in Afghanistan or here in Egypt.

Finn reached for his phone. Only one bar. "Hey, it's me," he said as soon as Harper answered. "I'll probably lose you when we leave the city limits. Maybe even before then. Service sucks."

"I've been trying to reach you," Harper quickly responded. "Natasha said the truck just took an unexpected turn and is heading in the opposite direction from the airport. But our drone is being pulled because the truck is still close to restrictive air space. Head east on Aswan Road once you reach it. You should be seven to ten mikes behind the truck. Pick up your speed."

"Roger that." Finn relayed the orders to Wyatt. "How's Jul—" *And she's gone.* No bars. "Let me get the boys on comms since we lost service and update them."

He handed A.J. and Wyatt their comms and positioned his own in his ear, then tapped it on, checking to see if Chris and Roman were connected. "This is Echo Five, do you copy, Three and Four?"

"That's a good copy, Five," Chris answered.

Finn noticed Wyatt lifting his left hand and removing his wedding ring he'd forgotten to leave back at the hotel. Was his hand shaking? What was that about?

"What's wrong?" Finn leaned forward once again, and Wyatt peered at A.J., then back at Finn.

"A lot on my mind, but I'll be fine. Don't worry." Yeah, that wasn't typical of Echo One.

"You sure, man?" A.J. asked as Wyatt stared at his ring on his open palm.

"I, uh, just have a . . ."

There was no way Wyatt would finish that statement, but Finn knew what he was thinking because fuck, Finn had a bad feeling, too.

* * *

"Do. Not. Open. That." A.J. enunciated each word through gritted teeth. "Seriously, brother."

Finn holstered his sidearm and knelt on the floor inside of the truck they'd taken over five minutes after the gunfight.

Echo Team had managed to secure the transport vehicle and take down the three men Tariq left in charge of the transport.

It'd almost been too easy.

Nothing was ever that damn easy.

And he'd yet to shake that bad feeling in his gut.

Finn lifted his flashlight to Echo Two's face to see A.J.'s shemagh lowered to show more than his eyes, and it was clear A.J. wasn't ready to call this night a mission success yet, either.

"You all need to confirm and take photos of the weapons inside the containers before we blow up this truck. Ignore Echo Two," Wyatt said over comms from where he was positioned outside the truck in case anyone in the vehicle had managed to radio for reinforcements before they'd been taken out. Doubtful since not even Echo Team could get one bar on a cell phone out there.

Chris crouched next to A.J. and slapped him on the back. "You're going to find weapons inside there, man."

"Yeah, but these are not typical containers." A.J. held his hands up, stood, and backed away from the coffin Finn was on the verge of opening. "And," he added while pointing, "that's a warning carved right beneath that Pharaoh-looking dude with the bad goatee."

The entire truck was filled with knockoff sarcophaguses. Twelve of them stacked up.

"Are you seriously worried about some bogus hieroglyphics?" If they weren't in a hurry, Finn would make a few jokes and laugh this whole thing off.

"I heard on the news that a research group moved some mummies from where they were found last year, and bad things started to happen. A curse," A.J. went on, and was the desert heat making him hallucinate? "King Tut's sarcophagus said something like death would come on quick wings for those who disturb his peace."

The movie Julia loved, *The Mummy*, popped into Finn's head. He was pretty sure there was a curse involved in the plot, and a surprising smile cut across his lips at the memory of her sharing that with him. He hoped one day they'd have a chance to watch each other's favorite movies together. *And where did that come from?* He blinked and swiped a hand over his brow beneath the scarf, finding his skin sweaty.

"Since when are you an archaeologist or historian?" Chris lowered his shemagh to scratch his beard. "These things are fake and probably sold to tourists."

"Oh sure," A.J. went on, looking at Finn and shaking his head with a *Don't do it, brother* look in his eyes as Finn stood poised to shove off the top.

But for some reason, now of all damn times, that woman's words of warning on the dock earlier today hit him.

123

Her admonition about Osiris and the prediction Julia would die if she continued to pursue her current path.

If anything cursed them, it was most likely the woman's words, not the weapons they'd find inside the knockoff sarcophaguses.

"And how do tourists bring these things on their flights home, Captain America?" A.J. teased. "Carry-on luggage or baggage check?"

"Just open the bloody thing before I come in there and do it myself," Wyatt rasped over the line. "You all have lost your minds in this heat. I'm sending you back to Afghanistan for a few weeks to remind you of the SEALs you're supposed to be." His tone was half teasing and half team-leader tough.

At that, Finn finally pushed the lid off, which was heavier than he expected for a fake.

"If a mummy pops out of there, I'm—" A.J. let go of his words, and Finn stared in surprise at the contents inside the coffin.

Definitely not weapons.

Or some dried-up dude.

Finn shut his eyes as memories of the past took over and robbed him of his ability to override and operate.

This time, his past didn't just reach out and pull him back, it sucked him up fast like an F5 tornado and threw him there.

Now he was in his older brother's bedroom back on Arden Road in Pasadena. At nineteen, his brother still lived at home despite having signed a record deal with a major label. *What are you doing?"* Finn recalled asking, pointing at the small bottle in his hand. *"Those pills you're taking?"* He'd rushed forward and tried to snatch the bottle, but his brother had a few inches on him. *"Are they Mom's benzos?"*

"Get the fuck out of my room! You tell Mom about this, and you're a dead man."

"Finn?"

He vaguely heard someone calling his name, but he was stuck inside those four walls decorated with posters of rock bands.

"Finn. You okay?"

"Finn?"

Different voices called his name this time.

None were his brother.

Not one.

"It's okay. I got you." A hand wrapped over his shoulder.

Finn slowly opened his eyes at the familiar sound of Roman's voice. The man who had become like a brother to him knew what was wrong. Finn was close to everyone on Echo, but only Roman knew exactly what was happening.

Those pills.

Those damn fucking pills inside the mummy coffin were the problem.

"They're not weapons? What do you mean?" Wyatt asked over the comms, which meant someone had already shared the news with him during Finn's trip to the past.

Roman hooked an arm beneath Finn's and helped him rise to his feet, then pinned him with narrowed brown eyes. The team may have been on a tight timeline, but Roman wouldn't budge unless Finn gave him the signal that he was okay.

Finn lightly nodded, letting him know he was solid. Or he'd force himself to be for the sake of the team and the mission.

"Check all of them. The weapons should be here," Wyatt ordered over comms.

Once Roman left his side, Finn took a knee again and reached for one of the bags of pills. "We should bring a bag back with us to identify the drugs."

"A negative on the weapons," A.J. said a minute later as

BRITTNEY SAHIN

Finn stood again. "They're all drugs. We still blowing this truck sky high?"

"Shit, okay. Charlie mike. We don't need a bunch of drugs winding up in the wrong hands, either," Wyatt instructed.

"If the arms dealer sold drugs instead of weapons to Tariq," Roman began, "this must be that drug Captagon." And, of course, his best friend would know that. "Syria was the major player in manufacturing the drug for their soldiers, but Sudan has recently gotten into the business, too. And they're just south of the border."

"This is the Jihadi drug of choice," Chris said as they began wiring the rig to blow, and Finn managed to pull his shit together long enough to follow orders.

"Yeah," Roman responded in a low voice and took the bag of pills out of Finn's hand he hadn't noticed he still clutched.

"Wrap it up and collapse back to me," Wyatt commanded.

"Roger that." The response came out like two brittle, breakable words from Finn's mouth, but he managed to follow his teammates out of the vehicle and over to their parked Land Cruisers, which were a safe distance away from the truck.

"These the drugs that make soldiers paranoid and violent?" Chris asked as they knelt for cover behind one vehicle. "Keeps them awake for days? Shoot a guy, and he keeps coming at you like a zombie?"

"Great. Zombies," A.J. guffawed. "I was wondering if 2022 would bring us zombies or aliens. I'm thinking both, at this rate."

"Aliens are already here, brother," Chris said with a light laugh.

The sand dunes of the Nubian Desert were their only

companion as they waited for Roman to detonate the explosives. That and the bright half-moon hanging on its back in the sky.

Complete silence until Roman blew up the truck, and Finn stared at the flames bursting into the air as if searching for their last dying breath.

"How am I going to raise a child in this world with the way shit has been going lately?" A.J. asked a beat later.

"I'm right there with ya, brother. I don't know," Wyatt said as he opened the driver's side door, opting to take the wheel this time.

"Something going on with Gwen?" Finn asked.

Gwen was the daughter Wyatt hadn't known existed until recently. She was an adult now, but Finn assumed that didn't ease a parent's worries. Hell, it might have made them worse.

"No, I, uh should probably tell you that, uh . . ." Wyatt's words trailed off when his gaze cut toward what appeared to be movement in the distance. "Are those camels?" He grabbed a pair of night vision goggles from inside their vehicle and slipped them on.

Finn checked his phone. If he had no bars, no one else out there did either. "Shit. No way they called in reinforcements."

He grabbed his own NVGs to see what they were about to go up against. A dozen men on camels, because why the hell not, were heading their way armed to the teeth from what he could tell. "I think we're about to face an actual rebel group." *Like the kind we're pretending to be.*

"This is not what I wanted to be dealing with." Wyatt pushed the NVGs to the top of his head and turned toward the team to direct them into positions.

"Damn it. They've got an RPG on them," Finn quickly told them.

"An RPG on a camel," A.J. said as he faced Finn and

reached for his heavy .50 cal. "Well, shit, you don't see that every day."

"There are two guys with rocket launchers," Wyatt said over comms as they fanned out. Not much high ground, so they'd be using the burning truck for cover. "Echo Four, you take the one on the left. I've got the right." Wyatt was the best sniper on Echo, and hell, one of the best in the world. But Roman was damn good, too.

"Too late. Incoming," Finn alerted as the rocket-propelled grenade made contact, and he watched their Land Cruiser blow up. "Everyone good?" he called out over the roaring sound of destruction as their second vehicle exploded as well.

"There goes our rides. These boys aren't looking to mess around. They're out for blood," Chris hissed over the line after everyone announced they were solid.

"See," A.J. chided, "I told you not to open that damn coffin. Now we're cursed."

CHAPTER NINE

AFTER TEXTING MYA WITH AN UPDATE, JULIA SET HER CELL phone on the dresser, a Victorian-era piece made from dark wood polished to a shine and decorated with elaborately carved vines, flowers, and an occasional cherub. Afraid to go into too much detail, Julia only mentioned that she'd seen their "target" and had obtained access to "the list," meaning the surgeon's encrypted client list.

Julia's fingers traced over the top of her ballerina jewelry box sitting next to her phone. It wasn't something she normally brought along when she traveled, but she was in Egypt to help Tucker's brother, so she wanted Tucker's military ID tags with her.

Lifting them out of the box as if they were fragile, she held them in her palm and let her thoughts slip back to the past.

"What are you doing? Did you just throw them away?" The panic she'd felt at the sight of Tucker tossing his tags into the trash had long since been replaced by a deep ache. At the time, she and Tucker had been at his apartment, which

was close to campus, and she'd frantically begun digging for the tags.

"I'm out. I don't need them. Fuck it." Tucker had grabbed hold of her arm and pulled her away from the trash.

Stunned and confused, she'd said, *"I'll keep them. You made it home alive. Not everyone did. I want them. I just do."* She would never forget the moment she'd looked up at him, tears in her eyes, and caught a whiff of booze. *"Have you been drinking? It's three on a Tuesday."*

"It was one beer. I'm not working. Chill, babe." He'd released her and pinned her with a hard look. *"And fine. Keep the damn things if they mean so much to you."*

Julia's stomach hurt at the memories, and as she placed the ID tags back inside the box, she paused at the sight of the flower pendant Finn had bought her today—technically yesterday since it was now after midnight.

Maybe Julia should thank Mya for bringing Finn into her life?

She felt . . . something for him. Something unexpected, and more than just physical attraction. She couldn't explain it, much less understand it. She was also certain and kind of terrified that his work was more dangerous than he let on when he first started watching over her two weeks ago.

But Oliver's life was on the line, so there was no time for dissecting thoughts and feelings about Finn or his mysterious job.

"How long will they be gone?" Julia asked as she closed the jewelry box. When Harper didn't answer, Julia glanced around the room to find her on the balcony, one arm resting over the railing and her phone clutched in her hand. "Something wrong?" She stepped out to join her.

Finn and Roman had made a hasty exit hours ago, but during the last forty-five minutes, Harper had barely spoken a word. She'd made multiple trips out to the balcony as if she were struggling to find a breath, and surely that wasn't a good sign. And Julia was at a loss about how to help since Harper wouldn't talk about whatever had her on edge.

"Okay, so maybe you're not allowed to tell me what's going on with the guys, but my nerves are getting pretty strung out watching you try and keep your shit together for my sake." Julia eased around the circular table to stand next to her.

Harper's shoulders fell, and she hung her head, then whispered, "They should have been back a long time ago, and I can't get ahold of them. The cell service is pretty bad in the city, but if they're still outside the city limits, it's basically a no-man's-land for phones."

"Oh." Julia gripped the railing at the realization her worst fears regarding Harper's silence and restlessness might possibly be coming to life. "What can I do? How can we make sure they're okay?" She did her best to keep herself together and maintain a steady tone because it was fairly obvious Harper was hanging on by a very thin thread. And if a woman like Harper was that worried, then . . .

"When I went to my room twenty minutes ago, it was to make a call to a friend at the CIA." Harper peered at her with brows drawn tight.

"What'd they say?" Julia's voice cracked.

"My contact managed to get a drone over the spot where the guys are supposed to be since they took a different route from the airport than planned, but there were no signs of life on the ground. No movement."

Little dots appeared in Julia's vision. When had she slammed her eyes shut? Why was she seeing freaking stars?

No. No, no, no.

"The boys' vehicles appear to have been destroyed,"

Harper continued. "Maybe by an RPG. So, that could be what's taking them so long. They needed to find an alternate means back to the hotel, and there's no way to update me. And if they're on foot, fifteen-plus miles outside the city limits will take time."

"And do you think that's the delay, or do you think something else happened?"

Are they dead? Were they taken hostage? A million other shit thoughts raced through her head and had her knees buckling. She forced her eyes open to find Harper shaking her head, and she wasn't sure how to interpret that answer.

"I refuse to accept any other possibility than they're on their way back, and it's simply taking them longer to arrive."

"What if we go search for them? Can we rent a car? What can I do?" Julia strode back into the room in a hurry in search of her purse, ready to buy an entire fleet of vehicles or a plane. When she spun around, Harper was right behind her, a torn look in her eyes.

"That's not really how this works."

This? Julia tipped her head, eyeing a woman who was maintaining her cool despite the circumstances. "I'm just . . ."

Harper slapped a hand over her mouth, and her eyes grew wide moments before she jetted straight for the bathroom.

Food poisoning?

Seeing the door to the bathroom open, Julia entered, knelt beside Harper, and held her hair back as she threw up.

Harper wasn't as invincible as she made herself out to be. She was human.

For that matter, so was Finn. There were no superheroes in real life. And that meant, God forbid, there might come a day when Finn didn't make it back home. If tonight's events were any indication, it was clear his bodyguard gig had simply been a favor to Michael. *This*, whatever he was doing tonight, was his real job.

"I'm sorry." Harper winced and shifted back onto her bottom a few minutes later, setting her back to the wall behind them.

"Don't apologize. Never." Julia wet a face cloth with cool water and handed it to her.

"This isn't nerves. I don't think it is, at least." Harper tipped her head back and shut her eyes. "I think I may need to move the wedding date up."

Julia sat next to her. "What do you mean?"

"I'm, um."

"Ohhh, you mean you're . . . pregnant?" Julia bit her lip, unsure whether to say *Congratulations* or *Oh, dear*.

"I don't know for certain, but I haven't told Roman yet. I need to buy a test to be sure."

"You should do it together. The test, I mean. Maybe tomorrow."

"Things will be difficult if I am. Don't get me wrong, I want to be. But Knox and A.J.'s wives are pregnant. And well, this is just between us, but Wyatt's wife, Natasha, told me she's pregnant, too. Wyatt hasn't mentioned it to anyone yet because he's doing the our-world-is-too-dangerous-for-a-baby freak-out at the moment. So, if I am pregnant, we might need to bring on more staff."

"Oh. Um." Julia didn't know what to make of the confession. So many babies. Harper was right. And the world was dangerous and scary, so she didn't blame Wyatt for freaking out. "Everything will work out." What else could she say? That no, life didn't always work out the way you planned? That good people died for no freaking reason?

Harper smoothed her hair back and adjusted her tee, which read *Being a functional adult every day seems a bit excessive.* "Come on, let's go find them," she said like she hadn't been puking her guts up five minutes ago.

Julia shook her head, then stood and reached out a helping hand.

Harper grabbed it and easily sprang to her feet. "You wouldn't happen to have any mouthwash, would you?" she asked sheepishly.

A few moments later, Julia snatched her purse, so she'd have funds accessible if they needed it, then followed Harper into her room.

"You know how to use one of these?" Harper showed Julia a gun inside what appeared to be a black purse holster, and Julia accepted it.

"I do, actually." She carefully tucked it inside her oversized purse, thankful it was big enough to conceal the weapon.

Harper hid her own gun at the back of her dark jeans, then covered it with her shirt. "Let's go."

When the elevator doors opened in the lobby, the sounds of sirens met her ears, and her heart jumped into her throat. "It's not because of them, right?"

"No, those sirens shouldn't be about our guys."

Our guys. Were they mine too?

Finn feels like mine.

Why does he feel like mine?

She shook free the crazy thoughts and followed Harper's lead, sweeping her eyes over the lobby that shouldn't have been so crowded at midnight. Whatever was going on outside had people gathering the same way cars slowed to view an accident alongside the road. Nosy.

They worked their way through the crowd, and Julia clutched her bag containing the Glock tight to her side.

Harper seemed unphased now by her bout of vomiting.

She was a woman on a mission. To save the father of her child. *If* she was pregnant.

They exited the hotel and immediately stopped.

Police cars and ambulances, their lights flashing, filled the *porte cochére* where cars usually pulled up for valet service. Walkie-talkies squawked, and police hollered at people to move along.

Two men in paramedic gear were lifting a black body bag onto a stretcher that still lay low to the ground. Julia held back a gasp when she spied Giorgio Ferrari's face just before it was covered by the zipper.

"Was that the surgeon? Did you see that, too?" Harper whispered as the police tried to shoo them back inside.

"Police only. Go back in," a uniformed officer said in what she assumed was Arabic, then repeated it in English, but Julia was frozen in place at the sight of another bag on a stretcher, this one already zipped tight.

Was that Lorenzo? What in the hell happened?

"Get inside," the officer prompted again.

"We'll need to go out the side exit of the hotel," Harper suggested, grabbing Julia's arm and urging her back into the lobby. "Does anyone know what happened?" Harper raised her voice to the lobby in general, most likely hoping someone would answer.

"Both bodies were thrown from the fourth floor," a woman who appeared to be an American replied.

"I heard they were killed before their bodies were tossed. Surprised their faces weren't too messed up after that fall," a man with a British accent spoke up.

"We'll have to deal with this later," Harper murmured to Julia as they rushed to the far side of the lobby. At the end of a long hallway was a sign above the door with the familiar Exit sign lit up in red. Harper reached the door first and flung it open. Julia, hot on her heels, nearly ran smack into Harper's back when she came to a full stop. Julia leaned to the side to see what had happened. And there was Roman, standing on the other side of the door with his arm extended as if he were about to swipe his way into the building.

Harper leaped into his arms, and Julia's shoulders fell with relief at the sight of the other four men behind Roman.

"Sorry," Roman rasped. "It was a hell of a night."

CHAPTER TEN

ALL FIVE GUYS, PLUS HARPER AND JULIA, WERE CRAMMED inside the hotel elevator, and despite the tight space, Julia wanted to throw her arms around Finn the same way Harper had greeted Roman downstairs, but she assumed it wasn't her place to do something like that. Not only did she barely know the man, but she'd been an absolute Queen B to him for the better part of the past two weeks.

But there was a sad, almost haunted look in Finn's green eyes as he leaned against the gold mirrored walls and peered at her while the elevator made its way to their floor. And that look had her desperate to bury herself against his chest and hold him. Even if he smelled like an animal. As a matter of fact, the entire car had taken on a pungent aroma that reminded her of a trip to the zoo as soon as the doors had closed.

Finn's hair and clothes were a mess. Sand in the laces of his boots, his hair, and smudges of dirt on his cheeks. And she was betting there was sand in other places not visible to the eye. *But* he was alive, and that was all that mattered.

"I need to get hold of Natasha and let her know what happened and that we're okay," Wyatt said in a low voice.

"Our phones didn't work. I'm sorry." Roman had spoken softly, and Julia glanced over to see him caressing Harper's cheek before she focused back on Finn.

"And if you're wondering what that smell is," A.J. piped up in his Southern drawl, "it's camel. We smell like fucking camels because that's how we got back here."

"The only guy in the bunch with experience riding horses," Chris began as Wyatt motioned for everyone to exit the elevator, "had the hardest time on the back of a camel." He jerked a thumb casually A.J.'s way as if whatever the hell happened to them wasn't a big deal.

"Camels and horses are not the same, my friend," A.J. said once they were all inside Roman and Harper's room.

"Everyone's okay, right?" Harper surveyed the guys while Roman hooked an arm around her back to hold her tight to his side.

The guys collectively looked straight at Finn, which had a small alarm going off in Julia's mind. He appeared the most exhausted of the group as he stood with both hands in his pockets and a grimace on his face.

"Yeah, we're good. But Finn took a bullet. Thankfully, it hit the chest plate, but it narrowly missed clipping his shoulder." Wyatt brought a phone to his ear and walked toward the balcony.

"You took a bullet?" Julia's voice squeaked as she scanned Finn's broad frame for the injury. Had she really heard Wyatt correctly? How was Finn still standing? How was the man okay?

"He's fine," Chris said as if Finn had merely scraped a knee. "Just hope you love purple. Our man's chest might be that color for a few days."

Still talking like it was no big thing.

Who were these guys? For real, for real?

"The, um, getting-shot thing happens often?" Julia found herself asking as Finn steadied his gaze on her once again. There was a blank expression on his face, and his eyes looked almost vacant. Was this an effect of getting shot? Was he in shock?

"We've all taken a bullet or shrapnel at some point. Only one of us . . . well." A.J. dragged a dirty palm down his face, then abruptly left the hotel room.

"What just happened?" Julia asked, not sure what she'd missed.

"Um." Finn looked to Harper as if allowing her to take point on an answer.

"One of our teammates was killed in action a few years ago. Jessica's husband, Asher, replaced him on the teams," Harper explained in a doleful tone.

"Oh." Julia turned toward the door, wondering if she could also make a quick exit the way A.J. had done. The entire time Tucker had served, she'd been terrified of receiving that very news. Same with her brother, as well as Oliver.

"You all do smell pretty bad." Harper scrunched her nose.

Roman hauled her close and purposefully pulled her face against his dirty shirt.

Way to diffuse the tension, Harper.

"But I don't care. I'm just thankful you're back," Harper mumbled into Roman's chest.

"What happened out front, though?" Wyatt asked once he rejoined them while tucking his phone in the pocket of his pants.

"It looks like the plastic surgeon and maybe his assistant were murdered," Harper beat Julia to answer. "We need to confirm, though. Why don't we all get cleaned up, call our loved ones, then we regroup in thirty?"

"I'm gonna go check on A.J., then call Rory." Chris lightly patted Julia on the shoulder before leaving the room.

"Everything will be okay," Harper said, her words directed at Julia.

But Julia wasn't ready to accept what felt like such a foreign word to her now. *Okay.*

She was far from okay. Finn had been shot. And also, her best lead had apparently been thrown from a fourth-floor balcony.

"I'll verify Giorgio and Lorenzo were the ones killed, then try and wrap up decrypting that client list in the meantime." Harper's gaze remained on Julia. "We never planned to talk to Giorgio anyway, so let's at least check out his client list and see who'd want him dead."

"He met with Tariq earlier. Could he have something to do with what happened?" Roman asked. "While we were gone, did Natasha provide a status update on him?"

Tariq who?

Julia looked at Finn, standing off to her left, for his reaction to Roman's questions, but he remained silent. She was just about to turn away when he folded his arms over his chest, winced, and slowly lowered them to his sides again. Good grief, had the man forgotten he'd been shot?

Shot. She still couldn't believe it. He wasn't in the military anymore, but he was still getting shot.

"Yeah, as far as we know, Tariq's at the hotel. But he's on a flight to Dubai tomorrow," Harper told him, which was news to Julia.

"Hang on." Julia lifted her hand. "You just said he's heading to Dubai tomorrow." Her stomach muscles squeezed tight. Perhaps Finn was right and whatever his team was working on was connected to her mission somehow.

When Finn swiveled his focus her way, she continued laying out the pieces.

"You all are here following this Tariq guy. I came to Egypt hoping to meet up with the surgeon, Giorgio Ferrari." Julia paused for a moment before continuing. "You saw Tariq in the lobby talking with the surgeon, and now the surgeon is dead. And Tariq is going to Dubai."

"What are you getting at?" Harper asked.

"Doesn't that seem like more than just a coincidence?" Julia was about to gnaw on her thumbnail but stopped herself. Instead, she fired off a round of questions. "What's Tariq's full name? Who is he other than some rich guy who funds terrorists?"

Roman scratched his beard with his free hand, eyes darting to Finn, then back to Harper. "He has ties to the Saudi royal family."

"What's his last name?" she rasped, drawing a hand to her stomach as if that'd help dull the pain there.

"El-Baz," Finn answered. "Why?"

Julia took two quick steps back as if she'd been shoved by the news. "The wife of Ario Zare, the man Oliver is accused of killing. Her maiden name is El-Baz. What if she and Tariq are related?"

* * *

"Harper will figure out what's going on," Finn said in a distant voice once they were alone in their hotel suite. "We'll double-check that Kaira is related to Tariq. Connect all of the dots. Don't worry." He turned and headed for the bathroom, moving more easily than a man who'd taken a bullet should be able to. "I just need, um . . . a minute."

"Of course." And that'd been hard to say because she wanted to help him. She had no clue how to do that, though.

She ditched her purse, nearly forgetting the Glock still inside, then watched Finn disappear from sight.

A moment later, she heard the water running in the shower and looked to see that Finn had left the bathroom door open, which didn't seem like something he'd do. Had something else happened out in that desert?

Was he thinking about the teammate who hadn't made it home years ago?

Finn's health and safety were a priority. She had to put her thoughts about Oliver on the back burner for now. To momentarily forget that this terrorist financier, Tariq, might be connected to Oliver's case.

"Finn?" She slowly crept closer to the bathroom and covered her eyes when she reached the doorway. "Dalton?"

She hesitantly lowered her hand, and the sight of Finn behind the glass shower wall filled her vision. A very clothed Finn. He still had on his short-sleeve shirt and khaki pants. Boots and socks were all he'd discarded before stepping into the shower.

His face was tipped up toward the showerhead as water cascaded over his body, his clothes clinging to his powerful frame.

"You okay?" *Dumb question.* He was definitely not okay. Damn that word. It was going to be scrubbed from her vocabulary because nothing had been okay lately.

Finn roped a hand around the back of his neck, still keeping his chin turned toward the water as it pelted him in the face.

"Talk to me." She moved to stand at the entrance of the

shower. *Fuck it.* She kicked off her sandals and stepped inside to face him. "Why only take off the boots and socks?" Small talk as an opener? Why not?

"Hate getting my shoes wet," he answered in a low tone a moment later, then slowly opened his eyes, dropping his head to look at her.

"What are you doing?" he asked in a husky voice, his gaze lowering over her clothed body.

"Isn't it obvious? I'm worried about you."

Droplets of water continued to roll down his tan cheeks. "Don't be."

"You're standing in the shower with your clothes on. Did something bad happen out in that desert?"

"Nothing bad went down. We won. They lost."

"You were shot."

"Shit happens. Why are *you* in here?"

"Because you're in here," she answered honestly, her throat growing thick as she thought about the fact she could have lost him tonight. "Because I missed the signs with Tucker, but I can see them plain as day with you."

"I thought you avoided military types because you were worried you wouldn't see the signs if something's wrong." The back of his hand caressed the contour of her cheek, and she leaned into his unexpected touch. "And yet, here you are."

"So, you admit there are signs I should notice?"

His brows lifted as if he were surprised, too.

"Something is hurting you. *You're* hurting." She eased closer to him when he lowered his hand from her cheek. "Not just from getting shot."

She joined him beneath the water and reached for his left forearm, unsure where he'd been hit.

"I'm not Jaden. I'm not going to . . ." He closed his eyes,

pulled free of her grasp, and turned away, setting his clenched fists on the stretch of tiled wall.

She'd expected him to say he wasn't like Tucker, but she was clueless about who he was referring to. Her hand went to his back since he'd rejected her touch on his arm. "Who is Jaden?"

"I just need a minute, okay? Please. I'll be fine." He lifted one hand from the wall, and she thought he was going to wave her off, but instead, he squeezed his palm into a fist and placed it on the wall again. "Just go." He looked at her from over his shoulder, a mix of rage and anguish filling his dark green eyes that glittered like wet emeralds. "Please go. I'm going to get naked now. So, unless you want to be here for that . . ."

Feeling defeated, she dropped her hand from his back and turned to leave. But Finn took her by surprise when, faster than she thought possible with an injury, he grasped her wrist and firmly tugged, whirling her around to face him.

He raked his gaze down the length of her body, his eyes flaring at the sight of her red dress that was now soaked and plastered to her skin. And no doubt her hard nipples poked through her thin bra. Before she could say a word, he pulled her flush to his body and held her tight as his chest heaved with deep, anguished breaths.

And then time slowed when he eased up on his hold and slowly skated his palms up the sides of her arms, stopping at her biceps. His gentle touch was a contrast to the storm of emotions brewing in his eyes. Anger competing with something else. Lust? That couldn't be, though.

"Tell me what's wrong?" she whispered as his gaze dropped to her mouth. "Let me help you."

At those words, he released her and backed up just enough to lift his shirt over his head. He peeled it off slowly, then tossed it over the glass partition. Before she had the chance to appreciate his exposed chest, her eyes landed on the purple bruising already starting to form. It looked like someone had taken a baseball bat multiple times to the upper part of his left pectoral muscle. Thank God he'd been wearing protection beneath his shirt, or he'd be in the hospital now or worse.

She stepped forward and gently touched the marks, half-expecting him to snatch her wrist again, but he lowered his focus to where her hand raced over his muscle, water continuing to glide over them both.

"You should go," he said gruffly.

"What if I don't want to leave you alone?"

"I'm in the shower. About to get naked. And I'm just . . ." He took a few shallow breaths as his gaze slowly drifted from her eyes down as far as he could view.

"You're just what?" she whispered, breathless. Her world felt condensed down to this very moment, fully clothed inside the shower with Finn, while everything outside of their room was spinning out of control.

With his large palm on her lower back, he quickly pulled her closer to him, trapping her arm against his chest.

Ohhhh. She felt the bulge in his pants. The hard, hard bulge. "Are you thinking about, um, angles?" Was it stupid to attempt a joke now? Probably. But she would do anything to help ease his tension and stress. To help him. She also had no idea why he was turned on right now.

Okay, that was a lie.

She was aroused, too, even if she had no right to be. But here she was wet between her legs and not only from the shower.

"You need to go," he murmured darkly. "Please, go. I don't trust myself."

"I trust you," she answered without a second thought, and a fluttery sensation filled her abdomen. "I trust you," she said again in a softer voice, tipping her chin up to find his eyes.

His eyelashes were wet and dark, enhancing those stunning green eyes. "I'm thinking about a lot more than angles, Jewels."

Jewels?

Why did that name turn her on so much? No one had ever called her that before. It somehow felt fitting coming from him.

"You were shot. And something else is bothering you. So, why would you want . . ." She couldn't even finish her line of thought. It felt absurd to say what she assumed he wanted. Sex. Because hell, what if she was reading him wrong?

But his cock was ridiculously hard. And big. So, yeah, she shouldn't second-guess herself.

"I'm angry and tense. And you're soaking wet in that dress. And I need to escape the past before it swallows me whole."

The past? Her breathing picked up, and she wanted to hug this man and take away his pain. Both physical and mental. Whatever was hurting him. She wanted to erase it.

"I will *not* use you to escape." And with that, he looked to the floor and let go of her.

"See," she added in a soft voice. "I knew I could trust you." She licked her wet lips. "But what if it wouldn't be using me? Because what if I need to feel something other than my pain, too?" Her eyes closed as she struggled with how to go on. "I haven't felt anything in so long. I've been numb. But when I'm around you, I-I don't know. You make me feel things."

"Julia." The use of her name felt like a warning, but a warning about what?

"I haven't even been able to get myself off when I touch myself," she confessed and opened her eyes to find him staring at her, his mouth drawn tight. "I—"

"What?" he hissed through barely parted lips. "You can't tell me something like that and . . ."

She turned her cheek, suddenly regretting her honesty. "I'm sorry."

"That's not a word you use often. Don't start now." The back of his hand once again traced her cheek, and he drew her back in to face him. "You can't get yourself off?" he prompted, his voice still low and deep.

She shook her head in response, afraid she'd say even more crazy shit if she opened her mouth. This wasn't the time to push him into saying something he might regret tomorrow. He could have died tonight, and he needed a safe space to handle that.

He closed his eyes for a moment, then lifted his lids as if they were heavy. And the next thing she knew, he was walking her backward to the tiled wall, and based on his hard jawline, he was biting down on his teeth as if he were pushing through his pain. "Lift your dress."

"What?"

"Lift it," he said again like an order.

Without hesitation, she gathered the skirt of her dress and lifted it to her waist. His big hand skated up the inside of her thigh as he leaned in so close she felt his breath against her cheek. She cried out when his fingers feathered over her wet panties.

Was this actually happening, or was she dreaming? Maybe she fell asleep while Finn was gone, and this wasn't real.

"Can I touch you?" he whispered in her ear, the water

147

bouncing off his broad shoulders and back, shielding her from getting sprayed.

"You already are." She wanted to grip his biceps, to hold on to him before her legs gave out, but she kept her grip on her dress. He was ignoring his pain to pleasure her and give her something she hadn't had in so long. Putting her needs first while he was suffering.

Then again, maybe this was the escape he appeared to so desperately need. A win-win. The moment was too intimate to only translate to them using each other, though.

"Beneath your panties. Can I touch you there?"

"Yes." She arched into him. "Please."

He set his forehead to hers the moment his finger dipped beneath her panties and touched her damp folds. "You feel like silk down here. Fuck, Julia."

"Jewels," she murmured. "I like that."

When he lifted his head and looked into her eyes, she knew she was truly fucked. This man was going to break her. But she wasn't sure if it'd be in a bad or good way.

His work was dangerous and—*no, don't get inside your head again*. She needed this release. She needed this man to touch her more than she needed anything else right now, even if that was insane.

"Jewels," he said on an exhale before inserting not one but two fingers inside her pussy, and she bucked against his hand, wishing the panties were out of the way.

She let go of her dress and set her hands to his abdomen instead of his chest, not wanting to hurt him, and he backed up one step.

Her fingers went to the straps of her dress, and she pushed them over her shoulders, then removed the rest of the saturated material while steadily holding his gaze. Her panties went next, leaving her in only a nude strapless bra.

His eyes snapped down to her breasts. "Bra, too. I mean, if I'm going to get you off, let's have you fully naked while I do it."

"Confident, huh?" she asked with a surprising smile as she unhooked her bra, and he leaned in, bringing his mouth dangerously close to hers, but he didn't lay a kiss on her lips.

"Very," he responded as the bra fell to the tiled floor.

He had her against the wall again in a heartbeat, the cold tile sending a shiver up her spine. His hand wandered over her flat belly down around the curve of her ass before finding its place back between her legs, never once breaking eye contact.

His fingers felt like a seductive dance over her soaked center, as if he already knew every intimate detail of her body and how she liked it. And maybe how she never knew she liked it.

Fingered by my bodyguard in Egypt. What title of an erotica film was she lost in right now? This couldn't possibly be her life.

"You in pain?" she asked before moaning when she felt his thumb on her bud while he continued to pump two fingers inside of her.

"What pain?" he answered with a cocked head and heated look in his eyes. "I'm distracted from every fucking thing except for you, Jewels."

She was going to come.

Too soon. Too fast.

And after not having the ability to find pleasure for so long, she didn't want it to end because who knew when or if she'd be granted sweet surrender again.

"You feel so good."

Out of the corner of her eye, she saw his palm against the wall twitch as if fighting the urge to keep this from escalating further. And was it wrong that she wanted to feel the heat of his mouth on her breasts? Have him take off his pants and fill her deep in one fast thrust?

"Finn, please, don't stop. Don't. Oh. God." Her back arched off the wall, bringing her pebbled nipples against his chest, and she cried out, forgetting what it was like to come. She was breathing heavily, gulping in the damp air as she came down from the ride of ecstasy and whispered, "Let me help you with your tension, too." It wouldn't be quid pro quo. No favor. She wanted to touch him. To feel him.

His mouth snapped shut. Jaw tight. The veins in his arms popped as he now had both palms against the wall on each side of her as if he needed it for support, worried he'd collapse onto her. "No, I needed that to happen for you."

"You needed it for me?" she asked softly. "Why?"

"I needed to see you fall to pieces from my touch. To see you lose your control."

"You going to help put me back together?" Her legs were rubber, but she was temporarily relaxed.

Finn's dimple appeared for one quick second as he brought his mouth to her ear. "You're not the kind of woman to need help from any man."

When he started to pull back, she slid her hand over his right pectoral muscle free of bruises. Then she lifted her chin and found his eyes. "And what if I want help?" *What if I want you?*

CHAPTER ELEVEN

WHAT THE ACTUAL FUCK JUST HAPPENED? FINN TOWEL-DRIED his hair in the bedroom after changing into jeans and a white polo. How had he gone from his heart feeling as though it'd explode from painful memories, not to mention the bullet he'd taken in the chest, to fingering the woman who drove him crazy?

Enemies-to-lovers romance. Wasn't that what Harper had said at that bar in Tribeca, the night of Julia's "date" with Lorenzo?

He liked a challenge. Loved it, in fact. Thrived on it. Being a SEAL was all about challenges.

So, when Julia said she couldn't even get herself off, how could he not see that as a personal challenge? He'd been burning to touch her for weeks, and her admission was like pouring gasoline on the fire blazing inside him.

And yet, he'd been so angry after the op. Not just that it was a bust, but about so many things out of his control. And he didn't want to accidentally hurt her if he lost control of himself. Sex with her had to be off-limits in his current state of mind.

Inside that shower, he'd seen some of himself in Julia. The pain from losing someone. The guilt because she blamed herself—he could relate to all of it.

It was clear he still struggled to move on from his own guilt. But did anyone ever actually move on, or did they just bury it beneath a pile of platitudes and bullshit their way through life?

Although, how many times over the years had his mom blamed him for what happened? How many times had he blamed himself for not telling his parents sooner about Jaden's problem?

I can't look at you. How can I ever look at you again after what you did? his mom had asked Finn before slapping him across the face. But he'd been too numb on the inside to feel the sting.

Finn dragged a palm down his face as if it had just happened, hating that his thoughts landed in the past yet again, especially after the erotic shower scene had pulled him to the present.

He was usually okay, well, whatever okay really meant. It took a lot to get his mind to slip like that. But those pills. Damn those pills.

And it was this crazy night that led him to make the split-second decision to touch her. Wrong or right, he wasn't so sure, but he'd done it. Fueled by anger and pain, yes. But also driven by the feelings he'd developed for her far too fast for his comfort.

Finn carefully lowered himself to sit on the bed, a hand to his chest as he did so. The dull, achy throb ratcheted up a notch. Thank God he'd already been numb by the time he had to ride that camel because the side-to-side swaying motions of the enormous beast would've made him feel worse.

Emotionally and physically numb. It'd become an art form he'd perfected over the years.

Lost a friend during the war. Numb.

IED. Fucking numb.

Marcus, Bravo Three, dying at the hands of terrorists. Numb, numb, numb.

Throw in some humor about anything and everything to hide the fact he was numb? Check.

Until little by little, over the last six months, the numbness had begun to fade.

Everyone on Echo Team had been seeing a therapist, a strength-in-numbers kind of thing to support Chris with his PTSD, and it turned out Finn was benefiting from the help, too.

After the op went sideways tonight, he was worried he was on the verge of slipping back into his old routine— numbness hidden by humor.

In that shower, Julia somehow saved him from losing himself.

He felt a connection with her, and it scared the hell out of him.

But he would inevitably hurt her because of his job. And she admitted she couldn't be with someone like him, so while she might have felt spectacular in his arms and helped ease his pain, he couldn't risk hurting her.

He refused to add another layer of guilt to what he already wore.

So, no touching her again. He needed to erase the memories of the shower from his mind. Forget what she sounded like when she came. How her naked body felt beneath his palm.

She got off, and I've got painful balls. And now I need to focus on giving her the help she really needs.

Moving on would be a hell of a lot easier if what he felt for this woman was purely physical, but he knew it ran so much deeper than that. She was more than just an assignment despite how she came into his life for the second time.

Harper may have had the best of intentions when she tried setting them up, but she didn't know about Julia's issues, and only Roman knew about Finn's. *Scratch that.* Jessica and Luke knew his past, but they were unaware of the fact that he still carried it with him like a rucksack on his back everywhere he went.

Finn rose from the bed just as Julia walked out of the bathroom wearing white cotton shorts and an oversized pink sweatshirt. *Fuck.* All thoughts of forgetting her vanished as he gave in and allowed his gaze to dip over her tan, silky legs. He wanted to drop to his knees and devour her, lose himself in her again. Feel something other than the numbness that was slowly creeping back in.

"Hi." The little word floated with unease from her lips. She was nervous, probably unsure how to act after what they did in the shower.

It'd honestly be better if she went back to pretending as though she hated him, even if her attitude had made his dick stir. Then again, everything about Julia made his dick stir.

He took a step closer, desperate to wrap his arms around her, but stopped when Julia flattened her back to the wall next to the open bathroom door as if she sensed his intentions.

"I'm sorry. I don't know why I shared what I did. I honestly don't know what came over me." Her hands slipped behind her back as if she needed to pin them down to prevent reaching for him.

She was so damn adorable that he couldn't fight the few dangerous steps he took her way.

"People have a tendency to tell me their secrets. It

happens," he admitted, his body feeling heavy again, weighed down by memories and guilt.

"That can be a burden. Being a secret keeper." Her blue eyes held him captive as he remained a good ten feet away, hoping that was far enough to keep himself from pulling her into his arms and kissing her like he'd wanted to do in the shower. "People must trust you, though."

That hit him like a brick to the face. Or a bullet to the chest. He reached up and set a hand on his pec where he'd been shot. "Maybe they shouldn't."

He was about to turn and escape to the balcony, but she said, "Tell me a secret, then. Help me lift whatever burden it is I see you carrying."

"My problems are mine. You have enough on your plate." He slipped his hands into his pockets, still worried he'd go to her, the same way it appeared she needed to pin her arms behind her back to keep from reaching for him.

"Can you tell me what happened out there?" Her tone was gentle, almost like she hoped to coax the truth out of him.

"Are you asking if I think what went down might be connected to Oliver?" Speaking of Oliver, Finn needed to hear the full story to determine whether the dots did connect, but he'd wait until Harper was in the room.

"No." She freed her hands and came closer, which had him drawing in an uneasy breath. "I'm asking because I care about you. Something obviously shook you out in that desert, and I want you to tell me what it was."

"Why do you need to know? You hated me up until we arrived in Egypt. Maybe even until five minutes ago."

"You know full well that was an act to drive you away. I had no idea my friend set me up, and she's the reason my brother hired you. I was worried you'd get in my way, so I wanted you to ditch me."

Friend, huh? His brows lifted in surprise.

She pulled her bottom lip between her teeth for a split second, eyes falling to the floor. "I'll explain everything like I should have done a long time ago." Her shoulders dropped, and he recognized that look.

Guilt.

He didn't want her to feel guilty.

"Julia." He couldn't bring himself to call her Jewels again. It'd happened on a whim during an intimate moment, and he needed to separate himself from that now. He wished like hell he could be the man Julia deserved, the man she needed. The only man he was pretty sure he'd ever be was an operator, though. A Forever Single Guy. "You—"

"It's me," Harper called out while knocking, and Julia's face fell as if disappointed by the interruption.

"It's better you share with her here, anyway," Finn said as he went to the door.

"We need to talk," Harper announced as she strode into the room while throwing her hair into a ponytail. She was sporting a new tee, one of her signature ones that had Finn surprisingly smiling. Her black T-shirt said, *I have a "WTF is wrong with people" moment at least 4 x's a day.*

"Why do I feel like I should sit down?" Julia asked hesitantly.

"You might want to do that," Harper replied softly.

He couldn't handle the suspense any longer. "What is it?"

"Well, the good news is that I accessed the doctor's files, and there's a treasure trove of bad guys on there that multiple nations will be happy to go after. And some women, too, actually," Harper said, leaving out the main subject Julia was interested in, which had Finn worried. "The bad news is that Tariq is already on the move. He must have heard about what happened with—" She stopped mid-sentence and cut a look to Finn, silently questioning how much Julia knew about the op. "He's gone. His private plane took off ten minutes ago. Still scheduled to arrive in Dubai, just earlier than planned."

"Have we been able to verify who was killed here tonight? Was it the doc and his assistant?" Finn glanced at Julia, who was now seated on the bed, hands firmly on her thighs as though she were preparing herself for the first big drop of a roller coaster.

"It was Lorenzo and Giorgio. The security cameras were taken out, so we can't confirm who killed them. But for whatever reason, I think Tariq had them taken out. And I double-checked, Tariq is Kaira Zare's brother."

"What's the *rest* of the bad news? Well, aside from my only lead being murdered." Julia stood. "I can feel it coming."

"Ario and Kaira Zare did have a meeting with Giorgio two days before he died, and they were on Giorgio's schedule for plastic surgery. But both surgeries were canceled," Harper shared. "They were scheduled for January eighth, and Ario was killed on the sixth. According to the doctor's calendar, the procedure was canceled because Ario had died. I need to try and get ahold of the coroner's report, but . . ."

"Someone could've altered it? That's what you're going to say." Julia's shoulders collapsed.

"No, I was going to say that Giorgio kept before and after records on his clients. Along with their new identities. I guess he was a full-service shop, not just a face changer. I'm sure his clients didn't know he kept such detailed records, though," Harper delivered the news. "There were no before and afters for Ario."

"So, you'd been hoping the cancellation note on the schedule for Ario was a ruse, and for some reason, he went through with the operation without his wife?" Julia asked.

"But since there's no new identity listed for Ario, you don't think it's possible."

Harper nodded and asked in a low tone, "And you're sure your friend didn't really kill his boss?"

"No, he would never do that. I don't care what the report says. All lies. Oliver is a good man. There has to be something I'm missing. Maybe it's related to the wife's brother, Tariq."

"Since you accessed Giorgio's calendar, who was he supposed to meet here in Egypt?" Finn asked, trying to keep the conversation moving in a direction that wouldn't have Julia feeling helpless or without hope.

"It wasn't Tariq. Well, let's put it this way, I don't think Giorgio *knew* he was meeting with Tariq," Harper responded.

"What do you mean?" Julia asked.

"I have to do some more digging, but I think Tariq used an alias to draw out Giorgio. Then he changed the meeting location at the last minute. Did Giorgio look surprised or uneasy at all when you saw him talking to Tariq in the lobby yesterday?"

Finn thought back to that moment, but he'd been so shocked to see Tariq with the doctor he'd lost his focus. "I don't remember." He turned to Julia. "You?"

"Maybe. I-I don't know."

"What I'd like to know is why a man with Tariq's status and reputation felt the need to use an alias to get a meeting? Wouldn't Giorgio have jumped at the chance to help him? Big name, lots of money." Finn hoped Harper already had an idea or two on that matter.

Harper crossed her arms and let go of a light breath. "Unless Giorgio had a reason to fear him."

"Wait, what if Giorgio *did* perform the surgery and Ario is really alive? And when Tariq confronted him in the lobby, he panicked and altered his files on Ario, expecting Tariq would want to see them?" Julia quickly proposed. "Maybe Tariq began to have suspicions that Ario was still alive, and he tracked down Giorgio for Ario's alias." There was energy in her voice. Shoulders back with hope.

"I doubt Giorgio would be stupid enough to believe Tariq would simply take a peek at his records, discover the surgery was canceled, and be satisfied with that information." Harper looked to the ceiling for a moment. "Tariq may not believe Ario is really dead for whatever reason, and maybe he tortured Giorgio to find out what he knows." Harper paused as if continuing to deliberate the theory. "There's a big time gap between Ario's supposed death and now, though. So, either Tariq only recently found reason to believe Ario faked his death, or he had a hard time getting Giorgio to meet with him," Harper pointed out. "I'm leaning toward option one if that's the case."

"Fuck, I don't know what to think." Finn grimaced. "But we'll figure this all out," he told Julia. "It's what we do." His words earned a surprised look from Harper. A "you're saying too much" kind of stare.

Before Finn could respond, Julia's phone rang from the bedside table, startling her. As she went to grab it, Finn exchanged a quick look with Harper, who peered at him with sad, apologetic eyes.

"It's my brother," Julia said, looking down at the screen.

"Calling this late? Something wrong?" she asked Julia.

"He doesn't know I'm here. It's six hours earlier in New York."

"Right." Harper frowned, and from the looks of it, her nerves were on point with Finn's.

"Hey." Julia turned her back to them and answered, her

tone guarded as if worried her big brother was on the brink of catching her in a lie.

Phone to her ear, Julia listened quietly for a few moments before she abruptly swung around to face Finn, her eyes wide. In one surprisingly fast move, she dropped to her knees. Finn rushed to her side and dropped in front of her, catching her by the elbow as the phone fell to the floor.

"You're going to need to fill him in." Finn handed the phone to Harper, and he waited for her to leave the room before pulling Julia toward him and cradling her in his arms. "What is it? What'd he say?"

She looked up at him as he looped her arms over his shoulders, her face near his. Eyes shimmering with the threat of tears. "He said the Saudis made a deal with law enforcement in Dubai to have him transferred and executed there."

"What?"

"He's being moved to Saudi Arabia in a week," she cried. "Michael said once Oliver is in Saudi Arabia, the chance of helping him before it's too late is next to none." Her eyes fell closed as tears began to roll down her cheeks. "Oliver's going to die, isn't he?"

And damn, that bit of hope she'd had moments before had now been extinguished from her eyes.

CHAPTER TWELVE

"From the beginning," Finn said softly. "Please." He sat down next to Julia on the bed, hoping to provide some support while she shared her story.

Harper was back in the suite, but she hadn't mentioned how her conversation with Michael had gone, though Finn had some guesses. Most importantly, Julia had calmed down a bit from the shocking news she'd learned from her brother, and now Finn hoped she would be able to shed some light on what the hell was going on.

"And for now, let's act as though Tariq's not involved. I want to hear what you knew before tonight," Harper added.

Finn reached for Julia's hand and laced their fingers together. Probably not what he should have done since he needed to change course away from any kind of intimacy with her and remain professional, but she was hurting, and he hated seeing that. Anything he could do to help her, he would.

"When Oliver got out of the military last year, he was adrift." Julia had to be drawing parallels to Tucker, too. It couldn't be easy for her to share this. "He wasn't sure what to do. How to handle civilian life."

Finn couldn't relate since he wasn't technically a civilian, but some of the guys he'd stayed in contact with from his old platoon, before Echo, were out now, and they struggled.

"I was worried he'd, um . . ."

End up like Tucker? He squeezed her hand gently to remind her he was there.

She looked up at him and lightly nodded. "I heard about an international security firm that hired veterans for different gigs, but mostly to be bodyguards. A chance to travel and experience the world and not from behind a scope this time. I knew one of the owners of the firm, and I connected them." She paused. "There was an opening in Dubai, and I encouraged Oliver to take the job last year."

And there was the guilt. The blame.

Unwarranted, but would he feel the same way if it'd been him in her shoes? Probably.

"His first client was Ario Zare. The whole thing is just strange because Oliver said he liked him and his wife," she explained.

"Did anything change before he was arrested?" Harper asked. "Did he say Ario had changed, I mean?"

"No, not at all. So, when my brother called me after he'd learned through his government contacts that Oliver was in jail for murdering his boss, I thought it was a cruel joke."

"What proof is there?" Harper continued the questioning, and Finn was relieved she was able to do the back-and-forth with Julia. He wasn't sure if he could handle it.

"Security footage from the office building across the street showed Oliver arriving at the construction site and entering the building at eight in the morning. He usually accompanied Ario to work, but for some reason, Ario went without him that day."

"I can't imagine Ario was the only one there when Oliver arrived," Finn spoke up.

"No, Ario and Oliver weren't alone. And the only reason the U.S. was granted access to anything related to the case is that Oliver's an American. And even that took time. Michael was finally able to look at the footage and read the statement, but they won't let anyone talk to Oliver. It's killing me."

Yeah, Finn would lose his damn mind if a friend was locked up and he couldn't even hear his side of the story.

"So, um, ten minutes after Oliver was inside," Julia continued, "Ario was supposedly pushed, and Oliver exited the building shortly after. The cameras across the street caught the fall. No cams inside yet since the skyscraper was under construction, but there were five crewmen on the tenth floor that day. Two said they were physically near Ario when Oliver showed up and . . ."

"So, they have witnesses to verify Oliver pushed him?" Harper probed when Julia let her words hang, words she clearly didn't want to say.

Julia nodded. "They said Oliver started yelling at Ario in English, backed him to the ledge while yelling, and then just pushed."

"What were they arguing about?" Finn asked.

"The workers don't know English. They weren't sure what was said." Julia frowned. "But Ario's wife, Kaira, said she knew why they were fighting."

Another pause. Another moment of silence that had Finn worried Julia was afraid to share something.

"What is it?" Harper asked in a near-whisper.

Julia's blue eyes vanished behind her lids. "Kaira said Oliver showed up to pick Ario up for work, discovered he'd already left, and found her badly beaten that morning. He became enraged and went to find Ario to confront him. In her statement, she also said she believed Oliver had fallen in love with her," Julia answered in a somber tone as if her words might serve as the final nail in Oliver's coffin.

Coffin? No. Damn it. Memories of pills in the sarcophaguses haunted him yet again.

"The United Arab Emirates recently overhauled its Islamic personal laws in 2020 if I'm not mistaken," Harper said. "It's an effort to draw tourists and businesses. So-called 'honor crimes' and 'honor killings' are now punishable just like any other kind of assault."

"I'm still guessing a man like Oliver wouldn't let wife abuse fly, especially if he considered Ario part American," Finn remarked. "Not that some Americans don't beat their wives even though it's illegal there, too."

"Regardless," Julia said while opening her eyes, "Oliver wouldn't commit murder because of it." She stood, and Finn released her hand. "I-I don't think he would. But Michael believes it's possible."

"Well, the incriminating factor is that Oliver fled the scene of the crime instead of offering himself as a witness," Harper said.

Why run if he was innocent?

"Maybe he knew he was being set up?" Julia's proposal sounded weak, but he wanted to believe her faith in her friend was well-founded. "If Ario's really alive, he would need a fall guy, right? And surely Ario has enough money to buy off someone at the police station to ensure they identified him as the victim. His body and face were badly damaged from the fall."

"Possible, and given who Kaira's family is, there's most likely a lot more to this story than the police report let on." Harper's comment seemed to relax Julia a bit. "Especially when you throw into the mix the plastic surgeon showing up in Egypt and then murdered shortly after being seen with Tariq."

"Tariq wouldn't need Ario's money for anything, right?" Finn asked. "Not if he's wealthy enough to throw money at terrorist groups over the years as a hobby."

"True. But Ario had billions. Tariq's only thirty-three, still living with his parents, and his money comes from them. Same as his twin and his other unmarried brothers," Harper answered.

"Maybe they cut Tariq off because he's too Western for their style, similar to Kaira." God, this was some next-level silver-spoon-rich-boy issue if that were the case.

"I don't know. We'll find out." Harper pinned Julia with a curious look. "How did you find out about Giorgio and the possibility Ario faked his death?"

Julia pivoted to the side to put eyes on Harper. "My friend is a freelance journalist and basically a crime solver these days, and I asked her to dive deep into the Zare family. Anything irregular that stood out within the timeframe nearing Ario's death."

And you took self-defense lessons from me in case you . . . He couldn't finish that thought. The idea she'd anticipated putting herself in danger made him sick.

"By dumb luck, Mya happened to recognize Giorgio Ferrari in some surveillance footage she'd had a friend pull from Ario's main office building. She knew him from a previous case she'd worked where a criminal faked his death and used Giorgio to do it."

"So, you thought maybe Ario faked his death, and if he was really alive, then there was no question Oliver was innocent, and that's how you'd save him." A good lead. A shaky one, but it was better than nothing, and he was rather impressed Julia and her reporter friend had gotten so far.

"It took a lot of time to track down Giorgio, and I had to bait his assistant into wanting to date me. I cloned Lorenzo's phone and sent the intel to my friend, and that's when she found out where Giorgio would be next."

"Damn." A quick, impressed smile ghosted Harper's lips. "Sorry, didn't expect to hear you talking about mirroring phones. Your operative skills are top-notch for a businesswoman."

And had Julia always wanted to be a businesswoman? Or a photographer? Had she set her dreams aside when she lost Tucker? Was that when she put down the camera?

"I also recently found out my friend was the one sending death threats to my office because I refused to take her advice and hire protection. She was worried I would get hurt the deeper I looked into this, especially when she discovered Kaira was related to the Saudi royals. I didn't know Tariq's name because Kaira has seven brothers from what I remembered from Mya's research. I didn't consider that Ario's death might be connected to her family somehow, and I assume Mya's investigative skills wouldn't have turned up the whole financing-terrorism thing by Tariq, either."

"No, she wouldn't have found that out." *Not unless Mya's secretly CIA.*

"My brother promised to handle things by going through the proper legal channels, and *I* promised him I would stay out of it. But despite how compelling the evidence is against Oliver, I know in my heart Oliver is being set up."

"What'd Oliver say happened?" Finn asked. "I assume Michael read that in the report even though no one can talk to him."

"Oliver said he went there to confront Ario about the abuse, which matches Kaira's statement, and by the time he'd made it to the tenth floor—there were no working elevators yet—Ario had already fallen."

Finn drew a hand over his face, wishing he still had his thick beard, as he processed the news.

"Did you look into Oliver's background? Did they check for anything suspicious at his home? Or—"

"Yeah, the report said they found, um." Her blue eyes were hidden, this time by her palm.

"What?" Finn tensed, but why did he already know what she was going to say?

"Alcohol all over his condo. Empty bottles."

Shit, that couldn't be easy for her to learn. Did she think she missed the signs again?

"And there was more," Julia whispered as she lowered her hand. "They found pills."

"Pills?" He stepped back but hit the bed and wound up sitting when he lost his balance.

"The toxicology screen said he had fenethylline or something like that in his system. I don't believe Oliver would take drugs, though."

Finn's head was spinning now.

"You're sure that's what it said?" Harper asked in a low voice, and it took Finn a moment to put two and two together.

"What is it?" Julia looked down at Finn.

"Fenethylline is a codrug of amphetamine and theophylline." Harper's shoulders sank at the unexpected news.

"And it's also known as the brand name Captagon," he hissed.

167

CHAPTER THIRTEEN

"We can't take her with us. That's a non-starter." Wyatt looked up from where he was packing his belongings in his suite. Echo Team had arranged for a private flight to take them to Dubai, once again bypassing the domestic-only flight situation in and out of Aswan. Wheels up at zero five hundred hours. "Her brother is catching the next flight out, and you'll watch her until he gets here. Then you're on a flight to Dubai the second Michael has her."

As soon as Michael learned the truth about what Julia had been up to, he flipped out at the team for taking her to Egypt. And *after* he calmed down, he pleaded with the guys to keep her in Egypt until he could personally escort her home since they'd politely told him they couldn't force her on a plane back to the States when she had every intention of going to Dubai.

She was a woman on a mission to save a friend, and the only reason Finn considered standing in her way was because it'd be a death sentence for her if she got involved with Tariq. People who tangoed with the royal family died an ugly death.

"What if Oliver was set up and someone found out Julia's been looking into Ario's death?"

"Julia said Mya did all of the leg work, so we can put in a call to make sure she has protection, and as for Julia, Michael will keep her safe." Wyatt zipped the duffel bag and stood. "Harper and Jessica will do what they do best and track Tariq's last movements as far back as they can. And if the man so much as takes a shit from here on out, we'll know about it."

"I think we should talk to Luke. Convince him to let us bring Julia along." Finn held up a palm, hoping to ward off another protest from Wyatt. "Hear me out. Julia is desperate to save her friend, and she's disappointed her brother hasn't been able to make any headway, so she may not have high expectations of us, either. But she will damn well find a way to Dubai, I guaran-fucking-tee it."

Wyatt settled his hands on his hips as he processed Finn's words.

"Think about Natasha and the lengths she went to in taking down the man she'd been after for years," Finn reminded him how his wife had gone rogue to pursue a notorious cybercriminal. "Julia has that determination. She'll go to Dubai without any plan. And out of sheer desperation, she'll most likely go straight to Ario's wife herself for answers." That scared the hell out of him.

"Natasha is Natasha." Wyatt took a seat on a nearby chair as if his legs were going to give out. "I can't stop that woman no matter what, even when she's . . ."

"She's what?" Finn stepped closer to his team leader, trying to get a read on him since he'd been acting a bit off all night.

"Nothing." He set his elbow on his jeaned thigh and rested his palm against his face.

"Doesn't look like nothing, man."

"She's pregnant." Wyatt slowly lifted his head to meet Finn's eyes. "And the woman won't slow down. And I . . . shit, this is our first op since I found out, and I, um." He curled his hand into a fist and placed it over his heart. "There's been something inside of me I'm not used to feeling when we're working an op. Fear." He lowered his hand. "I'm terrified I'm going to leave that baby fatherless someday. I already missed out on Gwen's childhood, and I don't want to miss out on this kid's."

Ohhh. What was he supposed to say to that?

"Not to mention the world is nuts. Hell, the guys might be right about an imminent zombie apocalypse. We know UFOs are a thing. And 2020 and 2021 were a damn disaster. I just can't handle the stress."

Finn stepped before him and set a palm over his shoulder to try and calm him down with the conversation taking an unexpected turn. "I thought you wanted a baby with Natasha."

"I do." He closed his eyes and hung his head. "But I need to find a way to put the baby in a bubble. Gwen, too. Natasha. And everyone I care about." Wyatt's voice cracked, and Finn had a feeling Wyatt hadn't shared this news with anyone else yet.

He didn't mind Echo One opening up to him. He was happy to be there for him. But Finn really was beginning to think there was something about him that brought out confessions.

"Should've been a priest," he accidentally whispered his thoughts aloud.

And there was the humor he'd grown so accustomed to falling back on, same as Chris had done over the years to hide his PTSD.

"Sorry, I didn't mean to lay this on you. I just have this bad feeling in my gut I can't seem to shake."

"Like a storm is coming?" Finn asked. "Because that's how I feel."

"Remember that sandstorm we were caught in back in Gan a few years ago?"

Finn thought back to the desert in Afghanistan. A herd of horses had been racing across the sand to God only knew where, fleeing because they'd instinctively known what was coming.

"Like we're going to choke to death on sand?" Goose bumps rose on Finn's arms at the memory.

"I feel like I have sand in my throat, and I'm struggling to breathe. Stuck in a storm that's not even here yet, but it's coming."

Wyatt may not have been his brother by blood, like Jaden, but he was family just the same, and Finn was glad to push his own problems aside to help him out. As a matter of fact, for the last nine years, Finn had considered Bravo and Echo his only family. "You can't think like that. Everything will be okay."

Why did that feel like a lie? And why the hell did Julia have to choose the Osiris statue that came complete with an ominous warning? Another reason he wasn't ready to fly off to Dubai and assume she'd listen to her brother and not go to the end of the world to save her friend. He knew exactly what was motivating her. She was trying to absolve herself of the guilt she'd been hauling around for years. Guilt that was not her responsibility to carry.

He understood her more than she'd ever know.

He'd be lying if he didn't confess to himself that one of the reasons he joined the Navy was penance for his own guilt.

To try and save as many lives as possible. But all the lives he'd saved didn't undo the one life he couldn't.

"I'll snap out of it. Override." Wyatt blinked a few times, his blue-gray eyes a touch glossy. That was also new.

"According to our therapist, we're not supposed to override. Well, not unless we're on an op," Finn said, recalling Dr. Logan's words from a few weeks ago.

"We are technically on an op, so." Wyatt cleared his throat, an announcement that he was done with the "feelings" conversation, stood, and brushed past him. "I'll call Luke and run your request up the line. Bravo is en route to Dubai in the morning, too. We'll be splitting up in the city, staying at different hotels, though."

"Yeah, you, uh, already told me." Finn stared at his team leader, worried about him.

Wyatt's eyes narrowed. "Oh, right."

"And thank you for trying. Let me know. I should go check on Julia."

Finn made his way to the door and clutched the handle when Wyatt asked, "About the pills, what do you think Tariq is up to?"

"Weapons. The jihadi drug of choice. Money. Sounds like he's building his own private army." Finn did his best to answer like an operator and not a man broken by his past.

"That's what I'm thinking, that this is more than him simply funding activities. Tariq seems more involved than usual."

Finn opened the door and turned to put eyes on his team leader. "We'll stop him. It's what we do." He nodded, then left the room.

A.J. was on the balcony with Julia when Finn walked into their hotel room. "Hey."

A.J. turned around at the sound of Finn's voice and

started his way. Julia kept her attention fixed off in the distance. The hours and days were all blending together at this point. He was losing track of time.

He checked his watch. It was zero three hundred. The time when he was originally supposed to spin up. But what day was it?

Her date with Lorenzo had been on Monday. They flew out Tuesday. Arrived Wednesday. So, yup, it was technically Thursday now. When did that happen?

"Thanks for keeping an eye on her."

"Of course." A.J. tipped his head. "You good?"

"I should be asking you that," Finn replied in a low tone so Julia wouldn't overhear.

"You know how I get when we talk about Marcus. I thought I was better since I still swear the man is haunting me —in a good way—but you know."

"I do know," he said apologetically.

"I'm square, though. Gonna go pack." A.J. jerked a thumb back toward Julia. "She ain't happy about her brother ordering her to wait for him to fly back to New York."

"Can you blame her?"

"Not really. She's got a personality like my Ana," he said with a smile. "Well, good luck, brother." He slapped Finn on the back and left.

"Julia." *Jewels* didn't feel appropriate when he was expecting tornado Julia to make landfall any minute in retaliation for the fact that she was being handled. Told what she could and couldn't do, and the woman hated that.

"He said no, didn't he?" Her ice-cold tone had him pausing midstep, just as she whirled around, the look on her face thunderous. "I'm not waiting for my brother, and you can't keep me as a prisoner until Michael arrives. That's illegal. I'll find a way to Dubai on my own from here."

"Oh, you will, will you?" It took every ounce of effort to keep his voice steady because that was exactly what he was worried she'd say. And it wasn't an empty threat. She'd somehow find a way to give him the slip, and that thought fucking terrified him.

Julia planted her hands on her hips and stared at him with icy eyes.

"I have orders, Julia. The kind that runs all the way from —" *The President.*

She ate up the space between them and lifted her chin, confidence flowing so fiercely he wondered if maybe she could go head-to-head with Tariq and the entire Saudi monarchy. "Who do you really work for? Tell me and I won't give you a hard time."

Well, damn. Too bad he wasn't a liar.

She crossed her arms and squeezed her brows together as she stared him down, or more like up. She stared *up* at him.

"What's it going to be, sailor?"

"Are we back to that?" He cocked his head, waiting for her to take the lead. If he weren't so broken-hearted for her about it all, he'd find her attitude amusing. Also sexy as hell.

"You're standing in my way again. You know how I feel about that."

"Yeah, I feel like we're heading toward DEFCON 2 status in about three seconds."

"More like DEFCON 1 if you try to stop me from helping Oliver." The woman didn't miss a beat. She even knew DEFCON 1 was the most severe level of military readiness— many thought that was DEFCON 5, which was peacetime readiness.

Her brother is Michael Maddox, he reminded himself. But he still avoided answering her.

"You can't blame yourself for what happened to Oliver."

"I can do whatever I please. And now that I'm not keeping any more secrets from you, you shouldn't keep any from me."

"None? Really?" He fake-frowned. A distraction attempt to keep her in the room so he wouldn't have to physically pin her down. "I was hoping for a few salacious secrets. Or, at the very least, something juicy. But nothing? Zilch?"

She relaxed her arms only to slap him in the chest, then she winced and covered her mouth. "Oh my God, I'm so sorry."

"It's okay." He'd forgotten he was in pain, actually. "You hit my right side. You know, the right-right side of my body." A fake laugh went about as well as his fake frown five seconds ago—zero response aside from a look of annoyance.

"I was just trying to playfully swat you." She grimaced and turned away. "I'm sorry."

"You and your habit of hating me one second and apologizing the next. Woman, you give me whiplash."

"I'm doing it to myself, too, then." Her shoulders fell, and he wanted to walk up behind her, set his hands on the sides of her arms, and rest his chin on top of her head. Comfort her. But he'd decided on distance, hadn't he?

Finn had to come up with a way to keep her in the room until either the President agreed to Julia joining them in Dubai or Michael arrived. It'd be a hell of a long wait for her brother, which meant A LOT of distraction attempts that didn't involve fingering her in the shower. Too bad for that.

"I refuse to believe Oliver is guilty. But no matter what I think, in one week, he'll be stoned to death or shot by a firing squad or something equally horrific after he's moved to Saudi Arabia. He's accused of murdering a man who, in addition to being a wealthy and influential business leader, was also married to a woman related to the royal family." Her voice was thick with emotion, and he was unable to stop himself from going to her and doing exactly what he'd visualized.

He lightly gripped the sides of her arms and rested his chin atop her head. "Shhh, it'll be okay. I promise. I won't let him die." *And why the hell did I just make a promise I may not be able to keep?* But damn it, now he had to. Because he wasn't a liar. "If I have to break him out of jail, then so be it."

CHAPTER FOURTEEN

Finn wasn't sure if he was in the depths of a nightmare or if this was his reality. He was moving in slow motion, his trigger finger so stiff he was unable to get a shot off as he stared into the eyes of his enemy in the desert.

A hot wind blew relentlessly, and the swirling sand felt like vicious bits of glass as it pelted him. And yet, the man kept coming as if the sandstorm carried him to Finn.

His enemy was on horseback, and his face wrapped in a black shemagh.

And Finn was going to die if he didn't get his finger to move.

The horse slowed to stand before him, front legs prancing up and down as the sand whirled around them. The man slowly lowered his headscarf.

"Jaden?" Why was his brother on that horse? Why was he raising his rifle and—

Finn jolted upright with a gasp, blinking against the brightness in the room, his eyes feeling gritty. *Shit, shit, shit.* He'd fallen asleep on the couch when he was supposed to be keeping an eye on Julia to make sure she didn't pull a fast one

BRITTNEY SAHIN

and skip out on him. POTUS had nixed the idea of Julia catching a ride to Dubai with Echo Team, and she'd been a little miffed, to put it mildly.

Finn's petition that Julia accompany the team had been sent up the chain from Wyatt to Luke and on to POTUS, who struck it down. Luke shared that he'd been made privy to the fact that Michael had spoken to the President and made the personal request she *not* go to Dubai.

The hotel room was lit up well enough for a plane to land in there as the sun shone through the window by the couch, and it wasn't until he stood that he noticed the bed unmade and empty.

She had to be in the bathroom. He wouldn't accept any other option.

His heart hammered as he shook off the dream and prayed he wasn't stepping into a real nightmare, one where Julia had taken off without a word, without him.

"Julia?" he called out, scanning the room for her suitcase or purse as he moved with hurried steps to the bathroom.

He slammed his hands against the doorframe and looked inside. Empty.

"Damn it, woman." He was still dressed and wearing his boots, so he grabbed his gun and rushed out of the suite and to the stairwell, not wanting to wait for the elevator.

He couldn't have been asleep for long. The last thing he remembered before nodding off was the sun just beginning to rise. He'd head for the airport and the private hangars since a private plane was her only option to go from Aswan to Dubai. *How did you manage to get a plane, Jewels?*

She'd been texting someone last night after they'd turned off the lights and she was in bed, but she promised it wasn't Mya.

She lied to me. She lied, damn it.

He was too worried to be as angry with her as he should be right now. There was still the chance someone had learned about Mya's investigative work and connected the dots to Julia. No doubt, there was a cyber footprint of Julia and Oliver's relationship as well, and it'd take all of a minute to discover who her brother was and how important Michael was to the U.S. government.

Finn darted out the front doors of the hotel, yellow caution tape from the crime scene still strung across the area, but Giorgio's death felt like a distant memory now.

He needed a ride to the airport, but all the valets were busy, and he didn't have time to wait. So, he ran outside of the hotel gates hoping to find a taxi, or worst case, he'd hijack a car. He'd pretty much stop at nothing to get to her in time.

He was overwhelmed by a wave of relief when he spotted Julia standing at the curb a hundred feet away, a gentle breeze blowing the skirt of her pink sundress.

She must have felt his presence because she turned and dropped her suitcase at the sight of him. Even from a distance, he noticed her shoulders collapse once she'd fully faced him. He cautiously walked toward her, wanting to run the distance, but he was worried she'd sprint away like a frightened deer if he moved too fast.

Julia went for her bag, and he said a mental *thank you* that it appeared she wasn't going to take off.

And then everything happened in slow motion like in his dream . . . and why wasn't he going for his gun?

Why couldn't he move when a man jumped from the passenger side of a nearby blue sedan and grabbed Julia.

Move! Fucking move! Panic drove him toward Julia as the man dragged her to the back of the vehicle and threw her into the now-open trunk.

The sound of her scream and the image of Julia's outstretched hand just before the trunk slammed shut would be forever burned into his brain.

Finn managed to reach them and slap a hand on the trunk before the car lurched forward.

"No, no, no." He ignored all of the chatter and voices raised in surprise from the people gathered around who had witnessed an abduction happen right before their eyes.

Now desperate, Finn jumped in front of the next car coming down the road, grabbed his gun from the back of his pants, and pointed it inside the driver's open window. Then in Arabic, he commanded the man to hop out or die.

The driver quickly surrendered and stumbled out, and Finn slid behind the wheel to pursue.

"Come on, come on." The little white two-door car sputtered as if the engine might croak from the desert heat as he tried to catch up with the sedan.

Did Julia remember any of the skills he'd taught her in class?

The sedan was too old to have a trunk release like he'd taught her to use if the situation were ever to arise, and she was in a locked trunk. Not that he'd ever imagined this moment in a thousand years or that he'd ever *let* it happen. But it had, all because he'd hesitated. Those two seconds he stood frozen like in his dream might cost Julia her life, and that was guilt he'd never walk away from unscathed.

Praying there was a screwdriver or a tire iron in that trunk, and she recalled the lesson, Finn knew she had a shot. As long as she didn't freeze the way he had.

"You got this, Jewels," he whispered under his breath as if he could actualize what needed to happen. "Open the trunk. Come on. Come on."

Finn slammed the heel of his hand against the steering

CHASING THE STORM

wheel when his car struggled to keep up. He didn't have time
to ditch this one and hijack another.

Both his car and the sedan in front of him left the city
limits a few minutes later, and they headed into what felt like
nothing but desert surrounding the Nile.

"Don't be a mirage," he rasped at what appeared to be the
trunk . . . *opening*.

The driver of the sedan suddenly slammed on the brakes,
probably realizing what Julia was doing.

That's my girl, Finn thought as his heart pounded
erratically.

The trunk had started to bounce closed again when the car
lurched, but Julia's slender arm reached up and caught it.

Finn came to an abrupt halt and jumped out of the car
when he saw Julia struggling to climb out of the trunk. He
knew it was only a matter of seconds before the driver and
passenger of the sedan would be on them.

He went for his piece and rushed toward her, practically
throwing her behind him the moment he reached her. "Get in
the car," he hollered, shielding her from a bullet that just
missed clipping his shoulder as he felt it speed by.

Without delay this time, Finn snapped out a round, hitting
the man who'd discharged his weapon and was still leaning
out of the passenger side window right in the face.

One more to go, and he needed him alive for questioning.

Finn quickly glanced behind him to verify Julia was out
of danger, then crouched behind the open trunk of the sedan.

Worried the man might escape, Finn took the chance to
make a move, keeping his head low as he crept alongside the
vehicle. He checked to ensure there were no surprise guests in
the backseat, then aimed his weapon at the driver, who
clutched the wheel with one hand and pointed a gun at Finn
with the other.

"This is not your day to die," Finn growled through the open window. Sweat poured down the driver's cheeks, and he gave off all the signs of an amateur, not someone Tariq would send. Not like the skilled men he and his team had faced last night. "But it can be if you move a fucking muscle."

Maybe the guy didn't understand English, but the look Finn read in his eyes said he wasn't going down without a fight.

With his weapon still aimed at the driver's head, Finn swiftly reached inside with his free hand and grabbed the man's wrist. The asshole fired out the window and into the sky.

Finn knocked the weapon free next, and fueled by adrenaline, he pulled the man through the window and tossed him like the trash he was to the ground.

"Who sent you?" He crouched over the guy, fisted his shirt, and shouted the question in Arabic.

The man continued to struggle silently, attempting to fight back. He was lean and lacked upper body strength. Or hell, any kind of strength or skills to go up against Finn.

The memory of Julia being taken and him watching it happen kept circling in his mind as he pummeled her assailant.

"Who? Tell me! I need a name," he screamed before kneeling alongside him.

The guy opened his mouth and spat out a mouthful of blood.

Seething, Finn cocked his head and hissed, "So, it's going to be like that?" He sent an elbow to the man's face, and it was lights out for the asshole.

CHAPTER FIFTEEN

T HE DISASTROUS EVENT FROM THIRTY MINUTES AGO PLAYED on repeat in Julia's mind. She figured it was going to be a long time before those images and emotions faded away, if ever.

The shame she'd felt when Finn caught her trying to leave him.

The terror of being grabbed and thrown into the trunk of a car, which was every woman's nightmare, and one reason she'd taken Finn's self-defense classes.

The precise headshot to the man who'd snatched her from the sidewalk so fast it had taken her a moment to process what the hell had happened.

And then, of course, what Finn had done to the driver. He'd done more than beat the guy up. He'd destroyed him. Most likely brought him to hell and back a few times. Delivered round after round to try and get answers out of him.

She'd looked on in horror as Finn's clothing became spattered in blood as if he were the canvas and the man the paint.

"I can't be sure, but based on what he told me," Finn said into the phone as she walked past him, "they're only in the business of kidnapping rich-looking tourists. But I texted Jessica a copy of both IDs to be sure. I also took a photo of the driver but couldn't get a clear image of the one I had to shoot."

Because there was nothing left of his face.

Julia's stomach wrenched so she pinned her forearm across her abdomen and went to the balcony for some fresh air.

Finn had called Luke Scott after they'd arrived back at the hotel since the rest of his teammates were currently in the air on the way to Dubai. But before that, Finn had quickly washed his hands and taken a wet towel to his face and throat, saying he'd get to the rest after he made his call.

Finn had the wherewithal to wipe his prints from the car he'd hijacked. And after his interrogation of the driver, they'd left him in the Nubian Desert, then drove to the city limits and ditched the car. Finn called in an anonymous tip to the police about the attempted abduction and the men's location.

Julia rested her arms over the railing and continued to listen to Finn talk behind her. The only thing he'd said to her since the incident out in the desert was *I'm sorry* and a half dozen *Are you sure you're okay*?

"A lot of people on the street witnessed what happened. I'm going to need Jessica to try and cover my tracks with the police, but we need to leave this hotel before I face questions that can't be answered. We can wait at the airport early, maybe?"

Julia swung around at the news.

"Yeah, it's a long wait until Michael arrives, but I don't feel comfortable staying here," Finn went on as if Luke had shot down the "wait at the airport" idea.

Her shoulders dropped upon realizing Finn still planned on waiting for Michael, and she turned back toward the view of the Nile. This trip officially ruined Egypt for her and tainted the memories of her favorite childhood movies about the location, too.

Damn statue that woman sold her.

And, oh my God, Julia suddenly remembered she'd left her suitcase and purse on the street when she'd been taken.

"Tucker's ID tags." She peeled off the balcony and went straight for the door, only to have Finn hook her arm with his hand to stop her escape.

"Your bags are at guest services downstairs," he calmly said. "I'll get them in a minute."

"Wait, what? How?" Puzzled, she faced him, and he released her.

"I gotta call you back," he said to Luke, then ended the call and slipped the phone into his pants pocket. "When I was washing up in the bathroom, the front desk called. Someone saw you leave the hotel gates before getting grabbed. A *good* someone. They returned your purse and suitcase. They also reported that an American-looking man stole a car to chase after you. The concierge checked your purse for a passport. Your name isn't in the hotel's system, but someone on staff downstairs must have made a connection between us to call me."

"Oh." *Ohhh.* "That's why we need to get the hell out of here." *The questions we can't answer. The man you shot in the face. The other man you almost beat to death.*

"Yeah, so I'm going to pack really quick, and we'll leave."

"I've never seen . . . something like that before," she said, noticing a spot of blood he'd missed on the side of his neck.

"What part?"

187

BRITTNEY SAHIN

Julia thought back to the other day when Finn ordered her to change out of the white sundress, saying it was too revealing and he'd lose his temper if some guy on the street harassed her.

Do you have a temper? Or was that Finn on autopilot to protect and serve as a SEAL?

"You killed that man. I've never seen death so up close and personal before."

"I've killed a lot of men. Does that bother you?"

Why was he asking her that? Did he think she'd look at him differently? "I'm sure it's because you were saving someone. Like you saved me this morning."

A quick smile crossed his lips. "Pretty sure you saved yourself."

"You taught me how to escape. There was a tire iron in the trunk, thank God." And luckily, her kidnappers hadn't had time to bind her wrists together, which made it easier to get the trunk open.

His brows drew together, and he placed a hand on her shoulder. "You lied to me. You were going to run."

Unable to meet his eyes, she turned her head and looked away, struck with guilt by the sting of his words. "Yeah, but in the end, I couldn't do it. I mean, before I even knew you'd found me, I sent away the taxi I'd hailed and was just standing on the sidewalk, feeling numb. And then I felt your presence."

"Numb," he whispered, the word laced with pain.

Julia turned to face him once again, and the look of sadness in his green eyes swamped her with more guilt.

"I'm so sorry I went behind your back to arrange the . . ." Without thinking, she fisted the front of his polo. "Wait, we can still make it," she whispered with desperation in her tone.

"The plane, I mean. The flight doesn't leave until nine. It's only eight."

"What?" His head jerked back as if she'd both insulted and slapped him.

Her eyes fell to the fabric still tight in her hand, and she swallowed and let go. "Um. You said we couldn't stay here, and you know I'll find a way to Dubai one way or another. I'll slip free from my brother once you turn me over to him."

"Turn you over to him, huh?" He lightly dragged his knuckles down the side of his cheek like he felt a burn from the slap that never happened. "Sounds like a prisoner transfer."

"No," she whispered. "But that's what's going to happen to Oliver soon, and it may be game over. And it's my fault."

"*Not* your fault," Finn said firmly, then unexpectedly reached out and gripped her shoulders with a gentle touch. "I need you to hear me." She could get lost in those green eyes as they stared down at her, and now wasn't the time to lose herself in a moment. "Tucker's death wasn't your fault. Neither is Oliver's situation. Please, you have to know that. You can't live your life being weighed down by guilt. I don't want that for you. I don't want you to feel like—"

"Like you?" She angled her head, and he tightened his grip a little.

"Like me," he rasped, then let go of her and looked away. "How'd you get a plane, anyway? Did the same friend who faked the death threats help you? Why would she do that if she was worried enough about your safety that I wound up on your doorstep because of it?"

He didn't want to talk about whatever guilt was clearly eating at him, and she was okay with tabling the conversation of her own for now. So, she didn't press. "Mya didn't help. She couldn't. And wouldn't."

"Because she cares." He faced her with a dark look in his eyes.

"I texted an old Special Forces buddy of Oliver's, and I told him I'm desperate and needed a ride to save Oliver. He spent a few hours speed-dialing all of his contacts this side of the Atlantic and hooked me up with a ride for a hefty price," she admitted.

"All of this while you were in bed." He stroked his jaw, some of that tension appearing to melt away as he closed the space between them and lowered his gaze, which for some insane reason made her stomach feel all fluttery. "Are you sure you're not a spy?"

"I wish."

When his palm caressed her cheek, she did her best not to lean in and respond to his touch the way she'd done in the shower. "You're going to get me in so much trouble."

"I am?" she whispered. "Why?"

He retracted his hand and stepped back, a torn expression crossing his face, but he said in a low voice, "Because we're going to catch that flight of yours to Dubai. And then your brother and my team leader are gonna have to play rock-paper-scissors to decide who gets to kill me."

* * *

"I'M PRETTY SURE THIS NEW KNOT IN MY STOMACH IS FROM even more guilt," Julia admitted quietly aboard the Cessna private plane an hour into their flight. Two-ish more hours to go. "I don't want you getting in trouble because of me."

"I'm a big boy. I make my own choices. I'll handle Luke and your brother."

"Yeah, my brother doesn't like to be handled." *Nope, he's*

not hand-able. Hand-something. Oh my God. My brain is not working.

Sleep deprivation. She'd barely slept since leaving New York.

That's all it was. Not her shot nerves about Oliver. Or that she was worried about her brother flipping out when he'd land in Egypt. Or the storm inside of her that materialized whenever she caught a glimpse of Finn's very masculine hands and remembered what he'd done to her with them last night in the shower. Her first orgasm of 2022, and was she supposed to regret it? Wish it hadn't happened? Not a chance, even if that unforgettable moment between them was brought about by insane circumstances.

"I'll tell Michael and whoever it is you report to that I refused to let you keep me prisoner and that you had no choice but to come with me. I'd say I held you at gunpoint, but I gave the gun back to Harper before she left."

He unbuckled his belt and turned in his seat. "Wait, what? She gave you a gun?"

Julia shrugged. "Yeah, we went to go look for you last night, but y'all showed up as we swung open that exit door."

Finn gave her a look of surprise. "You're serious? You were going to come rescue us, huh?"

"Why is that so amusing? I might be a question mark, but I'm pretty sure Harper can handle herself."

He cupped his mouth as if imagining such a rescue, and his eyes crinkled at the edges. "While I appreciate your chivalry, Luke and Wyatt won't believe your story."

"Why not? They know how stubborn I am."

"So, you admit you're stubborn?" He arched a dark brow.

"When it comes to helping those I care about, yes, and I think you're the same."

His mouth closed tight, the crinkles at the corners of his

eyes now gone, and she immediately mourned the loss of the softer, more playful, happier side of him.

"Why wouldn't they believe my story?"

"Because they know if I didn't want you getting on this plane, you wouldn't."

"You're so sure about that?" She angled her head and leaned closer in challenge. "How? How would you have kept me prisoner?"

His lips tipped up into a smile, and desire pooled in his irises, causing her stomach to ache in a surprisingly good way.

Oh my God, am I turned on by violence?

No, not violence.

It was the lengths to which Finn would go to protect others. Protect *her.* He'd made it clear in both his actions and his words how devoted he was to fight bad guys and the injustices in the world. He was a hero.

But he's still vulnerable, the fight-or-flight mode in her mind reminded her. No magic armor unless she counted the chest plate that saved him from a bullet the other night.

More questions filled her mind, but she needed to pull herself back to the present before the quicksand of insecurity dragged her under. "I'm just so sorry you're now in the middle of all of this."

"And I can't imagine what would have happened if your reporter friend hadn't put me here." He leveled her with another dark look, one that said he was thinking about the moment she was nabbed off the street and that *he* felt guilty about it. "I froze," he said as if knowing she'd follow along with his thoughts.

"I did, too."

He shook his head. "I'm not allowed to freeze like that." He reached for her hand, interlocking their fingers for the briefest of moments, then abruptly let go of her palm. "Sorry, I'm trying to—"

"Keep some distance between us?" Yeah, she was still following along with his thoughts. They were riding the same wavelength. On the same frequency. "I'd had a similar idea after the, um, shower." A shower she'd never forget. And she'd be reliving that memory over and over.

Finn cleared his throat and remained quiet, avoiding eye contact.

"You shouldn't feel guilty for what happened," Julia told him a few minutes later, clasping her hands in her lap and facing forward inside the small private jet piloted by an American ex-pat living in the UAE. Thankfully, they had the cabin to themselves.

"Those two seconds could've cost you your life," he answered gravely. "Two seconds I can't ever get back."

"The only seconds that matter are the ones right now. Because I'm here on this plane, thanks to you. If you hadn't found me on the street—"

"Please don't finish that sentence." Finn stood and set his palm on the ceiling, which was only a few inches above his head. He rubbed his right quad with his free hand and grimaced.

"Sore from the camel ride?" she asked to lighten the mood a bit. But instead of answering, he hung his head like a man who'd failed.

But he hadn't failed.

He was keeping the promise he'd made to help her save Oliver, and he was bringing her along like she'd begged him to. She owed him so much and more.

"I don't want to imagine any situation where something bad happens to you," he murmured darkly in that deep, take-no-prisoners tone he'd been using since they left New York.

She considered unbuckling her seat belt and standing to loop her arms around his hips while looking up at him to say, *Same. So much the same.* Especially now that she'd seen him in action in a very literal sense. Shooting. Fighting. What if something had happened to him? What if Finn hadn't been wearing a plate the other night when he got shot? Or he'd been struck in the face? No, she couldn't handle it. *Not handable. Nope.*

"You really think those men were only trying to abduct me for ransom like that man said?" she found herself asking, trying to break through her dark thoughts.

Finn drew his arms across his chest, but the plane hit some turbulence at that exact moment, and he was thrown in her direction.

He quickly caught hold of the chair arms, maintaining his balance while leaning over her. Fast reflexes.

He stayed there, leaning in close, adjusting his balance as turbulence continued to jostle the plane. But that pensive, dark look in his eyes had her inhaling a shaky breath.

Her gaze journeyed to his lips which were inches from hers, and unable to stop herself, she asked, "Why didn't you kiss me in the shower?"

The turbulence stopped, and he took the chance to escape their too-close position to stand upright.

"Don't tell me you're gonna pull a Julia Roberts in *Pretty Woman* on me and say kissing is too intimate and—"

"In this scenario, am I the prostitute or Richard Gere?" He grinned, and just like that, those happy smile lines by his eyes were back, and she'd give anything to keep them.

"I'm impressed you've seen that movie since you haven't even seen *The Mummy.*"

"Okay," he said while holding a palm out, "*Pretty Woman*

is kind of a classic from our generation, and *The Mummy* ain't no *Star Wars*."

She chuckled, forgetting about her problems for a tiny moment, and allowed that handsome mouth to free her thoughts and blot out her worries.

"I'll have to be the judge of that." But would they ever have a chance to watch a movie together? Would they become friends after this? After they pulled off a miracle and saved her best friend?

Finn dropped into the seat facing her this time and stretched out his legs. Thankfully, he'd changed his pants and shirt before their flight. No more blood visible on him, either.

"Not going to answer me about the kiss?" she whispered a few quiet moments later.

"Should I have kissed you?" He brought his legs closer to the seat, bending his knees and setting his forearms flat on his thighs, then lifted his chin and pointed his stunning green eyes her way as he waited for an answer.

"I don't kiss people I work with, so I guess not," she said with a shrug, trying to play it off as no big deal.

"So," he began, straining to bite back a laugh, one that would surely be deep and husky, and she'd love to hear it, "you just let them—"

"Don't you dare finish that," she warned in a playful tone.

"Mm-hmm." He sat upright, leaned back against the seat, and crossed his ankle over his knee, sitting more casually now and less like a man contemplating life's greatest mysteries. "What about friends? Do you kiss friends?"

"I don't, no. Are we friends?"

"At this point, I'd say I've already fired myself as your bodyguard, so we don't work together. As for friends, I don't know, Jewels."

Jewels. There went her stomach again—book-boyfriend

butterflies provided by a real man. And yes, Finn was all man. Every inch of him.

"But Oliver's your friend, and we need to save him." Finn swept his attention to the ceiling as if it were more entertaining of a view. "You mentioned ID tags back at the hotel. You panicked when you thought you lost your luggage. Were they Tucker's?"

"Yes, and I wore them up until Oliver made me take them off about five years ago." She closed her eyes. "Oliver became like a second brother to me after Tucker died. While he was in the Army, we stayed in touch, and once his service ended, we talked every week no matter how busy our lives became. Life is about connections, and I'll fight to the death to protect the ones that are important to me." She grimaced. "Wrong choice of words because I can't let him die."

"If he's innocent, I promise I won't let that happen."

Julia's eyes flew open. "*If?*" She couldn't have anyone working with her doubting Oliver's innocence, not with Michael already starting to question it. "If only the police would let me talk to him. It's driving me crazy that he never got a phone call."

"Dubai has one of the lowest crime rates in the world because their laws are pretty damn harsh. But Harper and Jessica will find out the real story."

"Jessica will be in Dubai, too?"

He nodded. "Bravo is en route. They'll land before Echo Team. But we'll be splitting up. Not all staying at the same hotel. We don't have any safe houses to use, so we'll be posing as tourists again."

"Bravo. Echo. Safe houses." She crossed her arms and narrowed her eyes. "Who are you really?"

"If I tell ya, I'd have to . . ." And for obvious reasons, he opted to cut off that famous line. "Why don't you get some sleep. Real sleep. No faking it like you did while you masterminded a scheme to get us on the plane."

"I'm not a liar. I mean, I did lie. But it was for Oliver." She reclined her seat but didn't lie down with it. "I'm still sorry."

Finn shrugged as if it were no big deal, but she wasn't buying that. Or the smile he allowed to sit on his lips like a crescent moon. "You can apologize to me after your brother punches me in the face."

CHAPTER SIXTEEN

DUBAI – UNITED ARAB EMIRATES

"IT'S SAFE TO SAY FLYING OVER DUBAI IN A HELICOPTER IS definitely getting added to my bucket list," Julia said from the passenger seat of the Range Rover she'd rented at the airport on arrival.

Dubai was known for a lot of things, including luxury shopping and glitzy nightlife, but expensive cars were at the top of that list from what she'd heard. And a Range Rover wasn't even considered all that luxurious in this city of astonishing wealth. Finn was behind the wheel, and the spectacular view of the city raced by as they made their way from the airport to their final destination.

"The aerial view is pretty impressive. I experienced it but not in a chopper." Finn peeked over at her, lifted his shades, and shot her a cocky wink, then dropped them back into place.

"And that means?" Julia laughed, enjoying this playful version of Finn so much she momentarily forgot they were in this stunning city to save a life and not a romantic weekend getaway.

"HAHO."

"Hey what?" She smirked.

"Sorry." Using the heel of his hand, Finn rotated the steering wheel to make a left turn and pulled onto the E11. They had a forty-minute drive to get to the islands from Dubai International Airport.

How did he make driving look so sexy?

"High-altitude parachuting," he translated. "Parachute is deployed within fifteen seconds of jumping instead of falling first."

"And was this for fun?" Would he answer truthfully? "Or were you still in the Navy?"

She watched his profile and noticed the movement in his throat as he swallowed hard like this was a difficult question.

"Um, for the Navy. We inserted over the islands where we're going now. Long story. Classified, as well." His tone became more matter-of-fact, which told her she ought to drop it.

But she didn't. "Like when you were still active duty with the SEAL Teams or doing work for the Navy with your current team? You know, clandestine ops for the President?"

Finn unexpectedly swerved, nearly missing a white and green Lamborghini, before regaining control of the Range Rover. *Wait, was that a police car? Right. The police drive insanely expensive vehicles.*

"I have no idea what you're talking about." Finn coughed purposefully a few times.

"Yeah, okay. That was a fake cough if I've ever heard one. Choking on bullshit, huh?" She had no idea what possessed her to spill her theory that there was way more to his job than he and his teammates let on. Bravo. Echo.

Working with the CIA. *Mm-hmm.* "My brother told me he believes the government has covert operators running missions that the military can't get green-lit or something like that. You're the guys, right? My brother doesn't know, I assume."

"I have no idea what you're talking about," he said again, "and that was desert air I was choking on."

"Desert air? Hm. We're in an air-conditioned vehicle, so I—"

"Julia, please." He looked over at her before changing lanes. "I can't talk about this."

This. So, was her theory correct? Correct or not, she'd respect his wishes and drop it because he was currently risking his neck for Oliver. If Finn took his orders from the President himself, could he be fired because of her? Or hell, worse? You didn't *just* get fired from the Navy for breaking orders—the penalties were much more severe. "I'm sorry."

"You trying to give me whiplash again, Jewels?" Finn whispered in a lighter tone, then turned on the radio. A song she didn't recognize was playing, the lyrics a mix of English and maybe Arabic, and since the refrain *"One Night in Dubai"* kept repeating, she guessed that was the title of the song.

"So, back to the helicopter ride," she deflected for both their sakes, "I'll come back and stay here for fun once Oliver is safe. Maybe take some photos."

"You want to take up photography again?" he asked, sounding a bit surprised.

She was a little surprised, too. She wasn't sure where that thought had come from, either. "Maybe." Her gaze went to the ultramodern architecture out the window and over to the skyscraper, the Burj Khalifa, which dominated the view. She'd taken a few architecture courses in school and was well acquainted with this amazing feat of architecture that still held the title of the tallest structure in the world. "I wanted to travel the world and observe it through the eye of the camera lens. There's something so real about looking through an unfiltered lens and finding beauty in unexpected places," she said softly, feeling sad at the loss of her dreams.

What she did now with her brother, helping veterans, was more than she could ever hope for, but she'd set aside her passions long before she and Michael built the business to what it was today.

"You still can, you know. The great thing about dreams is that it's never too late to chase them. Unless you want to be a SEAL. I'm afraid your expiration date for joining has already passed."

Out of her peripheral view, she spied a small smile grace his full mouth—a mouth she regretted hadn't touched hers in that shower.

She wanted to ask what the retirement age was for covert operators who technically didn't exist . . . but she bit her tongue. Sore subject and all. Probably off-limits if her brother was correct in his assumptions about there being an off-the-books team. Oliver's life was in the best hands, though.

"So?" he prompted.

"Maybe I'll travel more. See the world. Take my camera with me. I guess I can work from anywhere. Do both things."

Finn was quiet for a moment, and she wasn't expecting him to ask, "How'd you meet Tucker?"

He must have been thinking about the fact she'd given up photography when he died, but did he really want to talk about another guy? *It's not like we're dating. He only finger-fucked me and . . . No, it's more than that between us now. Who am I kidding?*

"I was between my freshman and sophomore years at

UNC, and I was on summer vacation in Wilmington. No surprise, I was taking photos on the beach while my friends lounged around working on their tan lines, or lack thereof, I should say. Tucker was there for the weekend and bumped into me while playing football with some friends of his from Fort Bragg where he was stationed," she revealed, her tone low and somber. The pain of his loss still hurt, but it'd been a long, long time since he was taken from the world. Time healed wounds, but the scars never went away.

"He won you over, huh?"

"He worked hard to do it. Maybe too hard." She smiled. "He was a decade older than me, so I was hesitant. But the man was persistent. And he told me he only had one more year in the Army, and he wasn't re-enlisting. We really didn't see each other much that first year we dated. But he fell in love with me, and as you know, he clearly won me over." She thought back to her time with Tucker and the memories they'd made together. "Whenever he visited, he was always grabbing my camera to take photos of me. He knew I hated being on the other side of the lens, but he would always laugh and say the view was much better than some beach."

"I mean, I can't disagree with him," Finn said.

Julia whipped her focus his way, and chills chased over her spine and down her arms at the sound of his deep, husky tone. "But when he died, I couldn't get myself to pick up the camera again. And soon after, my focus moved to helping veterans alongside my brother. And when I commit to something, I go all in. I can't really divide my focus all that well."

"I can relate to that. Teamguys aren't known for balancing their personal and professional lives all that well." His tone was remorseful. Did he have regrets about his life choices?

"Have you given up anything for work?"

He kept his eyes on the road. "Love."

Wow, that made her heart hurt.

"I think the idea of love is appealing, but the reality of it is messy and painful." His confession was unexpected and cut deep.

"Who hurt you?" Julia let go of a sharp breath before quickly adding, "Sorry, not my business."

"My mom," Finn surprised her with an answer that dug even deeper. "She, um, has barely been able to look at me, let alone talk to me in twenty years. My dad is sort of the middleman between us even though they're divorced now." He cleared his throat, bringing a fist to his lips. "They fought all the time when I was growing up. Usually about my . . ." He let his words drift into the air, and he surrendered to a deep, clearly needed breath. "I was the one always trying to keep the family together, even when I was ten. Or fifteen."

"That can't be easy." *But what happened to make your mom stop talking to you?* Could she ask that?

"Anyway."

Annnd nope, you want to change subjects.

"Can I ask you something?" He pinned her with a quick look before channeling his attention on the road and maneuvering between cars as if he were in a street race.

I would like to ask you quite a few questions, too. "Yeah, of course. No secrets, remember?"

The Range Rover felt as though they were gliding on air left and right. The man knew how to work a wheel. "How are you—"

"I wanted to be Vin Diesel in *Fast and Furious*," he said with a laugh, the mood suddenly much lighter now. "Give me any car or SUV, and I would make the perfect getaway driver."

"Let's not go rob a bank anytime soon," she responded

when he stole a quick look at her. They may have a prison break to coordinate, though. "So, um, what did you want to ask?"

He smiled and peered ahead again. "You said you might take photography back up. Well, what made you fall in love with it in the first place? Maybe if you remember that, it'll help reignite your passion for it again."

"Ah." An instant smile touched her lips at the question. "My dad. Photography was his hobby, and he taught me everything I know. I was always so excited to go to the store and get my rolls of film developed every weekend. To find out what beauty I'd managed to capture for all of time," she said, feeling as though she were glowing while reliving her past. "I even hid a few rolls inside a box at my parents' beach house, like a time capsule hoping one day when I was older I'd develop them and . . ." She chewed on her lip for a moment at the memory she'd suppressed over the years. "My dad eventually built us a darkroom so we could develop our own film. There's something so raw about being alone in that room, watching the images magically appear during the development process. Alone with the moments you captured. It was my safe space."

"Sounds nice. You're close with your parents?"

She nodded. "Yes," she added in case he was being good and keeping his eyes on the road and off her.

"And then Tucker died. And the last time I went into the darkroom at my parents' summer house . . . I was surrounded by photos I'd developed and left behind, the last photos Tucker had taken of me. I didn't like the woman I saw in those pictures, and I was hurting, so I asked my dad to lock up the room. I didn't want to see it again."

She expected a sympathetic *I'm sorry* from Finn, but instead, he whispered, "I don't think that's what Tucker would've wanted. He wouldn't want you to give up on yourself and what you love because of him."

"Maybe you're right." She released a shaky exhale. "But the dead can't want anything, can they?" Her eyes fell shut. "Can we, um, maybe talk about something else?"

He turned up the volume of the radio a bit in response. "Of course," he answered, his tone a touch distant, like he struggled with something himself.

They listened to music for a bit as they headed for the man-made archipelago, Palm Jumeirah, part of a larger series of developments called the Palm Islands.

Sand had been brought in to create the man-made islands in the shape of a palm tree that were now home to the uber-wealthy.

Mya had done her research on Kaira, and since she was such a public figure because of her billionaire husband and her royal connections, there was a Wikipedia page on her, which helped construct the big picture as to who she was. But it hadn't helped Mya discover what went wrong back in January that landed Oliver in the middle of everything.

Kaira and Ario had purchased their home fifteen months ago after briefly living in Florida. They owned a fifty-million-dollar four-floor mansion on the island. From the photos Julia had viewed, it was more modern and eclectic than Arabic in design.

"Kaira still lives in that huge mansion on the islands by herself. I was expecting she might move after her husband died," she spoke her thoughts aloud twenty minutes later after deciding the silence was too much to handle.

Finn peeked at her for a second before eyeing the road. "And that's why Wyatt and the others are staying at a hotel on the island. With Harper's intel reporting that Tariq showed up at her house today, we should stay as close to them as possible."

"How did Wyatt react when you messaged him while I was asleep on the plane?"

"DEFCON 1," he quickly said. "He didn't buy the story that you abducted me," he teased. "But he did believe you were stealthy enough to arrange a flight, and you'd go with or without me."

"I know my brother is still on his way to Egypt, but did they get word to him via message that I'm not there anymore?"

"Luke did." Finn's voice was now somber.

"Go that bad?"

"He got the angry, all-caps kind of message back."

"Ah. Very shouty, then." She thought about her overprotective brother. He'd forgive her. Maybe not Finn and his men, though.

"Very." Finn's smile was unexpected when he peeked at her for a moment, careful not to swerve again.

"I promise to stand between you two when he shows up here. Protect you from a punch." She thought back to her abduction and those men Finn had handled. "Not that you can't protect yourself." She swallowed. "Um. How's your chest?"

"Still purple." He sounded so nonchalant.

"And has that happened to you before?"

"Yes." He delivered his answer with a hint of hesitation, as if afraid to admit it, causing her stomach to turn.

"I'm sorry."

"Don't be." His mood shifted like the summer winds on the beaches of North Carolina when a storm was about to roll in. He looked at the GPS on his phone, which was mounted to the dash of the vehicle near the wheel. "Shouldn't be too much longer." He leaned to the side a bit, slipped his hand into his pocket, and produced a ring box she was clueless had been there.

He'd changed into khaki cargo pants and a white tee before the flight, so the pockets were large enough to conceal it, she supposed.

"What's this?"

"Wedding rings," he said as if that were totally normal.

Two gold rings were inside the black velvet box. "You carry rings with you wherever you go?"

"You never know when you need, um, a prop for a . . . job."

Job, huh? "Why do we need the rings? I thought unmarried couples are now allowed to stay in the same room together. Live together, too."

"It's a little iffy. And I'd rather not draw suspicion."

She slipped the gold band onto her ring finger, a touch loose, so she hoped it didn't fall off. She handed Finn his ring once they pulled off the highway, and he put it on at a red light.

"What's my name? I assume you thought that far ahead, too." The man must have done a lot of planning while she was asleep.

"Checking in as Evelyn and Richard O'Connell."

"You're kidding?" She lightly laughed, but he kept his eyes on the road as if he had no clue why that was so funny. "You looked up the movie, didn't you? *The Mummy*? I'm Evie and you're my hero."

"Hero? No, I'm no hero. If a mummy comes swirling out of the desert at some point, I'm hiding behind you, missy," he said in a serious tone.

"Right. A gun wouldn't work. And your fists—you'd be swinging at sand."

"Exactly." He smiled this time, his focus on the road, and she was unable to take her eyes off him as he maneuvered the Range Rover after pulling through the now-green light as if they were in a Lamborghini.

"What am I going to do with you?" she teased.

He stopped at yet another red light, rested his forearm over the wheel, and focused on her this time. She wished his sunglasses weren't shielding his eyes so she could get a better read as to what was going through his head. "And you see, that's exactly what I'm trying to figure out about you."

CHAPTER SEVENTEEN

JULIA STOPPED ALONGSIDE FINN AND TOOK A DEEP BREATH, expecting him to immediately walk inside the suite. Instead, he set their bags down outside the door, then reached out, lifted her chin, and pinned his eyes on hers. She was so distracted she'd barely noticed the opulence of the hotel, located right on the Arabian Gulf, as they checked in as Evie and Richard before making their way through the lobby and up the elevator.

"You okay?" The look on his face had her stomach tensing up. A sweet, almost tender expression took over his hard features. A handsome contrast. "Nervous?" He dropped his hand and gave her a small smile when she'd yet to answer. "I should be the nervous one. I'm about to get chewed—"

"Very nervous," she finally answered. "Also, I feel bad that you're about to get chewed out."

"But you wouldn't change anything, am I right?" he asked as his smile grew.

"No." Julia returned his smile. "Does that make me a bad person?"

As his gaze held hers, she noticed that his irises were the

same color as the emerald leaves on the palm trees outside surrounding the pool that seemed to disappear into the sea.

"I don't think you could ever be a bad person even if you tried." Finn closed his eyes for one second, most likely remembering her icy act during those first two weeks. "Although I will say you were very good at being mean and making me a little crazy because you were trying to save a friend." When his lids parted, he lifted a hand between them. "Don't apologize for that again," he said, shutting down the words that were about to leave her lips.

If she'd had a camera with her right now, she would have taken a picture of him. Of how he looked in this exact moment. There was something about his expression as he studied her that she wanted to capture. Or maybe it was the way she felt when he looked at her that she was seeking to capture and keep.

God, she missed being behind the lens of her camera where she could trap a moment forever. Immortalize a perfect memory or transform a not-so-perfect one into something unexpectedly beautiful.

She thought back to the darkroom her father had kitted out for her as a teenager. That'd been her safe place, her haven. She'd never had an active social life. Not a lot of friends, either. Her shy personality and preference for reading had other girls thinking she was stuck up or unfriendly. "Pictures are also an interpretation, I guess. They can be misunderstood."

"What?" Finn's brow lifted, and she remembered he hadn't been in her head to follow along with the detour she'd taken in her thoughts.

"Sorry, I um. I've been misunderstood my whole life because of my shyness. By almost everyone, I think." Her tongue pinned to the roof of her mouth for a brief moment.

"People rarely gave me the chance to show who I really am, and so I guess I just stopped trying to let them see me. And I spent my time behind the camera looking at everyone else, feeling like an outsider. Just observing. Wondering. Trying to find some peace, I guess."

"Julia," he said softly as if her name was somehow painful to say. Then he cupped her cheek in his large, rough palm. It was warm and inviting, comforting. And the memory of their conversation in the car not too long ago came to mind. The way he studied her now was as if he were behind the lens himself and seeing her from a different angle.

"Angles?" she murmured, not referring to her ass. Not even a little.

Finn kept his palm on her cheek, studying her with those soulful eyes . . . had anyone ever looked at her that way? Had Tucker? Had she ever felt so understood, so *seen* before?

When the door opened behind her, Julia nearly fell inward, and Finn abruptly dropped his hand and cleared his throat.

"You're here," Wyatt announced in a growly voice.

Julia wished they'd had one more minute. Even one more second so she could snapshot and freeze whatever moment had happened between them in that hallway.

Wyatt ushered Finn into the bedroom without giving him a chance to do anything other than set their suitcases inside. Yeah, he was pissed.

She looked around at the rest of Finn's teammates crowded in the bedroom, too.

Her shoulders startled back at the sound of the door closing shut, and she lost sight of her lifeline, of Finn.

Now she was alone with Harper in the living room of the suite, standing there, awkwardly waiting for her to look up and say something.

BRITTNEY SAHIN

"Hold off on telling him for now," she heard Finn say, his tone barely below a shout.

Ouch, not good.

"Tell who what?" Julia peered at Harper, hoping she'd finally talk. The silence sucked.

Harper sat at the desk in front of the window. From the looks of it, the room had a killer view. She walked by the U-shaped gray sofa to peer outside at a stretch of white sandy beach and shimmering turquoise water.

"Tell who what?" Harper responded by playing coy and repeating Julia's question.

Julia strode to the Nespresso machine positioned next to the TV stand on the other side of the room and inserted a pod to make an espresso. She was desperate for java. It was late afternoon now, and she could count the hours she'd slept since Tuesday morning on both hands, and it was Friday. Or was it Thursday? *Great. I've lost track of time.* She turned to the side to observe Harper while she waited on her drink.

Wyatt, A.J., and Chris were sharing this particular suite. Roman and Harper had their own suite next door. And she and Finn, being last-minute additions, would be staying one level above them.

"So, you're sure those men who tossed me into that trunk weren't connected to all of this?" Julia asked, seeing as how she didn't think Harper would answer the *who* question anyway. Plus, she hadn't had a chance to hear Harper's thoughts on the matter of the now-dead man lifting her like a feather, chucking her into a foul-smelling trunk, and zooming off. And everything else that followed.

"Looks like a crime of convenience. An amateur group of locals who abduct rich-looking people from expensive hotels to either traffic or ransom them."

214

"Traffic." She tried not to let the idea of being sold rattle her when she needed to focus.

"But we still need to keep a close eye on you just in case." Julia heard the unsaid *Don't run away again* message loud and clear.

"Did you happen to find out if Tariq was in Dubai at the time of Ario's death? I think we ruled him out as being the murderer, but I was curious."

Harper leaned back in her seat and closed her laptop. "No. Well, maybe yes." She frowned. "Tariq wasn't there, but his twin brother flew in a few days before Ario died, and he left the day after he was murdered."

"Oh. And what do we know about his twin?" Julia never had Mya dig into Kaira's royal family ties.

"He's fairly conservative, unlike Tariq. Helps run the family oil business. Dots his I's and crosses his T's from what I can tell. Not like his sociopath brother."

Mya hadn't mentioned a twin. Hmm. Then again, why would she? They had no clue Oliver's case was connected to Kaira's family.

"So, you don't think he's involved?"

"I wouldn't rule anything out. We'll examine everything from all angles, I promise." Harper straightened her posture. "So, while the boys talk, I can fill you in on the plan."

"Okay." Julia snatched her drink and disposed of the used pod. If only she'd confessed the truth to Finn sooner about what she'd been up to, like two weeks ago, they'd have more time. Maybe Oliver would already be free by now. His team was uncovering information so much faster than she'd been able to up until now. "And, uh, what is the plan?"

"Kaira left her home on the island an hour before you arrived. Owen and Liam have eyes on her at the Al Habtoor Resort and Club where she checked in for the weekend," Harper explained. "Our people are splitting up. Focusing on both her and her brother. Luke wants Roman and me to check in at the resort. Keep tabs on her while she's there for the weekend."

"Are you hoping to try and talk to her? Or is this going to be a wait-and-see kind of thing?" Did she have the patience for that, knowing Oliver was locked away somewhere in this city? God, he must have felt so alone all these months. She prayed he knew she was on the outside doing everything in her power to save him.

"Actually, we've been instructed not to talk to her."

Shit, because of her family.

"But it does look like Kaira is meeting with an American couple that's in town this weekend. They're hosting an equine fundraising event Saturday night. A costume party. Dress up as your favorite eighties movie character. I managed to get the invite list, and Kaira is on it."

"The resort is also an equestrian club?"

"Yeah, horse riding is huge here. Horses are strongly connected to Emirate history, and there's a big equestrian training center and camp at the resort where Kaira's at now. Her brother didn't go with her, though. So, the rest of Bravo has eyes on the mansion for when he makes his next move."

"I can't imagine her dressing up in some eighties outfit either, even though Oliver said Kaira doesn't wear a burqa or practice her religion. She appears to be somewhat of an outcast from her Saudi family."

"Same story as Tariq."

Julia sat on the couch facing the floor-to-ceiling window viewing the water. "Who are these Americans?"

"I'm doing my homework on them next to see how and when their paths have crossed before."

"What if we get an invite to the party?" The idea of her

and Finn playing dress-up seemed absurd, but her life felt a bit unreal in general lately.

"I'm considering trying to get an invite in case we need to pin down the couple for questions before they leave town. If they're close to Kaira, they might know something, too, but—"

"I can get us on the list. I'll make a big contribution. It wouldn't be unrealistic. I can say I was in town on vacation and heard about the event and wanted to donate. Is there anything planned between now and Saturday night to help me get their attention somehow?"

Harper opened her laptop again. Was she hacking the hotel's system? *Probably.*

"Dinner reservations for three tonight at the steakhouse," Harper announced.

"You think Kaira might be the third?"

"Maybe." Harper began typing again. "And tomorrow, they have some sort of safari adventure booked through the hotel out in the Lahbab Desert. Looks like Kaira is going as well. So, she must be fairly close to them, not simply a guest to the event."

"I need to be at those places to try and win over this couple. I can do this. Plus, what if you, um, get sick?" she whispered the last part, wondering how Harper was feeling and if she'd told Roman about possibly being pregnant. "You shouldn't risk going if you're . . ." She let Harper fill in the gaps. "I can also try and get close to Kaira. Get her talking without realizing she's sharing. You may not be allowed to, but I don't report to anyone."

Not the President. Or my brother, for that matter.

Harper frowned, but Julia could tell the way her brown eyes flitted from her to the floor she might be considering the idea. "You're not a spy. You're not trained. I can't send you on some op."

"Send her where?" Finn rasped, worry flooding his tone.

When did the bedroom door open?

The rest of his team filtered into the room and gathered in a line to stand opposite Julia, arms crossed as if they were a bunch of running backs prepared to stop her path before she made any headway.

Five special operators and one CIA officer . . . those were not good odds. *Perfect.*

"She wants to go to the resort, in my place. Try and get an invite to the party on Saturday," Harper explained. "We managed to secure one of the villas there. Technically, a few of us could go since there are four bedrooms in the villa. You don't need to be married to stay as a couple, either." She drew a hand over her abdomen.

Oh no, was she going to be sick?

"Absolutely not," Wyatt was quick to shoot down the idea. "Julia shouldn't even be here."

"I know, and I'm sorry for the position I've put you all in." Julia faced Wyatt with a plea in her eyes and tone. "If it was Finn locked in that prison, what would you do?"

Wyatt peered at Finn as if truly contemplating her words. But when she checked Finn's reaction, his gaze was pointed at her. A familiar look of worry there.

"I think Kaira knows what really happened or what Tariq is planning. You all need to focus on whatever reason you were in Egypt to begin with, right? Let me handle Oliver. And assuming Oliver's case is connected," Julia went on in a rush, worried she'd lose the nerve if she didn't, "maybe what I find out will help you."

"What makes you think you can get Kaira or this couple

to talk to a stranger?" Wyatt asked while the others fell back and allowed him to take the lead.

Finn broke from the line and crossed the space to stand beside her, and she wasn't sure if that was a sign of support or if he was about to beg her to back down. "Julia's rather convincing. She lured Lorenzo to New York, didn't she?"

Her heart launched into her throat at his words. He was on her side.

"I'll go with her. And you two can still go to the resort as planned. Better together than apart, right?" Finn continued, glancing over at Harper. Julia followed his line of sight as Harper abruptly stood, apologized, then threw a hand to her mouth while making a quick dash for her bedroom.

Oh no. Roman frowned, and based on his look of confusion, he was still clueless. He quickly followed her to the bedroom.

"She might be sick, so you need me," Julia added once the door closed.

"Michael is gonna lose his mind." Wyatt dropped his head, his hands going to his hips like a commander hating the decision he was about to make when it involved the lives of his people. Putting someone else's life on the line as opposed to your own had to be such a tough call. She couldn't begin to imagine the heavy weight of that responsibility.

"If Harper and Roman do join us, Jessica can continue to do the cyber work in retracing the steps of everyone who may be involved in whatever is going on," Finn said with a determined voice. "Let us do this."

You're on my side. Just hope this isn't the dark side. Well, wrong side. Her thoughts had her mind racing back to Finn's comments at the hotel in Egypt and his love for *Star Wars* films, and how he liked Darth Vader and that other guy better. They wore masks, right? Did he feel like he was wearing one? Did he want to shield his face? Had his mom made him feel like that?

She had no clue why she was thinking about this now, but her heart hurt for him, and he was such a strong, loving man who'd had his heart broken by his mom for whatever reason, and it crushed her to see.

"And my brother will just have to deal," Julia tossed out with enough conviction to stand up to *the* Darth Vader herself if she had to. "It's not up to him."

"You really are like Natasha, aren't you?" Wyatt covered his eyes with his palm and made a *tsk* sound. "Damn it. If we somehow land up shit's creek without a paddle, I swear—"

"I'll come save you with a life raft," Julia sputtered, and he dropped his hand.

"Save us, huh?" Wyatt asked, amusement in his tone, which was much better than anger. He looked from her to Finn, then back her way again. He shook his head but finally relented, "Fine."

"Really?" Julia turned toward Finn so fast she nearly slammed into that wall of muscles. "If I'm going to get the attention of this American couple, then we need to really go big on this."

"Go big, how?" Finn folded his arms, studying her with curious eyes.

"I can't go as myself because if anyone looks up my name and discovers my brother's identity, the plan will backfire. Can you whip up an alias?" She looked at the wedding ring on her finger. She'd need a Mount Rushmore–sized diamond to go with the band for the sake of appearances.

"We can keep the names I gave us," Finn said, and a strange tingling sensation filled Julia's chest at the idea of continuing the charade as husband and wife. Why did it feel so good to be his? Even to pretend?

You gave up on love. I think I have, too, though.

"And Harper or Jessica will create your background story," Finn went on, his tone sounding like her brother when he was in operator mode. Focused. "Need a few hours, though."

"We can shop in the meantime. I'll need a new wardrobe. Something flashy without getting myself into trouble in Dubai. Plus, we'll need something for this party on Saturday."

"Anything else?" Wyatt cocked a brow, still hanging on to his foul mood.

"I would probably have a bodyguard, and if we can swap the Range Rover for a Bentley, that'd be ideal. We need to flaunt my money. Get this couple to notice me." She wasn't that type of woman, but she'd act the part if need be.

"And who is going to be your bodyguard?" Chris asked. "I'm not dressing up in an eighties costume."

"Oh, come on," A.J. said in a teasing voice. "Tom Cruise. *Risky Business.*" He acted as though he had a camera in his hand as he eyed Chris like he was doing that vogue thing. "I can see it now. Or maybe some *Top Gun* action. Was *Cocktail* in the eighties?"

"You have a man-crush on Tom Cruise I don't know about?" Chris joked back and rolled his eyes.

A.J. snapped his fingers and smiled. "*Ghostbusters.* There you go. The big marshmallow guy."

"You're going, brother. Not me." Chris winked at A.J. "You can be the green blobby thing."

Julia's attention bounced back and forth between the two comedians as they spoke before Wyatt remarked, "Ignore them."

"We'll rock-paper-scissors the situation, then." A.J. put his hand behind his back as Chris stepped forward.

"Are they serious?" she asked Finn, who was smiling, but hadn't he said something similar to her at the hotel before they'd left Egypt? Maybe this wasn't a joke.

Finn shrugged. "Probably."

"Hell, our boy here drew the short straw when it came to you, so—"

"A.J.," Finn hissed.

"The short straw, huh?" Julia leveled Finn with a quick look.

"Anyway," Wyatt said, and Finn appeared relieved to have the attention off him. "I guess that means I'll be the one waiting for Michael when he shows up. I'll have to take one for the team." He set his eyes on Julia. "I'll be taking the punch from your brother."

CHAPTER EIGHTEEN

Finn kept his gaze riveted to the storefront of the designer boutique inside the sprawling Mall of the Emirates, where Harper and Julia had disappeared almost an hour ago. It was after eighteen hundred hours, so they were short on shopping time. Dinner was in two hours.

He'd decided to hang back with Roman on the bench outside the store, while A.J., who lost the intense battle of rock-paper-scissors, was inside with the women as they tried on dresses for the steakhouse tonight.

"Harper okay? Is she coming down with something?"

Roman pulled his attention from the store to Finn. "She thinks she might be pregnant."

Finn's spine went straight at the news.

First, Wyatt's big reveal. Now Harper and Roman might be having a kid?

"Oh. Um." He scratched his jawline, the growth starting to come in a bit more since he'd trimmed it. "That's what you all want, right?" Was Roman going to go into panic mode like Wyatt?

"We do. If she has morning sickness, that might be a

challenge. Plus, do I want her out in the field with my child in her?" His shoulders collapsed, and he positioned his gaze to the left, then to the right, checking their surroundings.

The mall was filled with a mix of modern versus traditionally dressed people. Some women had on the abaya, a loose-fitting black cloak. Others dressed in the latest fashion while adhering to Dubai's strict dress code. No exposed shoulders. Nothing above the knees.

Many of the Emirati men had on the kandura, a white, long-sleeved, ankle-length garment. They also wore the gutra, a variation of the shemagh Finn had worn in Egypt, but it had a white-and-red-checkered pattern on the headdress instead. Tariq was rarely seen in traditional clothes, unlike his brothers, which had always made it easy for the CIA to ID Tariq on his funding-terrorists escapades over the years.

"I'm happy for you both. We'll work things out," Finn finally spoke up once Roman had decided there were no visible threats around them.

"How?" Roman asked in a low voice. "Knox can't operate with Bravo right now. He has to hang back. So, Bravo is down a man."

Their last operation, which ultimately brought Roman and Harper together, also led to Knox getting shot. Although he'd recovered from his injury, Bravo Five was also the President's son, and his father and pregnant wife felt it best he keep a low profile for now. So, Knox had been placed on "desk duty," only allowed to hang back on ops with Jessica in the command center.

"Wyatt told us on the plane that Natasha is pregnant. He said you already knew. Not surprised he told you first. Everyone seems to tell you everything, man."

"Tell me about it." Finn lightly laughed, but on the inside, he was in pain. In pain because of the secret he'd kept when he was younger and wished he hadn't.

"A.J.'s wife is due, too. We'll—"

"I think it's time we take up POTUS's suggestion that we bring on new members," Finn finished what he was sure was Roman's line of thought after a couple walked past and moved out of earshot. "Recruit five new guys. Either they can rotate between our teams, or we start a new one. But that doesn't mean we retire." None of them were ready for that.

"I'm not sharing my call sign," Roman said. "But Wyatt did float the idea on the plane. I guess this baby thing has the man shook. Never seen him so off."

"Agree."

"Harper is going to buy a test while we're at the mall. If it's yes, it's probably good you and Julia are with us this weekend in case my head isn't in the game."

If Harper was pregnant, that meant everyone except him had moved forward with their lives and started a family. Marriage and babies. Well, Chris and Rory had a dog for now as their child, but that counted in Finn's mind.

He'd no longer be the only single guy, he'd be the only one in the bunch alone with no likelihood of becoming a parent anytime soon. And he wasn't so sure how he felt about that fact. Hell, he was hanging on to thirty-nine by a thread with forty just around the corner.

When Finn lifted his gaze from the tiled floor, he spied Harper exiting a dressing room inside the store, and out of the corner of his eye, he spotted Roman zero in on her in the red dress. "I'll be right back," Roman announced.

"Hey, no PDA allowed here, remember? So, no getting caught hooking up in the dressing room," Finn teased, but really . . . that'd be a crime in Dubai. They didn't need anyone else locked up.

Roman tossed a dismissive hand in the air, already on the move.

A.J. exited the store, swapping places with Roman. "He tell you?"

"About Wyatt?" Finn didn't want to accidentally spill the Harper news in case no one else knew.

A.J. sat next to him on the bench. He had on a black ball cap, dark jeans, and a black tee as his bodyguard-look. Finn still had on his pre-flight khakis and shirt, but he definitely needed a shower before dinner tonight. Probably should shop for clothes, too. "And the new team idea."

The guys needed some relief as their families grew. They'd made a commitment not to put their families on the sideline for the sake of an op. If you didn't make time for your family, what were they even fighting for? "I think it's a good idea. Some new guys to boss around," Finn said in a light tone, trying to push aside his sadness about the fact he was feeling more alone these days.

A.J. looked around for possible threats as he said, "I could get on board with having new guys buy all of our drinks for the next year. Do the grunt work." He looked at him over his shoulder for a moment. "But how are you holding up? The whole mess of Julia running off and then getting taken this morning must have done a number on you."

Finn thought back to the morning, which now seemed like weeks ago. To the fear that'd swelled as he watched Julia get grabbed and kidnapped within a split second. God, he'd never forget the look of terror on her face.

"I hesitated," he confessed. "I never hesitate."

A.J. slapped Finn's back. "Honestly, if I saw that happening to Ana, I'd probably turn into a deer in the headlights too for a hot second. But she's okay. So."

No way would Echo Two freeze. Finn didn't believe that. But he appreciated the attempt to make him feel better.

"We've all been a bit off on this trip, I think. And I'm blaming the mummy curse. Opening those coffins . . ."

"Sure, sure." Finn smiled and shook his head. Leave it to A.J. to lift his mood with talk about mummy curses.

Finn glanced at his watch, growing a bit anxious. He was awaiting a call from Jessica, who was cooking their backstory as Evie and Richard O'Connell from the hotel where she and the rest of Bravo were staying. Hopefully, the movie was old enough that no one they encountered tonight had seen it or remembered the character's names.

In the meantime, Chris was at the stables at the resort to keep an eye on Kaira before Finn and Julia, or rather Evie and Richard arrived.

"I wonder who this American couple is and how they're connected to Kaira," Finn said, trying to pull his focus back to the mission. "What are their names again?"

"Joan Wilder and Jack Colton. I guess she didn't change her name when they married," A.J. answered.

"Why do those names sound familiar?" Finn had the distinct feeling there was something off about it, but he dropped his thoughts and stood at the sight of everyone exiting the store with bags in hand a moment later.

Julia caught his eyes, and a small smile touched her lips before she made her way to his side. "I need a diamond. A big one. Then costumes."

"Costumes." A.J. grunted. "Maybe I don't need to dress up. I'm your bodyguard, after all."

"No, I would make you dress up if I were Evie." Julia winked A.J.'s way, a glow rising on her cheeks, and Finn's knees went damn near weak. Where'd that come from?

"Why don't we divide and conquer? The guys need

dinner clothes, and uh, safari clothes, too. You two go get the ring, and I'll pick out clothes with these guys." Harper offered her elbow, and Roman hooked their arms. "Can you find a diamond in fifteen minutes?"

Julia smiled. "Probably five since it's not like I'm actually saying I do."

"Perfect." Harper motioned for A.J. and Roman to head to the men's store two windows down, and Julia turned back to Finn.

"So, ready to get married?" she asked as easily as if inquiring whether he wanted an ice cream cone. Finn laughed, but his attention was suddenly pulled to the sound of live music drifting up from the level below. He walked away from Julia and toward the railing.

"You recognize the song?" She eased up next to him to view the band singing on a small raised platform in a courtyard area.

"A Bryan Adams song. I guess we're really having an eighties weekend."

Finn had a death grip on the railing, and his knuckles were probably turning white, but he couldn't let go. Or remove his gaze from the singers.

"Is that *Everything I Do*?" At the touch of her hand on his back, his muscles flexed, and he tensed.

"My brother used to sing his songs all of the time." Finn swallowed, trying to force down the lump of emotion as he remembered his brother playing the piano and singing into a microphone in their living room back in Mass when Jaden was twelve years old. "He did it for my mom. Bryan Adams was her favorite singer." His voice broke a little because that damn lump wouldn't move.

"Your brother was a musician? Hobby?"

"Professional. We moved to LA when I was fifteen

because my mom hoped he'd be signed by a major record label." *Why am I sharing this? Why, damn it?*

"Does he still perform? Would I have heard of him?"

"No." A quick gutshot answer, and now he needed to change subjects.

When the song ended, Finn released his grip and faced her. The brilliant blue of her eyes was overshadowed by her dilated pupils. She was worried about him, and that was the last thing he wanted. She had enough on her plate.

"Let's get the ring." He smiled, trying to replace whatever dark cloud had briefly hung over his head and rained all over him.

"Oh, okay. Um." Julia glimpsed Finn as they started for the nearest jewelry store. "Tell me about this 'short straw' thing."

Was she trying to help him override? Distract him from the darkness threatening to overwhelm him? "I, um."

"You didn't want the gig, huh? And that was before I was evil to you."

His phone began vibrating in his pocket. *Annnd saved by the boss.* "It's Jessica." *Thank God.* Hopefully, Julia would forget her question if he spent enough time on the phone. "Are we all set?" he asked upon answering.

"Yes and no. Your cover story should hold up. But Asher called and said Tariq left his sister's house and is now at the resort. Chris saw Tariq and Kaira at the stables, and he didn't look happy. Tariq escorted her to her villa from there," Jessica explained. "Luke and Wyatt have decided it'd be best if Asher and I also go to the resort this weekend now that Tariq is staying there as well."

"And he's not going to make her leave?"

"I just checked, and his name was added as a guest to the party."

"Well, I guess it makes sense that more of us are there. We may need to divide and conquer," Finn agreed. "We'll get you both something to wear to the party Saturday if we can pull off tickets for everyone. And don't worry, I'll pick out something ridiculous for the Big Guy to wear."

"You know me so well. The crazier the outfit for Asher, the better," Jessica responded with a laugh. "We'll meet you there."

"Roger that," Finn returned in a low voice. "Any word from, uh, you know who, about Julia being here?" he asked, not wanting to mention the President's name.

"He's . . . not happy. We've dealt with worse situations, though," Jessica said, an uncharacteristic hesitancy to her tone. "We'll deal. We always do. See you soon."

Finn ended the call and pocketed his phone, then gently urged Julia off to the side of the flow of traffic and near a storefront window to talk. "Tariq is at the resort. He was pissed that his sister was there from the looks of it. And now he's on the guest list for the party." He shook his head. "We need to figure out who the hell this Joan Wilder and Jack Colton really are."

"Wait, who?" Julia blinked a few times. What had he said? "Joan and Jack are characters from *Romancing the Stone*. An eighties movie I loved as a kid."

The fucking '80s again, and now the Bryan Adams song was back in his head along with the painful memories of his past, too. "Coincidence?"

"We're Evie and Richard, remember?" Julia lifted a challenging brow. "What if this couple picked out names for themselves from one of their favorite movies? And that's why their past is such a mystery?"

"Yeah, it's weird our facial recognition software couldn't ID them."

"I think this couple is as real as Evie and Richard." She squeezed the bridge of her nose as if a painful or alarming thought had filled her mind. "And I have a guess as to who a couple might have gone to if they needed a face change."

"Giorgio Fucking Ferrari," Finn said under his breath.

CHAPTER NINETEEN

THE GLITTERING, 3-CARAT PRINCESS CUT DIAMOND ON Julia's left hand caught Finn's eyes as they headed toward the resort.

A.J. drove their new rental, a 2021 silver Bentley Continental, which Wyatt had picked up for them and swapped for the Range Rover at the mall while they'd had their shopping excursion to make the best use of their limited time. The car had a price tag of over 200K if they were to buy it. Thankfully, Julia had plenty of cash to throw around to foot the bill for everything while they were there.

The ring on Julia's slender finger shouldn't have caused such a stir in his stomach. He and Julia didn't actually get engaged. And did men get butterflies? Was that a real thing he'd heard Harper and Jessica discuss over the years? He didn't feel sick, nor did his abdomen ache like he'd done a thousand sit-ups, but something was off.

Nerves? Maybe.

He was feeling something, that was for sure, and it wasn't numbness.

As A.J. turned into the resort, Finn looked up to find Julia peering at him from where she sat next to him in the backseat. Harper was on the other side of her, and Roman sat shotgun.

Julia's eyes were shielded by her sunglasses, same as his. But she knew he'd been staring at the ring, didn't she?

"Well, we're here. Ready for this wild weekend adventure in Dubai?" A.J. asked as if trying to lighten the too-quiet mood, which was typical of his brother. "Anything special you want me to do as A.J., the bodyguard? And wow, that sounds like the title of a bad eighties film."

Finn owed A.J. for Julia's husky, feminine laugh that had his dick twitching in appreciation.

"Just be yourself," Julia told A.J.

Roman looked back and smiled. "Probably not a good idea. He should act like a grown-up."

"Har har," A.J. responded as they waited for the valet to come to the car.

Can I survive this weekend? Could he make it three days as Richard O'Connell, the brave hero from *The Mummy* movies? Julia had filled him in on the details of the movies in case anyone recognized their names, and they needed to play it up somehow.

Harper was anxious to get to the villa and work with Jessica so they could go through Giorgio Ferrari's files to see if the American *Romancing the Stone* couple had had work done by the surgeon. They would try to match the couple's current photos to Giorgio's records that Harper and Roman had stolen in hopes their guess was not only correct but would also disclose who they were before becoming Joan and Jack.

What planet am I on right now? An '80s-themed weekend in Dubai? With a woman I can't have and shouldn't want next to me.

234

"Ohh, look. A rainbow of Ferraris," A.J. spoke as if cooing to a baby. "I guess this Bentley will stand out."

"Are you practicing baby talk for when A.J. junior is here?" Finn teased.

"He ain't gonna be a junior. And I'm not sure if we're having a boy, anyway. Ana doesn't want to find out the sex, remember?"

"I don't think I'd want to know, either," Julia said, and Finn noticed Harper drawing a hand to her abdomen out of the corner of his eye.

"Yeah, well, Ana is the boss." A.J. tossed back a look toward Julia accompanied by his signature smile. "It's showtime." He exited the driver's side when the valet appeared and handed off the keys before opening the rear door on one side while the valet opened the other side.

Finn reached for Julia's palm and clasped their hands to play the role of her husband. Was this considered PDA? Screw it. He was going to do it anyway. She didn't seem to mind, and her delicate hand fit perfectly inside his big one.

They followed behind Roman and Harper, with A.J. at their six o'clock, but Finn stopped at the sight of the two bronze horse statues in a fountain by the hotel entrance. He closed his eyes, his dream from the other day flashing to mind.

"You okay?" Julia's whispered words broke him from whatever weird spell he'd fallen under. Maybe A.J. was right and they were cursed. Or the desert heat was going to his brain.

"Fine," he lied, opening his eyes and urging them to head inside and check in.

It was hard to miss Jessica and Asher, already in the lobby waiting for them, considering the odd pair they made—a dark-haired mountain of a man standing next to a petite blonde with blue eyes. Asher's height and muscular build assured he stuck out in most places, but the fact that he loosely resembled that *Aquaman* actor, especially when he grew out his hair and beard, which Jessica loved, only added another layer of noticeability.

"Hey," Asher greeted them, his gaze swerving to Julia with curiosity. "You're no quitter, huh? I admire that." He gently elbowed his wife. "Reminds me of someone I know."

"I have to agree. Ballsy, though," Jessica added, then pulled Julia in for a hug. Jessica had transformed from a notorious Ice Queen to a mamma bear. It had been an interesting and promising sight to see. It gave Finn hope that people could change.

"Three has eyes on Tariq and Kaira's villa," Asher offered in a low voice after they checked in and were being accompanied outside to golf carts to be driven to their villa, which was in a separate location on the massive property.

Since Asher was Bravo Three, Finn knew he was referring to Echo Three, Chris.

Finn and Roman nodded in response before they all climbed aboard their own golf cart, and A.J. rode solo with his driver.

Finn released a shaky breath when Julia united their hands as they sat on the back of the golf cart and drove past the emerald-green polo lawns. Who was the act for? The driver? He doubted that. Maybe she sensed something was off with him?

He stared at that ring again. It was too big for her. Too gaudy. If he were ever to buy an engagement ring, he'd go with something simple. A classic solitaire. But did Julia like flashy?

He tore his free hand through his hair as some strands caught a sudden breeze. *What am I thinking?*

Julia squeezed his hand, a signal he found himself interpreting as *It's okay. I got you.* He was used to only his brothers and Jessica and Harper "having his back" and no one else. Why did his fingers laced with Julia's feel so comforting? So natural?

It took Finn a second to process that the golf cart had stopped outside the villa, and he gently pulled his hand free from Julia's, which *hadn't* been natural to do.

"Damn, we have our own pool. Not that we'll get a chance to use it," A.J. commented when they were all inside the four-bedroom villa.

Finn walked over to the sliding glass doors in the living room to view the swim-up pool that ran parallel to the villa. He looked left and right, curious which villas Kaira and this suspicious American couple were staying in. Harper would have that intel, though.

"You should hurry up and get ready. Reservations are soon for the steakhouse," Jessica pointed out.

Finn turned at Jessica's words. "I think you and Harper should hang back and work. Julia and I can handle tonight."

"I was thinking the same," Jessica agreed. "Asher and Roman can keep tabs on Tariq and Kaira if they're not at the steakhouse with the American couple tonight like we hope they'll be. Their reservations were originally for three, but I don't think Tariq is letting his sister out of his sight. I'm surprised she even showed up at the resort unattended."

"Yeah, well, Tariq wasn't far behind her," A.J. noted. "Like her shadow."

"Why not make her leave the resort, though?" Asher asked the million-dollar question.

"I'm guessing the reason has something to do with this couple," Harper responded. "So, we need to figure out what's the deal with them."

"But we'll handle that. You two get ready." Jessica shooed Finn and Julia away. "You two mind sharing a room?"

Am I okay with that? Yes. Also no. The one time he'd actually slept in the hotel room they shared in Egypt had resulted in her taking off. He didn't anticipate that happening this time, but he did worry something else might happen if he were alone in a bedroom with her.

"Yeah, if you are?" Julia asked Finn, and he forced a nod.

"You can use my shower while Julia gets ready," A.J. suggested.

Good call.

Because for a split second, he considered they could save time by showering together. It'd also give him the opportunity to finger her into another orgasm and kiss her like he wished he had last time.

As Finn kept hold of Julia's gaze, he witnessed a blush of color bloom on her skin, slowly slide up the column of her neck, then continue on to her cheeks as if similar thoughts had entered her mind as well.

He didn't need to be behind a camera to commit every inch of this woman to memory, to find the beauty on the other side of the lens. He saw her clear as day before him now. A stunning and independent woman he . . . fuck, he wanted her. So damn much.

"Hopefully, by the time you're finished with dinner, we'll have answers about this Joan and Jack mystery couple." Jessica pivoted to Harper, and when Harper cupped her mouth as if she might bolt, Finn let go of his thoughts.

"Not again." Harper began running for the nearest bedroom, and Roman shrugged as if he were clueless and went after her.

"Is she sick?" Asher stepped alongside his wife. "Or?"

Or is she pregnant? Finn kept his mouth shut and pulled the same shrug maneuver as Roman had.

Something in Julia's eyes as she'd watched Harper flee told him she knew the truth. Harper must have told her at some point on the trip, which was a bit surprising she'd opened up to Julia first instead of Finn. That honor was normally his.

"I'll be quick." Julia went to one of the bedrooms, and Finn took A.J. up on his offer to utilize his room to get ready.

Harper had chosen what he'd be wearing to dinner tonight. Khaki linen pants with a white linen long-sleeved shirt. Dressy enough without being too hot.

When Finn stepped into the fancy shower, he turned the water on so hot he nearly scalded his skin, which felt horrible on his chest. Ice cold would have been the wise choice on the bruises he'd gotten after being shot with a plate on, but he wasn't in the mood for a cold shower.

He also didn't have time to jerk off, but he was afraid if he didn't release all of his pent-up tension, he might lose his mind at some point soon.

So, he set one hand to the wall, bowed his head, and stroked himself from root to tip, growing painfully hard as he called up the memory of his hands on Julia's body during their shower together. The play-by-play unfolded in his head, and he squeezed his eyes closed when an unexpected tug of emotion, totally unrelated to getting struck by a bullet, filled his chest.

He released his cock and braced both hands to the wall at the realization he was falling for this woman more than he thought, and damn it, he was going to get hurt.

* * *

"Beautiful, yes?" The man couldn't take his eyes off Julia, and Finn didn't blame him.

Julia was stunning no matter what she wore, but tonight she looked like an elegant movie star, her hair falling like silk over her shoulders. The black and red fitted, knee-length dress she wore was modest, but Finn knew it had to have cost a pretty penny. The cinched waistline was embroidered with red flowers, and while the sleeves were sheer, they went to her elbows to follow local clothing guidelines. Gold, strappy heels made her long legs look even longer. The neckline of the dress was also modest, but that didn't stop Finn from thinking about how perfect her tits felt against his chest during that shower in Egypt. And if he had the chance for a repeat, this time he'd hold them in his palms, drag his thumb over her nipple, and—

"Yes, the stables and horses are both very beautiful," Julia answered the hotel employee who'd all but given them no choice but to take a quick pre-dinner tour after he picked them up in the golf cart ten minutes ago. "And there are over five hundred stables here?"

Finn pocketed the naughty things he wanted to do to Julia in the back of his mind in hopes he'd be able to eventually extinguish whatever flame she'd lit inside of him since he met her back in January. A flame that'd grown during the last two weeks to what felt like the point of no return.

"Yes." The man smiled, his thick, black mustache hiding most of his lips. "Nothing more magnificent than an Arabian horse. Their chiseled heads. Long, arched necks. A high tail carriage." He beamed as he motioned toward one of the chestnut horses in the closest stable inside the massive, well, whatever type of room he'd said they were in. "Equine passion is synonymous with Dubai. We care a lot for our horses."

Finn looked straight into the creature's big brown orbs for eyes and . . .

Jaden suddenly came back to mind.

Why now?

Why that dream?

"We have a saying," the man went on, and Finn pulled his focus back to Julia when she gently tugged his arm for his attention, obviously noticing something was wrong.

"And what is that?" Julia asked, her voice polished and a bit haughty sounding as she played up the rich-woman act.

Hell, she *was* a rich woman. And if Julia hadn't gone back to her true self and dropped the I-hate-you attitude she'd given him those two weeks in New York, he'd believe she was the woman she was pretending to be now.

Their impromptu tour guide appeared to relish Julia's attentive gaze. She was quite the actress. "The saying we have here is '*The devil will never dare enter a tent with an Arabian horse.*' They are a protector of people."

Protector? Devil?

When Jaden's face filled his mind yet again, Finn instinctively took a step back, pulling free from Julia's touch as he looked away.

But horses were everywhere he turned.

And he felt his brother's presence surrounding him, too.

The pills as well.

The fucking pills he should have told his parents about. Or Jaden's agent. Hell, anyone. He should never have made his brother the promise to keep his mouth shut.

Why didn't I make him get help for his addiction before it was too late?

How could he ever walk through that cemetery in Pasadena without God opening the heavens to strike him?

"I didn't say anything. I should have," he mumbled under

his breath as the room began to spin.

"I think he's hungry. Probably jet lag, too. Maybe we should get to our dinner reservations." Julia reached for Finn's arm and tugged him tight to her side. He sucked in a sharp breath and brought his palm to his forehead, finding it damp with sweat.

"Oh yes, let's get you to dinner," the man said.

"Richard. Mm. Rick?"

"Evie," Finn whispered in response when Julia reminded him where he was and who he was supposed to be.

"Yes, I'm starving. Got a bit dizzy," he lied and regained his focus, doing his best not to look in the eyes of any of the horses, worried he'd find his brother staring back at him instead.

Julia hooked her arm with his, and they followed the concierge, or whatever the dude's role was, to the steakhouse.

The hostess ushered them to a special table within a minute, and once they were seated, Finn spotted the American couple with not only Kaira but Tariq as well. Harper and Jessica had provided photos of the American targets to commit to memory before they left for dinner. Fortunately, Harper was feeling better, but Finn figured she'd be staying in the villa for the remainder of the weekend with her touch-and-go nausea.

"They're a few tables over," Julia leaned in and said after their server finished discussing the specials and left them alone. Something about Argentinian meat with roasted yada yada yada.

"Yeah, I see them."

"They don't seem to be following the dress code," she commented from behind the menu she held in front of her face, only her eyes visible over the top.

He glanced at the "they" she'd referred to.

Kaira was in a chic, sleeveless fitted white dress with her black hair down her back. Tariq, on the other hand, didn't seem to give any fucks, wearing jeans from what Finn could tell coupled with a black T-shirt. And the Americans didn't appear to care about clothing etiquette either. "Maybe the rules don't apply to the uber-rich at this resort? Does that mean we're exempt?"

"We will be for the costume party, I suppose."

He smirked at the memory of her chosen outfit. "*Wonder Woman.*"

"Not sure how Harper talked me into that. The movie is called *Wonder Woman 1984,* but I think it came out in 2020."

"Pretty sure *Wonder Woman* dates back to pre-2022, though," he said with a laugh, suddenly feeling better the farther away from the horses they were. *And* from his memories of Jaden. "I wish you would've let me get my Darth Vader costume. *Empire Strikes Back* was in the eighties."

"We need that handsome face of yours visible. No hiding behind a mask."

"Handsome, eh?" He set his menu down and looked around the restaurant. "You sure it's okay we didn't bring our bodyguard tonight?"

"Yeah, for tonight, I think we're clear. Tomorrow makes sense for him to come with us on the safari."

The server approached a moment later. "Ready to order?"

Hell if Finn could remember what he'd selected from the menu not two minutes later. And with the candles lit at the center of the table and the romantic lighting and ambiance, not to mention the soft tunes being sung from somewhere in the room—he was pretty sure it wasn't being piped in—this was the closest thing to a real date he'd had in forever. Aside from that dinner on the terrace in Egypt, he supposed.

"I think you'll make a great *Indiana Jones*," Julia said, returning to the conversation they'd been having before he'd grown distracted by A.J.'s absence. Not that they were truly alone. His guys were lurking around the hotel grounds in case any of their four targets left the restaurant and split up. They needed all hands on deck just in case.

Julia's brother wouldn't arrive in Dubai until tomorrow because he couldn't get a flight, and he was under strict orders not to show up at the resort. They'd have to find a way to meet with Michael the day after tomorrow since he and Julia would be gone all day, which her brother was going to hate.

"I'm no Harrison Ford, but I guess my inner child is happy with being Indiana." He winked, and the smile forming on her pouty lips made his heart sing.

That organ in his chest pumped harder than it should have from the sight of her smile.

Julia thanked the server for her red wine and once again waited for the woman to leave before speaking. Ramadan was over now, which meant they could drink and eat during the daytime in Dubai again. And although he was working, he'd take a few sips to calm his pulse that was jockeying too fast with her blue eyes on him. "Can I ask you something?"

"Guess you'll have to ask to find out," he teased.

"What is it with you and horses?" That was not what he expected. "The statues outside. The stables."

"It's not the horses." Finn considered how much to say. He'd nearly shared everything with her at the mall when he heard the Bryan Adams song. "When I nodded off on the couch while you were supposed to be in bed"—a*nd wow, was that THIS morning?*—"I had a shit dream. I was in a sandstorm, there was a horse. I don't know, it was pretty unsettling."

244

Julia's shoulders fell as if disappointed he wasn't willing to share.

It wasn't that he didn't want to. He was never the confessor but always the person everyone confided in. He never shared those secrets, and he certainly didn't share his own. Aside from Roman knowing the burden Finn carried and how much it affected him, he didn't go around talking about himself.

Finn stole a second to check their targets while he contemplated what else to say, knowing Julia wanted him to talk. But he also knew that, for him, opening up to Julia was as good as making a commitment to her. And while it might not be the case for most people, for Finn, it was a bigger step than sex. Bigger than a relationship. In his head, she'd have to be the woman he planned to marry for him to share his heart and his pain like that. His *guilt*.

"Um, they're dancing." He blinked in surprise to see "Joan" and "Jack" slow dancing between tables. A musician Finn hadn't noticed serenaded the room, singing in Arabic.

"Dance with me." Julia stood and came around to his side of the circular table.

"What?" He tried not to draw attention with his shock. But *what?*

"They'll notice us if we dance, too." She arched a dark brow and lightly nodded the directive to take her hand, but he remained in place. "Do you trust me?"

"Shit," he whispered in a low voice, thinking back to Elaina's favorite Disney movie, *Aladdin*. He'd watched the new version starring Will Smith how many times with her? Emily and Liam's eldest daughter was a radiant light. Also, more than a bit prophetic. Or psychic. Whatever it was called, she had *it*. "Another movie line. And here I am as Princess Jasmine this time." But he smiled and took her hand.

When he rose, he took charge and slung her arms over his shoulders, then framed his hands around her waist.

He felt the eyes of the other couples there on them. But for the moment, he was completely mesmerized by the woman in his arms. No PDA in Dubai. Did this not count? Maybe not in a restaurant with live music? And he also couldn't get himself to unglue her hands, fingers interlocked behind his neck if he tried.

"You really are a movie buff like me. My niece loves *Aladdin*." Julia smiled as if drawing up a memory. "My brother didn't think he'd be able to have kids. Miracles happen."

"They do, don't they? Sometimes, I guess," Finn said softly as they moved side to side to the tunes. "For some people. Not everyone."

"I think everyone gets one miracle in their lifetime. Hopefully more." Her blue eyes shimmered like the waters of the Arabian Gulf. So beautiful. So full of optimism. He was pretty sure she hoped saving Oliver would be her miracle. He wanted so many more for her. "They're noticing," she whispered into his ear, and her warm breath there had his dick stirring in his pants. *That* would probably get him thrown in jail in Dubai if he had an erection in public. And the team didn't need a second person to bust out of prison.

"Kaira is going to the ladies' room, I think," he said while watching the woman walk behind Julia, saying something quick to Joan on her way across the room.

"I should talk to her." Julia casually removed her arms from his shoulders. "Tip the singer. I'll be back."

"Jul—" He quickly stopped himself from saying her real name. "Evie."

"I got this." She winked. "You trust me, remember?"

CHAPTER TWENTY

JULIA RE-APPLIED HER RED COME-GET-ME LIPSTICK, THEN fiddled with the few contents of her clutch, trying to appear busy while she waited for Kaira to exit one of the two stalls. Her goal was to engage Kaira in a bit of casual small talk, but Julia also needed to step away from Finn for a few moments or else she'd burst into flames.

There was definite chemistry between them. So much so that she kept losing sight of why she was in Dubai. It was incredibly distracting, as was the haunted look that appeared in his eyes every so often, which made her heart hurt. She wished he would have opened up to her and shared whatever it was he was hiding about himself or his past.

At the sound of a flush, Julia put away her lipstick and began to blot her cheeks. Barely any makeup there, but it was hot enough that the natural oil in her skin had begun to appear.

In the mirror's reflection, she watched Kaira walk up toward the sinks, her nude heels a good four inches high. The woman was gorgeous. Oliver would have surely noticed her beauty, but he wouldn't go so far as to fall in love with a married woman and then kill her husband. That wasn't a possibility.

Kaira sent her a friendly smile in the mirror and began to wash her hands.

If the information Finn and his team had obtained was correct, this woman had helped set up Oliver, but there was something so sad in her eyes that Julia almost felt bad for her for some reason. She looked lost and a little scared. And Julia knew that feeling all too well.

Realizing she was probably staring, Julia tossed the paper towel into the bin.

"You're American?" Kaira startled her with the unexpected conversation starter.

"I am. From Florida." According to her research, Kaira had spent time there. A "connection" she'd hoped would get Kaira to open up if they had a chance to talk.

"I lived in Miami for about nine months while my husband worked on a project there before moving to Dubai." The heel of her hand went to her forehead as though a headache stirred.

"You okay? I have Advil if you need it."

Kaira lowered her hand. "You're sweet, but no, I . . ." Her slender neck went tight as if combatting stress or trying to keep herself from talking. "My husband died in January."

"Oh, I'm so sorry." *Okay, this is progress, right?* Now, if only she could cut to the chase and ask Kaira what her brother was really up to and why he framed Oliver for Ario's death. *Assuming that's what happened*, she reminded herself. *And is Ario really dead?*

"We weren't married for long, but I fell in love with him. I didn't expect that to happen."

Julia resisted letting another "oh" fall from her lips like a broken record.

"Arranged." Kaira shrugged. "Not by my parents, though."

Tariq?

"I have said too much." Kaira pushed away from the counter and brushed past Julia, then turned back before exiting. "There's something about you that makes strangers open up, yes?" Was that a question or an observation?

Before Julia had a chance to say anything, she was gone.

Was Finn's secret-spilling vibe rubbing off on her?

Julia pulled herself together and rejoined Finn at the table just as dinner arrived.

"How'd it go?" he asked, his gaze shifting to the table where Kaira was sitting alongside her brother again. The Americans were eating as well.

"Kaira sort of struck up a conversation with me," she said in an excited whisper, leaning forward to keep from being overheard. "And it sounds like Kaira was forced to marry Ario. You think it was about his money even though her family is already uber-wealthy?"

Finn focused back on Julia and shook his head. "I guess we'll find out soon."

After dinner ended, a meal Julia noticed Finn merely picked at, they headed back to their villa since that's what their targets appeared to be doing as well.

Once they were back, Harper announced, "We have news. But before we share, how'd it go? Make any headway?"

"We got their attention. Hopefully, we'll have a chance to chat with them on the safari," Finn spoke up, popping the top two buttons of his shirt as if he were suffocating. He looked so handsome and dashing in that white linen shirt, which, incidentally, was similar to what Rick O'Connell wore in *The Mummy*. His dark hair was a little disheveled now from all of the times he'd run his fingers through it between dinner and their golf-cart escort back to the villa. She scolded herself for wishing it'd been her fingers instead of his when she was supposed to be focusing on Kaira and the others. "Where's Chris? Eyes still on the other villas?"

"Yeah, I'll rotate with him soon," Asher responded.

"So, what do you know?" Jessica prompted a beat later.

"I lucked out and spoke with Kaira in the ladies' room. I'm fairly certain Tariq is the reason she married Ario three years ago. She told me the union was arranged but not by her parents, and she hadn't expected to fall in love with him. She truly appeared to be in mourning," Julia shared what Kaira had confessed.

"I can see that happening," Jessica said thoughtfully.

And as Julia stood among Finn's colleagues, who obviously meant more to him than just work friends, it felt almost as if she were also part of their mission. It was strange, yet at the same time normal somehow.

It was comforting to have an elite team working to save Oliver and stop whatever malicious plans Tariq might be devising. When Julia messaged Mya with an update, she was careful to be sparse on the details, but her friend was relieved the "professionals," as Mya called them, had taken over.

"So, what news do you have to share?" Finn directed Julia to have a seat on the couch, where A.J. sat with his feet on the coffee table in front of him.

Jessica removed her black-framed glasses and folded her arms. From the looks of it, she was going to take point on the conversation, and Harper appeared relieved. She was a bit pale again. Morning sickness was more like any-time-of-day sickness from what it looked like.

"Your intuition was right about Joan and Jack. Harper and I found a match in Giorgio's files. The *after*-surgery photos led me to the *before* ones. Strangely, there's no connection between Joan and Jack when they were Stacey and Doug aside from a mutual love of art. They didn't live in the same city. Stacey was an art teacher in New York. Doug, an art broker who traveled the world. No criminal record for either. No red flags. I'm stumped as to why they changed their identities."

"*But*?" Finn dragged out the word as if waiting for more details because Jessica seemed to love suspense-building. He sat next to Julia, and why did she get the feeling he was working hard to keep his eyes off her legs that were more exposed with her seated on the couch? Why did his attention thrill her so much? Why did she want to raise her dress some more (when they were alone) and show him what else was beneath?

Too many whys. Focus, Julia.

Jessica looked to Harper, then back at Finn. Had Harper taken a pregnancy test? If it was yes, would she share the news?

"They lived as Joan and Jack in Miami at the same time Kaira and her husband were there," Jessica said. "I assume that's how they met, and for whatever reason, they most likely shared Giorgio's name with Ario and Kaira."

"But would a billionaire like Ario want to fake his death to begin with? That's what we're assuming happened or was supposed to happen, right?" Finn asked.

"Still working on those answers," Jessica said.

"Since Kaira told me she didn't expect to fall in love with her husband, maybe that wasn't part of the plan. What if Tariq forced her to marry Ario, but he had no intention of allowing him to live that long?" Julia proposed, trying to unravel the mystery like she was in a real-life game of Clue but didn't know who all the players were.

Finn pivoted to face her a bit more. "You think Kaira tried

to save Ario by faking his death? She was on the calendar, too, though. And, well . . ."

She's still alive. "Is it a stupid idea?"

"No, not stupid. Still possible," Jessica was quick to say, which made Julia feel a bit better. "We really do need to get close to Joan and Jack this weekend. The fundraiser they organized and are hosting was a last-minute event thrown together. Maybe Kaira contacted them because she needed their help, and the event was a good excuse for them to come to Dubai in hopes it wouldn't draw Tariq's notice."

"But then he unexpectedly showed up here after his quick kill-a-surgeon trip in Egypt," A.J. joined the conversation, sitting upright from his slouched position.

"I have an idea as to how you might get invited to the party." Harper pushed back from the desk, and Roman set both hands on her shoulders and gently squeezed, giving her a massage.

Julia was pretty tense, too. She could use a massage, but she wasn't about to ask the sexy SEAL Finn to do it. She probably needed sleep more than anything.

"Since both Joan and Jack seem to be into the eighties given their name choice and party theme, and they appear to love art, what if you happen to mention tomorrow during the safari that you have a piece of art you'd like to auction for charity? Something that'd catch their attention."

Julia closed her eyes for a second, rummaging through her head for what she might own that would do the trick. "I should have something. I can have my assistant head to my place and take some photos of the paintings I have. Or other collectibles that might pique their interest."

"I wonder . . ." Roman's voice trailed off as if an idea had popped into his mind. "Anyone remember that art thief in the news a few years back? Interpol believed one person was responsible for some of the more notable stolen items, but no one had a clue as to his identity. Then one day, he just stopped. Dropped off the grid."

"*I* don't remember that," Asher said in an exaggerated tone. "But of course you would."

Harper turned in her chair to eye her fiancé. "You think Jack-Doug was that guy? And do you remember the year this famous art thief retired, by chance?"

Roman shook his head as if disappointed with himself.

"Maybe we're dealing with a love story?" Jessica proposed, her eyes moving to the man she loved.

"*Romancing the Stone*," Harper said softly. "Jack's character in the movie was a thief."

"And Joan's character was a writer, I think. Not a teacher, but maybe Doug and Stacey fell in love, and he gave up stealing art for her. And if they have a shared love of the eighties . . ."

Julia continued Harper's line of thought as she drew to mind the few memories of that childhood movie she'd loved.

It made for a good romance, that was for sure. The guy giving up his wicked ways for the woman he loved. What about a good guy? Would he give up his passions for a woman?

No, don't think that. Don't even consider Finn giving up his work for you. You can't let him do that. And wait, love? That's nuts. Sure, she and Finn had spent nearly every moment together for the last two-plus weeks, but she wasn't falling in love with him.

Julia did her best to ignore the strange, nagging feeling in her gut and refocused on the main issue at hand. The Americans.

"It's possible," Jessica said.

"I think more like probable," A.J. added his two cents and

joined Asher on his feet. "But why don't you two get some rest since you've been going nonstop?"

"Agree." Jessica directed her head toward the stairs leading to the suite Julia and Finn would be sharing.

"There are more than enough of us in Dubai working leads. Rest," Harper added.

"Since it's earlier in New York, I'll shoot a message to my assistant to head to my place for a look-see at what I might donate, so I'm prepared for the safari tomorrow." Julia rose, and Finn did the same.

"There sure as hell better not be any camel riding." A.J. grimaced. "I'm still sore in places I'd rather not discuss from the other night."

"You and me both, brother," Finn said in a light, easy voice. "Wake me if you learn something. Or need me." She noticed him glancing at Jessica and Asher, then moved his gaze around the room.

"*Goodnight.*" Jessica exaggerated the word as if to say *Sleep, damn it. Let me handle the rest.*

"Thank you again for everything." Julia smiled, and Jessica tipped her head but remained quiet.

Once inside the bedroom upstairs, Finn shut the door behind them and slid out of the leather loafers Harper had bought him at the mall to go with his outfit.

Julia removed her engagement and wedding rings, a reminder this was all an act. But earlier on that dance floor, when he'd been holding her, it'd felt far too real.

"You sure you want to share the bed? We're not really Evie and Rick."

Julia took off her heels, trying to buy herself some time. How would she answer? Sleeping next to a man she was more than just attracted to would be a challenge, but there was no other place she'd rather be than alongside him.

Julia pulled her gaze up his long legs and to his fingers deftly moving over the buttons of his shirt. Those veined hands made short work of the buttons with quick precision, and his shirt parted to reveal his golden six-pack. *And* the purple bruises on his chest.

"It's a big bed," she said, her voice a little hoarse at the sight of his body. "And I don't bite."

Finn's grin reached his eyes the way she loved, and, God help her, she wanted those lips to cover every inch of her body. But it was the husky depth of his voice when he said, "That makes one of us," that had her wondering how long she'd last before *she* made the next move.

CHAPTER TWENTY-ONE

THE LAHBAB DESERT SAFARI HAD TURNED INTO SOMETHING unexpected and, well, fun. A forty-minute drive had transported them from the sophistication of Dubai, with its skyscrapers and fast cars, to a desert oasis of sorts. It may have been nothing but sand and more sand, but the austere beauty held a peacefulness that was somehow calming to Finn.

And despite never losing sight of the fact that he, Julia, and A.J. were technically working, Finn found himself enjoying the day's activities. Julia was clearly having a good time, and she seemed excited to be behind the lens of a camera again. Seeing her in action, the way her eyes lit up when she discovered a new subject to capture, had his stomach doing those little flips, a sensation he'd only ever experienced with Julia. She'd snuck in photo after photo of him as well, laughing when he shielded his face from the lens and shooed her off, encouraging her to photograph the ripples of sand instead.

Throughout the day, which had started with dune bashing —driving over the dunes at increasing and decreasing speeds

—before driving deep into the desert, he'd been unable to forget what it'd felt like to sleep alongside her last night. She'd snuggled herself inside his arms at some point while she was fast asleep, and he hadn't resisted. She'd felt warm and soft and amazing cradled against his chest, her face tucked beneath his chin. Not wanting to wake her, he'd barely moved a muscle when she'd positioned herself that way sometime around three in the morning, which had roused him from sleep. It'd taken forever to fall back asleep because he'd wanted to relish the feeling of her pinned to his body so intimately. Finn couldn't even pretend that Julia didn't affect him physically. But what was probably even more terrifying about holding her in his arms was the gamut of emotions it brought to life.

"You okay?" Had Julia sensed he'd let his thoughts wander the same way the sand rolled whenever there was a breeze?

"Thinking about sandboarding," he lied, and then wanted to kick himself. White lies were okay, he supposed. White lies didn't get people killed.

"Mm. You said you'd never do that in a million years. Same as A.J." She smiled as they walked beneath the setting sun and took a photo of their path as the light hit the sand in a unique way Finn lacked the words to describe. He remembered this phenomenon from Iraq, but he'd been under heavy gunfire instead of walking alongside a beautiful woman with stunning blue eyes wearing a red scarf wrapped around her head to protect her face from the sun and the sand when needed.

Finn glanced back at A.J. trailing behind them, playing the role of dutiful bodyguard to a T. Then he reset his focus ahead as they followed their tour guides from where the Land Cruisers were parked to the Bedouin-style camp for a late meal and show. "When you've had sand in places where sand should never be, then you avoid it when possible."

"BUD/S?" Julia lowered the Nikon Finn had brought and peeked at him, and he nodded.

"You were a pro," Finn told her. "Sandboarding like you were on snow."

"Not a pro. But at least falling didn't hurt as much as when I've tried snowboarding in the past. You did great."

"Ha." Finn laughed. "I just did my best not to fall, because sand."

"At least we didn't have to ride camels," A.J. spoke up from behind.

"Or you'd be even grumpier?" Julia surprised Finn by teasing A.J. and shooting him a quick look over her shoulder.

"Darling, I am not grumpy. I'm just not a desert kind of guy. Give me a Southern sunset and a horse, sure, but this heat and sand? Nah, I'm good," A.J. replied as they neared the campsite, trailing a few couples behind their targets. When they'd booked the trip, Finn hadn't realized this was an overnight adventure. And now he'd be sharing a tent with Julia in one of the "desert chalets," whatever those were.

Looking ahead, Finn saw the campsite coming into view like a mirage. Asher and Chris were out there somewhere with eyes on them as backup in case anything crazy went down with Tariq there.

He and Julia hadn't yet had the chance to strike up a conversation with the Americans, and Tariq's close eye on his sister made it impossible to speak to her. The way the man held Kaira's elbow and pulled her tight to his side whenever she steered away by more than a few feet was a bad sign.

At this point, Tariq had to know the weapons he'd purchased in Pakistan had been destroyed, same as the drugs in Egypt, and yet, he opted to remain glued to his sister's side for a weekend retreat. It didn't add up. Unless he had reason to fear her or something she might do. Which raised the question of whether or not the Americans were there to help her. The fundraiser they'd organized and the trip to Dubai were both scheduled within the last two weeks. Events like that usually took months to set up. Had Kaira phoned them for help of some kind, and Tariq spoiled her plans?

There were still so many questions they needed answered, including Tariq's ultimate goals, but tonight, he and Julia had one mission: get an invite to the party tomorrow evening. It was there they hoped to pin down Joan and Jack, find out what they knew and how deeply they were involved in whatever the hell was going on. They couldn't kidnap two Americans in Dubai, but now that they knew the couple changed their names and faces, Finn would leverage that to get them to talk. The team agreed they had a better shot getting intel from the Americans than from Kaira, especially with Tariq as her shadow.

"Finally. Hot damn." A.J. lowered the shemagh from his mouth as they closed in on the site, an elaborate setup nowhere near what Finn had in mind.

He'd heard of something referred to as "glamping," a ridiculous blending of the words "glamorous" and "camping." But this was a mini resort with ten "tents" that looked a hell of a lot sturdier than any tent he'd ever slept in. Bigger, too. There were five tents on one side of a courtyard-like area and five on the other.

The courtyard was set up with six tables, sitting low to the ground, with pillows covered in red silk for seats. The tables were loaded with covered, silver platters placed down the middle, and the aroma of smoked meat wafted through the air, which seemed to catch the Bama boy's attention.

"I could get used to this," A.J. drawled and slapped his hands together.

"Maybe we should change before dinner? I think that's what everyone's going to do. Which tent is ours?" Julia asked.

A.J. reached into his pocket for the itinerary. "You're in the one at the end. Five. I'm in number four next to you. No-key entry, which I'm not crazy about, but we've got overwatch, so I guess we're okay."

"Overwatch?" Julia blinked. "Right. Never mind."

Finn set a hand to Julia's back as her "husband" probably would and escorted her to their tent. He found the split at the center of the "door" and unzipped it. This wasn't ideal. No door. No lock. But when they entered the tent and he sealed the flimsy door, he turned and was pleasantly surprised by the inside.

Red silk draped the wall behind the bed, which was low to the ground and covered in colorful linens. There was real hardwood flooring beneath their feet and a small bathroom off to the side. Hell, the lanterns by the bed were most likely for effect because there was plumbing and electricity. "An A/C unit." He pointed to the wall, then removed his shemagh and quickly pulled off his damp white tee that had clung to his frame.

"This is quite the tent. Not that I did much tent camping while growing up, my parents were too urban for that, but this is great. Minus the not-having-a-real-door thing."

Julia turned to face him, and her eyes widened, obviously taken by surprise to see him shirtless. He used his tee like a towel and dabbed at his bare chest to try and clean up like he'd have done if he were in Iraq. This was a step up from those days. A big-ass step up.

"I used to go camping a lot," she said a moment later, and

261

Finn tried not to smile as he watched her effort to look anywhere but his chest with little success. Finally forcing her eyes away, she placed her hand on the column of her throat and took a deep breath before removing the headscarf she wore. "I love it. The fresh air. The blanket of stars overhead. A fire to keep you warm."

"You paint a pretty picture. I'll have to go sometime." *With you, maybe?* But he left that question unspoken. "You can change in the bathroom." He looked around and found their one small travel bag had already been placed in the tent by one of the tour guides.

Not packing a weapon had made Finn uneasy, but he reminded himself Asher and Chris were out there, and they'd be carrying if Tariq became a threat.

"Sure." Julia reached into their bag and pulled out something pretty and pink.

She disappeared behind the door. At least the bathroom had a door. He'd prefer the tent had one, too, instead of an insubstantial zipper.

While she was getting dressed, he did the same. More linen, this time a bright blue shirt and khaki pants similar to last night's, courtesy of Harper's mall purchases. He left the top two buttons undone, rolled the sleeves to his elbows, and was in the middle of swapping his shoes for loafers when Julia exited the tiny bathroom in a pale pink wrap dress with nude-colored sandals. She was also wearing the necklace he'd given her, and it gave him pause.

"This okay? Angles shouldn't be a problem with the sun setting, right?" A smirk cut across her lips.

"Maybe you should spin around for me just in case." Finn winked at their shared joke, hoping it came off as silly rather than suggestive, and twirled his finger. But damn, he wanted to peel the dress off her and have a nice hard look at those "angles" of hers.

Her cheeks flushed a bit before she gave him a quick twirl, and *fuuuck* was that a terrible suggestion on his part. The material of her skirt lifted as she spun, exposing those deliciously toned legs that he knew would be silky smooth to the touch. Did they really have to go to dinner, or could he find a way to lock the zipper of their tent and finally get a taste of Julia?

"You're good," he managed to work the words free from his parched throat, knowing the dryness had nothing to do with the desert heat and everything to do with his unquenched desire. "You ready?"

"To try and win this couple over and earn ourselves a ticket to the event? Yes. But what's the backup plan? We going to abduct them?" She squeezed her eyes closed as if the memory of her own abduction had hit her thoughts like a two-by-four to the head.

He reached for her waist, not sure what possessed him to put his hand there, but it had her lids parting. "We're most likely going to need to corner them either way, but if we can earn their trust and get them alone that way before we, uh, pounce with the questions, that'd make things easier."

"And you think they'll have the answers we need?" she whispered as if his hand on her hip somehow affected her vocal cords.

"Tariq won't let Kaira out of his sight from the looks of it, which means she's probably a threat to whatever he's doing one way or another. But I do think this couple knows something, so we have to take it one day at a time."

"Oliver doesn't have much time."

He released her and took a step back at the reminder of what, more like who was on the line if he failed.

"We're not allowed to touch Tariq. Or his sister. We have orders. But maybe we can create a distraction to pull him away from her so that we can talk to her. But we can't take her."

"Because of her royal connections?"

He nodded. "One day at a time. I promise it won't take too many days. I know our sands of time hourglass has already flipped over, and we have yet to figure out what's going on. But you have Jessica and the others going back over the case file and the reports about Oliver's arrest." The walls were thick enough, but he kept his voice low.

"Hopefully a fresh set of eyes will help."

"Not to mention they'll access the reports not provided to Uncle Sam," he said with a small knowing smile, letting her know they'd hack the records to get to the bottom of things.

"Oh." She peered down at the floor. "But you also have to stop Tariq from whatever he's planning, not just save my friend. I understand that."

"It's going to be okay." He set a fist beneath her chin to guide her eyes up to his face. "I won't disappoint you."

"I don't think you could ever disappoint me." She brought her hand between them to hold on to her necklace. "I can't stop thinking about that woman's words to me in Egypt, though."

He shook his head. "You are not going to die. I won't let that happen."

"But she said a storm is coming, and why do I get the feeling she's right?"

CHAPTER TWENTY-TWO

"A Warhol? You have an Andy Warhol self-portrait that only cost you four point five mill?" Jack appeared incredulous, but Julia was happy to see his eyes light up with obvious enthusiasm.

"I really, really do." Julia sipped her drink and casually pointed her gaze in Jack's direction. The first thing she'd thought upon meeting Jack Colton was that, sadly, he was nothing like the dashing Jack Colton from *Romancing the Stone*. This Jack was tall and reasonably good-looking, even a bit funny, but he lacked that devil-may-care, swashbuckling charisma, whereas Finn . . . was every bit the Rick O'Connell from her favorite movie.

Stop daydreaming and get your head in the game, Julia.

Fortunately, while she and Finn were changing for dinner, A.J. had stealthily secured their seats at the same table as the Americans. Kaira and her brother were at the opposite end of the ten-person table and Joan and Jack were almost like a buffer between Julia and Finn. Julia's white-painted nails may have been short, but she wanted to rake them down Tariq's face anyway. Her gut told her Oliver was in prison because of him.

A.J. had joined their table only after Julia made a formal invite for her "bodyguard" to sit.

"My wife loves Warhol." Finn reached for her hand on the table and gave it a squeeze. The small gesture took her by surprise and had her momentarily forgetting where they were and with whom they were sitting. "So very avant-garde," he added the line Julia had fed to him in preparation for the evening.

Jack leaned forward, his brown eyes glossy in the light from the nearby flickering torches. "His use of silk screening was absolutely brilliant." He bit into his knuckles, which had Julia laughing. "Ugh, what I wouldn't do for a self-portrait."

"Mm." Joan rubbed her husband's arm like she was trying to calm down a puppy that had just seen a squirrel run by. "He gets a bit excited, as you can tell."

"Well," Julia began, searching Finn's eyes, pretending to seek permission for what she was about to suggest, "I have two Warhols, and I was planning to sell one, but if you have a charity in mind, I'd be more than happy to donate instead."

Joan and Jack copied Finn and Julia's shared look with one of their own. "We're hosting a fundraising event tomorrow evening at the resort. It's a themed costume party, and we'd love to have you there. I might even have to bid on your Warhol myself. What do you say?"

"We have another couple staying with us at the villa, or I would say yes," Julia said as rehearsed. "But thank you."

"The more the merrier, right?" Jack smiled and reached for his wine.

"I think you have enough guests tomorrow, don't you?" Tariq spoke for the first time, and the deep timbre of his voice had Julia casting him a hard look, one she hoped to tamp down before she gave away her hate for him.

"Never." Jack flicked his wrist toward Julia in a come-hither gesture. "It's settled. You and your friends are our guests."

"How do you feel about the eighties, by the way?" Joan asked, opting not to regard Tariq with a look.

"Love the eighties. Is there any other way to feel about them?" Julia flashed her white teeth, trying to play the part of the rich socialite that everyone assumed she was back in New York.

Rich? Yes. Social? Yes. But not an uppity snob who looked down on other people. Her parents were teachers, and they often lived paycheck to paycheck while growing up. She didn't have an uppity bone in her body, and her parents would have knocked it out of her if she'd grown one.

"Jack and I have a love for the eighties. And movies. So, it's a movie-themed party. No dress code tomorrow, either. I'm sure you can find something last minute in Dubai," Joan went on, and Julia nodded. "So, tell me, how'd you two meet?" Her quick change of subject had Julia understanding the feeling of whiplash she'd so often given Finn in the last few days.

This was something she and Finn had also rehearsed in case it came up, thank God. And Finn had wanted her to take the lead.

"Well." Julia turned a little on the pillow where she sat cross-legged. The skirt of her dress covered her, so she didn't expose her inner thighs or panties. She peered at Finn with what she hoped was a convincing "starry-eyed in love" look for the Americans, but . . . was she acting at this point? Feelings for him had steadily been working their way under her skin with each day they spent together.

"We were both in Egypt traveling," Finn began, as if worried she'd forgotten, so she set a hand to his shoulder.

"And this guy bumped straight into me while I was on a tour inside the Pyramid of Giza," Julia picked up the story. "I knocked into some old artifact and it clattered to the ground, almost breaking. I was certain he'd cursed me," she said with a polished smile, trying to play the part of Evie to the best of her non-acting abilities. "He thought I was a stuck-up drama queen after that."

When Julia stole a look at the couple, Joan was the one leaning forward this time. She loved romance as much as Jack loved art, so it seemed.

Julia pinned her gaze back where it belonged. On Finn. "*But* it turned out we were staying at the same hotel, and one thing led to another." His eyes were riveted on hers as though he were also hanging on to her every word. "And we—"

"Fell in love," Finn finished for her, holding her stare for a few more seconds before he turned to look at Joan.

"Wow. You two really love each other, don't you?" Kaira spoke up for the first time, her tone melancholy. She sounded like a woman who'd lost the love of her life.

Did that mean Ario was truly dead? Or was he alive, and Kaira didn't know it? Too many questions, and yet, all Julia wanted to do right now was be alone with Finn.

"We do," Finn said, drawing Julia's eyes back to him.

"Ah, the dancing is about to start," Jack suddenly remarked and motioned his hand toward the women who appeared in the aisle between the tables. "Belly dancers. Egyptian style. How perfect."

"Right. Perfect." Julia swallowed, her focus cutting back to Finn, whose eyes were on her and not the beautiful women who moved their torsos and hips like they had the hand of God directing them.

The eight dancers wore the traditional bedlah—a beaded bra, fitted hip belt, and a full-length skirt. Their hips undulated with grace during their torso-driven dance. Each staccato movement punctuated by the tunes playing. Beat by beat. Hip drop by hip drop. Between the music, the dancing, the atmosphere and the magic of the night with a sky populated by stars—she nearly forgot Oliver was locked up forty minutes away.

The thought of her best friend produced a sharp pang of guilt. She had no business enjoying herself with Joan and Jack, and especially not with Tariq at the table, when Oliver's life was on the line.

"They dance beautifully," Joan said. "The way they drop their shoulders and move their hips makes me wish I was in my twenties again. My forty-year-old body protests if I try to move like that now."

"Your body moves just fine for me," Jack teased.

When Julia peered at the happy couple, she couldn't help but wonder if Jack really had been an art thief in his previous life, and had he given it up for her? Did he give up everything for love? She'd never be able to ask someone to do that for her. Of course, Jack's passion was most likely illegal, so maybe Joan saved him from life in prison or worse.

When she found Finn's eyes again, her heart rate tripled in speed.

"You want to kiss her, don't you?" Joan's question to Finn was almost lost in the music. "We're in the desert, just do it," Joan urged.

"Kiss the girl," Jack said in a singsong voice.

Are we in a movie right now? she was beginning to wonder.

"Yeah, kiss the girl." It was A.J. piping up this time.

They were already turned on their pillows and practically

facing each other instead of the show. Finn was well within kissing range, but . . . should they? Would he?

Finn's brows pulled together as if torn about the decision. He knew he needed to kiss her to keep up the act, especially with Tariq there, but why was a kiss so difficult for him? He'd already touched her intimately but setting his lips to hers seemed to mean more to him.

Maybe she understood it. Kissing, if done right, was almost like a form of art. And she appreciated art and beauty.

Assuming he wasn't going to make the move, she began to turn, but he set a fist beneath her chin, guiding her focus back to him, and she found his mouth waiting for hers when he did.

The kiss was soft at first, hesitant and unsure. They had an audience, after all, and they were in a country that didn't allow PDA.

But they were also situated around a bed of gold and orange sand that somehow felt like a private cocoon.

When his tongue slipped between her parted lips, she lightly moaned against his mouth, unable to stop herself.

The moment had her feeling incredibly exposed. As if she were in front of a camera lens herself for all to see when really, she just wanted to be away from everyone, alone with Finn and exploring where this might go. For tonight she *needed* this. Needed him.

When Finn broke their kiss, the world fell silent as his lips lingered near hers and their eyes remained connected.

He'd felt that, too, hadn't he? Whatever happened between them just now had eclipsed their hot shower scene. And it'd been from a kiss.

"Will you excuse us?" Finn rasped, and without waiting for a response or apparently giving a damn, he stood and offered her his hand. Julia rose and allowed him to take the lead, her heart pounding a frantic rhythm.

A.J. stopped them just outside their tent, exchanged a quick word with Finn she couldn't hear, then headed over to his own tent as Finn quickly pulled her inside and sealed the door shut with their only line of defense. A freaking zipper.

He was breathing hard when he righted himself and faced her, and a hand went through his hair, disheveling the locks. What was he going to say? Do?

Why did her stomach hurt so much at the idea that he'd say this was a mistake? She didn't want to overthink anything. She didn't want to overanalyze for once. She just wanted to live in the moment. The freeze-frame movement she'd mentally captured outside beneath the stars.

"I think I've been right, and there is a storm coming," he said while stalking closer to her with confident strides until she bumped into the bed, not realizing she'd been walking backward. "But I think that storm is you, Jewels."

The way he said Jewels, she knew he meant it like jewelry, not Jules. It was like she was precious to him. Priceless.

But she also knew . . . "I know there are reasons why we can't be together." She started to turn to escape the rejection she felt coming, but he snatched her wrist and spun her into him.

Her palms went to his muscular chest, finding his heart beating almost as erratically and wild as hers. He leaned in and brought his mouth to the shell of her ear, her body shuddering at his proximity. "You've misunderstood, Jewels. I want you. The rain. The thunder. Whatever you bring, I'll take it. And the sunshine after the storm, too." The huskiness and total honesty in his voice had her closing her eyes and nearly crying at his tender words. "I need you tonight."

Her free hand slid up to his shoulder and around to his back so she could draw herself closer to him. "You have me," she confessed, and he groaned at her words, freeing her wrist only to hoist her legs up and around his hips.

Finn turned and walked them to the tent wall, finding a hard surface beneath the sheer white material, thank God. She tightened her thighs and rolled her hips, desperate to feel his body moving against hers. That seemed to be the go-ahead he needed because, in the next instant, he palmed her ass and lowered his mouth to hers in a bruising kiss. He drew her lip between his teeth for a moment and pulled, which did something to her erogenous zones she didn't know was possible. Her body was about to explode with his hard cock pressed into her as he kept her pinned to the wall.

His tongue slid between her lips and danced with hers. The music still pulsed outside, and she'd swear they were matching the rhythm with their kissing the way the dancers had moved their hips to the beat.

"You taste like heaven," he murmured against her mouth between kisses before he untangled her legs from his hips and set her feet to the floor.

And then he dropped to his knees and placed his hands on her waist, the heat of his touch warming her all the way to her core. Not breaking eye contact, he slowly undid the tie at her waist, letting the panel of fabric fall to expose the tie on the other side. But this time, he leaned in and worked the knot free with his teeth, and her dress fell open. Finn placed his lips to the inside of her knee and kissed a trail up her thigh to her center, his facial hair scratching along her skin and heightening the sensation.

"You smell like sex," he gritted out, sliding her barely there lace thong down her legs and helping her step out of it.

"And you're so fucking wet. I could eat you all night and it still wouldn't be enough."

"Yes, please," she cried out, feeling sexier and more turned on than she ever had in her entire life.

The fantasies she'd had about him in the last few weeks wouldn't hold a candle to this man based on his kiss alone.

His tongue slowly skirted her sex like a delicious tease, and she bucked against his mouth, remembering those beautiful full lips of his. Two fingers went inside of her as he lapped at her sex with his tongue. And she'd swear the "*One Night in Dubai*" song she'd heard on the radio the other day played outside.

This was her one night in Dubai. It was far better than any moment captured by a camera. It was a memory she'd hold on to forever.

"Yes," she cried, trying not to be too loud with people outside and a tent on the other side of theirs. "Oh, yes. Finn."

He paused for a moment and said, "Call me Dalton tonight," before kissing her wet center again, playing with her folds with his talented tongue as if he hadn't just asked her to call him by his given name for the very first time.

She didn't want to get into her head and out of this moment to decipher what that meant, so she squeezed her eyes closed and sank into the pleasure that was quickly working its way through her body, making her moan before saying, "Make me come, Dalton." And the moment she said his name was all it took. Her sex pulsed and her legs tightened as she came.

He continued to touch her and pleasure her even past her orgasm before coming out from beneath her dress.

"Do you have protection?" she almost panted out as he stood, still trying to catch her breath. Did that really happen?

He slipped his hand into his pocket and produced a

condom. "Just the one. I wasn't prepared but, um, A.J. carries them for our rifles in the event we ever . . . forget what I said." A sheepish grin cut across his face.

"Condoms and rifles? Kind of hard to forget."

"Snow. They help with snow. Hell, maybe even a sandstorm if, ya know . . ."

"Hm." She began to work his buttons undone, enjoying this man, a master with his tongue, appearing to grow flustered talking about condoms. Or maybe it was bringing up rifles in the bedroom? "I thought I was the storm."

"Right." He hooked his arms behind her back once his shirt was open. "See? So, I'll be needing it." He angled his head. "If you want it, that is?"

"Oh, I do." *So, so much.* "I want you. I need you."

"You need me?" Why did his voice break when he asked that as if surprised by this?

She brought her hands to his face and framed his cheeks between her palms. "I never thought I needed anyone before. But I find myself needing you. Needing this moment with you." She'd define and figure out the "everything" else part she was leaving unsaid after Dubai and their missions were both complete.

"You're full of surprises, Julia Sophia Maddox." Ah, right. He knew her middle name, but he'd never said it until now.

"Call me Jewels," she reminded him, then brought her mouth to his neck and kissed his throat by his ear.

Before she had a chance to do what she wanted to do— feel and taste him—he took back the control. He guided her dress down her arms and scooped her up before positioning her on her back on the bed. His quick movements and alpha behavior in the bedroom were more than appreciated, and her

274

arousal was heating right back up again as if she hadn't had his mouth on her moments ago.

She still had her sandals on, and he knelt at the edge of the bed, which wasn't high off the ground, and carefully removed them. Then he stood and kept his eyes framed on her face as he took off his shirt and finished undressing down to his boxers.

Her lip went between her teeth as she sat up on her elbows to take in the view. Rippling abdominal muscles. A deep V that disappeared beneath his boxers. Strong quads she couldn't help but wonder how they'd feel caging her on the bed as he buried himself inside of her.

The man was vascular. Veins in his arms prominent as he stared at her while slowly moving his hands to the waist of his boxers. And wow, the veins on his . . .

She blinked in surprise at his hard length very much alive after he rid himself of his boxers.

He worked his hand from root to tip a few times before joining her on the bed, and her fingers twitched with the desire to take him into her hand.

He climbed over her, and she felt safe and secure beneath him.

"Bra." He cocked his head, eyes falling to the only article of clothing she still wore. "Off."

His caveman-like orders made her sex even wetter.

She sat up as much as his body hovering over hers would allow, and she only now noticed he'd tossed the condom at some point onto the bed, and it was near her hip bone.

Using her core strength thanks to Pilates, she kept herself at an angle, unhooked her bra, and then fell back down to the mattress.

"Beautiful." He slanted himself over her, shifted down her

body a little, and placed her puckered nipple between his teeth.

"You really are a biter, huh?" she whispered, remembering the love bite of her lip.

"A little pain—"

"Is good with me."

He lifted his eyes from her breast, and that broody, dark look had transformed the green into something beastly. Something so damn hot, too.

One brow cocked as if pleased by her response, then he lowered himself to his forearms, his cock pressing perilously close to her center. He teased one nipple between his fingertips while sucking the other, which had her gripping his back and arching into him.

"I'm going to slip inside you if you keep moving like that," he said darkly.

She wanted that to happen. To feel him in such a raw and primitive way, but she knew that'd be dangerous for so many reasons. One being she wasn't on the pill.

"I want your mouth on mine," she cried a moment later, missing his kiss and the connection she felt with him when his tongue had touched hers. "And I want you inside of me. I-I don't want to wait."

"We only have one condom and one night," he said, his tone deep as he lifted his face closer to hers.

One night? "How's your stamina?"

He grinned, and that brow rose once again as if that were a challenge, one he'd gladly accept. "I guess you'll soon find out."

His lips crashed to hers once more, and she clung to his shoulders as they kissed passionately and for so long that she'd nearly forgotten her need-it-now plans because his kiss truly gave her a connection she'd never known she'd been so desperate for until now.

"You ready for me?" he whispered into her ear as he slid a hand between their bodies, his cock still heavy against her. His hand skated over her seam, drawing her slickness onto his finger. "You're really, really ready."

She swallowed and nodded, unable to get the words loose.

He sat back onto his knees, freed the condom from the wrapper, then rolled it over his rock-hard cock, which glistened in precum.

"I want you on top." He swapped their positions without waiting for her answer.

She shimmied against him without placing him inside of her yet. Her hands went to his abdomen, careful of the bruises on his chest, and she did her best not to let her thoughts drift to ones of worry about his safety. About future bullets and future bad guys he might encounter.

"What if I want you to take me how *you* want?"

He reached for her and twirled a lock of her hair in his hand. "You struggled to get yourself off for months. I think it's important you take the control back." He held her captive with those green eyes, and she understood what he was saying. What he was trying to give her. "I need this for you. Trust me, I'll enjoy it. And there will be another time."

Thank God for that.

"And I promise to—"

"Fuck me hard?" she finished for him, surprised by her dirty words, and his cock jumped in response. Yeah, they were on the same page.

She reached between her legs, positioned his tip at her center, then she slowly sank onto his length inch by inch. Her eyes squeezed tight from the momentary pain of his girth. So thick.

Her eyes peeled open, and there were tears there. She wasn't sure if it was from the shock of his size or the sense of ecstasy at having him inside her.

"You okay?" he rasped as if he were barely hanging on.

"I'm amazing," she whispered before lifting up to slam back down on him. He grabbed hold of her hips as she remained sitting upright, her back arched and breasts on display, which turned her on that he was able to soak in the sight of her while she took control.

She ground against him, and between the friction and being so full of this man, it was seriously going to test her stamina.

"You might get to take over soon because I'm already going to come," she cried a few minutes later, barely able to hang on to a steady breath as she grew sweaty and tense, her body on the verge of orgasm.

"Sweetheart, I'm biting down on my teeth right now to hold back from coming. I'll save the stamina for next time. Just waiting on you." And his jaw really was clenched, his brows drawn tight. Eyes broody as if he was almost in pain.

That look. That pensive, sexy look was what sent her right over the edge.

She did her best not to scream as she rocked her way into orgasm, feeling the warmness inside of her despite the condom as he released.

Totally sated, a bit confused and scared from whatever she was feeling for this man, she collapsed on top of him. Their bodies were sticky from sex and the desert heat, but this moment was as picture-perfect as it got.

And she prayed there really would be another one.

CHAPTER TWENTY-THREE

IT WAS WELL PAST SUNRISE, AND THE TENT-CHALET WAS bathed in the soft, early morning light. Finn slowly shifted to his side and propped his head on his hand to observe Julia as she slept.

His gaze snared on the necklace he'd given her, lying on the small nightstand by the bed, and he wondered why he hadn't noticed she'd taken it off last night.

Because you ravished her body, you idiot. Had the best sex of your life, too.

The sheet slipped from her body when he shifted a little on the bed, revealing her ass to him since she was also on her side, her face the other direction.

He bit down on his back teeth at the sight and resisted the urge to grab hold of her and press his growing erection against her firm body, which was also soft in all of the right places.

"Beautiful," he whispered to himself.

"What is?"

"You're awake," he said in surprise, and she slowly turned to face him, now giving him another view. Two perfect breasts with rosebud nipples he remembered swirling his tongue over last night. *And* in the middle of the night.

She covered her mouth while yawning. "I am. What time is it?"

Her sleepy, morning voice was hot as hell. He was about to respond in military time, sometimes forgetting the rest of the world didn't operate that way. "Eight."

"Breakfast is soon, and then we head back to the villa," Julia said, a note of regret in her voice.

"And to meet with your brother shortly after."

Her face blanched. Had she forgotten that small detail? Her brother had arrived while they were on their "adventure" yesterday, and surely, he'd demand a meeting. They had plenty of time before the party tonight, but facing Michael Maddox wasn't high on his to-do list.

"We should, um, meet him in a public space," Julia suggested. The way she scrunched up her nose was cute as hell and made him smile.

"So he can't clock me?"

Before Julia could answer, the sound of a horse neighing somewhere outside hit Finn like a crack of thunder, propelling him to roll to his back and squeeze his eyes closed.

Why had Jaden appeared on a horse in his dream? The closest to a horse Jaden had come was riding a pony at a neighbor's birthday party when they were kids.

"Where are you? I've lost you." Julia's soft voice coaxed his eyes open, and at the feel of her lacing their hands together on top of his chest, he peeked over at her. Worried blue eyes met his, and his stomach knotted. "The horse?"

"It's not about the horse. It's about my brother." Was he going to do this? Tell her about Jaden? There'd be no coming back from that for him if he did. "I've been off since the night I was shot out in the desert, and not because of the close call," he slowly revealed. He remained on his back, his gaze moving to the ceiling of the tent, which was pitched at the top with a circle of red silk. "We expected to find weapons, but instead, we found coffins full of pills." He tensed at what he was about to share next. "Captagon, to be exact."

Her hand went lax in his. "Like the kind they found in Oliver's place? Why didn't you tell me?"

"I wanted to." *No, that's a lie. You didn't want to talk about the damn pills.* "But it's um, classified," he added a moment later, hoping she hadn't noticed his thoughts had derailed.

"And it's still classified, so why are you telling me now?"

He rolled his head to the side to peer at her again. "Because I care about you, and yes, I am . . . who you think I am." This was *also* not something he'd expected to share. He was violating his oath to the job. To the President. But the woman was intelligent, and hadn't she called him on it already? Why fight telling her the truth? *Because telling her changes everything. Shit.*

Revealing everything to Julia was the same as declaring that diamond ring on her finger the real thing. None of the guys on the teams had told anyone about their real work without winding up in a together-forever situation afterward. And by revealing the truth to Julia, was he hoping that'd keep her in his life until he punched out in the time card of life?

"So, you're, um, still active duty?" she whispered as if processing those words like she was walking across broken glass to get to him on the other side of the room, and she was worried she might bleed out before making it.

Why did her reaction hurt so much?

Fuck.

"I am." The two words pinged around in his head a few

times as he waited for her to say something. As he waited for her to declare last night was a mistake.

"I'm not surprised, but I'm—"

"Disappointed?" He swallowed.

Her mouth softened into an O-shape as if prepping herself to say the right thing. "Not disappointed in you. Not at all."

The art of the dodge.

Her eyes fell closed for one moment before a pair of stunning blue irises met his gaze. "Tell me about your brother. And the dream."

Ah, on to part two of the reveals that'd probably wind up with him getting his heart broken, but he'd already taken the plunge from the cliff and was free-falling. At this point, he had no idea if she was interested in being his parachute to save him from hitting the ground. He could only hope.

"Jaden was riding the horse in my sandstorm dream, and he was about to shoot me. But my brother has been dead for over twenty years. He died in 2000. A drug overdose. A combination of pills."

He gave her a moment to process his reality. More doses of truth.

"I think he was always a little depressed, taking after my mother. She managed anxiety and depression her whole life. Not long after we moved to LA, I caught him sneaking some of her pills." He sucked in a deep breath, trying to steady his pulse and get through this, then freed the air from his lungs and looked at Julia, finding tears remaining captive in her blue eyes.

Tucker died due to alcohol abuse.

Jaden died from drug abuse.

They'd both lost people they cared about, and Finn knew she understood his pain. His struggles. His guilt. Not that she should have felt guilty about Tucker, but he also knew he'd never be able to talk her out of that guilt since no one had talked him out of his.

"Jaden made me promise not to tell anyone. He said it was a one-time thing. But there were more times after that. More promises to remain quiet." He kept his voice steady as best he could. "The stress from the music industry got to him. The pressure. The popularity that came with it. He couldn't handle it. I-I should have done something. Told someone."

Julia applied more pressure to their linked hands in support.

"Before you remind me I was only a teenager, well, I know . . . but a broken promise to my older brother who I'd idolized would've—"

"I understand," she whispered. "I get it."

Why did that feel so much better to hear than an *It's not your fault?*

"After he died, I broke down and told my parents I knew about his problem. Even the night before, um . . ." He went stiff at the memory. "My mom blamed me. She said she couldn't look at me again," he confessed, his voice hoarse, and were there tears in his own eyes?

"You don't think your parents knew? His manager or agent? You really think you were the only one?"

Finn closed his eyes and felt a touch of warmth on his cheek. Shit, he was crying. "They said they had no idea."

"If he was taking pills from her bottle . . ." Julia let her words trail off, allowing him to draw his own conclusions. "I think it was easier for her to blame you instead of herself," she added softly.

Finn had never considered his mom had known. The way she'd treated him the last twenty-plus years, placing all of the blame on his shoulders—she wouldn't do that if she'd had a clue her son had abused pills, right? A mom wouldn't do that.

"I'm so sorry you lost him," Julia whispered, and when he opened his eyes, his gaze was obstructed by more tears threatening to fall.

"I—"

"Guys, you awake?" A.J. called from outside.

Shit timing or perfect, Finn wasn't so sure. He sat up and swiped the backs of his hands over his cheeks. "We're up."

"Are you decent, though?" Finn heard the smile in A.J.'s tone, and he looked over for a last glimpse of Julia's naked body before she covered herself with the sheet.

Why hide the fact they'd slept together from A.J.? He was the one who'd saved him with a just-in-case condom last night.

Finn drew the blanket over his naked body as well. "Come on in." He watched as the zipper moved to part the "door" so A.J. could enter.

A.J.'s cheeks were a touch red, and Finn doubted it was from the desert heat. He remained just inside the tent and crossed his arms. "Tariq slipped away last night. I followed him. No cell service here, so it looks like Tariq kept on the move until he got a signal. Not sure who he was calling, but after that, he returned to the campsite. I called Asher while I was there, and he had eyes on both of us from his position as well."

"And?" Finn prompted.

"Jessica got word two law enforcement facilities, which happened to house major seizures of Captagon pills, were simultaneously hit last night. One location in Turkey, and the other Italy."

Finn's spine straightened at the news, and Julia sat upright. He noticed her clinging to the sheet out of his peripheral view.

"A hell of a lot more Captagon at those two sites than, um . . ."

"She knows about the mummy coffins," Finn told him, knowing the truth would soon come out that he'd revealed that intel to Julia anyway. "What the hell is Tariq going to do with all of those pills?"

"And we're still assuming Tariq is responsible?" Julia asked, and A.J. turned his focus her way.

"The timing of Tariq's call matches up as if he knew at around zero two hundred that something big was going down, and he needed to verify it was mission success," A.J. said. "CIA intercepted the intel in real time when the facilities were hit. A clean in-and-out job with no witnesses left behind. Surveillance cams went offline at both places in Turkey and Italy around zero two hundred as well."

Finn felt Julia reach for his hand beneath the blanket with her free one, and he welcomed her touch. His heart rate was out of control.

"I don't know what this fucker has planned," A.J. began in a grim tone, "but Tariq now has enough pills to make it rain."

CHAPTER TWENTY-FOUR

THE BURJ AL ARAB LUXURY HOTEL, FAMOUSLY SHAPED LIKE a sailboat, served as the background on the silky beach as Finn and Julia waited in their swimwear for Michael to show up that afternoon at the hotel where he'd chosen to stay.

Julia had on a sexy but simple black bikini and seeing her in that had managed to ease his thoughts about the heavy conversation he'd hit her with that morning before A.J. had dropped the hammer on him about the stolen Captagon.

But if Tariq needed more pills in a pinch, it made sense he'd hit the two sites where the largest drug seizures had occurred in recent years. The team needed answers as to what he was planning, and Jessica and Harper were working round the clock to try and get them.

Tariq may have still been off-limits. Same with Kaira. But they'd be cornering the Americans tonight and pumping them for intel. *Hopefully.*

As he and Julia waited inside a private cabana on the beach for her brother to arrive, Finn checked out her legs, golden and oiled up with tanning lotion, before drawing his focus higher. Memories of their time together making love filled his mind when he should've been thinking about the mission. Those long legs had straddled him while she rode him and he pumped inside of her. He was growing hard thinking about it now, so he stealthily adjusted himself. He didn't need a raging hard-on when Michael showed up, or he'd be getting more than just decked in the face.

He also preferred to focus on the physical moments they'd shared rather than the emotional ones because he had no clue if Julia was ready, or willing, to take any next steps, whatever they might be with him, given what he'd told her.

She'd made it clear that she wasn't disappointed *in him* but hadn't mentioned a word one way or the other when he confessed that he still served in the military. What did that mean? Why was his gut warning him he was screwed on so many levels?

"I'm beginning to hate one of my favorite movie series." Julia brought her fruity mocktail to her mouth and sucked through the pink straw.

"Why?" He sort of knew, but he was curious where she was going with this.

"Sounds like Tariq is making an army of the dead. You know, turning soldiers into a zombie-like state for whatever hellish reason." Harper had explained the effects of Captagon to Julia back in Egypt when he'd been unable to get himself to talk about the drug. "Reminds me of Anubis and his army of the dead from one of the movies. And . . ." She lowered her drink a moment later and closed her eyes. "The woman in Aswan, what if she was right, but her message was lost in translation?"

"What?" He thought back to the moment when Julia had purchased the Osiris statue, which felt like forever ago.

"What if her warning was about Tariq? He's Osiris in this scenario. Guardian of the dead, or well, undead soldiers." She revealed her eyes a moment later and set her drink on the little table between them.

Why couldn't they just be on a beach relaxing and enjoying each other's company? Why did they have to be stuck in such a shit reality where the world kept sucking at every turn because of bad guys? Why did she have to be so afraid to date men who served in the military? *Why didn't I tell someone about Jaden? Why'd I leave him alone that night at the party?*

"You're not going to die, so that woman's words are meaningless to me." And that was as much solace as he could offer, as much truth as he was able to deliver at that moment.

"I wasn't honest with you at the time I bought that statue. So, I'm not worried about *that* part of her message, now that you know everything and I have you on my side."

"I definitely won't let that happen." He reached for her hand and linked their palms, and as he held her eyes, his stomach wrenched at the idea of losing her after the op was completed. Would they forever only have Dubai?

"Ahem."

Finn immediately released Julia's hand at the sound of a throat clear. Of course, her brother had to show up now.

"We're pretending to be married," Julia explained, obviously feeling the need to justify the hand holding to her brother. She stood and Michael hugged her before turning his attention to his main target.

"Hi." Finn rose from the daybed, but he wasn't sure if he was supposed to offer his hand or turn his cheek for the punch he most likely deserved. "I'm sorry," he offered, which felt weak and not all that heartfelt.

"Don't be angry." Julia quickly stepped in front of Finn, as she'd promised to do on the flight from Aswan to Dubai. She stood facing her brother, but Michael still had a clear view of Finn since he was much taller than her. "I would have come for Oliver no matter what."

"I know." Michael stepped away from Julia and stared down Finn. "Thank you for rescuing her when she was abducted."

Finn wasn't expecting a thank-you, especially since he was still beating himself up for almost losing Julia because of his two-second delay. "I'm sorry it happened in the first place."

Julia turned to the side and glanced back and forth between the two of them, a look of relief on her face since it appeared her brother wasn't planning to punch Finn.

Michael was in a white tee and green swim trunks, but with his tight jawline and eyes unhidden by shades, he looked more like a Marine on a mission than a relaxed beachgoer.

"Now that you've seen me, verified I'm alive and in good hands, I say you head back home where you belong. You just moved and Kate needs you," Julia said with a soft plea, and although Finn only had her profile, he sensed that when she fully faced her brother, she was pulling out some puppy dog eyes for extra impact.

"I'm not leaving you in the middle of some storm."

Storm. Why did that word keep coming up?

"You're going to help us get Oliver out of prison, then?"

Michael folded his arms, his biceps popping under the sleeves of the white tee. "I've been trying to do that for months."

Julia set a hand on her brother's chest. "Legally, and I'm worried you're starting to believe he's guilty."

"Not anymore, not after Wyatt filled me in at his hotel on what you all have discovered." He paused. "I'm sorry for doubting you. But I'm still . . . just in shock you did all of this."

"How could I not? Oliver is like a brother. You think I wouldn't move mountains for you if you were in trouble?"

Would she move mountains to be with me?

Michael's shoulders fell. "Of course, but you should have told me what you were up to. Mya's a journalist, not CIA. Thank God she had the sense to fake the death threats. You would have gone to Egypt alone, and those men who threw you in the trunk would have . . ." Michael let go of his words, and Finn didn't blame him.

How did one finish that line of thought when it ended with Julia being trafficked for sex or killed?

"We have this handled," she went on, ignoring Michael's concerns. "Go home to your wife and kids."

"Julia, please," Michael said, and he was the one with a plea in his voice now. "You'll get in the way or get killed. These guys have it handled. I want you to come home with me until this is over. You'll stay with us. And Mom and Dad pulled the house in the Outer Banks from the market if you want it. You can go there."

And work in the darkroom again? Maybe it'd bring about a rebirth of sorts, like the blue water lily on the pendant he'd bought her, and she could start over. *Hell, can I do that?*

Finn didn't want to see Julia leave, but her brother was right. It was the safest option. They already had the invite to the party, so he could go alone. Or worst case, his people would break into Joan and Jack's villa after the party to question them.

"I'm not leaving until Tariq has been taken down and Oliver is out of jail. They go hand in hand from the looks of it." Julia folded her arms, standing up to her brother, and Finn stepped alongside her.

"Julia, you know my team can handle this." *You know who I really am.* "Maybe you should listen to Michael."

Relief filled Michael's blue eyes, but when Julia turned to set her attention on Finn—there was that feisty, angry woman he'd encountered back in New York. Tornado Julia was upon him, and she was about to leave some major damage in her wake if he sided with her brother. But her safety was more important.

"I'm not leaving, and if you think for one minute I'd turn my back and walk away, then you don't know me at all."

Was that directed to me or Michael? Probably both of us.

Julia maneuvered around her brother's firm statue-like stance and started toward the water gently lapping onto the sand.

Finn held his hand up to urge Michael to give her a minute to cool off. He kept his eyes locked on to her as she stepped into the water. He wouldn't let her get taken a second time, that was for damn sure.

"She's stubborn," Michael hissed. "Like me."

That almost made Finn laugh. He pocketed his hands and moved out from under the cabana to maintain his line of sight on the woman who drove him nuts. "If you give up on something you believe in, did you ever believe in it in the first place, then?" He cast a quick look at Michael to see him frowning.

"I can't stay here. The President doesn't want me mixed up in what's going on. He thinks I poked around enough with the case, and he doesn't want my presence here raising any red flags." Michael was also responsible for designing many of the U.S. government's intelligence software programs and still assisted with the technological application from time to time, and the last thing POTUS would want is for a man like him to make the news.

Finn returned his focus to Julia, who was now waist-deep in the ocean. There weren't sharks here, right? He hated freaking sharks just about as much as A.J. did. "I won't let anything happen to her. You have my word. It's not like we're going to take her with us when we take down Tariq's operation." *If we get the green light to do that. God, what if we don't because of the prick's royal connections?*

Michael's chest lifted and fell from a deep breath. It was clear he didn't want to give up control, and this was killing him. But Finn had a feeling Michael knew he didn't have a choice. Julia was Julia. "You know I'll go to hell and back to unleash on anyone who hurts my sister, right?"

Hell.

The Underworld.

Army of the dead.

Mummy coffins and curses.

It was all so strange.

Finn nodded. "I'd expect nothing less of her brother," he finally said. "Now, I'm going to go get her out of the water before she goes in too deep." He started to walk past him, but Michael grabbed his arm, and Finn cut his focus back his way.

"She likes you."

Finn's brows snapped together at his unexpected words.

"So don't die," he rasped. "She can't handle more heartbreak."

Shit, man, neither can I.

CHAPTER TWENTY-FIVE

LATER THAT EVENING, IN THEIR BEDROOM AT THE VILLA, Julia jumped when Finn rapped on the bathroom door and called out, "How long are you going to be mad at me?"

She set her palms on the vanity counter and lifted her eyes to her reflection. "I don't know." *Am I really mad? Or still reeling from . . . everything.*

Why couldn't she actually be Wonder Woman and not a girl in a costume pretending? Her gaze cut over her outfit as she pushed off the counter to stand.

"That's not reassuring," he answered. "How about we say you stopped five minutes ago. Like we retroactive this situation."

She tried not to laugh at whatever he was trying to say to break through the tension with humor.

"Wonder Woman wouldn't stay mad."

"No?" she said while smoothing her hands over the red bodice lined with fake gold armor that molded to her body. "Would she get even?"

"Only if someone hurt her loved ones." He paused. "Like

295

Oliver. I know. Shit, I'm sorry I suggested you leave, but I'm only trying to protect you."

She absorbed his words and opened the door, curious as to how he'd react when he saw her in the costume. "Wonder Woman is stronger than you, Indiana Jones," she said once he had her in his sights. "So, maybe I need to save you."

Finn had one hand braced on the frame of the bathroom door, blocking her exit. He silently lowered his eyes from her face to her feet. His attention lingered a bit longer on the short blue skirt attached to the red top with a gold belt at the center. Her armband matched the belt, but there'd been no boots at the store, so she'd need to slip on some gold heels to match the look.

She had to admit, she did look smoking hot. She'd done her makeup and hair more Gal Gadot style than circa the '80s.

"Of course, since I assume Scott and Scott is basically your version of Clark Kent's glasses, you're a hero, too." Her sexy, gorgeous hero.

Finn pushed away from the doorframe, removed his fedora to run his fingers through his dark locks for a brief moment, and eyed her intently. She wasn't sure if he was buying himself time to ponder life's greatest mysteries or contemplating ripping the costume off her with his bare hands.

He also looked every bit Indiana Jones in his khakis, brown fedora, and leather jacket opened to reveal a black tee. The plastic coiled rope at his hip and satchel strung over his shoulder were most likely the parts of the costume he wanted to object to.

"You were pretty quick to agree to let Michael take me away," she said, finding her way back to the original question as to why she'd been giving him the silent treatment since the beach that afternoon. "It hurt." And that wasn't easy for her to admit.

Finn's eyes fixed on hers as he set his hat back in place.

"Will you always let me go that fast?" *Shit, why did I ask that? Because I'm scared.* Would there be a tomorrow or a next day with him after Oliver was free and Tariq was in prison?

When the muscle in Finn's jaw tightened, and he turned away from her, it wasn't the response she'd expected. Why did a cold bluster of air suddenly cover her body in chills?

"It'll be you that drops me," Finn said, his tone low and startlingly deep. "You'll be the one who walks away. You don't need to worry about it being me."

Oh. How could I be so stupid? He was scared, too. They were two grown adults who'd had their fair share of trauma and pain, and now they were terrified of encountering more.

His mother had struggled after Jaden died, and unfortunately, Finn paid the price. Julia knew that was why Finn had just responded the way he did. "Do your teammates know?"

"Know what?" he asked a bit gruffly, his mood sliding to a darker place, the place she'd been in that afternoon when she'd felt like Finn had so quickly cast her aside at her brother's request.

"About your brother. And your parents . . ."

"Of course they know Jaden died of an overdose," he whispered back, still not facing her. "And that my parents are divorced."

When she lowered her gaze, she found his hands now set on his hips, gaze still pointed out the window that overlooked lush polo lawns. "But only Roman knows about my guilt and how it's affected me. Until you."

His words were soft and yet boomed loudly in her head.

Only Roman? And now me? He'd probably violated some major oath to the President that morning by confessing she was right about his occupation, and now this. *This, this, this.* It was a big deal to him to share, wasn't it? Bigger than his job.

"Finn, I—" She stopped herself at the sound of someone yelling downstairs.

"Abso-fucking-lutely not."

Finn grimaced. "That's Asher."

"I can tell." Julia turned toward the closed door.

"We should go see what's going on." Finn apparently saw this as his opportunity to escape and rushed past her, but she managed to grab hold of the sleeve of his leather jacket.

"Dalton." She felt like this moment required his real name. "Can we talk later?"

He looked back, a dark brow arched, and asked, "I don't know, Julia. Will there be a later?"

He was prepping himself for what he believed would soon be her rejection, wasn't he? *I told him I wouldn't date anyone on active duty, damn it. Why did I say that? But hell, can I?*

She let him leave the room without another word, knowing in her heart that she was well past the development stage in regard to her feelings for Finn. She was fully immersed. Swimming in emotions.

Julia quickly slipped on the heels sitting at the edge of the bed where she'd left them and went downstairs to see why Asher was so pissed.

She arrived in time to witness Asher in his costume slashing both arms through the air in the shape of an X.

Harper had picked out his and Jessica's coordinating outfits from *The Princess Bride* movie, another classic. He had on all black, including boots, a fake sword at his hip, but he didn't have the face mask on yet. Jessica was dressed in a

298

red princess dress with her hair in a side braid and a little gold crown at the top of her head. A.J. and Finn had hoped for something more ridiculous for Asher to wear, but the guy looked fairly cool and also intimidating in the costume.

A.J., on the other hand, looked hilarious in his Marty McFly from *Back to the Future* outfit. Jeans, high-top sneakers, a plaid shirt and a red puffy vest on top. Roman had insisted on the costume while they'd been at the mall on Thursday.

Wow, it was Saturday night already? *At least I remember what day it is now. Also, what is Asher saying?* He'd been talking and she'd started to zone out with Finn's green gaze cutting straight across the room her way, almost as if he were angry at himself for being so damn angry. He let out an audible huff of breath and turned toward the doors leading out to the private pool none of them had used yet.

"Let's not argue about this." Jessica held a hand in front of her husband.

"No way in hell is my wife seducing a terrorist. Or any man for that matter," Asher seethed, and Roman slapped a hand on his shoulder after striding up behind him as if trying to calm down a wild animal.

"We need Tariq away from Kaira. We need a diversion. And the man has been glued to his sister's hip, and she's glued to the Americans. So—"

"No," Asher cut off Roman and spun to face him, which had Roman releasing his hold and raising his hands in surrender.

Roman stole a look at Jessica that said *I tried.*

"He likes blondes. He's always with a blonde," Jessica reminded her husband.

"Yeah, well, you're my blonde. So, no. New idea." Asher folded his arms and stood firm.

"The plan is still to try and lure the Americans back here, right?" Julia asked, hoping to diffuse some tension in the room. "To say I have photos of the Warhol on my computer that I left at the villa, and then hope our *Romancing the Stone* couple will want to take a look for themselves prior to the auction, which is later tonight."

It was a plan on the fly, and she had a feeling they didn't usually do "on the fly" in the military, but maybe they were in uncharted territory, especially with Julia along for the ride.

Harper left the desk where she'd been sitting and joined the center of the room where Asher had started pacing. Finn was still looking out the window, and she wished she knew what was going on in his head. *Maybe I do know.* "Yes, and we'd love for you to get Kaira to join them."

"Since you aren't supposed to talk to her, I'm your loophole." Julia smiled, and Harper tipped her head as if to say, *exactly*.

"But we need to distract Tariq for it to work. To get them away from that man," Jessica noted, and A.J. shot her a sideways look like he was worried for all of their sakes that Asher might unleash on Tariq if the man so much as touched his wife. Then the plan would be blown.

They had a backup plan, according to Harper, if the Warhol thing didn't happen, but the backup also required a Tariq diversion, so, from the looks of it, they needed to get Asher on board.

"Well, I'm not blonde, and I found out the other day that I'm pregnant, so I can't do it." Harper's abrupt declaration had the room shifting to face her in surprise. "Elaina said we'd be having a girl, remember?" Her hand went to her abdomen.

Elaina? Ah. Liam and Emily's daughter. *Hadn't someone said she was prophetic?* And shit, that reminded her of the

Osiris statue and that woman on the dock. She didn't want to think about bad omens or curses or whatnot now, though.

"That explains a lot." A.J. walked over to Harper and pulled her in for a hug. "Well, hell, you, Ana, and Natasha will all have babies around the same age. This is great."

The tension seemed to deflate in the room as everyone congratulated Harper and Roman, and Julia waited her turn to do so.

"Wonder Woman can't do it because we need her to bring the others to the villa," Harper said a few minutes post-congratulations to redirect the conversation to the pressing matter. "So it has to be Jessica. Unless you think he'd be more into Marty over here," Harper teased, tossing a thumb toward A.J., and he grumbled.

"Not drawing the short stick on this one or playing rock-paper-scissors." A.J. showed both his palms to the room. "I'm not seducing Tariq."

Asher turned from the room. "Seducing."

Annnnd we're back to square one. Thank you, A.J.

"Won't he wonder why my wife is hitting on him while I'm there?" Asher asked, and at least maybe he was considering the idea.

"Might make her more appealing. Some men like to conquer another—"

Asher spun around at A.J.'s words, which had A.J. immediately letting go of his comment.

"Good job," Jessica whispered sarcastically and then went to her husband and grabbed him by the arm. "Give me a minute." She urged Asher to head to their bedroom, and once the door was shut, Harper dropped onto the couch as if she were exhausted.

"That should go well." Roman elbowed A.J. when he walked past him to sit next to Harper.

"Swimmingly," A.J. joked.

Finn was laser-focused on the pool once again, appearing to want to look anywhere but toward Julia. "Something has been bothering me," he said in a low voice. "If we really think Ario is dead, and he's dead because Tariq wanted him dead, then why go after Giorgio? And the time gap between Ario's death and Tariq coming out of the woodwork looking for Giorgio is still a question mark. Five months is a long time."

"What are you thinking?" Roman asked him.

Finn finally gave his attention to the room and said, "Tariq was after someone else on Giorgio's client list, wasn't he? He was looking for another name."

Harper nodded, and Julia took a step closer to where she sat.

"If Tariq had a hand in Ario's death, then he had no reason to question Giorgio," Harper began, seemingly aligned with Finn's concerns. "But Giorgio would still have a reason to avoid Tariq. He may have been worried Tariq, being Ario's brother-in-law, was pissed that Giorgio was in on the plan to fake Ario's death. Perhaps Tariq had tried to reach out to the doctor before, and when he was shot down, he arranged the meeting in Egypt as someone else."

"So, he needed Giorgio, but Giorgio didn't know why." Finn stroked his jaw and looked down at the floor. "Drugs," he said in a low, solemn tone. "We need to find someone on Giorgio's list who's connected to drugs of any kind."

"Like an old cartel leader who may have gone into hiding?" Roman pitched.

"Tariq has his hands on a lot of drugs now." It couldn't be easy for Finn to talk about drugs given his brother's history, but he continued, "What if he isn't trying to build an army of terrorists. What if he's trying to monopolize the region's drug trade?"

"So why reinvent the wheel," Roman began, rising to his feet as if the idea was a damn good one, "if there's someone out there who already knows all the best drug trafficking routes?"

Julia pinned her arms over her chest when chills chased down her spine. She wanted to go to Finn, to hug him and comfort him. She now knew how hard this was on him. But more importantly, this time she could see the signs that he was hurting. And unlike with Tucker, she felt them in her bones.

"Make it rain," A.J. whispered. "Tariq wants to pull a Noah's Ark–type move, but instead of water, he wants to flood the world with pills."

Roman faced A.J. "But why?"

Finn's focus moved straight to Roman. "You don't need terrorists to destroy your enemy when drugs can do it for you."

CHAPTER TWENTY-SIX

"You look stunning, by the way. Not sure if I told you that, Wonder Woman." Finn's husky voice, and him playfully calling her Wonder Woman as he held her in his arms on the dance floor, had Julia nearly collapsing against him with relief that he didn't appear angry anymore.

They'd arrived at the costume party thirty minutes ago, and this was the first time he'd spoken to her. She lifted her eyes and flicked the wide brim of his fedora with her finger to better see his eyes. "I'm sorry," she whispered, her shoulders sagging under the weight of his brilliant green gaze. Shakespeare had certainly gotten it right when he'd said the eyes are the window to the soul because Finn's were overflowing with emotion. "I don't want you mad at me." Julia dropped her eyes to his chest and drew her body closer to his. "I had no right to be upset with you on the beach, especially after everything you've done for me. It was a knee-jerk reaction to you wanting to send me away. I'm sorry."

Finn went stock-still at her words, and the lyrics to the '80s song currently floating through the room, *Nothing's Going to Stop Us Now*, struck her full force.

He brought his forehead to hers, as if exhausted or troubled, maybe both. She didn't blame him after the day he'd had.

His mission had become about the very enemy that had stolen his brother from him. Pills. And the guilt that he was to blame for Jaden's death was most likely bubbling back up inside of him.

"I'm mad at myself, not you." He placed his warm palm on her back and slowly slid it up beneath her mass of hair to cup the nape of her neck. Leaning back to find her eyes, he admitted, "I'm scared I'm going to lose you, so I guess I tried to push you away before it happens."

She blinked in surprise at his confession.

When was the last time someone was so straightforward and honest with her, so real?

"I can understand that." But could she tell him with certainty that she wouldn't leave him? Did she trust herself not to run when she was swimming in a sea of fear, terrified she'd lose him each time he was off fighting bad guys? How would she be able to survive that?

He didn't need to know about the war of indecision waging in her head. The push and pull of emotions that had been yanking her all over the place since the moment their bodies had connected inside that tent.

She knew in her heart that she wanted Finn, but she'd been running for so long, and old habits were hard to break, as he knew. Before she made a commitment to him, she needed to get her head on straight, or they'd both suffer the consequences.

"Tango One and Two are here now." The voice in her ear reminded her of the fancy wireless comm Harper had provided her before the party. Fortunately, Finn's teammates would only hear them if she tapped the comm to unmute it.

I didn't accidentally tap it, did I?

Finn stepped back and released her, then discreetly touched his ear. "This is Five. I see them."

Earlier, Julia had learned that his call sign was Echo Five and gotten a rundown of the call signs for each team member who'd be in her ear tonight.

Finn kept his attention on Kaira and Tariq as they made their way to the hosts, Joan and Jack.

Tariq wasn't dressed up, of course. He was wearing jeans and a solid black tee, and his black hair was gelled and a little spiky.

Kaira's costume was a simple pink dress and heels, which could have been from any one of the many '80s dance-themed movies. *Dirty Dancing* or *Footloose*, maybe?

Tariq kept hold of Kaira's arm as they made their way through the room, but tonight he seemed to be the protective brother, unlike the other times Julia had witnessed him with his sister when he'd given off an angry vibe that made her concerned for Kaira's safety. His eyes kept darting around the room as if searching for possible threats. What was that all about? Did he suspect someone knew the truth about him? And why didn't a woman like Kaira have a bodyguard in the first place? For that matter, why didn't Tariq have one? Unless they did but felt they weren't needed at the resort?

Julia looked around for Jessica and Asher, and despite being in a large event room surrounded by men and women in costumes, they stuck out. Well, Asher did.

A.J. was stationed at the bar to keep tabs on the hosts. And with Tariq now joining the party, Jessica was supposed to stop dancing with her husband and do her best to garner Tariq's attention. But would he let his sister out of his sights, even for a gorgeous woman? The way he held on to his sister had Julia growing worried their plan *and* their backup plan might fail.

It was all hands on deck, though. Wyatt and the others not at the party were still working on putting the puzzle pieces together and tracking leads behind the scenes, so she hoped by the end of the night, they found some answers and a resolution. A way to stop Tariq and free Oliver before it was too late.

"One and Two are sitting at their assigned table," A.J. announced over comms as Tariq pulled out the chair for Kaira. "Wait, he's leaving her and heading to the bar."

"I'll move his way now, then," Jessica responded.

Julia held her breath as she watched Jessica pull away from Asher and cut across the crowded dance floor, maneuvering between the framed movie posters that were fixed around the room.

The band was off to the side of the event space on a raised platform, which would also double as the auction stage when the fundraising part of the evening began. The auction wouldn't happen until later, not that they'd still be there for it, but auctions always reminded her of how her brother met his wife. She still felt bad about sending Michael off the way she had, but there were Navy SEALs and former CIA officers working the case, and Michael belonged back home with his family.

"I hate this," Asher hissed in a low voice over his comm. Julia detected a note of bitterness in his tone, and she was still a bit surprised he'd finally agreed to the plan.

"Targets Three and Four are talking to someone now," A.J. said, moving away from the bar when Jessica approached, making room to allow her to try and chat with Tariq. "Almost time to move in."

Targets Three and Four were Joan and Jack, who'd

dressed as the couple from *Top Gun*, another one of Julia's favorite films. But what woman born in the '80s didn't love that movie? Or *Dirty Dancing* for that matter? How many times had she written she loved Tom Cruise and Patrick Swayze in her diary as a kid?

Julia blinked back to reality and focused on Finn, who had his gaze riveted toward targets Three and Four.

"Ah, another Indiana Jones," Julia said softly at the sight of a man dressed similarly to Finn except with a button-down shirt beneath his jacket instead of a black tee. He was talking to Joan and Jack, nodding at whatever they were saying, but his eyes were set on Kaira.

"Guys, we, uh, may need to change our plans," Finn said, and Julia turned to find him staring straight at the other Indiana, who was now laser-focused on Finn.

Did they know each other?

"I see him, too," A.J. responded in a low voice. "What the hell is he doing here, and why is he talking to them?"

Julia turned into Finn and tugged at his shirt. "Mind telling me what's going on?"

Finn lowered his gaze to Julia. "I-I need to talk to him," he said instead, which was unsettling. Whoever the other Indiana was, his sudden appearance had clearly shaken Finn. But Finn wanted to talk to him, which meant . . . was this guy on their side? Team Good Guys?

Julia watched Finn walk away, debating on whether or not she ought to go with him for the sake of appearances. Before she had a chance to move, she spied A.J. heading her way. Maybe he'd have answers.

It appeared that Jessica had managed to strike up a conversation with Tariq, and when Julia searched out Asher, she couldn't find him. Knowing him, he wouldn't simply leave the room with his wife talking to a man like Tariq, though.

"Who is Finn talking to? What if he gives away our identities in front of Joan and Jack?" she whispered when A.J. was at her side.

"He won't." A.J. stroked his beard, and he peered around the room before putting his attention on Julia.

"How can you be so sure?" she asked, as Finn started their way with not just the other Indiana at his side but Joan and Jack, too.

"What's going on?" Julia asked A.J. in a low voice, more insistent this time. But before he could answer, the band kicked off a new song that had Finn stopping in his tracks.

Bryan Adams.

The songs by that particular musician were Finn's kryptonite, it would seem. A reminder of Jaden and the pain Finn still carried because of his death.

She wanted to wrap her arms around him and ease that pain. But they were on a mission, and when Finn found her face, he seemed to pull himself out of whatever spell he'd fallen under.

A.J. gently reached for Julia's elbow and brought his mouth to her ear. "*That* Indiana is Carter Dominick. Former CIA officer who went rogue. Both a pain in the ass as well as a badass."

Rogue CIA? "Why would he be with Joan and Jack?"

A.J. let go of Julia when this badass Carter arrived alongside Finn. "I guess we're about to find out," he huffed under his breath.

* * *

"THIS WAS NOT THE PLAN," JULIA HISSED AS SHE AND FINN

stepped out of the golf cart outside their villa. "Are we sure everything will be okay? And you're positive we can trust this Carter guy?"

"Yes, we've worked together before. Well, he sort of kidnapped Chris and Rory, and Harper and Roman . . ." Finn shook his head as if deciding that information was irrelevant. "He says he's here to help Kaira at Joan and Jack's request."

"Help her?" Julia peered over at the other golf cart as it rolled to a stop.

Apparently, Joan and Jack had enough pull that they all were permitted to leave their drivers behind and operate the carts themselves for a quick trip to the villas. Carter, Kaira, Joan, and Jack had driven in on one. A.J. drove Julia and Finn on the other. Asher and Jessica had remained back at the event, hopefully still distracting Tariq from the fact his sister had disappeared. Since they hadn't heard anything to suggest otherwise over their comms, Julia had to assume they were still safe.

But Carter was a curveball.

"I knew there was something about you," Kaira said when she caught Julia's eyes after stepping free from her ride. "And we can trust them?" She directed her focus to Joan and Jack, who then turned to Carter for an answer.

"One hundred percent," Carter announced with a firm nod, removing his hat, as Finn had done the moment they left the party. "Let's talk inside. Harper and Roman here?"

The ones you kidnapped? Yeah, she needed to know that story.

"Yeah, they're expecting us," A.J. spoke up before Finn had a chance.

Joan took a moment to scrutinize Julia and Finn, as if seeing them for the first time, before making the final decision they could be trusted, then nodded and agreed to go into the villa.

Harper and Roman stood from the couch at the sight of everyone entering, and Julia remembered Chris was positioned somewhere at the resort as backup for Asher and Jessica if they needed help with Tariq tonight.

"Carter." Harper moved across the room and hugged the man that'd . . . um, kidnapped her? Julia was still struggling to wrap her head around that one.

But when Roman gave Carter a quick one-armed manly slap on the back instead of decking him, Julia relaxed a bit. Roman was every bit alpha and growly when it came to the woman he loved, so if he was okay with this rogue CIA guy, Julia would calm down about this unexpected turn of events.

Either way, the first step of the plan had been successful —get Kaira, Joan, and Jack free of Tariq and to the villa to question them. *Maybe this is better.* Finally, a pinprick of light shining through the darkness that'd been following them around.

"Who are you all?" Joan asked, looking a little gobsmacked.

Jack, on the other hand, didn't seem all that suspicious or curious. He appeared to be looking around as if more interested in that Warhol self-portrait Julia had promised him. *Once an art thief, always an art thief?* Of course, they still had to verify that theory.

"You just need to know we're friends of Carter's, and we're trying to get to the bottom of a few things. I'm hoping our interests are aligned," Finn took point on the conversation, and he motioned for Kaira and Joan to have a seat.

"If you're here, and I'm here, I'm guessing we're both after Amin." Carter tossed the hat he'd been holding, then positioned his back to one of the white pillars in the living room and folded his arms.

"Amin? Kaira's brother?" Harper asked in a surprised tone. "Tariq's twin."

"Wait, I thought . . ." Julia let her words float and drift free from her mouth without finishing, worried she'd show her hand too soon. But weren't they after Tariq?

Carter and Jack exchanged a quick look, and Jack sat alongside his wife on the three-person white leather sofa. Kaira had jumped to her feet only seconds after she'd sat.

"You think Tariq is bad, don't you? I saw the way you were looking at him at dinner in the desert last night. I know what you must think." Kaira closed some of the space between herself and Finn as if assuming he was in charge.

"We know Tariq was in Egypt a few days ago, and we're aware of what he did there," Finn told her in what Julia had come to know as his Teamguy tone. The tone he used when he was focused on the job at hand and wasn't about to tolerate any bullshit.

"You have it all wrong." Kaira's soft voice trembled. "Yes, it was Tariq in Egypt, but he was following Amin's orders. He had no choice but to go."

"You're going to need to tell us more." Roman strode closer to Kaira, but Julia could tell he was keeping Joan and Jack in his sights as well. He also appeared to position his body between Harper's and where Jack and Joan sat as a buffer or protective layer between them.

"She's telling the truth," Carter spoke up, drawing Finn's and Roman's attention. "It's Amin that we're after, and it's Kaira I'm trying to help protect."

"You're going to need to start from the beginning if we're going to trust whatever you have to say," Finn said. "It seems you need our help, too. Yeah, you have plenty of people you work with, but—"

"I'm not going to step on your toes," Carter interrupted him. "Our missions are aligned, I'm sure. But it looks like you don't have the full story, so let us help you out."

"And what's the full story look like?" Harper asked.

Julia definitely wanted to know the full story of what was basically shaping up to be a Jack Reacher plot. Was this all really happening, or was it a dream?

Carter turned to Kaira and she closed her eyes. "It all started a few years ago when Tariq and I came up with a plan to escape our overbearing and controlling family."

Julia knew what she was going to say before she said it. "Ario," she whispered. "You used him for his money, am I right?"

Kaira opened her eyes and nodded. "Tariq and I came up with over ten prospects, but he's the one that, well, took the bait, I guess you could say, and we married."

Julia moved toward Kaira, unable to stop herself. "Yeah, and at what point did you all decide to frame my best friend for murder?"

CHAPTER TWENTY-SEVEN

KAIRA'S EYES STARTLED OPEN. "OLIVER'S YOUR FRIEND?"

Finn stepped alongside Julia, worried she might unleash her anger on their target and this whole night would go sideways real fast. They were too close to the truth to let emotions come into play. He reached for her forearm and gently squeezed to offer support.

"Yes, and you tricked him. Told him your husband beat you so he'd confront Ario in your defense, and now he's going to be executed," Julia responded with tears in her eyes, and Finn knew it was fear for her friend as well as anger toward Kaira that had a stranglehold on her voice.

"I didn't want to," Kaira professed, "and I was hoping this would all be resolved much sooner so he'd be freed."

Finn was well-versed in the art of bluffs and lies, and from where he stood, his gut feeling said Kaira was telling the truth.

But he also knew that wouldn't dial down Julia's anger. She needed answers and a way to get Oliver out of prison before it was too late, and his Wonder Woman wouldn't back down without them.

"I know you're upset," Harper said softly to Julia, "but let's see what they have to say, and hear how this all happened, and then we'll figure out the next steps."

Finn gently let go of Julia as she tore her angry gaze from Kaira, and looked to Harper instead, her shoulders sagging. Harper was their soothing voice of reason, and Finn breathed a sigh of relief that she'd gotten Wonder Woman to back down from a fight he firmly believed she'd win, especially after witnessing her in the self-defense classes he'd taught.

Why did that make him so damn proud, too?

"Tariq will come looking for me soon," Kaira said, sounding anxious as she moved to the glass doors that opened to the private pool. She looked fragile and vulnerable in her pink dress and heels instead of the sophisticated, confident woman in the chic white dress from just the other day. Was she feeling regret for what she'd done? Shame?

"We've got that handled for now," A.J. said and stood next to Finn.

Carter remained leaning against the pillar, and Roman joined Harper at the desk. Hopefully, after Kaira laid out all the pieces of her story, everything would add up, and they'd get a lead on where to go from there.

"The Warhol isn't here, is it?" Jack suddenly spoke up, and his question oddly broke the tension in the air. "But tell me it wasn't a lie, and you really have one to give."

Joan reached out and patted his hand in a soothing gesture, but also as if reminding him of the situation at hand. The man had tunnel vision. Had he really given up everything, whatever the hell that was, for Joan? It must have been seriously dangerous as well as illegal if it required a name and face change.

Finn had never bothered to check the files to see what Joan and Jack looked like as Stacey and Doug. But Stacey had said she was in her forties, and upon closer inspection, Finn was pretty sure Giorgio had erased whatever signs of aging she'd had. Her blonde hair was most likely dyed, and the blue of her eyes looked artificial, unlike Julia's gorgeous natural hue, which meant she was likely wearing contact lenses. And as for Jack, he was probably a decade older than his wife. His dark black hair was neatly trimmed and styled, and he gave off an air of refinement more reminiscent of Pierce Brosnan in *The Thomas Crown Affair* than Michael Douglas in *Romancing the Stone*.

Ah, *The Thomas Crown Affair*. Wasn't Brosnan an art thief in that movie, too? *Why am I thinking this?*

"Sorry, my husband can't always help himself, which is how we met Kaira and Ario in Miami," Joan explained, and okay, Finn wasn't expecting that. "How about I tell this part?"

Finn nodded but quickly adjusted his attention to Julia standing rigidly off to his side. He wanted to hook his arm around her and help her through this, knowing that with each passing hour, she came closer to succumbing to panic as she worried about Oliver. Finn was supposed to be her Richard O'Connell, her hero. Well, tonight, her Indiana, but he didn't feel much like a hero.

And what if he was unable to keep his word about saving Oliver? That promise, unlike the one he'd made to his brother, would result in saving a life, and Finn would do just about anything to keep his word. Hell, he would walk across the damn desert to make it happen.

"So, enlighten us," he heard A.J. say when Joan had yet to spill.

Finn forced his focus back to Joan, whose gaze flitted to her husband before journeying toward Kaira, who still had her back to the room. "We were new to the country club in Miami, and—"

"Pause." Harper held her hand in the air. "First, tell me how and why you changed from Stacey and Doug to the *Romancing the Stone* couple?"

Joan's face fell. "Oh."

"So, you know more than we realized," Jack spoke up.

"Are you the infamous art thief who disappeared without a trace?" Roman asked, checking to see if his theory was on point. "But why change your name and alter your face if your real identity was never discovered?"

"That was my idea, actually. Although I didn't recommend Giorgio," Carter interjected, which should have surprised Finn, but Carter operated by a much different set of rules than even Finn's off-the-books teammates did. "When Jack was still Doug, we had a brief encounter during one of his heists. He saved my life when he didn't have to and also helped me go after a much greater threat than someone stealing art from—"

"Bad guys. Everything I took was from really, really bad people." Jack opened his palms as if hoping for a "not guilty" verdict from his audience. "Well, aside from Ario and Kaira, but I wasn't supposed to be, um, stealing anymore at that point. And I had sort of assumed Ario wasn't a good guy until I got to know him."

"I encouraged Doug here to give up the life of crime before he got himself killed, but he didn't listen, of course." Carter waved a dismissive hand through the air as if this was no big deal, and if Finn didn't know the man so well, he would have thought Carter didn't really give a damn.

"Until he met me at an art gallery while planning a heist. Of course, I had no clue the entire collection belonged to some mafioso guy. Doug became more enchanted by me than the art, and instead of completing his objective, he took me out for drinks." Joan was surprisingly chatty. "I had no idea what he did for a living, if it can be called that, until the day he got down on one knee and proposed. He confessed the truth before asking for my hand." She was beaming, clearly in love with the guy despite his questionable career choice. "I said I'd forgive him for his past as long as he stopped stealing. And so, Doug reached out to Carter for advice on how to disappear. Mostly to protect me."

"And he recommended we both change our identities to ensure no one would discover who I was before I met Stacey," Jack explained. "Since I'd been stealing from criminals, Carter made a valid point."

"One of the criminals I stole from was Giorgio, so I took advantage of that, and I offered to, uh, find a piece of art stolen from him in exchange for the plastic surgery and new identities for both Stacey and myself." Wow, Jack was ballsy.

"So, you gave Giorgio back the painting you stole from him and made yourself look like a hero," A.J. commented with a light chuckle. "Damn. Not sure if I should be impressed or creeped out."

Same. But Finn was more interested in learning their connection to Kaira and Ario and how Ario ended up dead.

"I wasn't a fan of Doug's previous life of thievery, even if he was only stealing from criminals, so I've been slowly giving away the earnings he accumulated during that time," Joan explained. "But my husband has had some moments of weakness, one of which was when he discovered a Picasso in Ario's home. They invited us to a party shortly after we all met at the country club."

"We caught him in our house," Kaira said, spinning around to face the room with her first smile of the evening. "I did, at least. And he was so shocked, and I was so stunned by his bold move . . . we all somehow became friends. It sounds a bit odd, I know."

"And you told them the truth about your identities in Miami?" Finn spoke up.

"No." Joan shook her head. "It wasn't until Kaira reached out in December of last year saying she needed help and didn't know who to turn to that we confessed we had a contact who might be able to help. And actually, it wasn't until recently that we revealed who we really were to Kaira, either."

"The truth shall set you free," Jack said with a smile as if everything he'd done was water under the bridge.

"So, continue with the truth. We're listening," Roman said in an even tone, a hand on Harper's shoulder as she sat in the chair in front of him at the desk.

Finn did a quick check to see how Julia was holding up. Wonder Woman looked rattled as if she were struggling to keep her composure. Unable to stop himself this time, he hooked an arm around her waist, and she eased into his touch.

"Ah, Evie and Richard." Joan snapped her fingers. "*The Mummy*. I knew there was something about you two, but my husband heard Warhol and lost his mind. I was right when I called it, wasn't I? You two aren't faking being together."

Finn ignored her observation. This wasn't about him and Julia. "Please, tell us what happened, Kaira." He wanted her side of the story now that they knew how and why Carter, Joan, and Jack were connected to her.

"Tariq and I wanted out of Saudi Arabia and away from our family's control. We both tried making it on our own, but we weren't exactly great at making money. And to live the lives we'd grown accustomed to, if we wanted access to our family's wealth, we had to be people we didn't want to be." Her cheeks grew a touch rosy as if embarrassed.

Spoiled? Shocker.

"So, we came up with a plan to find someone with the

means to support the both of us. Tariq made a list of possible suitors who our parents would approve of and who wouldn't mind an independent and modern woman. That's how I ended up with Ario."

"He took the bait." Kaira wasn't so innocent, Finn decided. "You weren't supposed to fall in love, though," he said, recalling what she'd shared with Julia in the bathroom. And now, he found himself once again studying Julia. He wasn't supposed to fall for her, either, and here he was—dangling over that cliff.

"Even before I fell in love with Ario, getting rid of him was never part of the plan. But I also didn't want one more man telling me what to do in my life. My brothers, aside from Tariq, are as controlling as my father. Especially Amin. He hated both Tariq and me for our lifestyle choices. But Ario was different. He treated me like a partner instead of a possession. I helped him with the company, too. I had a sense of self-worth I learned by being his wife," she went on, her tone a bit shaky.

Finn glanced at Julia, and as their eyes met, his chest grew tight. Her absolute trust in him was conveyed in that shared look, which also served to awaken his fear that he would one day fail her.

"If your brother, Tariq, is so modern, why does he fund terrorist groups?" Harper interjected, stealing Finn's attention back to the room.

Kaira shook her head. "You have it all wrong. Tariq loves the West. He loves all things American, especially the women. But he also has another habit, one not so healthy."

"Drugs," Finn said under his breath, resenting the fact that this dark cloud kept hovering over his head. *Drugs.* He wanted them freaking eradicated.

"Tariq has fought depression for many years, but my

father considers taking antidepressants or seeing a therapist a weakness, especially in regard to his sons. Tariq was forbidden from seeking help, and with my father's connections, trust me, he would find out about it. So, Tariq sought out pills from other sources as a way to escape reality. He'd disappear for days. Is it called a bender? I'm not sure. But Amin would use Tariq's passport, dress like him, and he was the one behind all of that type of activity. Tariq found out after the fact, but no one in my family believed he was innocent."

What. The. Actual. Hell? What kind of brother was this Amin guy?

"I know it sounds crazy," Kaira went on. "But it's true. I promise. This was another reason Tariq wanted to get away from Amin. I think Amin got the idea to deal pills from Tariq's addiction. He denounced Western culture as greedy and selfish, and he said drug use would ultimately lead to their demise."

Finn needed to sit down.

Was the room spinning?

Roman seemed to pick up on the fact that all the talk about drugs was affecting Finn because he quickly started his way. *Well, that's not embarrassing. Twenty years, dude, and you still can't handle the subject.*

Finn held his free hand up to let Roman know he was okay, and he lightly squeezed Julia's side to reassure her as well. "I'm fine," he added, taking in A.J.'s concerned and confused expression once he was steady on his feet. "Go on," he urged Kaira once Roman hesitantly returned to Harper's side.

"Our parents slowly started weaning my brothers off solely relying on their inheritance. Yes, Amin worked for the family business, but he didn't put in as much effort as our parents wanted, and I think that's when Amin saw my husband as his way out from under our parents' financial thumb. I-I don't know if he ever suspected I'd used Ario for the same reason, but late last year, Amin started demanding cash infusions into his account. Ario put up with it a few times but ultimately refused to support yet another brother of mine. He was already funneling money to Tariq whenever I asked. Amin grew angry, and that's when he started to drop hints he'd kill Ario and remove the obstacle in his way to the billions." She took a deep breath as if trying to regain her composure. "I told Ario to remove my name as executor of his will. By doing that, Amin would have no reason to kill him, nor would he be able to get his hands on Ario's money should something happen to him."

"Ario didn't believe Amin would ever follow through with his threat to kill him, and he didn't get along with any of his family well enough to change his will," Jack spoke up as if sensing Kaira needed a break. "That's when she phoned me and explained she was dealing with a stubborn husband and a psychotic brother."

"I didn't know who to turn to, and my gut told me Jack and Joan would be able to help," Kaira added. "They suggested new identities and faces for both Ario and me, which would ensure we could stay together without looking over our shoulders forever."

"Why would Ario do that if he wouldn't even change the will?" Roman asked.

Kaira chewed on her lip for a moment. "You're right. My stubborn husband wouldn't do it. But he did come with me to meet Giorgio. In the end, Ario turned him down. I met with Giorgio on my own and told him to put us on his schedule anyway and that I'd quadruple his price."

"Did Ario ever learn the truth about the plan you and Tariq had initially cooked up?" Julia whispered.

"No. But as I fell in love with him, the guilt started to eat at me. If I hadn't schemed with Tariq to win over and use Ario as our means of escape a few years ago, he'd have been safe, free to live his life." She closed her eyes. "I'd hoped Ario would agree to my plan for both of us to change our identities and disappear, and even after he turned down Giorgio, I held out hope I could convince him somehow. But Amin killed Ario before I could change his mind. And now that he's really dead, it's like I murdered him."

"Had you intended for Oliver to be your fall guy?" Julia's voice lowered, fueled by her anger.

"No, throwing the blame on Oliver was never in my plan. We were going to 'die' in a boating accident." Kaira opened her eyes. "Hard to find bodies in the ocean."

Yeah, Echo Team had run across those types of faked deaths before.

"The day Ario died in January, Amin unexpectedly showed up at our house, angry that Ario was refusing to give him money. He was so mad . . ." Kaira whispered, visibly shaken. "Ario had already left for the day, so I was alone."

Tears ran down Kaira's face as she struggled to go on.

"Amin said he'd ordered Ario to meet him at the construction site that morning without Oliver, or else he'd kill me." Kaira let out a sob. "And then Amin beat me. Told me when Oliver arrived to pick up Ario as usual, to say the beating was by my husband's hand or else he'd . . . kill Oliver. So that's what I did. You can guess the rest of the story—Amin pushed Ario to his death, paid off the workers at the site to say it was Oliver, bribed the police to cover it all up and arrest Oliver." Kaira wiped tears from her face. "You know, I don't think Amin premeditated the murder. But I'm certain that Ario refused to give him money again, and his anger took over."

"Why'd you lie to the police? I assume he gave you no choice?" Harper asked, probably beating Julia to the question.

"Amin forced me to tell the police those lies in the report," Kaira said in a disappointed tone.

"You need to tell the police the truth." Julia stepped closer to Kaira. "They're going to kill Oliver."

"She can't," Carter spoke for the first time in a bit. "Not until we stop Amin first."

"He'll kill her and her brother." Jack stood and shoved his hands into the pockets of his *Top Gun* leather jacket.

"I'm still confused. Why'd Tariq go to Egypt? That was him there, wasn't it? And it's Tariq at the party tonight, not Amin, right?" Finn asked.

Kaira turned to Joan and Jack as if searching for the okay, and Jack nodded.

"You can trust them," Carter added.

Kaira's shoulders sagged. "Amin has been searching for someone. A name. I-I don't know the details. He's been forcing Tariq to do the legwork for him while he's off the grid somewhere. He knows how close Tariq and I are, so while he's off spending Ario's money on God knows what, he's making Tariq do his bidding under the threat that I'll be killed if he doesn't."

Finn's head was still spinning a little bit, but he managed out, "Did you know Tariq was sent after Giorgio?"

"I didn't know why Tariq went to Egypt until he returned to Dubai the other day all upset," she explained. "You see, I never told Tariq about my plan for Ario and me to run away. And it didn't seem necessary to do so after Ario's death."

"We felt it'd be better if no one else knew," Jack spoke up. "Not until later, when Ario and Kaira were living their

BRITTNEY SAHIN

new lives. And the plan was to leave Tariq in charge of the will. Executor of everything."

"So, when Tariq went after Giorgio as Amin instructed him to do, he stumbled upon your name and your husband's on that list, too," Roman said, putting it all together.

"Yes. He confronted me about it, and I told him everything. He was worried what Amin would think when he received the list and saw my and Ario's name on it," Kaira responded in a shaky voice. "He didn't want me to go to the resort this weekend, worried I was up to something again, and I'd get myself killed."

"Tariq saw the names of the hosts for the party this weekend, and he remembered them from Giorgio's list, which is why he showed up and wouldn't leave her side," Jack pointed out. "He put two and two together that we were Kaira's initial source in her plan to fake her death."

Julia stiffened against Finn's side. "So, is Tariq a threat to you or not? I'm confused."

Kaira peered Julia's way with apologetic eyes. "Tariq's been with me all weekend to protect me. You see, in his eyes, keeping me from defying Amin is also protection. For now, he thinks we have no choice but to do what Amin says or die."

Protection? Tariq was her protector. How was this possible? *How could a brother . . .?*

"I guess I don't understand why Tariq used a false identity to lure Giorgio to Egypt," Harper said under her breath. "If they'd never previously met or even talked."

"When I initially approached Giorgio, I explained that we wanted to change our identities because of Amin. Tariq didn't want to take any chances that Giorgio would fear he was like Amin and refuse to meet with him," Kaira replied.

"Do you know your brother's big plans? Does it have to

do with drugs?" Harper followed up with another question, and Finn was glad he had the support of his teammates there to help since he wasn't thinking all that clearly.

Kaira shook her head. "In the last few months, Tariq has done his best to try and win over our brother's trust by doing his bidding and acting as though he's been keeping tabs on me, all to try and figure out what Amin has been up to."

"So you can do what?" Finn asked this time.

Carter looked Finn's way and smiled. "Stop him, of course."

CHAPTER TWENTY-EIGHT

FINN MOMENTARILY LOST FOCUS OF EVERYTHING THEY'D learned an hour ago as Julia stood across from him in their bedroom and began removing her Wonder Woman costume.

"You were saying?" She bent forward and unbuckled the strap of one gold high heel, drawing his gaze to her long, tan legs. What he wouldn't give to have those legs wrapped around him right now.

"What?" He reached up to remove the fedora, forgetting he'd already tossed it earlier, then ruffled his hair instead before losing his leather jacket.

"You were talking about Carter. You think he'll get Tariq to spill everything?"

Oh. Carter. Right. Carter had surprisingly turned into their saving grace tonight since Tariq was still on their No-Go List. "Carter will get Tariq to tell him everything at his off-site location."

"You mean, torture him?" She discarded the shoe and switched to unbuckle the other one.

"Hopefully, it won't be anything more than a friendly chat

since his sister says he's on Team Good Guy. Jury is still out on whether I believe that, but we'll see."

"We don't have much time before Oliver is transferred, so unless you really want to plan a prison break, we need—"

"I know." He knelt before her and stilled her wrist before undoing the buckle and removing her shoe, his hand lingering on her delicate ankle for just a moment.

She startled at his touch and looked up, and Finn's first thought was that the Mediterranean Sea had nothing on the blue of her eyes. "We'll find out what Amin is up to and stop him."

"How can you be so sure?" she whispered.

"Because we always stop the bad guys." He smiled, hoping that was enough to ease her nerves for now.

Would he like to be at the safe house while Carter was questioning Tariq? Yes, but the guy was an addict, and his brother was planning on flooding the western world with drugs. Allegedly. So this op was torture on his ability to focus for many reasons, one of which had her eyes on him now.

Carter had intercepted Tariq an hour ago when he'd been searching for his sister and took him to an off-site location for questioning. "Tariq didn't put up too much of a fight. I guess that's promising." When she looked down to where his hand still held her ankle, he fought the urge to move his gaze to her cleavage, which was on full display in her outfit.

Tonight had been one for the record books titled "Strange," but despite all that had gone down, he couldn't seem to turn off his feelings, both physical and emotional, when it came to Julia. And with her literally in arm's reach, how could he not want to spend one more night with her in case she decided a future with him was impossible?

Who was he kidding? Losing her, regardless of the

reason, would hurt like hell no matter how much time they'd spent together.

"Where are you at? You don't seem to be with me now."

"I'm here." Finn cleared his throat. "Very much here," he added, his voice rough.

When she shifted onto her knees, Finn released her ankle and did the same.

"You want me." Her silky voice went straight to his heart before traveling south. Was that a question or a statement?

She skated her hands up the sides of his biceps and over the short sleeves of his black tee, then rested her forearms on his shoulders and drew herself closer to him.

"I do," he confessed. He had so much to seek forgiveness for, but wanting this woman didn't feel like a sin. Not even with so much on the line.

There was an entire team outside their room working the op, and for the first time in his life, he didn't want to be out there. He was right where he wanted and needed to be.

"I want you, too." She wet her lips, the little tease, letting her tongue linger on that pouty bottom lip he wanted to pull between his teeth. "But I'm scared. And I'm not used to being scared."

He leaned back a little to try and get a better read on her. "Why? Because of Tariq? Oliver?"

She shook her head and closed her eyes. "Us."

Us.

"Finn, the last thing I want to do is hurt you, and I don't want to get hurt either. But I don't know what will happen tomorrow or the next day. You of all people know there are no guarantees in life." The lip he'd wanted to suck wobbled, and was she on the verge of tears?

"I do know that." He drew a hand gently down her cheek and brought a fist beneath her chin, hoping she'd open her eyes. "And that's why I've stuck to being an operator. With the job, I know the risks, and I accept them. But in my personal life, the idea of the unknown is terrifying. I don't know how to bring those two worlds together because I've spent the last nine years living inside this one as Echo Five. In there, I'm not Dalton, and I'm not a failure as a son and brother." He had no clue if she was looking at him yet because his eyes had fallen shut as the truth escaped. He'd never shared those words with anyone, including the therapist they'd all been seeing.

What was it about Julia that had him spilling his secrets and sharing every part of himself?

She'd blown into his world like a storm and turned the life he'd locked himself into for years upside down. And he'd given her the truth last night when he declared that he wanted her and everything she brought with her—rain, thunder, lightning. Julia was his storm. He was caught right in the middle, and it was a place he found himself never wanting to leave.

"Dalton," Julia softly cried out and caressed his face between her palms. "You're not a failure. I've come to know you these last few weeks, and you're the most amazing man I've ever met. Someone I have no idea how I'll . . ."

"Say goodbye to?" Finn opened his eyes, wondering how they'd gone from nearly making love to heavy emotional stuff. But sex with Julia wasn't merely sex, was it? His emotions were involved and had been from the moment she joined him in that shower.

"You were shot." Was that her answer to his question? Probably. "You could have died in Egypt. What might happen on your next mission? I-I can't lose you forever-forever." She sniffled and released his cheeks, her hands settling firm on his shoulders as she held on to him like a lifeline she was afraid to use or lose.

"I'll, um, still be gone forever-forever whether we're together or not if that were to happen. You get that, right?" He was stumbling through this, but he was in uncharted territory, and this woman was the curveball he'd never anticipated. "Why don't we take it one moment at a time?" Was he really willing to put his heart out there like this, knowing she might crush it? He didn't see any other way around it. The risk was worth it.

She tipped her head and studied him. "Like with a camera, one shot. One frame."

He lowered his fist from her chin, forgetting it'd been there. "Yes."

A tear slipped down her cheek, a reminder she was also vulnerable and not a superhero despite the costume. He could lose her, too. Jaden hadn't served in the military, and he'd died. When Finn was in his twenties, he'd lost a friend to a drunk driver. So many others died, and it never seemed to make sense.

"Make love to me?" she asked, and instantly his thoughts switched from death to life. To her.

He'd picked up condoms earlier in the day. A pit stop at the store for a hope-so moment. And was this hope-so moment about to come to life?

She eased back, lowering her hands from his body before turning to the side. "Undress me," she requested without waiting for his answer.

He was vaguely aware of the muffled voices coming from downstairs. It should have been enough to snap him out of the moment, to refocus on the op, but all it actually did was serve as a reminder that he would need to keep her quiet because he'd be damned if anyone heard the sweet moans Julia made while coming.

Finn did as he was instructed and slid down the side zipper that ran the length of her torso. The belt was attached to the skirt and top, so the entire costume fell around her knees onto the ground. All that remained were her red, lacy bra and panties and the gold band on her arm.

When she shifted to face him again, his gaze caught her nipples poking through the thin lace of the bra.

"Touch me," she commanded in a breathy whisper, and fuck if that sound didn't go straight to his dick.

"On the bed." He guided them both up, and she stepped free of the costume. She removed her undergarments, then unhooked the armband and tossed it on their way to the four-poster bed at the center of the room.

Once Julia was seated on the bed, he kicked off his shoes. "I'm prepared this time," he told her, lifting his chin to point to the nightstand where he'd placed the just-in-case condoms inside the drawer.

A naughty look crossed her face. She'd transformed from worried and scared to turned on as fast as he had.

"I want you to take charge tonight. I want you to—"

"Fuck you hard?" he asked, remembering her words at the tent.

She sucked in a quick breath before lightly nodding and staring at his crotch as his hands moved to the buckle of his pants. He was painfully hard and in desperate need to lose himself inside this amazing woman, a woman he was falling for. *You already fell,* a voice in his head told him.

"Wait." She stood and came around before him, setting a hand to his chest, urging him to take a step back. When her eyes met his, she said, "I want to undress you." She continued to hold his gaze as she worked his belt loose, his heart pounding overtime.

Before moving to his pants, she lifted the hem of his shirt and guided it up and over his head before tossing it to the floor. Her attention briefly lingered on his chest as if the reminder of being shot was a bullseye of pain.

"Look at me," he said in a deep voice, not wanting to lose her to *what-ifs*.

She slowly dragged her focus to his face, and once their eyes locked, he could tell she was back in the moment. She worked her lip between her teeth at the corner of her mouth like she loved to do and slowly lowered his pants. As she dragged them down, she went to the floor, too.

He was going to lose his mind with her peering up at him from her knees. She hooked her fingers at the sides of his boxers and rolled her tongue along the seam of her lips before pulling them down.

She leaned in and circled her tongue around his head, giving it a light suck, and he almost lost it right there. Looking up at him, she ran her tongue from root to tip before taking him into her mouth.

"Holy fuck," Finn let out on a groan as she snaked her hands around his thighs to take him even deeper. It was somehow too much and not nearly enough, so he quickly wrapped her hair around his fist and guided her up and down his painfully hard shaft. He wasn't sure how much longer he'd be able to stay in place and keep from coming into her luscious mouth.

And then she moaned around his cock.

"Jewels," he hissed between barely parted lips. "I need to come inside you." His abdomen flexed and his quads tensed, but instead of backing off, she increased her suction.

Using both hands to pull her back, he finally slipped free

of her mouth. Her lips were puffy and red and glistened from her efforts, and if she kept looking at him like that, they'd never make it to the bed.

"I need to come inside you," he repeated while dragging his thumb along her lower lip.

"That's what I was going for," Julia said with a smirk, then her lips wrapped around his thumb, and her eyes fluttered closed, snapping the last bit of control he had.

"Stand up," he commanded, and her eyes flared with heat and lust and something else he couldn't name before she got to her feet.

He lifted her in one fast movement and had her pinned beneath him on the bed within a second. He splayed her legs apart with his knee, widening them in anticipation for what he wanted to do—rail into her, but . . . damn it, he needed a condom and to pull himself out of beast mode.

But she wants it hard, he reminded himself.

He pinned her hands alongside her head as he held himself over her, staring into those deep ocean-blue eyes. He leaned in and kissed her, her full tits touching his chest as he sucked on her lip before twining their tongues.

He freed her hands a few moments later and braced himself on his forearms while still kissing her. He raced one hand along the silhouette of her toned body before finding her soaking wet clit.

She yelped into his mouth when he plunged two fingers inside her. She grew wetter by the second, and this time, she was the one biting his lip.

"Dalton," she rasped as he continued to rub her sex, gliding her wetness all over her slit where he planned to soon plunge into and take her as hard as they both wanted and needed. "Please, I can't wait."

He understood that. Felt it in his bones.

He shifted off her for a second to secure the condom and roll it over his length.

Finn held her hips, prompting her to lift her pelvic bone up so he could sink his fingertips into the flesh of her ass cheeks. She arched her back, giving him what he wanted, and he squeezed and gripped her firm ass while staring down at her pussy. Her folds were swollen and pinkish from her arousal, and he wanted to bury his face between her legs and lick her, but first . . .

"Please," she begged again, her voice cracking this time. He lowered her back to the bed, set his tip to her center, and thrust into her in one hard movement. Her eyes rolled to the back of her head as she took all of him, and her insides clamped down around his cock like she was hungry for him, for this.

He bit down on his back teeth, his jaw tight, as he tried to keep his mouth shut so they didn't give the team downstairs a free show.

He rocked into her, trying to keep the pace steady and slow, but it was damn near impossible with her playing with her tits, eyes on him, and her tight pussy pulsing around his shaft.

Finn lowered himself back to one forearm to draw her lip between his teeth again before kissing her.

Her kiss was erotic and sensual. A slow dance. A tease to every nerve ending in his body. He drew himself in and out of her with hard pumps.

His free hand moved down her flat, soft belly and to her sex as they kissed, and the pad of his thumb shifted in circular motions to add more friction for her.

"Oh my God," she cried into his mouth before turning her face to the side, so he planted his lips on her throat by her ear and lightly kissed her there. "I can't hold back," she panted out a few minutes later after he continued to thrust inside of her, doing his best to hang on to this moment, worried she'd be unable to commit to forever-forever with him.

"Come for me, baby," he returned in a deep, husky voice as he did his best not to release yet.

"Look at me," she whispered, and he lifted his head to find her eyes.

"What is it?" he asked after letting go of a deep exhalation, on the verge of coming.

Her body started to quiver against him, and he knew she was on the precipice of her orgasm. "I like you," she said so innocently.

"I would hope so," he murmured.

"I mean," she added around a swallow, her eyes thinning, "I've fallen for you." Her words came out as part moan after that as she came.

The clenching of her sex triggered his own release, and he lost himself inside of her.

Finn pressed a kiss to her lips and collapsed off to the side of her, sweaty and a bit breathless. He reached for her hand and brought her knuckles to his lips.

He wanted to say something in return. Find the perfect words. But before he had a chance to figure anything out, there was a knock at the door.

"Hey, we're rolling out now. Get ready." It was Asher.

Julia slowly sat up, no sheet to cover herself since they were on top of the covers.

"Tariq already talked?" *That was fast.* "We got the green light?"

"Yes and no," Asher said through the door. "POTUS says if we go with Carter, we're acting on our own accord." He paused, and why were they having this conversation through the door?

Right. We're naked.

"But your theory about Giorgio's client list was right. He was searching for a European drug lord who'd gone on the DL a few years ago. He used to handle every major black market trade route for drugs in Europe. Amin located him in the Maldives, and then he took off back to his compound. And according to Tariq, we only have a short window before his brother's plans go into effect."

Finn looked to Julia, then back to the door. "Where are we going?"

Asher was quiet for a moment. "Amin is just over the Egyptian border in Sudan."

CHAPTER TWENTY-NINE

EGYPTIAN-SUDANESE BORDER – TWENTY-FOUR HOURS LATER

Finn made his way over to a collapsible table, the only furniture in the small space. On the table, alongside a wide range of weapons, there were a few bags of pills. Finn had no clue who had occupied the bunker-like compound before they arrived with Carter and his men, but he was certain Carter had had a team of people "clear it out" beforehand. He also assumed the previous occupants were taken by surprise, considering the drugs and weapons sitting on the table.

From this location, Finn and the others were thirty minutes from Amin El-Baz's compound, just over the border in Sudan. And now, Echo Team knew why those mummy coffins weren't headed to the airport the other night—they were supposed to go to Amin in Sudan.

Having been denied a green light for this op, Bravo and Echo were on their own. Well, technically, they were assisting

Carter, which was a bizarre twist of events in itself. But from the moment Asher knocked on the bedroom door announcing they were rolling out, Finn had felt as if he'd blinked away the last twenty-four hours. And he'd barely had a chance to talk to Julia about anything other than the mission since they'd left Dubai.

Bravo and Echo had spent all of their time with Carter prepping for the op that'd be happening in an hour's time.

Finn's teammates, both Bravo and Echo, were in the main quarters of the property, and at some point in the last few minutes, he'd found himself wandering down a corridor and into the room where he now stood.

Not the best room to wind up in. The reminder of who he'd lost and how much was on the line stared back at him from those bags of pills.

How many lives would be saved if they were able to keep all the drugs off the streets?

Amin now knew all the major drug trafficking routes in and out of Europe, and he planned to ruin the West. Destroy them by way of drugs. And that didn't take into account phase two of Amin's evil plan. Regardless of what it was, they'd end this now. Tonight.

Finn lifted one of the small bags of pills and noticed smears of blood on the table, most likely due to whatever happened before he'd arrived.

He had no clue how many pills were inside the clear bag. He'd never been great at that candy corn guessing game as a kid, and he wasn't about to try now. *And why does it matter?* He shook his head and grimaced when another memory of his brother surfaced, this one from the year 2000.

Jaden was having a party at the house he'd recently rented in Beverly Hills with all of his stardom money.

Most of the partygoers were at the pool outside, where a

DJ had just queued up a new song by Darude, *Sandstorm*. Jaden hadn't been among them, so Finn began wandering the sprawling property, a sick feeling in his stomach. He'd just entered the house for another look when he heard his brother singing upstairs. More like rapping, actually, which wasn't the norm for him.

These circle pills of heavenly devotion. Green, blue, but usually white. Pop one. Pop two. Pop fifty-two. Just do what ya gotta do. They taste so sweet and sometimes sour. Within each pill comes a special kind of power . . .

Finn had opened the bedroom door to find Jaden, wearing a bathrobe, letting go of the song lyrics he'd probably made up on the fly while three women lay naked and asleep, or passed out, on his bed.

Finn had looked away from the three blondes and to his brother. *What are you doing? You have a party downstairs. People are looking for you.*

I was having a little fun. You want one? Jaden jerked his thumb toward the bed. *You still a virgin, or you pop your cherry already?*

What are you on? Finn had asked instead, shutting the door behind him. *Tell me that's candy.*

Jaden looked down at the bag in his hand, then up at Finn. *I'm rolling, baby.*

Rolling?

MDMA.

What's that? But he'd known whatever the hell it was, it couldn't be good.

Ecstasy. And relax, they're a feel-good drug. Doctors used to give them to patients to get them to talk in therapy. He'd casually set the bag down on his dresser, and Finn recalled contemplating stealing it and flushing every last pill.

That had also explained why his brother had been so

chatty when normally he'd be yelling for him to get the hell out of there.

Did I invite you tonight? Jaden had asked in surprise.

No, I was checking on you when I heard through some friends you were throwing this party.

Jaden had stepped up to Finn, pulled him close, and rubbed his knuckles against Finn's head. *Always so worried about me, brother.*

I wish you'd stop. You're going to get hurt. You can't keep doing this to yourself.

I'll stop when I'm dead.

Finn opened his eyes and let go of the painful memory. The beats to *Sandstorm* now stuck in his head.

His brother had died the following morning. A combination of various drugs together with alcohol. If only he'd stayed at the party that night, maybe Jaden would still be alive.

"Hey, you okay?" The soft sound of Julia's voice from behind had Finn dropping the bag and seeking out her beautiful face.

She stood with her back positioned to the wall near the door, her head tipped to the side as her attention journeyed to the table covered in drugs and weapons. She had on jean shorts and a plain white tee with sandals, and she was a refreshing sight after his painful trip down memory lane.

"I'm fine." *At least, I think I am.* He placed his hands on his hips but didn't make a move. He wasn't sure why he didn't immediately go to her, other than the fact he was still unsure which way the wind would blow when it came to her decision about a possible *them* post-op. He needed to keep his head together for the sake of the mission, though. Attempt to override.

But how was one supposed to override and forget, even for a night, someone like Julia?

"This all happened so fast." She pushed away from the wall but didn't approach. "I guess that's good since Oliver is running out of time, and from the sounds of it, your teammates seem to think Amin plans to start pumping drugs into the streets soon."

"I guess it's a good thing Carter showed up, or we might not be here now since Amin is off-limits, and his target isn't the U.S." Not that that should have mattered.

"Can you run the op details by me one more time? I feel like I've heard you all discuss the plan a million times, but I still have an uneasy feeling."

He lowered his arms and removed the distance between them, unable to stop himself from going to her when it was clear she was worried. "Carter has three Black Hawks, no idea how he procured them, but Echo Team will be flying in one, Bravo in the other, and Carter's men in the third bird." Finn lightly braced her arms, the memory of the last time he saw his brother alive now clearing from his mind with Julia before him. "We'll fast-rope into Amin's compound at zero dark thirty, similar to the Bin Laden raid."

"But one of those choppers crash-landed." She sounded like a young girl instead of the strong woman he knew she was. She was scared, and it crushed him that her fear might be too paralyzing for her, which could ruin any chance at a future together.

"We'll be fine." He tried to reassure her by running his hands up and down the sides of her arms. "Choppers won't be landing inside the compound, so we'll be moving on foot to the HLZ a few klicks away after they wrap up their work at the compound."

"Once you're inside the compound, then what?"

"We destroy the drugs and clean house."

"Clean house?" Her eyes met his. "Kill everyone?"

Rules of engagement were a little different tonight since they weren't operating as SEALs but rather alongside a rogue CIA operative. "Most likely, they'll try and kill us, so we'll have to kill them instead." That was the best answer he could give, and he hoped it didn't escalate her worries.

Julia's eyes fell closed, and he stopped moving his hands on her arms.

"And as promised, after the op, Carter's men watching over Kaira and Tariq will take them to the police and share the truth about Oliver." He needed her to focus on the positive, on one of the outcomes of his mission tonight. Her friend's freedom.

"And what if the price of saving Oliver is losing you?" She opened her eyes and released a shaky exhale.

"I'll be in full kit. Eighty pounds of gear on me. Lots of protection." *Lots of weapons.* "You don't need to worry. This isn't like the last time we were in the desert. We have way more guns and backup."

"And the next time?"

Here we go. Fuck. "There's going to be a lot of next times," he admitted. "You need to decide if you can handle that."

Her mouth pinched tight, and her eyes crinkled around the edges as she stared at him as if unsure how to answer.

"You two lovebirds ready?" A rap at the door drew their attention to find A.J. there. "We're prepping now."

"Yeah, okay. Be right there." Finn nodded and waited for A.J. to leave.

"Focus on making it back safely. Right now, that's all that

matters, okay?" she whispered, pressing up on her toes and throwing her arms over his shoulders. He caught tears in her eyes before she pinned her body tight to his, and this was by far the hardest damn goodbye he'd had pre-op.

He pulled back and found her lips, brushing his mouth over hers before her tongue parted his mouth and met his. His hands slid down her back and to her ass as he held her firmly against him, kissing away her worries. Kissing away his own.

It took them a few minutes to detach themselves and make their way to the main quarters where Bravo, Echo, and Carter and his men were assembled. Everyone was already in their gear, except Knox, who was holding down the fort with Harper and Jessica since he was still "grounded" from operating. But it was a bit too crowded there for Finn's liking. More cooks in the kitchen than he was used to.

"Four horsemen, huh? Sounds apocalyptic," Chris was saying when Finn reached for Julia's hand and kept her at his side. He trusted Carter, but he didn't know his men, and he'd done his best to keep Julia as close to him as possible while in their presence since the plane's wheels touched down that day.

"Four horsemen?" Finn asked, trying to find out what he'd missed while sharing a hot but hopefully not a forever-goodbye kiss with Julia.

"Thermal imaging from the drone shows a guard on horseback posted at each corner of the compound," Luke said, taking point even though his people were "helping" Carter and he wasn't taking the lead on this one. "Not much movement inside, but Tariq says Amin will be wherever the most people are. He'll have himself surrounded by men willing to die for him."

Carter stroked his beard as he stepped alongside Luke, his

eyes moving to the map on the table at the center of their temporary command center. "Thirty heat signatures inside, and we have no clue if his boys there are doped up on those drugs."

"Zombies," A.J. hissed. "I knew all of our playing *Call of Duty: Zombies* would pay off."

"Leave it to you to joke at a time like this," Harper said while elbowing A.J. in the side with a smile.

"What's a mission without a little humor?" A.J. winked. "But seriously, if the sand starts turning into that mummy guy from that movie because we're cursed, I'm—"

"Running?" Chris cut him off.

"Damn straight. Not sure why I've got that *Mummy* movie stuck in my head. Well, maybe it's because of Rick and Evie over here." A.J. grinned, and why was this so helpful to Finn right now? Why did their kidding around make it easier for him to handle the gritty reality that they were going to take down Amin and his possibly drugged-up men while Julia stayed behind, terrified he wouldn't return?

"Too bad Bear isn't with us tonight," Chris said, referring to their new K9, and yeah, he would have made a great addition tonight.

"Tariq says there won't be any women or children inside, but be on the lookout anyway," Wyatt noted. And how was he doing? He looked a bit steadier and appeared more level-headed than during their last desert op, but nothing had changed since then, had it?

"Oh, and one more thing," Luke said in a grave tone. "There's a known Hamas terrorist cell not far away from Amin's compound, and it'd be best if we don't draw their attention tonight."

"Not that I wouldn't mind killing two birds with one

stone," Carter began, "but we're not prepared for dealing with a second enemy."

"Roger that," Chris responded. "Don't wake the other beasts."

"I hate I won't be rolling with y'all." Knox swiped a hand over his shaved head.

"We'll be okay. Plus, I'll feel better about you staying back with Jessica and the others," Luke said, lifting his chin toward Julia. "Michael would prefer his sister stay away from the gunfire."

"Of course he said that," Julia softly said, and Finn tightened their united hands.

"Let's go take this son of a bitch down and get your boy out of jail," Carter said, turning his focus on Julia.

But when Finn peered at Julia, her eyes were set on him. "Promise me you'll be okay?"

He looked around the room as if seeking help from his buddies who had experience with these types of goodbyes, but they were all busy with op details.

The last mission they'd been on like this was to save Jessica and Luke from a traitor in Afghanistan not too long ago, and now they were going after an off-limits Saudi royal who'd taken up drug trafficking as a new form of terrorism . . . when would it ever stop?

It won't. It won't ever stop.

"I can't promise that," he confessed. "I wish I could, but I can't." He had to be honest with her. She had to know the risks and fully understand them if they had a shot at finding out if there could be anything between them after tonight.

Her free hand went to the pendant around her neck that he'd given her, and she closed her eyes. "Then at least promise you'll do everything in your power to make it back to me."

He smiled and turned her into him, not caring about any onlookers. His free hand went up her spine and to the nape of her neck. He lightly gripped, tipping her head back to look up at him. "That's a promise I can for damn sure keep."

CHAPTER THIRTY

ZERO DARK THIRTY

"THE FOUR HORSEMEN NEED TO BE HANDLED BEFORE OUR super stealth birds are within visible range for the rest of the guys to drop in," Harper calmly explained as Julia peered over her shoulder with a tight knot of worry in her stomach. "We need to maintain the element of surprise."

Julia was glad Finn wasn't handling one of the horsemen. What if he froze up like he had done at the stables? She didn't need him hesitating and losing his life because he was haunted by a dream, and really, his past.

"Liam and Wyatt are two of the best snipers in the world. They'll take out the guards on the north and south sides," Knox added from where he sat in the swivel chair between Jessica and Harper, and it seemed he looked more on edge than Julia felt. It couldn't be easy for him to be in that room instead of out with his teammates. "And Roman and one of Carter's guys will handle the other two men."

"Then Finn and the others will drop in by rope from the helicopter?" How many times had she heard this? How many times had she played the scene out in her head to mentally prep for when it would happen? *It's happening now. Right freaking now.*

Finn was only thirty minutes away, but it felt like he was on the other side of the world.

"You sure you don't want to sit?" Knox gripped the black chair arms and turned to the side to look at her. "You look anxious."

Julia frowned. "So do you and you're sitting. Doesn't seem to be helping." She steadied her attention back on the laptop screen where they were observing the drone feed, or whatever that was called. The three helicopters weren't in view yet, but she could see the compound where the prick Amin was holed up.

Knox cracked his knuckles and grabbed the chair arms again as if he might break them off. "I can't stand being here while they're out there."

Jessica reached for his forearm and squeezed. "We can't have the son of the President of the United States killing a Saudi royal in Sudan."

"Bad optics, I know," Knox replied, and Julia spied a surprising grin sweep across his mouth before he returned his focus to her.

"I can't imagine how you make this work given who your father is. It can't be easy being the son of one of the most powerful men in the world," she found herself saying.

Knox shrugged. "No easier than spending half of my life having people mistake dear ol' dad for Denzel Washington, and women twice my age, when I was twenty, trying to give me their phone numbers because of it."

Knox was trying to help soothe her nerves, God bless him. But she was pretty sure nothing could distract her from thinking about Finn and the danger he was facing tonight.

And it was still hard to wrap her head around the fact that Oliver had been framed by the very man the President had sent Finn and his team to take down. They were brought together for a reason. Fate, she supposed.

"Your dad is a good man from what my brother says," Julia finally said, hoping to hear the sound of Finn's voice soon. *That* would put her at ease. A little, at least. Being able to throw her arms around him after this op ended was the only thing keeping her from throwing up right now.

"He has his moments." Knox winked and returned his focus to the laptop as Harper tapped at a few buttons.

"Two more minutes to go-time," Harper announced. "They should be online soon."

"You didn't have them on comms in Aswan for that other op, but I'm relieved you do tonight." She wouldn't be able to handle the silence and the waiting if that were the case for this mission.

But what about the next mission? She wouldn't be in their "TOC," tactical operation center as they'd called it, the next time. She would be back home making excel spreadsheets and holding meetings while her stomach was a shaky mess and she nervously eyed her phone, waiting for Finn to call and let her know he was safe.

How in the world did military wives handle deployments?

"It gets easier," Jessica said, shifting her chair to the side as if Julia had spoken her distressing thoughts out loud. "I mean, a little. But you have to remember that what they're doing out there is to protect those they love. To make the world a little safer."

"Sometimes it feels like we're using a toothpick to fight a dragon," Knox added, his tone solemn, "but better to fight with a toothpick than not fight at all. Can't let the bad guys win."

Julia closed her eyes and processed his words, hoping she might absorb some of his strength and be as fearless and powerful as the three warriors before her.

"Finn's worth it," Harper said softly without turning, knowing exactly what was on Julia's mind, just as Jessica had.

Knox peered at Julia. "More than worth it. That man will be your ride or die. He'll do anything for you."

"I know he would," Julia returned in a soft voice, her heart starting to race when she heard static pop over the line.

"This is Echo One. Zeroing in on the targets in three, two, one . . ."

Silence filled the line for a moment as she knew Wyatt, Liam, Roman, and Carter's guy were simultaneously sniping their targets. *Sniping? It's called sniping, right?* She needed to get used to the lingo, and . . . to this. She had to get used to it because what was the alternative? Saying goodbye to Finn? He was right. If he was going to die, he was going to die whether they were together or not.

She thought about Tucker's ID tags Oliver had removed from her neck five years ago. That'd been young love with Tucker, and what she felt already for Finn just after a few weeks felt like it'd become the forever kind of love. The ride-or-die kind, as Knox had said. But that was the root of her problem. She couldn't have that man die on her. And—

"H1 down." Wyatt's British voice popped over the radio.

H1? Horseman one, she assumed.

"This is Bravo Four. H2 is down." *Liam?*

"Echo Four here. H3 down." *Roman?*

"This is, well, hell, I don't have a fucking call sign . . . but H4 is down." And that had to be Carter's guy. Kind of funny, too. Southern drawl from the sounds of it.

"Moving over the target location now." *Finn,* and she'd

swear the voice of her inner child screamed with relief simply hearing him speak.

"This is TOC," Jessica said. "We have you in our sights now."

"Roger that," Finn responded.

Julia moved closer and set her hand on the back of Harper's chair so she could get a better view of what was happening. She had no clue how Carter had pulled off the drone, the SATCOMs, or any of this on such short notice, but according to Finn, were it not for Carter, Amin would remain a free man. Amin wasn't technically an American problem, which meant he was off-limits for Bravo and Echo. And Harper had said if anything went sideways tonight, the U.S. government wouldn't be able to help.

That wasn't exactly comforting. What kind of bullshit was that? Abandon the very people serving and protecting their country, as well as the world, because of optics?

"They're fast-roping into the compound now." Knox pointed to the screen and walked Julia through what was going on. "The birds are now leaving, and the boys will meet them at the HLZ extraction site."

Helo landing zone, she deduced.

Knox clenched his hand into a fist and rested his elbow on the table, then leaned in closer to the screen. "I really, really hate being on this side of an op. Not sure how you two handle it," he said, glancing over at Jessica and Harper.

Jessica swatted Knox on the back. "You're supposed to be comforting her, remember?"

"Right, right." He swung around in his chair and smiled at Julia. "I'm totally chill right now. Nothing to worry about."

Julia rolled her eyes, but for a second, she'd been distracted. Only for a second, though. "I wish we could hear them while they're inside the compound."

"If we can hear them in there, then the baddies will hear them, too," Knox pointed out. "So, it's radio silent until all targets are down." He set his finger on the screen. "But you can see the muzzle flashes a little. Just barely. People are getting shot. So, you know, progress."

Julia's stomach tightened. "Not our people, right?

"Nah." Knox eyed the screen. "Our people are doing the shooting, don't worry."

"You sound really convincing there," Julia replied sarcastically, sweat starting to drip down her back and not because of the heat.

"He's not so great at sitting behind a desk," Jessica said. "As you can see."

"I'm a shooter. A door kicker. A medic. A lot of things. Desk jockey sure as hell—" Knox let go of his words at the sound of static coming over the radio.

"Our HVT is down. I repeat, our HVT is down. I took the kill shot," Carter announced.

"Thank God," Jessica said under her breath as she wiped a hand across her forehead.

"That was fast," Julia whispered.

"Because our people are damn good." Knox semi-smiled.

"This is Bravo One," Luke said. "Compound is now secure. Tangos are all down. Preparing to destroy these damn zombie drugs."

"Yeah, these fuckers were so hopped up on that shit they may as well have been zombies." Julia immediately recognized the Southern drawl as belonging to A.J. "One guy took five shots in the chest and one in the head before he went down."

"At least some guy didn't bite you," Chris said. "Am I gonna have to get a rabies shot?"

"More like a tetanus shot, genius. How the hell did you

356

manage to let someone bite you?" Finn asked, and the sound of his voice had Julia releasing a quiet sob of relief as she hugged her arms around her torso.

"Boys," Jessica chided, sounding like a mom about to hand out a lecture. "Finish before Hamas actually shows up and sees the fireworks show."

"Pretty dusty out here tonight. I doubt anyone can see us." And based on the Aussie accent, that was Liam.

"Amin is really dead?" Julia wanted to hold on to that feeling of relief, but a nagging voice told her that it wasn't quite over yet. *You're overthinking. Over worrying. Over-everything-er. Not a word.*

"Yes. And see, we're all good." Knox settled back into his chair, appearing a hell of a lot more relaxed, so Julia would take that as a good sign and lose her worries. Or try to. "Now they just need to finish rigging the place to blow and make it look like it was Hamas's handiwork. Let the Saudis go after one of our enemies for us. 'Two birds. One stone' thing. You know, Hamas thinks drugs are evil, so they had to . . . yada yada yada."

"Drugs *are* evil." Jessica playfully swatted Knox again, and he laughed.

Okay, this is good. They're totally chill. Everything is okay. More than anything, Julia wanted to follow their lead and chill out, but her palms had become as sweaty as her back.

A few minutes later, an explosion lit up the screen.

"Heading to the extraction site," Luke said, a little breathless as if he and his men were running. "It's windy out here. We need to get these helos off the ground and fast. Kind of feels like a storm is coming."

"A storm?" Julia's stomach squeezed, and she backed away from where everyone sat.

"If it's a sandstorm, it's early enough. They need to get out before it turns into a solid wall of dust," Jessica said, her playful tone gone.

"How big of a wall are we talking? Like, a real wall?" Julia asked, dread taking over.

"Sometimes up to a thousand feet high. A mile or more wide," Harper answered, looking at Knox, a concerned expression on her face.

"What is it?" Julia stepped forward again.

"Bravo Two, I mean Owen, is flying Bravo Team. He's a skilled pilot. He can handle some sand," Jessica told her in a calm voice.

"And who is flying Echo Team? And the other chopper?" But she knew the answer, damn it.

"Carter's men." Knox faced the screen, and Harper made a few adjustments, zooming out a bit for a better look at what kind of storm they were up against.

"And what do we know about Carter's men?" *Nothing, right?* They knew nothing. Finn's life was more than likely in the hands of a stranger.

"You see that?" Harper pointed to the screen and quickly hit a few more buttons.

"Fuck," Knox hissed and grabbed the radio. "You have incoming two klicks from your location. My guess is you have some terrorists from that Hamas cell on your six."

"We're one mike away from the HLZ. We'll get out of here before they arrive," Wyatt said and began coughing. "They won't see us in all of this dust, anyway. We have coverage."

"You sure you can take off?" There was a rattle to Knox's voice as he stood tall.

"Not much of a choice, brother," Wyatt returned and coughed again as if he were swallowing sand.

And was he?

Now she was going to be sick.

The room was spinning. *Shit, shit, shit.*

A hand on her back had her slowly turning to see Jessica trying to console her. "They'll be okay. They do this all of the time. I . . ."

She was going to promise they'd be fine, so why'd she stop?

"I have faith in them," Jessica said instead, and she nodded as if trying to convince herself of that.

"Yeah." Julia lightly nodded, but . . . what if Finn's dream was prophetic?

A freaking terrorist group was closing in, and a sandstorm was upon them from the looks of it. Maybe Jaden had appeared in Finn's dream as a warning?

"Osiris. Fucking Osiris and the Underworld," she mumbled like a crazy person and squeezed her eyes closed.

"We're on the birds," Wyatt said. "Taking off now. Do you have eyes on the tangos?"

Julia's gaze flew to the screen.

"No, we've lost sight of the tangos. And we can't see you either," Harper responded, a hand going to her abdomen as her own fears of losing the father of her child were most likely settling in.

"Heading to you now." It was Finn.

"Be safe," Julia said, unsure if Finn could hear her.

The line cut back over, the noise of the helicopter chopping the dusty air almost overwhelming, but she heard Finn say, "Roger that, Jewels."

The radio went quiet for a few minutes, and every second of silence felt like her life was flashing before her eyes in slow motion.

From the first photo she'd taken with her Polaroid down to the last one before Tucker died.

To the moment she'd locked eyes with Finn at the karate studio in January all the way to their goodbye kiss tonight.

Freeze frame by freeze frame.

"We're . . ." Static. Who was that? "Repeat . . ."

Julia stood alongside Jessica and grabbed hold of her arm while Knox held on to the radio. "This is TOC. Repeat," Knox said.

"Engine fail . . . failure. Echo Team is crash . . . crash-landing."

CHAPTER THIRTY-ONE

FINN STRUGGLED TO OPEN HIS EYES, TO MAKE SENSE OF where he was and what had happened. His first instinct was to find his gun. Hamas was coming, weren't they? But . . .

"Finn!" someone yelled. "Echo Five!"

Finn forced his eyes to stay open but couldn't see a damn thing. Dust and debris filled his line of sight, and he knocked his NVGs over his eyes to shield them from the sand. "Everyone okay?" he called out, realizing he was still inside the chopper after the helo had lost control and they'd crash-landed in the desert.

"Finn, we need you."

Roman? "Where are you?" Finn secured his rifle and pushed up from the floor of the fuselage. He felt pretty banged up but had no injuries that he could tell.

The pilot was either dead or unconscious, but he didn't see the rest of Echo Team.

"Outside the chopper. Follow my voice," Roman yelled, competing with the sandstorm that'd snuck up on them and tried to eat them alive like that mummy in the damn trailer for the movie he never wanted to watch after tonight.

Visibility was shit, and Finn could barely see beyond his hand. He pulled up his shemagh to cover his mouth and nose, then he reached out and moved his arm back and forth to avoid running into something.

When he stumbled his way out of the Black Hawk, someone grabbed hold of his arm and jerked him to the left.

"Wyatt's down. He's hurt. He needs you." It was Chris this time.

"Wyatt?" *No, damn it.* "Everyone else on Echo okay? Bravo?" he asked as Chris guided Finn to wherever Wyatt was located.

The sand howled and swirled, an angry force trying to disrupt his attempts to get to Echo One.

"Everyone's okay. Owen managed to land Bravo Team before they crashed, so they're moving on foot through this shit to get to us, but they're under heavy gunfire. That Hamas terrorist cell is on their ass, which means if Bravo finds us, Hamas does, too," Chris answered.

"And Wyatt is in rough shape," Roman said while coughing. Finn was only just able to make out his face as Roman held the shemagh over his own mouth. He had on NVGs as well, same as Chris.

Chris and Roman led the way to Wyatt's location, and Finn knelt down beside his brother, finding A.J. across from him. "What happened?" *How long was I out of it, damn it?*

"He was thrown from the bird when we went down. Busted up his leg from what I can tell. He's got a pulse, but I can't see shit out here to examine him further, and he's not waking the fuck up," A.J. quickly explained.

"How long have we been down?" Finn removed his glove and found Wyatt's pulse. It was steady, but he wouldn't be able to examine him out in this mess.

"Thirty or so minutes ago," A.J. shouted back, his hands

on Wyatt's chest assessing for more damage, but the vest full of mags blocked his access.

"You get a hold of Jess and Harper?" Finn asked while continuing to monitor Wyatt's pulse.

"We lost communication with them after we went down, and Bravo shortly after that. But they'll find a way to get to us. And they know about Wyatt, so Knox will call POTUS. He'll force him to make the right call."

And the right call sure as hell better be to do whatever it took to get Wyatt to a hospital. But first, they needed to get out of this mess they were in.

"It's a fast-moving storm from the looks of it. Came out of nowhere," Chris shouted. "It's starting to blow past us, but that also means these Hamas fuckers will see us soon, and we'll be sitting ducks."

"We can't leave Wyatt out here, and I can't get a good look at him in this shit. We have to move him," Finn decided. "But if his spine is injured, we'll cause permanent damage if we're not careful."

Wyatt had had a bad feeling from the moment they'd arrived in Aswan, as if he somehow knew this day was coming. But Finn was going to save him come hell or high water. He hadn't fought hard enough to save Jaden twenty years ago, and he'd be damned if he'd let Wyatt's life slip through his fingers tonight.

"See if there's a transfer board inside the bird," he called out.

"Roman's already grabbing it," A.J. said, and Finn noticed A.J. reaching for something on his wrist, but he couldn't quite make out what he was doing.

"Hang on to this . . . buddy. You'll be ok-okay," A.J. said as if choking on a mouthful of sand.

The black band.

The lucky band Marcus had always worn, except on the day he died, the day Bravo lost him.

The guys rotated wearing it in his memory and honor.

A.J. slipped it onto Wyatt's wrist, and Finn's throat grew tight with emotion. The last time the band had been passed out of turn was to save the lives of Luke and Jessica in Afghanistan, and now they sure as hell needed to save Wyatt's. They needed some more of the good luck Marcus's band would bring them. Of course, Finn had never considered it good luck as much as it was Marcus watching over them.

They couldn't lose anyone else. One was already too many.

"He's going to be okay. Pulse is still strong," Finn said, and Roman appeared a moment later with the board.

Finn and the others surrounded Wyatt and gently shifted him onto it, doing their best to keep his spine straight.

"Easy, easy," Finn instructed as they cut through the dust that wasn't quite as thick now and had become more like wind kicking up a bunch of dirt in their faces.

"Pilot is still out cold, but he doesn't look injured," Roman said once they carefully set the transfer board down inside the helo, and Finn dropped to his knees to try and better examine Wyatt.

"We've got incoming," A.J. hollered a moment before gunfire crackled in the air. "We'll cover you. Just take care of Echo One."

"Be careful." The guys had no clue how many tangos were out there or what they were up against. But Finn knew Bravo would be close by. They'd never leave Echo Team out there alone.

Finn shifted his rifle to his side in case he needed to reach for it in a hurry, then knocked his NVGs to the top of his head to take a closer look at the damage to Wyatt's body.

His shoulders jerked when a bullet pinged inside the bird. And then another.

Finn shielded Wyatt with his own body, covering his face to protect Echo One to the best of his ability as more and more bullets flew around. He kept his head low and snatched his sidearm in one quick movement when he spied a tango approaching from around the bird, and he snapped out a shot and dropped the guy.

"They're surrounding us on all sides," Chris said as he took out two tangos while jumping into the bird. "We don't have enough coverage."

They'd been in jams before but not being able to see your enemy was a big disadvantage.

Chris remained on one side of Wyatt to protect him and Finn on the other. He'd have to examine Wyatt once they eliminated the immediate threats.

Chris reached for the radio. "TOC, do you come in? TOC, do you come in?"

Static cut over the line, the storm still blocking the signal.

Could the drone overhead see them?

"Bravo Five is . . . on . . . ." Jessica's voice came over the radio a second later, and Finn's heart jumped. "Air support . . . . stay inside the . . . bird."

Finn spotted another tango on approach, and he aimed for the head. Missed. Shot him again. *Stay down, please.* Unlike some of those pricks at the compound who'd kept coming like they were in a zombie apocalypse movie.

"Get back in the bird," Chris called out to Roman and A.J., who quickly appeared. "Jessica is telling us to stay inside."

"Knox must have made a call to his dad. We've got backup on its way," Chris told the guys, and they remained in positions to ward off threats, keeping their bodies around

Wyatt as a layer of protection for Echo One. They couldn't lose their team leader.

"Air support?" Roman coughed. "The Navy must have a ship on the Red Sea. No other way to get here that fast," he added before shooting a guy who came bursting through the dust, almost entering the helo.

"I don't know. I don't care who helps," A.J. answered, staying on guard behind his rifle. "They just need to get here fast."

"But can they see us and the bad guys? Can they fly in this shit?" Finn asked.

"It's clearing up," Chris said. "But I don't know."

"It's me. Don't shoot!" someone yelled a second later, and relief filled Finn at the realization it was Knox. He must have driven there with one of their Land Cruisers. Finding them was a miracle in itself.

As Knox hopped into the helo, Finn dropped a tango aiming at him. "Thanks, brother." Knox lowered to one knee with his rifle. "Five more minutes, and we should have air support clear a path for us. I'll drive you to where Bravo landed, and we'll medevac Wyatt to the ship."

Thank God for the Navy and Knox's connections.

"I have a feeling that when your dad found out you left your cushy TOC post to come play in the sand with terrorists tonight, he suddenly 'remembered' us," A.J. said but remained steady and focused, continuing to check for tangos.

"Something like that. Sorry it took so long to get to you. Damn sand." Knox peeked back at Wyatt on the helo's floor, and Finn was able to see much better, which meant their enemies would be able to soon as well. "Hang in there, brother."

"Where's Bravo? Carter?" Finn asked.

"They've been told to stand down and head back to their

366

bird while the pilots handle these pricks," Knox informed them.

A few minutes and about four more kills later, Finn heard the familiar scream of jets overhead and the explosive sound of sand being obliterated—hopefully along with the bad guys.

"If that ain't the sweetest sound I've ever heard." A.J. smiled.

Finn waited for the gunfire to stop, then turned back to Wyatt. "Let's get our man to safety."

* * *

FINN HADN'T BEEN ON A SHIP IN FOREVER. THE WATERS WERE choppy tonight, and his stomach did a few somersaults as he waited for news about Wyatt. All of Bravo and Echo were on board, but Carter's men had headed back to their TOC, and Finn hated he'd yet to see or even talk to Julia. First, he needed to hear that Echo One would be okay, and then he'd find a way to reach out to her.

"How many of us have had head injuries lately?" Roman cupped the back of his neck with one hand, pacing alongside Finn.

"Hopefully, he was only knocked unconscious, and his busted leg will be . . . well, let's hope he can still operate." *And survive.* Damn it, survive was the number one focus.

But Finn knew Wyatt wouldn't be able to handle news that he couldn't operate again. He may have been nervous with a baby on the way, but Wyatt was a SEAL. A warrior. He wouldn't know how to be anything else. Not anytime soon, at least. Same with the rest of them. And regardless of how terrified Natasha had to be after learning Wyatt had been injured during the op, she knew and understood her husband.

She knew the kind of man she married. And she supported him through and through.

Can Julia support me? Will there be an us?

The idea of losing her shredded him, but he had to focus on Wyatt. He couldn't think about himself right now. But his thoughts were also making him a little crazy. Or maybe it was the waiting that made him nuts.

"We didn't lose anyone. Amin is dead. And we also picked off a bunch of Hamas fuckers," A.J. said, joining them, "so stop acting as though we did lose someone."

"Wyatt will be—"

"Fine," Chris cut off Finn, which was probably for the best since he had no idea where that sentence was headed. But now, all of Echo, minus their team leader, paced like a bunch of crazies topside. "If Knox hadn't called his dad, and this ship hadn't been here, then yeah, we'd be in a different boat. You know, literally and physically."

Finn stopped walking, and his shoulders fell. "Wyatt had a bad feeling. He knew this was going to happen."

"Wyatt will be fine," Roman noted in a deep voice. "His pulse was strong. Chest looked okay when you examined him on the bird here."

No blood on his chest, but there'd been a lot on his head that the helmet had hidden, and his leg had been . . . in rough shape.

"How are we swinging the story of what went down?" Finn asked, needing a distraction.

"Luke spoke to POTUS," Roman began. "From the sounds of it, no one is claiming to know anything about what went down in that desert. Not the Sudanese, the Saudis, and sure as hell not POTUS. They're all feigning ignorance to keep shit peaceful, I suppose. Saudis don't want to fess up to what Amin was doing there any more than the Sudanese government wants to admit a known terrorist cell was there."

"So, no one will know Amin was really a terrorist, then?" Finn's shoulders dropped at the news. And what would that mean for Oliver? Would Kaira be able to convince the police in Dubai that it was Amin who had killed her husband? Or was Finn going to need to plan a prison break?

Roman grimaced. "The drugs are destroyed. A bunch of terrorists are dead. And we're all—"

"Okay." It was Luke. "We're all okay."

Finn abruptly spun, and his hands dropped to his thighs as he bowed his head. "Wyatt?" He lifted his eyes to look at Bravo One.

Luke stepped before Echo Team and crossed his arms. "Wyatt is going to be okay. It might take him a long time in PT to undo the damage to his leg, but he's alive. And the doctor says he should still be able to operate if he wants to."

Filled with relief, Finn lowered to a knee and closed his eyes.

"Oh, he'll want to," he overheard A.J. say.

"Thank God," Chris said under his breath.

Finn slowly opened his eyes to look at the man who'd recruited him back in 2013. He'd always said he'd follow both Luke, Wyatt, and any other person on his team to hell if he had to . . . and tonight, facing what had felt like Osiris's army of the dead, sure as hell felt like they had been in hell.

"How's Natasha?" Finn asked as Roman hooked an arm under his and helped him to his feet.

"Much better now that she knows her husband is okay. And I'm pretty sure she would have infiltrated the White House and threatened POTUS had he not made the right call to save our man tonight," Luke answered.

"Oh, she would have," Knox said, coming up behind

Luke. "I warned my dad you don't want to mess with a pregnant woman. I speaketh from experience," he said with a smile while slapping a hand to his chest, referring to his pregnant wife.

And the entire mood on deck was now much different. Because they hadn't lost any brothers tonight.

"We can't bring Julia to the ship, and now that we know Wyatt is good, Asher is catching a ride to Jessica." Luke looked to Finn. "You wanna go see your girl, too?"

My girl? "I need to put eyes on Wyatt first. Make sure he's okay."

"Wyatt would want you putting eyes on Julia to ease her worries, trust me. Echo One would kick your ass for staying here and leaving Julia there," Luke said, and how'd Luke even know he and Julia were a . . .

What are we?

"Roger that." Finn smiled, but his nerves were still all mangled from the night, and he also had no clue what this night had done to Julia.

He'd been shot in Aswan. His helo had gone down tonight, and they'd nearly lost Echo One. Would she be able to handle more of these nights in the future?

"Just a heads-up, there's a chance we might need to break Oliver out of jail in Dubai if Kaira can't convince the authorities that he's innocent." Finn looked around at his brothers with a serious expression. "I, uh, made a promise to Julia."

CHAPTER THIRTY-TWO

FINN HOPPED OUT OF THE HELO ALONGSIDE ASHER AND Roman, careful of the blades chopping the air, and watched as both men rushed to the women waiting for them.

Julia remained rooted in place, her back glued to the building exterior, and stared at him as if she were uncertain he was real. He wanted to run to her and lift her into the air the way Asher had with Jessica and Roman with Harper, but instead, he was suffering from another two-second delay. He felt like everything was happening in slow motion.

A new day had dawned while they were on the ship, and from the looks of it, the sand had given up its tantrum in the desert. If it weren't for Julia standing there, and he was fairly certain she wasn't a mirage, Finn might have thought last night was just another nightmare.

He desperately wanted to run to her but instead forced himself to walk across the courtyard to where she stood. Sunglasses shielded her eyes, and with each step closer, his heart pounded a little harder because he knew . . . he knew she was terrified. Or, at least, she'd been scared last night.

And he didn't blame her. But the terror still clung to her like a second skin, and he felt it strike him in the chest like a tidal wave.

"Hi," she whispered once he was within kissing distance. Finn lowered his gaze to her mouth as she worried her lower lip between her teeth.

He'd made sure to wipe any blood from his skin before he departed the ship, not wanting to freak her out the way he had after he'd pummeled her abductor in the desert a few days ago.

"Hi back." His voice was rough, his throat raw from the wind and sand. Out of the corner of his eye, he caught Asher and the others going inside, and Finn assumed Carter and his men were in the building as well.

"I'm going to kiss you now." The words tumbled out of his mouth as he reached to caress her cheek, unable to stop himself.

She lifted her chin, offering him her mouth, and that invitation was all he needed.

He framed her face with both hands and set his lips to hers. A soft kiss at first before he grew more ravenous and parted her lips with his tongue.

Could she taste his fear? The worry that he was going to lose her now that she'd had a front-row seat to the type of danger the teams encountered each time they spun up? Did she know how fast his heart was racing beneath his gear as the sun beat down on his back?

"I'm sorry if we scared you last night," he said against her mouth after breaking their kiss a moment or two later.

"I'm so glad everyone is okay." She set her hands on top of his as he kept hold of her face, and he wished he could see her eyes. But based on the wobble of her lip and break in her voice, tears were building up and threatening to spill.

"I can't lose another brother," he confessed.

She lightly nodded. "And I can't lose you."

But what did that mean? He hoped it meant that she wanted to go all-in with him. That she felt the same about him as he felt about her. But he needed to hear her say the words, needed to know that she could look at him and love him for who he was and without reservation.

"Hey, we've gotta get out of here in five." Carter poked his head out the door and motioned for them to get a move on.

Every time they were on the verge of sharing their feelings, they were interrupted. But for some reason, he found himself wanting to thank Carter this time because his gut was telling him that Julia was about to walk away from him. And the idea of that had his pulse beating out a panicky staccato.

"What about Oliver?" Finn asked Carter, knowing the question had to be on Julia's mind.

"I'm heading back to Dubai to meet with Kaira and Tariq. Would you two like to join me?" Carter asked.

Finn released his hold of Julia's cheeks, but he already knew the answer. "Of course."

Julia nodded, and Carter disappeared back inside.

"Let's go get your man back." *Why the hell did I say that? I'm her . . .*

Julia tipped her head to the side, removed her sunglasses, and the heartbreaking look in her blue eyes about did him in. "Finn," she whispered, but he held up a hand.

"Not now," he pleaded. "Tell me after." *Break my heart after.*

* * *

DUBAI – THIRTY-SIX HOURS LATER

Finn wasn't sure if he'd ever be able to watch '80s-era movies again. Not even *Empire Strikes Back*. And he sure as hell wouldn't be watching *The Mummy*. But damn, the '80s would forever remind Finn of the woman he fell for and . . . lost. He was jumping the gun on the "lost" part, but Julia had barely spoken a word to him since they'd left Egypt. *Of course, I told her not to, didn't I?*

They hadn't slept in the same bed last night, either. When he offered her the second bedroom in their suite at the hotel, she'd simply nodded. But the sadness in her big blue eyes, and the reluctant way she'd agreed, gutted him. And as he'd watched her disappear into her own room and shut the door, it'd felt like the answer to his question.

"Thank you again for helping Kaira." Jack shook Finn's hand after he'd said his thanks to Carter, and it felt a bit weird to be accepting a thief's thank you.

"If you're ever in New York," Julia said with an easy smile, "don't steal my Warhol."

The confirmation that her friend was on his way to see her had lifted a few layers of worry, and she was glowing. Thank God Finn had managed to keep that promise to bring her friend home.

"Ah, what the hell"—Julia waved her hand through the air—"you can have it."

"What?" Jack frowned, which wasn't the reaction Finn expected. Did Jack want the challenge?

"Or not." Julia winked, probably confusing the hell out of the poor guy. "But you managed to convince Kaira to help get my friend out of jail, so I'll happily donate whatever artwork you'd like in the future."

"Ah, I'd say your friends pushed the police into making the right decision. Not so sure if they would have listened to Kaira had Jessica not provided the evidence she did," Carter pointed out, and he was most likely spot on.

Oliver was en route to Kaira's house at the moment, being escorted by Carter's men. Carter had suggested Julia stay behind when they presented the new evidence to the police and asked that all charges against Oliver be dropped and that he be released immediately. The authorities were extremely cooperative and all too happy to oblige, most likely worried that word would get out that the famous tough-on-crime city had gotten it wrong.

Jessica had worked her magic once again and had managed to recover the original surveillance footage from the day Oliver had supposedly pushed Ario to his death. Footage that proved Amin was, in fact, the murderer. Between that, Kaira's statement, and the police then realizing that the timeline of events leading up to Ario's death was different than originally believed, they didn't have much choice but to let Oliver go.

Plus, it was all a bit messy with Amin getting killed inside a compound in Sudan that had traces of drugs—the Saudis wanted the entire incident swept under a rug. And it'd take an awfully big rug to hide that mess. In the end, though, the bad guys were taken out, and the drugs wouldn't flood the streets, so Finn had to accept the politics of it all and take it as a win.

"I'm so sorry again," Kaira apologized to . . . well, everyone in the room from the looks of it.

"What about Tariq? What happens to him?" Julia asked. The man had killed Giorgio and Lorenzo, but Finn wasn't sure what to make of him at this point. For years, he'd assumed it'd been Tariq funding terrorists.

Clearly, each family has its own issues, not just mine. He thought about his parents, knowing his dad didn't seem to hold a grudge against him, but his mom was a different story.

"I supplied Tariq with enough money to go off the grid and spend an indefinite amount of time alone." Kaira gave Finn a look as if he might challenge her decision to let her brother escape. But now that Oliver was free and all of his teammates had survived the mission, he was pretty sure he'd never think about Tariq again as long as the man stayed on the right side of the law.

Carter checked his watch a beat later. "My men should be rolling up now with Oliver."

Julia peered at Finn, and her relaxed look seemed to fade, which didn't make that much sense considering the good news.

Oh, she's thinking about me, isn't she? About what happens next. And that narrowed blue gaze had him clearing his throat and taking a step backward.

Finn walked past Julia to look out at the view of the Persian Gulf from Kaira's mansion. "Will the rest of your family leave you alone?"

Kaira joined him by the glass doors that led to the terrace. "I hope so. If not, I guess I know who to call." She jerked a thumb over her shoulder. "Just kidding. Don't worry, I'll leave you all alone."

Finn peeked at her and smiled. "Appreciate that. I try to stay out of family feuds."

"They're here," Carter announced, and Finn slowly turned toward the large, two-story living room to put eyes on the hall.

The moment Oliver stepped into the room alongside Carter's men, Julia rushed to him, and he lifted her into his arms. Finn's eyes stung for a second, and what the hell was that about . . . this wasn't about him. Although, to be honest, he was more than a little jealous at the sight of another man holding her, but he also felt a sense of relief because she finally had her best friend back, and she wasn't hurting anymore.

Finn took a moment to study Oliver, hating that jealousy lingered in the pit of his stomach. Oliver would be in Julia's life forever as her friend. But Finn doubted he could handle a "friends only" relationship with Julia. It'd hurt too damn much.

Oliver was about the same height as Finn. Similar build. Some ink on his arms beneath the short sleeves of his white tee. His brown hair was probably longer than normal and a little tousled as if he'd been clawing at it all morning while waiting for his freedom. But Finn definitely got the "good guy" vibe from him.

"I'm so sorry, Oliver." Kaira approached him once he'd let go of Julia, only to hook his arm around Julia's waist and pull her to his side, and ohhh, that was a damn knife to the chest.

They're just friends. Close friends, he told himself so he wouldn't go deck the guy.

Julia's attention shifted to Finn as Oliver and Kaira exchanged a few awkward words. She stepped out of Oliver's hold and started across the room to Finn. His breath froze in his lungs as he anticipated what she might say.

Crisp white pants hid her long legs, and she had on a silky, gold blouse with her hair in a braid hanging off to one side. Barely any makeup. So beautiful.

Mine. He wanted her to be his. Not Oliver's. And not any other man's. How did he convince her to want that, too? *I can't. She has to . . . want me, too.*

"Thank you," she said while pulling Finn in for an

unexpected hug. He squeezed his eyes shut for a moment and embraced her, setting his hands on her back and pinning her tight against his body.

When his eyes opened, they were met with Oliver's, and a big smile broke out on the man's face. Not a hint of jealousy there, only happiness for Julia. *Okay, so I don't need to hit you after I helped save you.*

"Finn helped bring you home," Julia informed Oliver once she'd released her hold of Finn and turned back to the room.

"It was all Julia," Finn said, not wanting the guy to feel as if he owed Finn anything.

Oliver left Kaira's side and made his way across the room, ignoring Joan and Jack as if they weren't there. "From what I heard on the way here, you had yourself quite the adventure." Oliver's eyes swept from Julia's over to Finn's as he reached for Finn's hand. "Thank you for keeping her out of too much trouble. The woman can be stubborn when she's trying to get her way."

Finn couldn't hold back the laugh that escaped. "That's for damn sure."

"Hey now." The smile parked on Julia's lips was priceless. "Can we have a second?" she asked Oliver. "Something I want to give you."

At those words, Finn's stomach dropped. *Ah, hell.*

"Here." Kaira quickly cut across the room and opened the glass doors, motioning for Julia and Oliver to go out onto the terrace.

Finn looked away and dragged a hand through his own hair to muss it up.

Carter came up to Finn. "You good?"

"Uh, yeah." Finn faked a smile, knowing the former CIA

officer and Delta guy wouldn't buy into his BS. *Probably shouldn't have mumbled uh, you idiot.*

"You look tense, pal. I think I know what you need. Give me an hour, and I can help you out before you catch that flight home." Carter's smirk gave Finn pause, but what the hell? What was one more adventure in Dubai?

CHAPTER THIRTY-THREE

JULIA STOOD ALONGSIDE OLIVER AND GAWKED AT THE TWO Lamborghinis parked side by side on a deserted road flanked by sand dunes. One ridiculously expensive vehicle was sunset orange and the other lime green. She bit her thumbnail in nervous anticipation of the race that was about to begin and hoped Finn and Carter knew what the hell they were doing.

She had no clue how Carter had pulled this off or why he'd even challenged Finn to a race, but maybe Finn needed it? He was tense. After what happened to Wyatt, of course. But Julia was fairly certain she was contributing to that tension, too.

She thought back to how Finn had handled the Range Rover as if it were a Ferrari when they'd first arrived in Dubai. What would he do behind the wheel of a Lamborghini?

"Who are these guys?" Oliver asked her, folding his arms over his muscular chest.

"Long story about Finn. But Carter's still a question mark to me." She looked around at Carter's men surrounding them, curious about their backstories and why they worked with

Carter. What exactly did they do when they weren't taking down terrorists, and from what she understood, they didn't have the government's blessing, so why'd they do it? And how'd they get paid? She doubted Carter offered stock options to his guys.

"Well, looks like you found a good man." Oliver nudged her in the side.

She lifted her sunglasses to peer at Oliver for a moment, so damn relieved and thankful she hadn't lost him. He had on Tucker's ID tags she'd given him an hour ago back at Kaira's mansion before they'd said goodbye to her, Joan, and Jack. Although, she had a feeling she'd be seeing the *Romancing the Stone* couple again down the road.

I think it's time I give these to you, she'd said to Oliver out on that terrace.

Oliver had lifted his brows in surprise. *You sure?*

She'd peered back into the living room at Finn as he'd talked with Carter and then nodded, knowing she'd never be able to put the past behind her and find a future with Finn if she didn't give up Tucker's tags.

"I care about him," she finally answered. "But what if he gets hurt? What if something happens to him because of his job?" *What if I miss the signs again?*

Oliver freed his arms from across his chest as she let her sunglasses fall back into place. "Baby girl, that's a lot of what-ifs." He circled her wrist with a large hand. "If he makes you happy, I say go for it. Life is too short to be afraid of what-ifs. Look at me, I almost—"

"That was my fault. You took the job because of me."

"You're not seriously blaming yourself for what happened, are you?" He scoffed and released her hand to remove his shades, ones Carter had loaned him for the insane afternoon race. "Don't. Even. Think. About. It." He tipped his head to the side. "Woman, I'm warning you." His tone switched to light and teasing, but she knew he was serious. He didn't want her carrying any more guilt.

She reached for the pendant around her neck Finn had given her and clutched it.

"I'm about to watch two strangers race some Lambos instead of waiting to get executed, and that's thanks to you. That's all I'm focused on."

"But what happens next for you?"

He put his glasses back on, and they both turned toward where Carter and Finn were talking by the cars. "The great thing about tomorrow is you just never know what's next. Life is exciting that way."

"I just don't want—"

"What happened to Tuck won't happen to me. Plus, you have my back. I know that. I'll let you know if I ever need you."

"You promise?" She needed double confirmation.

He hooked his arm around her back and then quickly let her go as if noticing Finn's attention on them. Finn was too far away and his beard was getting thicker, but she'd still swear she'd witnessed his jaw tense at the sight of Oliver's hand on her back. "He's a keeper. I wouldn't want another man touching my woman either."

In her heart, she knew she was Finn's, but maybe she needed to figure out who the hell *she* was first, to find the woman she'd lost before she could move forward?

She thought about the flower on the pendant. *Rebirth.*

"When did you two fall in love?" Oliver asked softly.

Love? She watched Finn climb behind the wheel of the green Lamborghini. *The two idiots weren't wearing helmets. Well, he better have his seat belt on.*

But seriously, they were in a city that was tough on crime,

and yet, Carter pulled some strings to make this impromptu race happen. Oliver was right. Who *was* Carter?

"I, um." Was she ready to drop that four-letter word yet? "My friend faked some death threats, and you know Michael, well, he asked Finn to protect me."

"Ah, glad your bodyguard story turned out different than mine," Oliver said with a laugh.

"Hey, now." Julia poked him in the ribs. "You're right, though," she added with a laugh of her own.

"You all ready?" one of Carter's men asked, approaching them.

His voice sounded familiar. "Were you the fourth sniper that took out the horseman guy?"

The man lifted his sunglasses and winked. She'd take that as a yes. "Engines are about to rev. These bad boys are going to tear out of here. Max speed of 325 kilometers per hour."

"And why are they doing this again?" she asked him as Oliver moved her off to the side of the road as the two vehicles' engines turned on and roared.

"She kidding?" The man looked at Oliver with a grin. "What guy doesn't want to race a Lambo in Dubai? A little *Fast and Furious* action."

Ah, another movie. "Okay, okay. But what woman doesn't want to race, either?" she teased.

He grinned and pointed to Julia. "I like her."

"Easy, she's taken," Oliver said, jerking his chin toward the green Lamborghini.

Sniper Guy allowed his sunglasses to fall back in place and raised his hands in playful surrender. "Go time."

When Finn tore past her, he was already cutting down the road so fast, and yet . . . she was pretty sure he'd looked straight at her, and her stomach dropped at what she knew needed to happen when he hit the finish line.

She watched his car disappear in the distance and remained on edge every second he was out of sight. "Y'all place bets?"

Sniper Guy smirked. "Delta Force versus the SEAL. Damn straight."

"I'm assuming you were a Delta guy?" she asked, and Sniper Guy only smiled in answer.

"Well, I'd normally put my money on the Army," Oliver spoke up, "but any man who can win over her heart has my money."

Julia faced Oliver. "I can't figure out if that's an insult or a compliment."

"Compliment," both Oliver and Sniper Guy said at the same time, then smiled.

When Julia heard the roar of the engines again, she looked off in the distance to see a speck of orange and one of green, growing larger and appearing, neck and neck as they came their way full throttle. Top speeds, from the looks of it.

Both cars blew past her a moment later, and she sure as hell couldn't tell who won. It was too close to call. Maybe that was better. A tie. But would these two be able to handle a tie? Probably not.

When Finn exited the vehicle looking sexier than hell, she wanted to run to him as if he'd won the big race and fling herself into his sexy arms.

In jeans and a black tee with shades on, he was smoking hot. And a man that could handle a wheel like that—well, damn.

"It's a tie. Going to have to go again," Sniper Guy hollered out and left her side to go to Finn and Carter.

Finn shoved his sunglasses into his hair and pointed his gaze at Julia. "I'll take the tie," he said in a low voice as she slowly approached him.

"Hi," she said in a soft voice.

"Hi back."

"That was pretty badass." She smiled even though her legs were weak, knowing what she needed to say soon.

"Ah, it was fun." Finn shrugged, but she knew he'd had a blast, even though he didn't look any less tense. "You ready to go home?"

She looked up at the clear blue sky before resetting her focus on Finn. Her stomach, chest, and well, everything hurt right now. "I, um . . ."

Finn captured her cheek in his large warm palm and steadied his eyes on hers. "Take your time," he rasped in a low, husky tone. "I'll wait for you forever."

CHAPTER THIRTY-FOUR

NEW YORK CITY, NEW YORK – THREE DAYS LATER

Julia lifted her glass and took a sip of her French martini, her sister-in-law's favorite, and studied Kate and Michael sitting across the booth at the bar in Tribeca. Michael had his arm wrapped adoringly around his wife, pinning her tight to his side, and Kate had her head resting on his shoulder. That was love. A sweet, forever kind of love Julia hadn't known she craved until . . . until Finn.

Until *Dalton*. Her thighs squeezed beneath the table at the memory of the first night they'd made love in Dubai. It'd only been three days since he'd raced the Lamborghini, and she missed him already.

"We lost you. Where are you at?" Fingers snapped in front of her face.

"Dubai," Julia whispered and followed the long fingers to her friend sitting beside her. She set her eyes on Mya, who'd helped not only save Oliver by leading her to Giorgio but had ultimately brought Finn into her life.

"You ever going to tell us the dirty details of what happened out there?" Mya waggled her brows.

"Can you save those details for when I use the men's room?" Michael released his hold of his wife, sat taller, and offered Julia his standard brotherly cringe.

"I would hope she'll need more time than the few minutes it takes you to use the restroom." Kate linked her hand with Michael's on top of the table.

Michael grabbed his beer with his free hand and closed his eyes as if trying to banish all thoughts of his sister doing things he didn't want to know about in the first place.

"You all really didn't need to fly to New York to check on me. You're still unpacking." Julia redirected the conversation away from her sex life, and her brother threw her a grateful look.

"Mom and Dad have the kids, and Kate and I have two quick nights away. It's not exactly a hardship to visit you." He smiled. "Plus, after everything you went through, I'm going to check in on my little sister."

"And you know for damn sure I'm checking up on you." Mya elbowed her, and Julia nearly spilled her drink on her silky blue blouse. "I'm just so relieved Oliver is okay."

"No thanks to me," Michael said under his breath. "Sorry again."

"Everything happens for a reason." How could she not believe that now after the last few weeks? "So, where is Miss Lois Lane off to next?" Julia once again changed the subject, unable to share the details about what really went down out in that desert or risk getting Finn and his teammates in trouble.

"We'll see where the wind blows." Mya flitted her hand in the air.

"Your father would prefer that the wind kept you local," Michael said in his predictably no-nonsense tone.

Mya's father was a judge in the city, and the man had to worry about her and her crazy adventures. He wasn't father of the year from the little Julia knew about him, but he was still a father. Didn't most fathers worry?

"You know I'll do the opposite of what dear old dad wants."

Julia set down her drink and looked around the room, half hoping to see Finn watching over her from the bar, the way he'd done the night she'd lured Lorenzo out for drinks. But no, he wasn't standing there, nor were Harper and Roman. And her heart sank a little. She'd really enjoyed hanging out with Harper and had even envisioned what it would be like to be friends with her as well as Jessica.

"How's Mason? I haven't talked to him in a bit," Kate slyly asked Mya, obviously poking around. Curious to know if they were still friends with benefits, which most of them seemed to know about even though Mason and Mya had tried to keep it on the DL.

Mya had just taken a sip of her drink and nearly spit it out. "He's good, I think."

"He's dating someone." Michael frowned. "The wrong someone."

"Ah." Mya shrugged. "She looks like a Barbie to me. I mean, she's a swimsuit model." She drummed the fingers of her free hand on the table. "Anyway, maybe I ought to get one of those water bungalows somewhere and just chill for a week or so. Just me, the ocean, and—"

"You'd be bored out of your mind," Kate cut her off.

"No." Julia smiled. "She'd manage to get herself into some trouble. Accidentally uncover a salacious story."

Mya looked at her and laughed. "You're right. I would."

"I think I might, um, head back home now, though," Julia announced a few moments later. As fun as it had been to spend time with everyone, she was in the mood to listen to sad music and wallow in self-pity. Or, more precisely, revisit the time she and Finn had spent together in hopes it would help her work up the courage to put on her big-girl panties and push through her issues so they could be together.

"You sure?" Michael tipped his head to the side and released Kate's hand to go for his wallet after she responded with a nod.

Once they were outside at the curb, Michael opened the door of the limo he'd insisted she take for safety reasons, and after she said her goodbyes to Kate and Mya, he gently laid a hand on her arm. "Julia."

"Yeah?" She lifted a brow, preparing herself to challenge whatever it was he intended to say using his big-brother tone.

"Finn loves you. I saw it in his eyes on that beach in Dubai." Michael glanced at a couple passing by. "But he could die." He briefly looked at Mya, who was a few feet away talking to his wife, ensuring they were out of earshot. "The work he does is dangerous. I don't see a man like him trading in his job for love, though."

"I would never ask him to." *Never.*

Her stomach did sad little flips at the message her brother was trying to drive home. *Be sure. Be absolutely freaking sure you can handle being with Finn before jumping into things with him. The forever kind of sure.*

"I don't want to see you in pain again. After Tuck died, I thought I'd lose you, too." He'd never confided that before, but until he met Kate, he'd been a one-night-stand, hide-his-emotions kind of guy.

"But you didn't lose me."

"Because you buried yourself in work with the company. And you let go of your dreams to do it." He set his large hand on her shoulder and lightly squeezed. "Maybe pick your camera up again, and see if things look differently through that lens."

She smiled. "When did you become all wordsmithy?"

He looked to Kate, the love of his life. *His* ride or die. "I think you know the answer to that." After he gave her a hug, she waved goodbye to everyone and slipped inside the limo to be alone with her thoughts.

Upon entering her condo, she reached for the light switch but realized the lights were already on. She frowned as a tingling sensation crept up her spine. "No one is here," she told herself.

But she'd go get her 9mm and clear the apartment the way her brother had taught her to do. And hope no one was in her bedroom already.

As she walked past her office on her way to her room, she halted. The light was on in there, and . . .

"That thief," Julia said, shaking her head.

She wasn't in danger. No, she'd been robbed.

She entered her office to find a note stuck to the wall behind her desk, where her Warhol had been, and couldn't help but chuckle.

She removed the hot-pink sticky note from the wall.

I couldn't help myself. Old habits die hard. Stealing is so much more fun. X, Jack

"Once a thief, always a thief." She set the note on her desk and left the room for her bedroom, still chuckling. Joan sure had her work cut out for her if she wanted her husband to stop his wicked ways. "Good luck," she said under her breath as she entered her en suite.

She grabbed her phone and discarded her purse, then turned on the shower, knowing exactly what she wanted to do. No, what she *needed* to do.

Julia opened YouTube on her phone to play the *One Night*

in Dubai song, removed her heels, then stepped into the shower fully dressed.

She closed her eyes and gasped when the water, still a bit cold, hit her.

Memories of joining Finn inside that shower in Aswan, both of them fully clothed, and him giving her the first orgasm she'd had in ages filled her mind. And she slowly lowered to her knees and bowed her head beneath the spray and prayed that walking away from him when their plane touched down in the U.S. hadn't been the biggest mistake of her life.

* * *

OUTER BANKS, NORTH CAROLINA

Julia stood inside the darkroom she'd asked her father to close up after Tucker died years ago and looked around. After her shower last night, she'd packed a bag and hopped on the first flight to North Carolina the next morning.

She'd known what she needed to do. Her brother was right. Finn had said the same thing to her in Dubai as well.

She needed to come there. To unlock the darkroom and find herself again. To find the woman she'd locked away, the woman who Finn had helped wake up.

Julia closed her eyes for a moment, drew in a breath of musty air, then waved off the dust that filled her gaze upon parting her lids.

She slowly walked around the room, at first just looking at everything and taking it all in. The enlargers, lenses, photo paper that was probably no good now, and tongs. Then she made a second journey around the room to physically touch it all.

Her fingers skimmed over the plastic trays she'd once used and onto the little bottles, now empty of chemicals.

Everything was still in its place, including her Canon she hadn't touched since Tucker's accident.

Before she'd opened the darkroom that morning, she'd stopped in town and bought a new camera. A fresh start. She'd gone with a Nikon, not only because she believed it to be a superior choice but because she'd used a Nikon with Finn.

As she'd clicked photo after photo in the Lahbab Desert with Finn, she'd been creating new memories, memories she didn't want to lock away and forget. And why would she?

They may have been working to take down a bad guy at the time, but she wanted to hang on to everything else that had happened.

Julia smiled as other happy memories filled her thoughts. "You're in a better place," she whispered her thoughts to Tucker, lifting her chin. "But I'm not ready for you to take Finn there with you. Okay?"

Would he answer? Probably not.

But she had to try.

After she cleaned up the room and prepped it for use, she went back into the house to retrieve her new camera and started outside for the beach.

It was a clear day. No clouds in sight. No storm on the horizon.

The sand felt good on her bare feet as she padded her way toward the water and lifted the camera to take a photo of the waves rolling in, creating a soft foam on the beach.

A few more shots and she was already feeling better. More alive.

She started to lower her camera when she heard a noise in the distance. The thundering thud of hooves pounding through wet sand had her bringing the camera back to her eye and pivoting around to see a wild horse running along the water's edge.

Her chest tightened at the sight, and she captured the moment, remembering Finn's comment about the photo she had over her couch back in New York the morning before they'd gone to Egypt.

And now, here she was.

As the horse neared her, she stepped back and removed the camera to take in the beauty of the animal catching her eyes the moment he passed, his silky mane blowing behind him in the breeze.

She thought back to Dubai, remembering Finn's nightmare.

This sign, this horse, was meant for him.

"And you're not here with me." Her stomach ached at the thought, at how much she already missed that man.

But she did her best to pull herself together and focus ahead, hoping Finn would be part of whatever was in store for her. A part of her tomorrow and every day after that.

CHAPTER THIRTY-FIVE

VIRGINIA

FINN HELD THE NECK OF HIS BEER AT HIS SIDE AS HE PEERED around the expansive backyard of Chris and Rory's house, where all of Bravo and Echo Teams and their families had gathered for a cookout and a celebration that Wyatt was alive. And another mission complete.

I'm still the only single guy. And as if their K9 heard his thoughts and didn't want him to feel lonely, Bear came barreling his way with enough force he nearly knocked him onto his ass. "What's up, boy?" He dropped to one knee, and with his free hand, scratched Bear behind the ears, then leaned and let Bear lick his cheek for a second.

"He missed you." It was Elaina, Liam and Emily's daughter. Finn smiled at her as she squatted on the other side of Bear to give him attention as well. "Do you think Uncle Wyatt is mad at me?"

"What?" Finn shook his head in surprise and set his beer in the grass, hoping it wouldn't spill. Elaina was heading into her teenage years—how the hell had that happened so fast—

and he knew Liam was going to lose his mind when she started dating. The kid was all kinds of special. "Why on earth would Wyatt be mad at you?"

She continued to pet Bear but set her eyes on Wyatt, who was standing on crutches, his leg in a cast, near the patio. Wyatt was talking to Gwen, his adult daughter he hadn't known existed until not too long ago, and he was laughing at something she was saying. "Because I didn't warn him about the storm. I didn't know about it. I should have known."

Finn's body went lax at her words. *Guilt. Hell no.* This girl was not going to saddle herself with guilt. He wouldn't allow that. No damn way. "That is not your fault. Not at all. Please, please do not think that." He dropped onto his ass on the ground and propped his knees up, and when Elaina copied his move, Bear ran off to jump around with Owen and Samantha's dog.

"I usually get warnings. I didn't this time. Maybe my mojo is gone."

"Mojo, huh?" Finn pushed his sunglasses into his hair, which was getting a bit longer and in need of a cut. And maybe he was looking more and more like Roman lately. "Do you want it to be gone?"

"Sometimes. But I could have kept Uncle Wyatt safe if I hadn't been on the fritz."

That made his stomach hurt. "You can't save everyone, Elaina, even when your mojo's not on the fritz. People make their own choices. Wyatt knew what he signed up for when he went out into that desert with the rest of us. He makes his own choices, and he knows what he . . ." Finn squeezed his eyes closed and damn near cried.

"You know, don't you?" Elaina whispered. A tear rolled down his cheek when her small hand grasped his. "You know it wasn't your fault now, don't you?"

She was talking about his brother, he was sure of it. But he didn't quite grasp how she was aware of Jaden. But one thing was for certain, her mojo was far from off.

"I'll forgive my brain for not knowing Wyatt was going to get hurt if you forgive yourself, too."

Finn wiped a tear free from his cheek and opened his eyes. He was choked up, damn it. "I should have saved him."

Elaina peered at him with her big brown eyes, the sunlight spilling all around her, making her look like an angel, a messenger from God. "You can't save everyone," she repeated his words, and he was going to have some kind of breakdown in two seconds. He could feel it. Dubai was only a week ago, and he missed Julia like crazy, and now hearing this . . . *Fuck.* "But you keep on trying, don't you?" A little smile met her lips. "So, I'll keep on trying too. I'll be like you." She tightened her grip on his big hand with all her strength, let go, then pushed up to her feet. "But I'm still going to go tell Uncle Wyatt sorry. Can't help myself."

This kid's wisdom was beyond her years and hell, his, too.

"I love you, Uncle Finn. You're going to make her a great husband."

"Make *who* a great husband?" He was sniffling, wasn't he?

Her grin stretched. "You know who," she singsonged before skipping away.

Finn quickly swiped at the tears escaping his eyes before his brothers saw his emotions leaking.

"Oh, she got to you, didn't she?" It was Chris, and he dropped down next to him with two beers and offered Finn a new one.

They both turned their attention to their teammates and

their families scattered about the yard, and Chris's gaze moved to Rory, to the woman who made him feel whole.

"Yeah, she got to me." Finn accepted the beer since it was cold, unlike the warm one he'd set down.

Elaina was now talking to Wyatt, and he rid himself of one crutch to hook an arm around her for a hug.

"What if Julia's never going to be ready for me?" he found himself asking after they sat for a few minutes in silence, which Chris must have realized he needed.

"Julia's the one for you. We all knew that when we had you draw the short straw to protect her." He lifted his sunglasses to wink at him, which had Finn rolling his eyes. "Plus, Harper says she offered her the beachfront house in North Carolina for us all to get hitched, so . . . we kind of need you two together to make that happen."

"You're hilarious."

Chris patted him on the back. "Totally not kidding. But maybe it'll end up being a triple wedding. Just not an accidental marriage this time, like with Liam and Emily."

Finn considered the insanity of his words. He knew Harper and Roman were going to want to get married ASAP with a baby on the way, and Chris and Rory had been undecided on their wedding location. *But me?* A wedding that summer to a woman he wasn't sure would be able to commit? Not going to happen.

"You never know, brother. You just never know what might happen."

Finn looked up as Luke and Jessica headed toward them, which for some reason brought him back to that shitty motel room in LA nine years ago when they'd recruited him. And he'd left Pasadena without visiting Jaden in the cemetery like he should have afterward. *Still haven't visited.*

Elaina wanted him to, didn't she? She'd just nudged him

to do so. To help him forgive himself for what she believed wasn't his fault. *Jaden chose to do drugs. How can I not be upset that I chose to keep his secret?*

"Why do you two look like team leaders right now instead of chill partygoers?" Chris asked once they stopped before them.

"Because POTUS called. We're spinning up." Luke grimaced as if this was the last thing he wanted, especially after they'd come close to losing Wyatt only last week. And then, of course, they were a man down if both teams were needed.

"Where are we going?" Finn grabbed his other bottle from the ground and stood at the news along with Chris.

"We're going hunting." Luke shrugged. "Or maybe fishing."

"What he means is POTUS wants us to find five new recruits. Scout them out. See who we want to form a new team."

"Wait, what?" Chris asked. "Like for real, for real? This is no longer just talk?"

Jessica removed her sunglasses, then exchanged a look with her brother before turning her attention back on Chris and Finn. "For real, for real."

"Charlie Team," Luke said. "I hate having a team called Alpha. Feels like they'd be in charge of us."

"Alpha males. Psh. You're all alphas," Jessica teased. "But Delta is reserved for us ladies when we join you."

"So, Charlie Team." Finn secured both bottles in one hand to free his other to shield his eyes from the sun and slide his glasses back in place.

Five more guys.

Was this really happening?

Finn immediately thought of Julia and her doubts about

whether she could handle all the worry and what-ifs every time he was on an op. He closed his eyes, and his entire body became weak. "You might need six," he added, his voice breaking at what that meant . . . he'd be leaving Echo Team.

* * *

LOS ANGELES, CALIFORNIA

Finn sat in front of the headstone with his brother's name etched above the gray cross and pulled up his music playlist on his phone. "Bryan Adams. *Everything I Do*," he said as he pressed play. "I heard it being performed while I was in Dubai recently. Thought of you, of course." He stretched his legs out in front of him, listening to the lyrics, and reached for the Nikon he'd asked Harper to give him back in Virginia before he'd left the party three days ago.

He clicked through the images he'd taken of Julia in Egypt. So beautiful in that sundress. He smirked as he recalled how outspoken she was that first day. She'd shocked the hell out of him, A.J., and Chris when she'd jokingly asked why men seemed to love doggy style so much.

"I fell for someone," he told his brother. "This girl is . . ." He shook his head. "No, Julia would prefer to be called a woman, not a girl. And she really is an amazing woman."

He scrolled through the images Julia had taken on the safari adventure, surprised to see she'd taken more photos of Finn than he'd realized. He swore he was looking at a different man seeing himself through her eyes.

And damn, did his chest ache.

He placed the camera on his lap and tipped his head back, absorbing the lyrics to the song. "Wonder Woman," he said under his breath. "You should have seen her in that costume.

Maybe you did. Maybe you're up there watching over me now." He closed his eyes for a second before turning his attention to the headstone. "Just, you know, don't watch us when we have sex, bro." He laughed a little.

Am I losing my mind? I hope not.

Finn wasn't sure what people did when they visited a loved one in a cemetery. He'd visited his fallen brothers, of course, but this was his first time one-on-one with Jaden. He assumed people talked, not that anyone could actually hear them. He didn't think so, at least.

Of course, A.J. insisted Marcus still visited him. And would Marcus's widow, Savanna, ever find love again? Or would she be forever married to Marcus in her mind?

"Can Julia move on?" he found himself asking Jaden. "Maybe you can put in a good word to Tucker for me? Let him know I'll protect Julia with my last breath."

He gathered in a deep pull of air and let it go, noticing his hand tremble a little.

"I visited Mom and Dad. Separately, of course. Mom is dating a pharmacist now, which feels kind of weird. Dad is with someone a decade younger but seems happy." He thought back to the moment he'd knocked on his mom's door yesterday before flying to LA. He hadn't expected his mom to immediately reach for him and hug him and whisper, *It's about damn time you visited.*

He'd built up the story of her hate for him in his head over the years to something much bigger than had been true, but she'd been too afraid to talk to him and apparently ashamed to make the first move. She'd been waiting for him to open the door to a difficult conversation about Jaden. The guilt he shared with his parents for not demanding Jaden go to rehab.

"I'm sorry, brother. I'm so sorry I kept your secret. I tried to stop you, but I didn't try hard enough. I've tried to save as many lives as possible since you died, though. I've done my best. I guess our best is all we really can do in this life."

He closed his eyes and secured the camera back into his hand, the weight of it somehow comforting as if he had Julia's hand instead to help get him through this moment.

"I love her," he found himself professing. "I was mesmerized by her the moment she walked into my self-defense class. But these last few weeks together . . . I can't imagine being with anyone other than her. I think—no, I know she's the one." He shifted to his knees, resting his butt on his calves, and set his free hand on top of the headstone. "I just don't know if she knows that." He bowed his head. "I should tell her, right?"

CHAPTER THIRTY-SIX

NEW YORK CITY, NEW YORK – THREE DAYS LATER

JULIA OPENED THE DOOR OF THE YELLOW TAXI AFTER PAYING her driver, her eyes set on the two-story brick building. Her stomach was in knots, and her nerves shot as if she'd knocked back a few espressos.

"It's pouring, ma'am. No umbrella?" her driver asked.

She looked at him and smiled. "That's okay. A little rain never hurt anyone."

The man pointed to the sky. "That's more than a little. Thundering, too."

"I'll be okay. Have a good night." She stepped out of the car and shut the door, and the rain began striking her with intensity.

A low rumbling noise sounded overhead as she stepped up onto the sidewalk, unable to take her eyes off the building in front of her.

I'm Lois, she recalled sputtering to Finn at the end of their first class back in January, the name slipping free from her lips a bit clumsily as she'd shaken his hand and found herself instantly attracted to him.

Dalton Finnegan, but you can call me—

He'd never finished his sentence because someone else had grabbed hold of his arm, demanding his attention. His green eyes had swung back to Julia, hesitation in his gaze as if he didn't want to walk away. He didn't want to leave her even then.

She swore it was like a bolt of lightning had struck both of them the moment she'd pulled her hand free of his to let him go that night. He'd stared at her as if he'd felt it too.

And then she let him go again after Dubai. And this time, he'd stared at her like she'd broken his heart.

Her pulse quickened as she focused on the building, not sure if Finn was teaching tonight. Was he even in New York?

Raindrops began to weigh on her eyelashes, but she couldn't get herself to move, to go inside.

If he were teaching, then class would have just ended, and he'd follow his students outside like he used to do, making sure they all got off okay in their rides. Always the protector.

I'll wait. She folded her arms and shivered when her pale blue sundress began to cling to her body. It was the same dress she'd worn the day they'd walked the streets of Aswan. She had on her necklace, too.

The crack of lightning from somewhere close by had her startling her shoulders back. But it was the sight of the door at the top of the six brick steps opening that sent her stumbling back and almost into the street.

Six women slowly filtered out, opening their umbrellas and bounding down the stairs, and behind them . . .

Finn.

He remained frozen in the doorway with his hand

propping the door open as he stared at Julia down on the sidewalk.

A tight knot formed in her throat, and she swallowed, hoping to maintain her courage for what she was about to do. And what she had to tell him.

He slowly stepped outside, allowing the door to swing closed behind him, but he remained at the top of the steps, still staring at her like she was a mirage in the desert.

Once the women had cleared out, she forced her sandals to move and swiped the beads of water from her face.

"Julia," he rasped as if finally realizing she was real. He dropped his duffel bag and ran down the stairs before she'd had a chance to climb them. "You're drenched." He grasped her upper arms and pinned her with his beautiful green eyes.

"I don't care." Tears were threatening to fall, but whether he noticed in the rain didn't matter.

She just wanted to bury her face against his chest and have him wrap her in his arms.

"I'm sorry," she whispered, worried he wouldn't hear her over the noise of the rain and thunder.

"No, I'm sorry." He smoothed his thumbs up and down her bare arms, gliding over the drops of rain. "I shouldn't have let you go. But . . ."

"But?" She tensed, worried he'd had a change of heart during their time apart.

"I told Luke I'm going to leave Echo Team. I want to be with you, and I can't—"

"No." She lifted her hands to his chest, finding his heart thundering like the heavens overhead. "Absolutely not. I forbid it."

"I'd do anything to be with you. Move any mountain." He looked down into her eyes and brought one hand to her cheek. "Anything."

Her body was shaking and not from the chilly rain. "I know. But I'll do anything for you, too." She sniffled, batting her eyelashes rapidly to keep them open during the storm. "And that means I'll support you and what you do. I could never be with you if you gave up who you are for me."

"Julia, I—"

"Jewels." She tipped her head and rolled her tongue between her lips, catching the rain. "You staying with the teams is non-negotiable."

"Wait." He blinked a few times. "You'd still want to be with me?" he asked as the rain continued to pour over them.

"I want you to be my forever-forever. My ride or die." She pushed up on her toes to draw their mouths closer. "*My* storm."

A smile touched his lips as he leaned in and cupped the back of her head. "We're in one now."

"And it's where we belong, don't you think? We can weather any storm together," she murmured before he crushed his mouth over hers.

When their lips broke apart, his eyes remained shut, but she slowly began to fall to one knee.

"What are you doing?" Finn started to reach down to hook her arms to help her rise.

"I want to marry you, Dalton Samuel Finnegan. And I'm stubborn and impatient. And I don't want to wait for you to ask me, so—"

His deep, husky laugh had her letting go of her words, and he lowered himself to his knees before her. "You are very stubborn, I'll give you that." He tipped her chin with a fist, and she noticed the rain letting up. She had no idea if anyone was around or watching them, but to her, they were alone and in a bubble. "But I'll be the one doing the asking."

"Oh." She started to lower her eyes to the sidewalk, but he lifted her chin again with his fist so her gaze met his.

"Marry me, Jewels? Be my forever-forever. I don't know how long I have on this earth, but I want those days to be with you."

Tears blurred her vision as she cried, "Yes."

This was her new beginning. Her rebirth. Her fresh start.

Being with this man was her second chance. And she knew in her heart she'd get it right this time.

"I love you," she said, realizing they'd skipped over that part, and he lightly chuckled as if remembering that "small detail," too.

He brought his mouth back to hers. "I love you," he said before bringing his mouth to her ear. "Let's get you out of this rain now. There are things I want to do to you."

He helped her to her feet and then surprised her with a little twirl before capturing her in his arms.

"We still haven't tried doggy style," she teased as he hugged her close.

Finn leaned back and waggled his eyebrows a few times. "We haven't tried a lot of things," he returned in a deep, rumbly voice that told her she was in for a hell of a ride. A wild, sexy, and amazing ride with this man.

* * *

THREE WEEKS LATER

Julia flung her arms around Finn the moment he walked through her condo door. He dropped his duffel bag and hoisted her legs around his hips and kissed her as if they hadn't just seen each other five days ago.

He explored her mouth with an erotic sweep of his

tongue, and she moaned against him. They'd had phone sex while he'd been away. At first, she'd sent him private Instagram stories of herself in front of a mirror, naked and touching herself, and then he'd become all panicky that someone would hack her phone and access them, so they switched to FaceTime, which still made him a little nervous. But they couldn't go a day without being together, even while he was away for work. She craved him. All of him. Always.

"How was Afghanistan?" she asked once he set her down, but he began peeling off his T-shirt as if he'd rather pin her to one of the surfaces in the condo than talk work.

"It was Afghanistan," he returned with a laugh as she reached for the buckle of his belt and made quick work of undoing it.

She ran her hand over the bulge in his pants. "You want me already, huh?"

He hooked an arm behind her back and drew her closer to him, then yanked loose the silk knot of her short red robe. His eyes soaked in her naked body from her tits to the smooth V between her legs.

"I want that sexy show you gave me in that damn Instagram story. We're deleting that app on your phone, by the way."

"Oh yeah?" She arched her brow. "So demanding." But damn, did that turn her on, and she shifted her hand back to his zipper to drag it down.

"Miss me?" he rasped.

"So much." She shoved down his jeans, forgetting he still had on his shoes. That was a potential obstacle to the bedroom.

She smoothed both hands over his hard pectoral muscles before grabbing hold of his biceps. "Tell me, though. Any luck? Find any candidates for Charlie Team?"

"Maybe." He smiled. "But I'd rather go down on my fiancée now than talk about work." He teased his brows up and down, then backed up a step to get out of his shoes and pants.

She helped him discard his boxers before her robe fell to the floor. He kicked everything out of the way to clear some space.

Oh, is this happening right here?

Still in the hall by the door, he swiftly spun her around to face the wall. She pressed her cheek against the cool surface as he leaned in behind her for a hot kiss before he returned his attention to her naked body.

"Keep your hands up."

"Been bad, huh?"

"Sending me those sexy videos of you touching your wet pussy," he murmured into her ear as his hands caressed her silhouette. "Very naughty."

Her sex clenched at the sound of his gruff voice and dirty words.

Julia closed her eyes and savored the feel of his rough hands as he glided them down to her hips, then knelt behind her and dropped kisses all over her bare ass before parting her cheeks and sliding his tongue to her clit.

What was it with men and that angle? But she loved how much he desired her body. He made her feel sexy and beautiful whether she was lounging around in an oversized tee watching *Stars Wars* movies, which he'd convinced her to do, or was naked like this . . . he loved her for her.

Her nipples pebbled, and she nearly clawed at the wall with her short nails as he licked and sucked. A moment later, he secured his hands on her hips while remaining on his knees. "Turn, Jewels."

She did as instructed, and he looked up at her with heated eyes.

"Lock your wrists together and keep them over your head."

"You want to punish me for those videos?" She bucked against him when he drew her sex closer to his mouth, and his beard tickled her sensitive flesh.

His eyes lifted to hold hers as her hips remained prisoner to his touch, and she wouldn't have it any other way. Her man was a bit more dominating in the bedroom than she'd known before they proposed to each other, and it was so freaking hot.

"Fuck yes," he murmured darkly, then leaned in and swirled his tongue between her legs, and it took all her strength not to reach down and fist his hair. "So wet for me," he said between kisses of her inner thighs as he tortured her by shifting away from her sensitive area on purpose. "Tell me what you want."

"Ugh," she cried out, her breasts lifting and her body tensing with the anticipation of an impending orgasm. She was definitely no longer broken down south. "I want you to fuck me. To take me hard and deep. Against this wall."

A devilish smile slid across his lips as he eased away from her and slowly stood. He leaned in and gently bit her lip.

Damn, she was going to lose it right there.

Lifting one of her legs and hooking it around his hip, he nudged her stance wider and positioned his tip at her soaked center, then plunged deep inside without a condom.

They'd made love for the first time sans condom before he left for Afghanistan, and how could they ever go back?

Finn gripped her ass, taking her raw and hard, and with each thrust, she moaned her pleasure.

Minutes later, she felt her pussy spasm around Finn's

cock as she came. He quickly followed her with his own release but kept her pinned to the wall as they both caught their breath. She was a mess as he gently lowered her one leg to the floor, both sweaty and still a bit breathless.

With his palms on the wall over her shoulders now, he caged her with his muscular frame, and his green eyes locked on to hers. A smile cut across his handsome lips as he leaned in and whispered, "My beautiful storm, let's do that again. This time in the shower."

EPILOGUE

OUTER BANKS, NORTH CAROLINA – THREE MONTHS LATER

"WE CAN ROCK-PAPER-SCISSORS IT."

"Wait, what?" Julia stretched her arms out to the sides and stepped between Natasha's brother, Gray Chandler, and the mysterious Carter Dominick. "You are not really fighting over my friend, are you?"

"What, I'm not worth the fight?" Oliver cocked his head to the side, clearly amused by what was happening.

"We both want Oliver to join our teams, and we can't both have him." Gray's eyes remained narrowed on Carter in preparation for some ridiculous rock-paper-scissors showdown.

"How about let Oliver decide?" Julia lowered her arms, but the "boys" ignored her suggestion, and Gray and Carter began the battle over her friend.

Gray Chandler had a security company on the West Coast, and although his work wasn't as intense as Finn's, it was still dangerous. And Carter? Well, that man was still a question mark.

Julia grabbed hold of Oliver's sleeve and tilted her head, motioning for him to leave Carter and Gray alone. "They won't notice we're gone."

"Eh, I don't mind being fought over." Oliver accepted a flute of champagne from one of the women working the wedding reception but handed it off to Julia. "I honestly can't choose. They both sound like good guys. Carter's more of a wild card, but you know I like a bit of excitement."

Julia sipped her champagne and peered across the backyard of her parents' beach home (well, now hers since they'd gifted it as a wedding present), where the reception was in full swing. She spotted her husband chatting with a few of his teammates near where the band played. He tipped his head back and clutched his stomach, laughing with the rest of them.

My sexy husband. Is this real? She'd almost thought they really would have a triple wedding, but Harper and Roman decided to get married back in June at the same church her parents, who'd long since passed away, had married. And Rory's family roped her into a big Southern wedding in Alabama since A.J. had robbed them of a wedding when he'd eloped with Ana.

When she and Finn decided on a super short engagement, he'd suggested only family and a few friends at the beach house beneath a canopy of stars.

They'd gotten married under the moonlight, barefoot and holding hands as they'd said their vows two hours ago. It'd been the most amazing and romantic moment of her life. She had a feeling there were many more moments to come, including their honeymoon.

They'd be leaving tomorrow for ten days in a water bungalow in Jamaica. They needed that time away.

He'd spun up a few times since he'd dropped to one knee and proposed that stormy night three months ago, and with the help of some of the spouses on Bravo and Echo who lived nearby, she'd successfully navigated those tough waters. It wasn't any easier each time he kissed her goodbye, but she doubted she'd ever stop worrying about that man. She loved him, and she could only pray he'd always come home to her.

Wyatt hadn't yet been cleared to operate, and the teams hadn't finalized all of their "draft picks" as they were calling them for Charlie Team, and it had Julia wondering if they were stalling for a reason. Were they not ready for this next generation of SEALs? Were they worried they'd take over for them one day, and well, wasn't that kind of the plan?

"Still can't believe you're married." Oliver stopped walking, his gaze sliding over to Mya talking to Mason, the friend who'd previously been supplying Mya with some benefits between the sheets. He'd broken up with whatever model he'd been dating a few weeks ago, and Julia wasn't quite sure what to make of how Mya really felt about Mason. She wanted her friend happy, though, as happy as Julia now was with Finn.

"She still single?" Oliver asked. "Or are they a sort-of thing?"

Julia looked at Oliver and smiled. How'd he know they'd ever been anything? Oliver had met Mya a few times over the years, but he'd been in the military at the time and hadn't shown interest in her then. Was he showing interest now? "Why do you ask?"

Oliver shrugged. "Just curious." He swiped his hand over his beard, keeping his eyes on Mya in her light pink sundress.

Everyone had decided to dress informally for the beach

wedding. No dress whites or dress blues for the servicemen, and no shaving beards . . . the guys had thanked her for that one a few times that evening.

She hadn't worn a traditional wedding dress tonight either. In fact, it was more of a simple white wrap dress similar to the one Finn had freaked out about back in Egypt months ago. So, tonight, she couldn't help but wear it, and she'd noticed Finn checking all of her "angles" at the reception as if ensuring none of his single buddies would be able to admire the so-called view.

Finn had on khaki linen pants and a white linen shirt with the sleeves rolled to the elbows. He'd looked perfect to her. The entire evening had been absolutely amazing.

Of course, Finn did get himself in a little trouble with Michael and Julia's dad since he'd dropped to one knee that night in New York without asking for her hand first, but she'd come to his defense explaining why that'd happened. And Michael and her dad forgave Finn.

"Hey, you have a delivery." Julia discarded the champagne flute on an empty table and turned to see her mom motioning for Julia to head to the house.

"Delivery, huh?" She squeezed Oliver's arm, letting him know they'd catch up later, and she joined Finn so they could go see why her mother had such a puzzled expression on her face when she'd announced the "delivery."

"You get me a surprise?" Finn teased while hooking his arm around her back. He took a moment to nuzzle his face against her neck and lightly nipped her earlobe. "Counting down the hours until I have you naked in Jamaica for ten days."

Her body shuddered from his breath. "Mm. You and me both." She leaned into him, setting her hand on his wall of muscles. "And no surprise from me, sorry to say."

"Trust me," he said while gripping her hip where his hand rested. "I have everything I could ever want and need."

She followed his gaze to where his divorced parents were chatting with POTUS, which was pretty surreal having the President himself at her wedding. "Together forever," she said in case his thoughts had gone dark with concerns they'd part ways one day like his parents.

Thankfully, Finn had returned to his therapy sessions with Dr. Logan, who happened to be a friend of Julia's and her brother's by way of her husband, Ben Logan. She firmly believed in talking through problems instead of burying them beneath the surface, and she knew Finn needed to continue seeing the doctor so he wouldn't let his guilt from the past come back to haunt him again. No more numbness. She wanted her husband to feel everything. Hopefully only good things, though.

Julia had also started talking to someone every week. For one, it helped her handle her stress about his job. She couldn't tell the doctor about his real work, but that was irrelevant. But also, she didn't want to fall victim to blaming herself for Tucker anymore.

"I love you," she found herself telling him as they walked up the steps to the patio, cutting through the crowd to get closer to her mom to see about the delivery.

"I love you, too, Jewels." He let go of her hip to lace their fingers together as they went inside the open French doors of the beach house.

Julia stopped in her tracks the second she saw the delivery, then set her free hand to her stomach as a surprised laugh escaped her lips.

"That's stolen, isn't it?" Finn said out of the side of his mouth as he lifted their joined hands to point toward the

Andy Warhol silkscreen of Marilyn Monroe resting against the couch in the living room.

"Probably." She released his hand, then went to check for a message.

"That can't be real, can it be?" Julia's mom asked, blinking in shock.

"I think it is." Julia smiled and then found a note stuck to the back of the Warhol.

A Warhol for Warhol. It's only fair. And don't worry, the bad guys won't miss it.

"Um." Julia handed the note to Finn.

He read it and grimaced. "I think we should get rid of this before its former owner notices it's missing and comes looking for it. I don't want any trouble in paradise."

"We'll deal with this tomorrow." She looped her arms over her husband's shoulders and pulled herself tight to his body. "Tonight is about us."

"Oh, is it?"

"And after the party, will that be all about us, too?"

She teasingly chewed on her lip before saying, "Hopefully, you'll be so far deep inside of me there won't be a you or a me. Just an us."

He closed his eyes and moaned, and she felt his dick harden against her. "Ugh. Damn. Is your mom still behind me? Can't move otherwise."

She peeked over his shoulder to see her mom's back to them, checking the Warhol as if trying to authenticate it. "You're good."

He reset his focus on her face, and his hooded green eyes told her exactly what he was thinking. He lifted a hand to her face and stroked her cheek before cupping the back of her head. "My naughty girl."

"For you, always," she whispered before moving in to let

him set her on fire with a kiss, the same way he did every time their mouths touched.

The same way he'd "sealed the deal" after they'd said their vows, and he dipped her dramatically to the delight of everyone before kissing the daylights out of her. She'd just about collapsed from the emotional high of finally being married to her forever guy. Sure, Julia knew how to take care of herself, she'd proven that in Aswan and Dubai, but there was no better feeling than knowing her guy would always be there for her. He'd always have her six.

When they were back outside with the guests, and she heard a Bryan Adams song being performed by the band, she froze.

Finn bowed his head for a second, then shifted his attention to his mom, and Julia noticed his mother staring intently at the band with a hand over her heart. "Dance with her. She needs that," she said, tears filling her eyes as she spoke.

"Are you sure?" He looked her way, his gaze narrowing. "I want to dance with my wife."

She reached for his arm and lightly squeezed. "And the great thing about marriage is that I'll still be your wife for the next song. But your mom needs you. And I have a feeling Jaden is looking down at us right now." Her stomach squeezed as emotion nearly robbed her of her ability to talk.

"I love you so much," he rasped and cupped her cheeks to kiss her, then she urged him to get to his mom before it was too late.

Michael sidled up next to her as she stood on the deck and watched her husband dance with his mom. And in that moment, it was as if little pieces of her heart she hadn't known were broken suddenly mended themselves. "How are you?"

"Amazing." She'd whispered the only word that felt right. Because she did feel amazing. "I'm married. Can you believe that?" How many times would she repeat that line so she'd know she wasn't living in a dream?

She'd pinched herself quite a few times in the last three months, struggling to believe she'd been so lucky to find love as well as rekindle her passion for photography. *All* the while continuing her work with her brother to support veterans. She'd never known it was possible to have everything until that very moment.

"That's all I wanted for you. To have an amazing life." Michael stepped before her and kissed her on the forehead. "Proud of you, sis. You're going to make a great mom, too."

She smiled. "Slow down there, Superman. One step at a time."

"At the rate you're going, you'll have more little ones than me soon."

The idea of a yard full of kids had her heart racing. "I might start with a dog first. We'll see how it goes from there," she teased. But of course, she and Finn had opted to no longer use birth control and see which way the wind blew —whatever was meant to be would be, they'd decided.

"You'll have a few little hurricanes running around, no doubt."

"Hurricanes, huh?" She couldn't help but smile at her brother's choice of words.

"I'm going to go dance with my gorgeous wife now." Michael set his hand on her forearm, looked her in the eyes with a big smile, then left her to find Kate.

Julia walked down the steps to head toward the makeshift dance floor in the backyard with the band off to the side and the peaceful sounds of the ocean muted by the music. She searched out Mya, finding her dancing with . . . well, Oliver. *Hm. Okay.*

She glimpsed Harper and Roman dancing there as well. Her baby bump wasn't quite showing yet, but she was about seventeen weeks from what the doctor guessed. They'd be finding out the gender soon. According to Liam and Emily's daughter, they were having a girl.

And A.J. . . . *well*, he said he wasn't naming his son after him, but he was having a boy.

"How's your leg?" Julia asked Wyatt when she joined him and his wife to look at the dance area.

"Doc says a few more months until I can operate again." Wyatt looked at Julia, then off to where his daughter, Gwen, was dancing with some guy Julia didn't recognize. The man was probably a good ten years older than her. "Excuse me." He'd lost his crutches, and he didn't move like a man who'd had his leg broken three months ago, but he was also a dad and apparently didn't like whoever his daughter was dancing with enough to have him fast-tracking to them without a care about his injured leg.

Natasha sighed. "He forgets his daughter is *twenty*-two, not two." She set a hand to her growing abdomen. She was only six weeks ahead of Harper, but she knew they were having a daughter, which would most likely make Wyatt crazier. *Two* daughters to freak out about when it came to the opposite sex. "Tonight was perfect, by the way. I'm so happy for you. And well, for Finn. But hey, all of Echo knew you'd end up together before you two knew it. They totally set him up for the short-straw drawing. Matchmaking is now their side hobby, so it would seem."

Julia chuckled. "Unless it comes to Gwen."

"Yup." Natasha swiped her hand through her blonde hair and pointed her gaze on her husband, and Julia looked over at him to see Wyatt, who had some Tom Hardy look going for him, folding his arms and staring down at the man who was no longer dancing with his daughter but eyeing Wyatt like a deer in the headlights. Poor guy.

The song stopped a beat later, and both Finn and Oliver left the dance floor and started their way. Wyatt seemed to reluctantly let Gwen's dance partner flee, and Gwen tossed her hand in the air like Julia imagined a pissed-off daughter would do.

She could picture Finn down the road with their own kids being all overprotective and growly and . . . *Oh, I guess I do want a big family. Still want a dog, though.*

And with all the sex they'd been having, it'd probably happen soon. The man had an insatiable appetite for making love, and his alpha attitude in the bedroom had woken an inner sex goddess she hadn't known existed before him.

"Hi, my wife," Finn said with a smile, the strings of lights strewn about all over the yard, alongside tiki lights, making his face glow as he joined her.

"Hi, my husband." When she reached for his hand, he gave her a quick twirl, which lifted her dress a little and made her think about Marilyn Monroe's famous movie scene. *Maybe I should keep the Warhol?* "Everything okay?"

Finn looked back at his mom, who now danced with her boyfriend to a new song, then returned his attention to Julia and nodded. "Better than ever, thanks to you."

"Well, that makes my heart happy."

He slid his hands to her hips and held on to her. "If your heart's happy, then so is mine."

"You two need a room and stat," Oliver teased, and she'd nearly forgotten they had an audience.

"So, who are you going with?" Finn turned to the side but kept his arm around Julia's waist. "Carter or Gray?"

Oliver looked out to where Gray and Carter were now on approach. "I guess we're about to find out," Oliver answered.

Wyatt strode their way as well, and he reached for his wife and whispered something into her ear that had her laughing.

"So, who won the epic battle?" Julia asked once Carter and Gray were there.

The two men exchanged a quick and curious look . . . *Oh no, another tie?*

"Neither," Gray said under his breath. "We have a different idea."

Julia lifted her brows, waiting for them to drop the "idea," curious what the hell it was. Oliver was her friend, and she needed to look out for him.

"It's crazy, but," Gray began while shaking his head, peering at his sister as if he were worried she might not approve, "we may join forces. He's got a fuck ton of money and toys."

"And he'll keep me a bit more in line with legal shit . . . *maybe*," Carter said as if the words were painful to digest.

"Wait, what?" Natasha untangled herself from her husband to step closer to her brother. "You're going to work for Carter?"

"No," both Carter and Gray hissed at the same time.

"Fifty-fifty. Partners," Gray said.

"Maybe like forty-sixty," Carter spoke up. "I do have the money and the toys."

Finn started laughing, breaking any possible tension, but before they knew it, Carter and Gray moved off to the side of everyone and began arguing over the details of the insane agreement.

"They for real?" Oliver jerked his thumb toward Carter and Gray.

Natasha smiled. "I honestly don't know."

"I'm kind of disappointed. I was at least hoping for some more *Fast and Furious* action to settle this. A race, maybe, but this time with me behind the wheel," Oliver teased. Well, knowing her friend, maybe he wasn't joking.

"I'm sure there will be plenty of face-offs considering these two are going at it like two little—"

"Don't you dare say girls," Natasha interrupted her husband and held a finger between them, and Wyatt tightened his mouth to keep out of trouble.

Finn secured his arm around Julia's waist again, and she settled into his embrace, feeling safe and secure. "Why do I feel like it's the end of an era for us?" he suddenly asked. "Charlie Team and now these two joining forces? What happens to us?"

"Nah, it's not the end at all." A deep voice flowed behind them, and the hair on Julia's arms stood as the President, who actually did look a lot like Denzel Washington, husky tone of voice included, circled them.

"No?" Finn asked, tightening his grip around Julia, and thoughts of their vacation swam in her head from his touch alone.

Naked . . . on a bed, inside a bungalow open to the ocean as they made love and . . .

She blinked her focus back to the fact the President was talking, but well, it was her wedding night, so she shouldn't feel guilty for fantasizing, right?

"Not an end of an era, at all." And now Liam was there. Where had he been, and how had he heard them?

Before Julia knew it, all of Finn's teammates were surrounding them as if they'd heard some silent whistle demanding their attention. Had Rory been training them instead of Bear?

They were a family. She felt it in her bones. And she was part of that family now, too.

Luke stepped alongside the President, and Knox stood next to his father on the other side.

"So, what is it?" Finn asked, and everyone put their eyes on the President.

President Bennett flashed his white teeth, opened his palms, and smiled. "New adventures." He nodded and looked from teammate to teammate, making eye contact with everyone. "And I know you SEALs say 'the only easy day was yesterday,' but maybe we focus on having an easy night since we're at a wedding, and we worry about tomorrow tomorrow."

A.J. clapped his hands together and stepped forward. "Amen to that, sir. And I know exactly what we need. But you have to participate, sir," he added, and when Knox set his hand to his stomach, already laughing at whatever was about to happen, Julia couldn't help but smile. She was clueless, but still.

"Nothing like a little two-step to Blanco Brown's *The Git Up* to lose your worries and have a good time," A.J. said, and like that, he was off to talk to the band.

"*The Git Up?*" The President angled his head.

Knox threw an arm around his father's shoulder. "Don't worry, Pops, I got you. Just follow my lead."

President Bennett smiled. "I always do, Son."

The guys all dispersed, and Julia glanced at Oliver now caught up in the middle of the Carter–Gray showdown to discuss the who, what, when, where, and how of this new plan of theirs.

"That's going to all work out, right?" Julia asked Finn, and he pulled her into his arms and hugged her.

"Absolutely." He gently kissed her lips and then stepped

425

back to hold her hands. "You know how to dance to this song?"

Julia grinned. "You forget I grew up in the South, and two-stepping is basically encoded into my DNA?"

Finn closed one eye. "How could I ever forget that?" He quickly pulled her back into his arms and lightly swatted her ass before squeezing it. "These, ugh, angles are gonna get me into trouble with your dad and brother here tonight."

"If there were ever a night for them to look the other way, it'd be our wedding," she whispered into his ear before setting her mouth to his neck and lightly sucking, not caring who might see them.

"Maybe we forget the dance and sneak away?" he murmured a second later, and she felt his cock growing hard against her.

"Hell no." She eased out of his reach, loving how much this would torture him to have to wait. "We're dancing." She pointed to the sky when the lyrics to the song began to play over the speakers instead of being sung by the band. "Ready to dance with me?"

A beautiful smile played across his lips as he held her hands inside his. And the President was right, wasn't he? There were only new adventures waiting for them. "Tonight," Finn said in a deep voice while holding her eyes. "And every night after."

CROSSOVER INFORMATION & BOOK NEWS

Crossover Information

I brought a few characters over from other series and books:

Michael & Kate Maddox - *The Safe Bet*

Carter Dominick was in *Chasing Fortune* (He will get his own book)

Gray Chandler was in *Chasing the Knight* (He will get his own book)

Mya - *My Every Breath* (She will get her own book)

Mason Matthews was also briefly in *My Every Breath* and *The Hard Truth* (He will get his own book)

What is Next?

It's not really goodbye to the Stealth Ops Series … but for

those who have been with me since book 1 - thank you so much. These guys have become like family to me.

Carter Dominick and Gray Chandler join forces in an exciting new series releasing October 2021. We'll see more of Bravo/Echo in this new series.
Join my newsletter and/or Facebook groups to stay up-to-date on news.

Wondering about Jesse & Ella from previous books?
(*Chasing Daylight/Fortune*) - They will get a book as well.

Stealth Ops: Next GEN - Charlie Team - coming down the road. We'll see more of Bravo/Echo in this spin-off series, too.
(Elaina and Gwen will also eventually have books)

Continue for a reading guide/timeline, music playlist, and Stealth Ops Family Tree!

READING GUIDE

Find the latest news from my newsletter/website and/or Facebook: Brittney's Book Babes / the Stealth Ops Spoiler Room /Dublin Nights Spoiler Room.

A Stealth Ops World Guide is available on my website, which features more information about the team, character muses, and SEAL lingo.

Stealth Ops Timeline
Reading Guide
Pinterest Muse/Inspiration Board

* * *

Stealth Ops Series: Bravo Team

Finding His Mark - Book 1 - Luke & Eva
Finding Justice - Book 2 - Owen & Samantha
Finding the Fight - Book 3 - Asher & Jessica
Finding Her Chance - Book 4 - Liam & Emily

Finding the Way Back - Book 5 -Knox & Adriana

Stealth Ops Series: Echo Team

Chasing the Knight - Book 6 -Wyatt & Natasha
Chasing Daylight - Book 7 - A.J. & Ana
Chasing Fortune - Book 8 - Chris & Rory
Chasing Shadows - Book 9 -Harper & Roman
Chasing the Storm - Book 10 - Finn & Julia

Becoming Us: *connection to the Stealth Ops Series (books take place between the prologue and chapter 1 of Finding His Mark)*

Someone Like You - A former Navy SEAL. A father. And off-limits. (Noah Dalton)

My Every Breath - A sizzling and suspenseful romance. Businessman Cade King has fallen for the wrong woman. She's the daughter of a hitman - and he's the target.

Dublin Nights

On the Edge - Travel to Dublin and get swept up in this romantic suspense starring an Irish businessman by day…and fighter by night.
On the Line - novella
The Real Deal - This mysterious billionaire businessman has finally met his match.
The Inside Man - Cole McGregor & Alessia Romano
The Final Hour - Sean and Emilia

Stand-alone (with a connection to *On the Edge*):

The Story of Us– Sports columnist Maggie Lane has 1 rule: never fall for a player. One mistaken kiss with Italian soccer star Marco Valenti changes everything…

Hidden Truths

The Safe Bet – Begin the series with the Man-of-Steel lookalike Michael Maddox.

Beyond the Chase - Fall for the sexy Irishman, Aiden O'Connor, in this romantic suspense.

The Hard Truth – Read Connor Matthews' story in this second-chance romantic suspense novel.

Surviving the Fall – Jake Summers loses the last 12 years of his life in this action-packed romantic thriller.

The Final Goodbye - Friends-to-lovers romantic mystery

PLAYLIST

Hurricane - Luke Combs

Rescue Me - OneRepublic

Echo - Yves V

Far Away From Home (feat. Leony) - Sam Feldt, VIZE

Crowded Heart - Samuel Jack

Capital Letters - Hailee Steinfeld, BloodPop

Bigger Than - Justin Jesso, Seeb

One Night in Dubai - Arash, Helena

Tear Me Down (feat. Philip Rusted) - Davai

Nothing's Gonna Stop Us Now - Starship

I Don't Know Why - NOTD, Astrid S

Slow Dance (feat. Ava Max) - AJ Mitchell, Ava Max (Sam Feldt remix)

Outta My Head - Love Harder, Julie Bergan

Letting Go - Hogland, KIDDO

Born To Be Yours - Kygo, Imagine Dragons

Last Hurrah - David Guetta remix - Bebe Rexha, David Guetta

Everything I do - Bryan Adams

Spotify Playlist

Mentioned in the book (not on the Spotify list): Sandstorm, Darude; The Git Up, Blanco Brown

STEALTH OPS FAMILY TREE

Luke and Eva Scott (daughter: Lara, son: Easton)

- Sister: Jessica (Scott) Hayes

Owen and Samantha York (son: Matthew), (Dog: Ollie)

Jessica and Asher Hayes (Twins: Juliana and Arabella)

Liam and Emily Evans (Daughter: Elaina, Son: Jackson)

Knox and Adriana Bennett (pregnant)

- President Isaiah Bennett (Knox's dad)

Wyatt and Natasha Pierson (Wyatt's daughter: Gwen), Natasha is pregnant

- Admiral Chandler (Natasha's father)
- Gray Chandler (Natasha's brother)

STEALTH OPS FAMILY TREE

A.J. and Ana Hawkins (pregnant)

- Beckett, Shep, Caleb, Ella (A.J.'s siblings)
- Niece: McKenna

Chris Hunter and Rory McAdams (married)

- Dog: Bear

Harper Brooks and Roman Riviera (married/pregnant)

Julia Maddox and Dalton Finnegan (married)
    Brother: Michael Maddox

In loving memory of Bravo Three:

Marcus Vasquez (His widow: Savanna Vasquez)

* * *

Stealth Ops Team Members

Team leaders: Luke & Jessica Scott / Intelligence team member (joined in 2019): Harper Brooks

Bravo Team:
    Bravo One - Luke
    Bravo Two - Owen
    Bravo Three - Asher
    Bravo Four - Liam
    Bravo Five - Knox (Charlie "Knox" Bennett)

Echo Team:

Echo One - Wyatt

Echo Two - A.J. (Alexander James)

Echo Three - Chris

Echo Four - Roman

Echo Five - Finn (Dalton "Finn" Finnegan)

Charlie Team: Coming at a later date

Stealth Ops Timeline

Chasing the Storm Pinterest/Inspiration board

WHERE ELSE CAN YOU FIND ME?

I love, love, love interacting with readers in my Facebook groups as well as on my Instagram page. Join me over there as we talk characters, books, and more! ;)

<u>FB Reader Groups:</u>
Brittney's Book Babes
Stealth Ops Spoiler Room

Facebook
Instagram
TikTok

www.brittneysahin.com
brittneysahin@emkomedia.net

Pinterest Muse/Inspiration Board